JAKON

KINGDOM OF FAIRYTALES
SEASON TEN

You all know the story of your favorite fairytale, but did you ever wonder what happened after the fairytale ending? Well we know. Not all afters end up happily, sometimes the real adventure starts much later...

Following famous fairytale characters, eighteen years after their happily ever after, the Kingdom of Fairytales offers an edge of the seat thrill ride in an all new and sensational way to read.

Lighting-fast reads you won't be able to put down

Fantasy has never been so epic!

Copyright © 2021 J.A. Armitage & Emma Savant
ISBN: 978-1-989997-32-1
Enchanted Quill Press

This book is a work of fiction
Any resemblance to actual persons is purely coincidental

Contaact the author at www.enchantedquillpress.com
Cover by Enchanted Quilll Press
Interior Formatting by Enchanted Quill Press
Editing by Rose Lipscomb

KING OF TRAITORS

9TH SEPTEMBER

I woke up in a cold sweat and flailed at the air. The strength of someone's grip tightened on my arms and their musky odor filled my nose with stink and fear. The ground spun beneath me and the darkness pressed in on every side, each shadow holding a new and horrifying possibility.

I clutched, searching for purchase amid fur and feather, and my hands closed over rough fabric.

No, not fabric.

Blanket.

I was in bed. I had slept here.

The dream still clung to me, made worse by the way it mingled with memory. Everything that had happened last night--that had been real. Wrong, and real. Terrifying, and *real*.

I held onto the blanket, like its flimsy weight would be enough to tether me to the ground if the monkeys came again.

I took several slow, steadying breaths, the way my mother had taught me. I'd been prone to panic attacks as a little boy, sudden bouts of beating heart and gasping lungs that convinced me I was at the very edge of death. Ma had always held me close and patted my back.

"Breathe, Jakon," she had said. "In, two, three, and out, two, three. Breathe with me. That's it."

I closed my eyes and listened for her voice in the gloom of my cell. I could almost hear her, just beyond the shadows.

She was an angel now, or so she'd told me. Angels were a Kansas concept, something people talked about in church or cross-stitched onto pillows alongside comforting phrases. Some angels were fierce with burning swords, Ma had told me, but others were kind and loving and watched out for the people they left behind. She'd be both kinds of angel, she'd promised, because much as she intended to watch over me, she always ended up in some battle or other and a flaming sword sounded like a nice kind of weapon.

Memories of my mother crowded in on me, each bright strand of my past replacing the images of the flying monkeys from last night. The sky lightened outside, visible only from a tiny rectangle high above. It was too far out of reach to climb to, and the wall seemed to be made of solid cement or maybe stone, too strong to break.

And of course it was. This was the Grand Prison, so nick-named, not because it was particularly luxurious, but because it was reserved for the worst criminals from all across the twelve kingdoms. Every nation had its own jails, but for serious offenses, there was the Grand, otherwise known as Urbis Prison, though it was nowhere near the walled city of Urbis, but off the north coast of Badalah. I'd never seen it before now, but everyone knew it was impossible to escape from. High, thick walls, magical and mechanical technology from around the kingdoms, and a veritable army of guards should have been enough, but this prison had the added security of being way out in the ocean, connected to the Badalah mainland only via a long, narrow bridge that was covered with guards day and night.

I knew about Urbis Prison. And I knew how I'd gotten here. I'd never seen flying monkeys. They'd been gone from Oz since I was an infant. But the flying monkeys that had stolen me away last night had been impossible to misidentify, and I wouldn't soon forget the sight of the earth and then the ocean speeding far below.

What I didn't know was *why*.

I pushed my blankets aside and stood. The thin socks I'd been given last night provided little protection from the cold of the floor. I changed from the drab gray prison pajamas into the drab gray prison uniform that didn't look much different and hurried to put on my shoes. These weren't much good, either, but at least they were thicker than the socks.

I put the used clothes on the cement bench across from the *other* cement bench, topped with a mattress that didn't quite deserve the name, which served as my bed. And then I banged on the heavy metal door. It rattled in its frame.

"Let me out," I shouted, hoping against hope that someone was out there to hear me.

I banged on the door again.

And then, to my surprise, it opened.

A guard glared down at me. I'd only ever seen a few ogres in Oz, but there was no mistaking this fellow as one. He hulked over me, tall and broad, and bared uneven yellow teeth that made my stomach turn.

"What?" he demanded.

I took a deep breath and stood up straight. Excellent posture, Ma had always said, could cover a world of insecurities.

"Why am I here?"

The guard glared down at me, but didn't answer.

I tried again. "What am I being charged with?"

The guard sneered. "Why should I know?"

The corridor behind him was as dreary as my cell, all cement walls and dim lights with a sickly greenish tint. Another door like mine was across the hall, no doubt holding another prisoner.

"I'm in prison and you don't know why?" I said.

"You think I keep track of the rap sheets of every piece of trash that comes through here?" the guard said.

"I'm not a piece of trash," I said. "I'm the mayor of Oz."

"Only trash ends up at the Grand," the guard said.

He cleared his throat, bringing up what sounded like a thick drag of mucous. He spat it at me, and the hot glob landed on my face and slid wetly down my cheek.

I furiously wiped it off with my uniform sleeve. "I demand to see the warden," I said.

"Ooh, he makes *demands*," the guard said.

I remembered rumors I'd heard here and there about how ogres liked to eat people. They'd capture lone travellers, the stories went, and string them up and roast them over a spit. I'd always chastised my little sisters for repeating the stories, asking them if they thought it would be right to talk about Munchkins or Winkies like that just because of their races.

Now, I wondered if I'd been too quick to come to the ogres' defense.

"I am the mayor of Oz," I repeated.

"Yeah, well, I got the king of Fancyland here two cells down."

It was a mediocre joke at best, but he laughed uproariously, baring his teeth. Lines of saliva stretched between his flabby lips and revulsion stirred in my throat.

"Thing is," he said, leering down at me. "Thing is, no one here cares who you are. Not anymore. You're at the Grand now, boy, and that makes you garbage."

"I trust your superiors will disagree." I considered adding that everyone, including the rats that were sure to find their way to my cell eventually, counted as *superior* to him, but the satisfaction of saying it wasn't likely to be worth the consequences.

I folded my arms and glared up at the ogre, doing my best impression of someone who thought he had any chips to bargain with.

The guard saw right through my charade. He cackled and wheezed. I started to wish I'd just stayed quietly in my cell.

But that wasn't an option. I'd been stolen away by flying monkeys. Who could say what those evil creatures were doing now? If they'd grabbed me from the street, there was no guarantee my little brothers and sisters were safe from similar attacks.

I had to get back to them. I had to protect them. And then I had to figure out how the hell flying monkeys had ended up back in Oz, anyway.

I switched tactics.

"Come on," I said, lowering my voice. "A smart guy like you? I'll bet you know everything that goes on in this place."

The ogre blinked at me.

"I'll bet we could make a deal. You tell me what I'm doing here, maybe I can make it worth your while."

He burst into another long peal of discomfiting laughter.

At least I was making someone's day more interesting.

"There's nothing you can offer I don't already have," he said. "I thought you were just ugly, but seems you might be stupid, too."

I bit the inside of my cheek and tried not to point out the irony in *him* calling anybody unattractive.

"You're a prisoner," the guard said. "Prisoners don't got nothing worth having."

I kept biting my cheek so I wouldn't point out the double negative.

"You sure could try to bribe me with that handsome suit you got on there, though," the ogre said, clearly finding himself hilarious. "Or maybe all those jewels you got."

I glanced down. My mayoral ring was gone, no doubt stolen by the monkeys or confiscated by someone at the prison.

"Or maybe you think you're going to do me some favors with all the power you've got here," the ogre said, cackling.

I fixed him with a stony frown. "If you're not going to help me out, why'd you bother opening the door?"

His face clouded over. "To tell you to shut up," he snapped. "The banging's giving me a headache."

I took a step back into my cell and swung the door

shut. There was no point trying to reason with him, and I didn't fancy the idea of another gob of spit on my face as punishment for trying.

A thin slot set into the metal door slammed open. The ogre's bloodshot eyes peered at me through the gap.

"You'll see the warden soon enough. You don't like what I got to say, you can go up against him."

He guffawed, and my stomach sank. His tone wasn't promising. If anything, it held a downright warning.

"Better put on your fanciest clothes," the guard said. "You being the *mayor* and all."

He indulged in another grating laugh and slammed the opening shut again.

The hours slipped by, and I had no way to track them except by the subtle changes in the blue outside my tiny window. I paced the cell, then laid on the thin mattress and stared at the ceiling, and then paced the cell again. A few times I heard footsteps and voices outside in the corridor, perhaps guards changing shifts or new prisoners being brought in.

I wondered how many of them had been brought here by flying monkeys. Perhaps I wasn't the only person from Oz. Maybe the monkeys had returned and gone rogue, and we'd all be released with apologies in a day or two.

It was a futile daydream, but I indulged in it anyway, if only to keep myself from panicking at the thought of my little siblings being locked in a place like this. Margaret could handle herself here. She could handle herself anywhere. In fact, Margaret probably wouldn't have let herself be taken by flying monkeys in the first place. If anyone in all of Oz could have fought them off single-handedly, it was my fierce, grumpy, wonderful sixteen-year-old sister.

Frank would be all right, too, or at least he would pretend to be all right until I could figure out how to rescue him. Frank had always tried hard to be a man, and ever since Ma had died he'd seemed even more determined to be strong and rise to every challenge.

But the twins, Gertrude and Ethel, would struggle. Little Chester still woke up with nightmares about spiders most nights; a place like this would just about do him in.

And Lucy...

My heart clenched at the thought of anything happening to sweet little Lucy. She was only six, and she'd already faced too much loss. I couldn't bear the idea of her ending up in this austere prison--or worse. Who knew what the flying monkeys were up to? For all I knew, they'd *eat* someone as little as my baby sister.

Goosebumps prickled all across my skin, and I marched back and forth across the cell with renewed vigor. This tiny square was barely three steps wide, and my head soon spun from turning around that often.

I dropped back onto the mattress, and then, finally, a key sounded in the metal door.

I jumped up, heart pounding. A new guard, also an ogre, opened the door and stared at me without much of an expression on his lopsided face.

"The warden wants you," he said gruffly. He turned and walked out, leaving the door open.

Was I supposed to follow him? I waited for a moment, then darted out the door. I looked both ways down the corridor. On the left, the guard trudged with a club slung over his shoulder. On the right...

Nothing.

I could run.

"Don't think about it," the guard said without turning back. "There are more guards, and that hall opens right out onto the ocean anyway." He shifted the club to his other shoulder. "Guess you could go that way. If you want the man-eating sea dragons to get you."

I weighed the possibility of a lie against the threat of man-eating dragons and decided to give the warden a try first. This whole thing was clearly a mistake, and surely the prison boss would understand that and do his best to get me on my way home.

I jogged to catch up to the guard. He was a brisk walker, and it wasn't long before we were in a large foyer that looked slightly nicer than the corridor I'd been in before. A door was propped open, showing a small meeting room. This was clearly the part of the prison meant for outsiders to see, diplomats and dignitaries and maybe merchants who had contracts to supply the prison with food and these depressing uniforms.

We walked across the hall and toward a polished wooden door with a brass nameplate. *Warden Skrag*, it read, in tidy block letters.

The guard knocked.

"Enter," someone barked.

The guard pushed open the door and shoved me in. I stumbled, ran into the back of a chair, and grabbed onto it to steady myself. I looked up at the warden.

He was another ogre, but he was better put-together than the guards I'd seen. His pinstripe suit had been tailored to fit his broad shoulders, and his pocket watch looked of a decent quality.

"Sit," Warden Skrag said without looking at me. He shuffled papers on his desk, frowned at one of them, and put that sheet to the side. He waved the guard out. His nails were neatly manicured, but filed to a sharp point. My stomach churned.

I sat in the chair I'd almost toppled myself over and straightened my shoulders.

"Warden Skrag," I said, as politely as I could muster.

Finally, he looked up.

"Why am I being detained here?" I asked. My voice stayed calm. *People tend to match your attitude,* Ma had always said, *so keep yours good.*

"Jakon Gale," the warden said. He picked up another stack of papers and started paging through. "From Oz, right?"

"That's right," I said. "The mayor of Oz."

"You're here for treason," the warden said. "You've been brought in as a traitor to Oz and you've received the maximum sentence of life in prison."

My heart felt like it fell right through my stomach and onto the floor, but I fought to stay steady.

"That can't be right," I said. "I'm the *mayor.*"

"Who's a traitor to Oz, yes," the warden said. "It's right here on your papers."

He picked up one of the many sheets of paper on the table and shook it vaguely at me. I reached for the page, but he snatched it away.

"No touching."

"I'd like to see evidence of these *charges*," I said. "I haven't even had a trial. And how can I be a *traitor* to Oz? I rule Oz."

"Rulers are often corrupt."

He seemed more interested in the sheaf in front of him than in me. I cleared my throat, but he didn't look at me.

"I'm Jakon Gale," I said slowly, as if he hadn't just

told me that same information. "I'm Dorothy Gale's son."

This didn't seem to mean anything to him. He shrugged and, finally, looked up.

"I have orders from the Wizard," the warden said.

I frowned. "The Wizard of Oz?"

"How many other wizards do you know who have reason to be in your business?"

"There must be a mistake. The Wizard hasn't been seen since before I was born. He left Oz. If the stories are true he left this world entirely."

The warden shrugged. "All I know is what's in your file. You don't like it, you can take it up with the commissioner."

His dull mouth cracked into something like a smile. Whatever the joke was, I wasn't in on it.

"Then I'd like to see the commissioner."

He barked a laugh. "We'd all like to see the commissioner, boy. No doubt he's sipping some fruity concoction on a beach out in Skyla." He shook his head. "You won't see him. You're likely to die here. Best make peace with it."

I opened my mouth to argue, but the warden called out, "Ready for you" before I could get a word out. The guard who had escorted me here came back into the room and, with a glare that told me I'd better not make a fuss, escorted me back out.

I'd expected to be taken back to my cell, but now, the guard led me in a different direction. I couldn't make sense of the inside of the prison; it was all identical cement corridors and thick metal doors and flickering greenish light.

We stopped in front of a new door, and the guard took out a key.

"This isn't my room," I said.

"Oh, it's not your room," he repeated in a mocking tone. "Your room is where I say it is, rat. You've been moved. You were in Intake before. *This* is where you live from now on."

He swung the heavy door open to reveal another dull gray cell. This one was a little bigger than the first one, at least. It had a window, slightly larger but also slightly higher than the one in my previous room, and there were two large cement shelves here, each one topped with a thin straw mattress. My clothes had already been moved here and set on a rickety-looking metal storage rack, or perhaps they weren't my clothes at all but just another set from the prison's communal stash of uniforms and pajamas.

One side of the room was bare except for the mattress and the clothes. The other side was its mirror image, aside from the young man sitting on the bed with a book in his hands. He looked up as we entered, his shoulders tense and his dark eyes taking everything in. He was wearing the same uniform as me, but he looked better in it, blessed as he was with strong shoulders and beautiful dark skin.

"Meet your new best friend," the guard sneered. "Hope you don't snore."

I wasn't sure which of us he was speaking to, but it didn't seem to matter. He shoved me in the center of the back, pushing me further into the room, and retreated, chuckling to himself. The door clanged shut, and the stranger and I were alone.

The man carefully marked his place and set the book to one side. His movements were graceful and measured, as if he wasn't about to exert energy that could be better spent surviving in this place.

"Welcome." His face was a little guarded, and he was still examining my features for clues about where I'd come from and, perhaps, what kind of roommate I'd be.

I stepped forward and held out a hand. "I'm Jakon Gale."

He shook it. His hand was larger than mine, and warm and dry.

"Clement Pace."

I caught a glimpse of a silver bracelet, but it was quickly hidden again by the too-long sleeve of his uniform.

"So," I said awkwardly. "What are you in for?"

A second later, I shook my head and held up a hand.

"Sorry. I was trying to make a joke. I guess it's rude to ask people why they're in prison. Is that rude?"

Clement kept studying me. And then, to my surprise, he smiled.

"I have no idea," he said. "I'll admit I'm probably not up to date on the latest prison etiquette."

"Thāt's probably a good thing."

"Probably."

He kept smiling, and my stomach wobbled a little. Something about him unsettled me. Ever since the flying monkeys had scooped me up from the streets of the Emerald City, my skin had felt as if it were vibrating with adrenaline and nerves. I'd tried to fight off the monkeys, and I'd been brutally aware of how little good it would do me to fight any of those enormous ogre guards.

For the first time since I'd arrived, I was faced with someone who didn't make me feel as if my life might be on the line, and the relief of it swept through me hard enough to just about knock me over.

"You all right?" Clement asked.

13

"Just a little dizzy. Been a long day."

"You should sit." He nodded at the bed across from me. "Everyone feels a little unsettled when they first get here. Everyone with magic, anyway. It takes a while to get used to having your powers suppressed."

I sat gingerly on the mattress across from Clement's, and he sat back down on his mattress, too. He crossed his legs and leaned back against the wall. The cell was big enough that there was plenty of space between us. For the first time since last night, there was enough space to *breathe.*

"I don't have powers," I said. "I think I'm just overwhelmed."

Clement's eyes narrowed, and he seemed to study me even more intently for a moment. "I definitely sense it on you."

"You can sense magic?"

"Of course." He grinned. "I'm from Enchantia."

I'd always wanted to visit Enchantia. Oz had magic of its own, but Ma had always said that the Enchantians were something else.

"Is it true that you all have magic over there?" I said. "Even little children?"

He laughed. "I should hope so. Our way of life and government are so steeped in magic, it'd be hard to get by without it." He laced his fingers together and rested them in his lap. "I guess immigrants don't always have abilities and they get by. Not sure how. Charms and talismans can only take you so far. You, though--I would have sworn you have magic."

I shrugged. "None I know of. My mother always said that was its own strength, that not having powers of our own forced us to think more creatively." I smiled ruefully and gestured at the walls around us. "Not sure

I agree right now."

Clement shook his head. "Magic wouldn't do you any good here. If it did, I would have shapeshifted and escaped a long time ago."

I shifted on my mattress. A straw pierced through the mattress and poked my leg. "You can shapeshift?"

"That's my magic."

Even if he couldn't use it, Clement still spoke with pride. I liked the strength in his voice and the bright look on his face; his magic was clearly part of him in a way I couldn't quite empathize with.

He rested more of his weight against the wall. Slight crinkles appeared at the corner of his eyes. "What about you? Where are you from? And, uh, what are you in for?"

Laughing in a place like this felt wrong, but I couldn't help myself.

"I'm from Oz." I grimaced. "I'm the *mayor* of Oz, in fact, but that doesn't seem to carry much weight around here."

Clement's eyebrows went up. "The mayor? You're a man of distinction."

"Not so much." I leaned against the wall, too. The cement pressed hard against my spine. "I didn't get the job on merit or anything. My mother was the mayor before me, and... Well, it's called a mayorship because Ma insisted on it, but in practice it's more like a monarchy. Passes from parent to child. I'm the oldest in my family, so the job fell to me."

Clement considered this. He seemed to be trying to picture me as some kind of makeshift king, and I wasn't sure he was able to get the mental image to form.

I didn't blame him. I didn't look like much of a ruler. I was short, compared to most men my age, and I didn't have the muscles or the loud voice or the confident bearing of a great leader. All I had was a sharp mind and a commitment to Oz that resonated deep in the marrow of my bones. That was enough, Ma had said, and better than some kingdoms had.

I wished she were still here to help me figure this situation out. She'd been kidnapped by flying monkeys more than once, if memory served. She'd fought her way out of those situations and many others besides.

I shared her love of Oz, but I wasn't so sure I shared her fighting spirit. That had all gone to my sister Margaret. Each of us had inherited pieces of Ma, despite none of us being related to her by blood. I missed them all. Worry for them gripped me.

"And why are you here?" Clement asked. There was something in his voice, some edge I didn't know him well enough to identify.

I leaned my head against the hard wall and stared up at the ceiling. Light from the window had given the ceiling a slightly lighter tint than the rest of the room, but it was still gray, and still dull.

"Treason," I said at last. "Apparently."

He shifted, as if he was having as hard of a time getting comfortable on his mattress as I was on mine. "Apparently? You don't know?"

"I've never gone against Oz in my life," I said.

"No trial?"

I shook my head, and Clement pressed his lips together.

"Me neither."

We stared at each other from across the room.

"I'm a political prisoner," he said at last. "Also *apparently.*"

"Grim."

"Very," he said. "Welcome to the Grand, I guess?"

I did feel welcome, in a strange way. Ma had always said there was no place like home. She'd also said that home was where your friends were.

I wasn't sure *that* was true. Home to me meant emerald skyscrapers and yellow brick roads and the happy chaos of my siblings talking over one another and trying to get my attention all at once.

But I had one friend here now, and it was leagues better than being alone.

10TH SEPTEMBER

I slept in the next morning. Or, rather, I got the impression I'd slept in, based on the way Clement was already up and dressed by the time I opened my eyes.

It was impossible to tell what time it actually was. The sky outside was the same blue it had been the day before, and I hadn't been here long enough to interpret the angle of the light coming through the high window.

"How long was I asleep?" I asked blearily.

Clement glanced up from his book. He shrugged and gave me a gentle smile. "As long as you needed to be asleep, I guess."

"One day in prison and I'm already getting lazy."

"It can take a while to recover from the stress of

getting booked in here."

I leaned up on my elbow. "People do eventually get over it, then?"

Clement grimaced. "That might be stretching the truth. People get accustomed to life at the Grand. Calling it *recovery* would be generous. I don't think we'll get there until the ogres who run the place stop handing out beatings for no good reason."

I flopped onto my back and stared at the ceiling. The flat cement seemed to go on for miles. Its featureless surface looked alarmingly like my future here.

"What do people do around here?" I said. "Do we just sit in this room all day?"

"Some days." He placed a slender finger in his book to mark his place and let the pages fall closed against his hand. "We get to go out for meals most days, unless there's a riot and they want to keep us in our rooms."

My heart skipped a beat. "Are riots a big problem here?"

He shrugged. "Best to just stay out of the way when the weather feels like it's changing. Keep away from the troublemakers and you'll do all right."

I'd heard more reassuring pieces of advice. Above me, the gray of the ceiling seemed to press down onto my soul.

"We get to go outside most days, too," he said. "Spend more time in than out some weeks. That can be nice."

"Is it?" I gave him a skeptical look. "I thought Badalah got pretty hot."

"Badalah's hot," he said. "But we're out in the middle of the water. We get some nice ocean breezes here, and you'd pay a lot to live with this view of the sea anywhere else."

"Lucky us," I said. "We get to enjoy it from prison."

"You've got to take the silver linings when they come," Clement said.

I got the feeling he was talking as much to himself as to me.

I sat up. The thin blanket fell away, not that it had done me much good anyway. I glanced at my uniform, folded on the metal rack, and idly wondered whether it really mattered if I got dressed. Would anyone care? Would anyone *notice*? Aside from the pinstripes on the pajamas, the clothes all looked about the same.

"I can't stay here," I said. "My little brothers and sisters need me."

Clement raised an eyebrow. He seemed to do that a lot; the concise gesture carried a weight of meaning. This time, he seemed curious.

"You mentioned you were the oldest," he said.

"Of seven," I said. "Four sisters, two brothers. The youngest is only six."

"And your mother," he said, somewhat cautiously. "You said you inherited the role of mayor from her. Is she...?"

He trailed off, unwilling to finish the sentence.

I didn't blame him. It had been almost a year now, and I still had days where I couldn't say the word aloud.

Today, though, in prison and surrounded by gray gloom on every side, was not one of those days.

"Dead," I said flatly. "She's dead."

"Your father?"

"Never had one," I said. "Not as long as I can remember, anyway. We're all adopted. Chester's the only one who remembers his birth parents, but he still came to us pretty young."

"So you're in charge," Clement said. "You're the one who takes care of all of them."

It wasn't a question. If my words hadn't given him all the information he needed, I was pretty sure my frantic heartbeat was loud enough that he could hear it across the room.

"I need to get back and make sure they're all right," I said. "The creatures that kidnapped me--I have to make sure they don't take my siblings."

"Are your siblings politically active?" Clement asked.

I frowned at him. "What? Of course not. They're children."

Well, except for Margaret. She could be a bit of a loudmouth. But politics weren't one of her interests. She'd already told me flat-out that if I ever fell off a bridge or something, she wasn't going to take on my job because she couldn't think of anything more boring.

"Then I suspect you don't have anything to worry about." Clement opened his book again, but didn't start reading. "The prisoners at the Grand have almost all been political ones lately. Just like you and me."

"What do you mean, political?"

He pursed his lips, as if trying to figure out what to say, or how much. "I haven't been here as long as some of the others, but the old-timers say that most of the people who've been arriving over the last few months are here because they couldn't keep their mouths shut about changes happening in their kingdoms. They're all people like me: They had opinions and got too loud about sharing them."

A vague anger washed over the pit of my stomach, its heat mellow but deep. "How can you get *too loud* about sharing your opinions?"

"You know." Clement shrugged. "Talking on street corners where enforcers can hear you. Writing things you shouldn't in newspapers. That sort of thing."

"Oz isn't like that," I said. "We're governed by principles of free speech. Ma was very outspoken about that."

"Not every kingdom is Oz," Clement said. "And not every kingdom has been holding to its own rules."

The thought that I might have been thrown into this awful place because I'd dared to share my opinions about my kingdom was enough to make that anger inside me start boiling.

I didn't get angry easily. Margaret, feisty as she was, had always claimed it was one of my biggest failings. But the idea that I'd been accused of treason because I'd had strong opinions about how things were going in Oz made me sick.

What could it have been? Was it my insistence that the Munchkins should receive another representative in Parliament after the Artists' Guild had tripled in size? Or was it my refusal to add funding to the army's budget until the stretch of yellow brick road between Winkie and Quadling country had been fixed? I couldn't think of anything I'd done that would have been serious enough to land me *here.*

"If I'm here for something as stupid as having opinions, that's even more reason I need to get out of here and go home," I said.

Clement sighed. "Good luck. You'd have an easier time conjuring a golden sailboat out of thin air, and I'm saying this assuming that your claim that you don't have any magic is true."

"This isn't very encouraging."

"Trust me, if there was a way to get out of here, I'd have found it already."

"There's got to be a way through the walls," I said. "I saw them when I got here. They aren't that thick."

The image of the jail whizzing along below me as the monkeys had descended onto the island prison filled my memory. Cold wind had whipped the hair across my face, but I'd still made out the high stone wall that circled the island. It had seemed delicate, even flimsy; perhaps I could chisel my way through if I found a spot the guards didn't much notice.

"It's not the walls," Clement said. "They're tougher than they look, but a few guys have managed to climb over or under them over the last few years. They all drowned."

"I'm a strong swimmer."

Ma had made sure of that. She'd had a life of adventures. *You have to be prepared for anything,* she had proclaimed whenever she'd enrolled us in swimming lessons or oil painting classes or a horseback riding course or whatever whim had struck her fancy.

Clement shook his head. "That won't help you. The waves crash against the rocks and you'll get dashed to pieces long before you make your way past them. There are whirlpools all over the place. And if you manage to dodge *those,* you still have the sea monsters to deal with."

I studied his face. "What kind of sea monsters? Sharks are much more docile than most people realize."

A sudden memory accosted me, of the small garnet sharks at the Emerald City Menagerie. They'd been timid animals with shimmering blood-red eyes, and when the zookeeper had allowed my siblings and me to carefully pet them in their shallow pool, their skin had surprised me with its sleek softness. Ma had draped herself along the edge of the pool and stroked them, then glanced up to meet my gaze. Her immediate smile had been gentle and knowing; she knew I liked creatures of all kinds, and I'd realized in that moment that she'd arranged this private menagerie tour mostly for me.

My heart clenched. I missed her in a way I'd never imagined could be possible.

My siblings missed her, too. I had to get back to them.

"Fine, then," I said. "I'll fly."

It was impossible to outrun grief or anxiety. The wizard knew I'd tried. Even so, I jumped up from my bed and paced across the small room.

"There's got to be a way to get a message out," I said. "I don't know anyone who can fly personally, but I'm sure the Scarecrow could come up with a machine. The Urbis Express zeppelins get around in the air well enough. Perhaps he could design something based on those."

Clement stretched his legs out and rested his hands in his lap. "Who's the Scarecrow?"

"He's... Well, he's the Scarecrow," I said. "That's his name. He keeps trying to find a more conventional name, but none of them stick." Personally, I'd been partial to Constantine. It suited him. But in the end, we'd all just kept calling him Scarecrow, and he kept letting us.

Clement still looked confused. I hadn't answered his question.

"He's one of my godfathers," I said. "And one of my advisors. He's brilliant. The Wizard gave him brains a few decades ago and he's put them to nonstop good use. If anyone could invent a flying machine that could pick me up and get me out of here, he could."

This seemed to interest Clement, or at least he looked a tiny bit less skeptical.

"That still leaves the problem of how you get a

message out," Clement said. "They don't let us send letters here."

"Isn't that a violation of our rights?"

He stared at me, then burst out laughing. "What rights?"

Back in Oz, everyone had rights, written into our national laws and fiercely protected by the leaders of the guilds and committees and charters that ran the different provinces. Ma had been passionate about that sort of thing, saying it was an important part of her Kansas heritage.

But I wasn't in Kansas. And I wasn't in Oz anymore, either.

I was in jail, and the walls were closing in.

I sat on my bed and let myself fall back onto the pillow. It wasn't much of a pillow, barely a few pieces of fabric stuffed with what felt like old rags.

I turned my head to stare at Clement, who seemed tranquil. I couldn't imagine being at peace here.

Perhaps it wasn't peace. Perhaps he was just resigned to his miserable fate.

"Aren't you going crazy with wanting to get out of here?"

Clement smiled. It was an almost condescending expression, like the face adults always made when children claimed they'd *never* want to take naps when *they* grew up.

I waited to feel rankled by his look, but instead, a blanket of sadness descended over me.

"Of course I want out," he said. "I want a lot of things, though. I suppose I've just gotten used to disappointment."

He held up his wrists. His silver cuffs shone dully in the maybe-afternoon light.

I wrapped an arm around my pillow, gathering it up as best as I could and snuggling it. The pillow provided a bleak sort of comfort. It wasn't cozy or soothing, but it reminded me of other things that had been--puppies, and the Lion's cubs the week after they'd been born, and my little brother Chester back when he was a cuddly toddler.

"Disappointment that you can't use your magic here?" I said. "I guess I can see how that would be discouraging."

"Not so much that," he said. "Disappointment that I ended up here at all."

He examined one of the cuffs, but his eyes didn't really focus on the metal. It was as if he'd already studied it so many times that there was no point looking anymore.

"Enchantia has always been a place of rules," he said. "We need them to keep everyone on a level playing field."

I frowned, asking for clarification with my eyes, and he seemed to read my mind.

"When so many people have magic, it's easy to let it run the show," he explained. "People with stronger magic can easily overpower people with weaker magic, even without meaning to. I once saw a telepath accidentally end up at the front of a line at the market. He hadn't meant to use his powers to persuade everyone to let him go ahead; he was in a hurry and his mind was wandering and it just happened. We all laughed about it, but without laws about magic it's easy enough for that kind of thing to happen on a larger scale, and then you have powerful sorcerers running your town and no one else gets a say."

"I could see that being a problem."

"Even when everyone's magic is about the same strength, it still sometimes interacts and causes problems." A slight smile tugged at his lips, and I got the feeling he had stories he wasn't telling me. "So legislation is good. Controlling our magic is good. I'm not denying that."

"But?"

He sighed. "But sometimes the people making the rules are the wrong people."

I waited for more, but he seemed lost in memory.

"Is that what happened to you?" I prompted.

He nodded, but not with much confidence.

"I think so?" he said at last, voice quiet with uncertainty. "I was accused of a theft. I didn't steal anything, but the jewels were dumped when the criminal fled and I happened to be nearby. I'm a shapeshifter. I can look like anyone, and I was in the area, so it must have been me, right?" He looked down at his hands in his lap as if hopeful to discover he was holding the answer without realizing it. His hands stayed empty. "The evidence was circumstantial at best, and I didn't even get a trial. They just brought me here in this tiny cart and dumped me." He shrugged. "And here I am."

I stared at him. "That's awful."

"It's weird, is what it is." He glanced up at me, as if unsure how much he should say. Finally, he seemed to decide that, for whatever reason, I was a safe enough person to talk to. "I think it might be because I'd made some political statements in public earlier that night."

I pulled my pillow in tighter. "What do you mean, political statements?"

He glanced up at the window. The rectangle of blue was unchanged.

"It was nothing," he said. "It's stupid. There's been

some rumbling in Enchantia lately, just malcontents making trouble. I said I supported Queen Snow, and this guy across the pub gave me this *look*. It was like a hawk spotting its prey. Next thing I knew, I was being hauled in and accused of being a jewel thief."

Anger flared in my chest. At least Clement had been accused of something specific, but still: Neither of us should be here.

"So we didn't do anything wrong, and we didn't get trials," I said. "What a great justice system."

"I don't think anyone's ever accused it of being spectacular," Clement said, lips turned up in a wry smirk. "Except maybe the ogres."

A bell rang out in the hallway. Its dull, clanging sound echoed down the cement corridor. I jumped and sat up, my heart pounding.

Footsteps sounded outside, and a key turned in the lock. I froze, waiting for the door to open, but the footsteps just continued down the corridor.

"That was the lunch bell," Clement said. "Come on, I'll take you to the cafeteria. The food is awful, so at least we have that to look forward to," he added dryly.

My hopes for the cafeteria had been modest. When I walked into the room, it became immediately clear that I'd still set my sights too high.

Cement walls, cement floors, thin windows that only provided a view of the stone walls that encircled the island, and long metal tables that looked like they hadn't been cleaned in a lifetime--it was a depressing sight. And if I'd thought the visuals were bad, the smells were even worse. An unpleasant aroma of old beans and boiled cabbage filled the room. I gagged. Clement clapped me on the shoulder, pity written all over his face.

"Like I said, it's not much to look forward to," he said. "The best part is the walk down the corridor. It's a chance to stretch our legs."

"How is this legal?" I muttered.

Clement only laughed.

We took our place in the long line at the far side of the room. A long table was laden with dishes, but shielded from us by a metal grille that made it difficult to see the food. A line of ogres stood on the other side of the table, dropping sloppy spoonfuls of unrecognizable mush onto trays.

"Don't try to make requests," Clement said under his breath. "Trust me, just take whatever you're given and say thank you."

I did as I was told. The ogre who handed me my tray didn't even bother to look up at me; to him, I was as good as a rat dropping on the floor, not worthy of his attention.

The person directly in front of me accidentally jostled another larger man, who spun around and got in the first man's face.

"What are you looking at?" he demanded. "You have something you want to say to me?"

The first man backed up, holding up his tray like a peace offering. "It was an accident. Didn't mean to run into you, and I'm not staring or nothing. I'd never push you on purpose, Crowbar, you know that."

"You'd better not."

"You know I wouldn't, Crowbar. I wouldn't disrespect you like that."

Crowbar grunted and marched away to a table. The

smaller man's shoulders relaxed, and he scurried away to the other side of the room.

"Word to the wise, don't bump into people if you can help it," Clement said.

I didn't need telling twice. I watched my step as I followed him to the table, all the while trying to avoid breathing in the scent of the gloop on my tray.

A few men at the table Clement chose nodded at us. They all had silver bracelets on, and the man sitting across from me fixed his gaze on me. He had a rectangular face with a sturdy jaw and small eyes that seemed locked in a perpetual squint.

"Who's the fresh meat?" he demanded. "Don't see cuffs on him."

"This is my new cellmate, Jakon Gale," Clement said. "Don't be elitist, Digger, it's not a good look on you."

"Didn't think we ate lunch with mundanes, that's all."

Clement picked at his food, sitting straight and seeming to intentionally avoid looking at Digger. "You know I don't like that kind of language. Don't use it about my friends, please."

Digger muttered a sort of vague apology and shoveled into his food. Clement pointed around the table as he introduced the other men. Canine was a middle-aged man with shaggy dark brown hair threaded with gray. Barnabas looked to be only a few years older than me, and his posture was like Clement's, erect and fluid. He had golden hair that fell in elegant waves around his face. Stoker, who I was fairly certain was a vampire, had his long black hair tied back in a low ponytail, and he nodded politely but slowly at me, like he'd prefer to be asleep somewhere than making new acquaintances. Bear was the oldest of them all, but despite his white hair and lined face, his bright eyes and broad shoulders suggested an inherent strength I'd never seen in someone his age.

"We all have some kind of magic or other," Clement said. "But that's mostly coincidence. Lots of prisoners have abilities of some kind."

"Including *most* of the recent additions," Stoker said. He stirred his mush around on his plate, disgust curling the corners of his mouth. "I don't suppose anyone here got any meat?"

Clement picked through his gloop. "I think it's just eggs and beans."

Stoker sighed and kept stirring his fork in lazy circles.

"Where are you from?" Barnabas said. He seemed the most energetic of them all. I couldn't tell if that was just his personality or if he just hadn't been in here as long as the others.

I told them my story as briefly as I could, explaining who I was and how I'd gotten here. Bear watched me with quiet interest as I spoke.

"Flying monkeys, you say?" he asked after I was finished.

"Couldn't mistake them for anything else."

"No, I don't suppose you could. I thought they'd all been destroyed."

This piqued my interest. "I didn't realize anyone outside of Oz knew about the monkeys."

"I daresay most don't."

He didn't seem inclined to explain any more, but Clement leaned over to me.

"Bear here is from Aboria. They seem to be an educated lot over there."

"We're not so educated, we just know how to listen

now and again," Bear said mildly.

Clement seemed to suppress a smile.

"Lots of creatures what shouldn't be around are around again," Canine said.

"You'd know all about that," Digger said with a nod. He turned to me. "Canine here is a wolf shifter."

"Not so much anymore," Canine said darkly, raising his cuffed wrists.

A pang of sympathy darted through my chest like lightning, hot and painful. I had been separated from my siblings, and that was bad enough. I couldn't begin to imagine what it would be like to be separated from such a core part of myself. I didn't have magic, and neither had Ma, but one of her oldest friends was a witch and she'd told me enough about how it felt to move through the world with that extra sense. She would be devastated in a place like this. No doubt these men felt the same.

"None of us are what we used to be," Clement agreed. He shot me a wry look that was equal parts tragic and amusing. "It's a terrible place to be, but at least the company's good."

"I wouldn't go that far," Stoker muttered.

I laughed. He glanced up, caught my eye, and gave me a quick smile. His sharp teeth flashed white.

"Welcome to hell," Clement said, raising his water glass. He went to take a drink, then hesitated and fished out a stray hair. It was dark and wiry, clearly from the head of an ogre.

"To hell," Canine agreed.

We drank. The water was brackish and metallic on my tongue.

∼

Back in our cell, Clement and I stretched back out on our beds. There was nowhere to go and nothing much to do. He offered me the pick of his small library of books, and I selected a novel full of dragons and princes and adventures far from anywhere like here. We read in silence for a long time, the only sound the occasional turning of our pages.

Eventually, I glanced over at him. He was curled on his side with the book half-concealing his face. Above the pages, his eyes darted busily back and forth across the page. He was handsome; his high forehead and clear eyes gave him a look of nobility, and I had to stifle the urge to cross the room to run my fingertips across his rich skin.

He felt me staring and glanced up. I blushed, though I hadn't really been doing anything, and he smiled.

"What are you looking at?" he asked.

Unlike Crowbar in the cafeteria before, Clement wasn't asking to challenge me. His gaze was soft, his voice curious.

"Nothing, really."

I hoped the late afternoon light was dim enough to conceal the heat sweeping across my face. I'd never been much of a blusher. That had always been Frank's territory. I must have picked something up from him.

"I was just wondering if you've ever tried to break your cuffs," I said. "You or any of the other guys. Canine looks like he might be strong enough."

"They're solid metal." Clement held up his wrist and pushed his sleeve out of the way. I leaned forward to see, but we weren't close enough.

Clement sat up and perched on the edge of his bed, then leaned out across the space between our beds to show me the cuff more closely.

I dared myself to reach out and touch it. The plain, dull metal was warm from Clement's skin, but he was right; the cuff was solid, without so much as a seam that might have provided a weakness.

"They're magically attached," Clement said. "Ironic, huh?"

"What could break through silver?" I asked. "Or is it even silver?"

"I don't know." He rotated the cuff around his wrist, but every angle looked just like all the others. "There's a werewolf over in one of the other blocks and it doesn't seem to hurt him any, so maybe it's not really silver? I don't know if the silver thing is just a myth when it comes to werewolves, though. I've never asked."

"What's the difference between a werewolf and a wolf shifter?" I said, thinking back to Canine.

Clement shrugged and grinned. "Beats me."

"Do most of the inmates here really have magic?"

He nodded. "Seems that way. I imagine it's because most prisons can't keep magicians in, so they have to send us here. Me, I'd shapeshift and get out of here in a second if I could."

I set my book aside. The reality of having an actual real-life shapeshifter in the same room was more interesting than any imaginary adventure.

"When you say shapeshifter, what do you mean, exactly? Can you change your features or, like... could you turn into a chair?"

Clement laughed. "I can't turn into a chair. Although that would be a great trick to pull out at parties. I can shift into anything living."

"Could you look like me?"

"Absolutely," he said. "You'd be fun to shift into. You've got great arms. Much better than mine."

I blushed again and took a deep breath to try to keep the redness from completely taking over my face.

"You've got nice arms," I said, which didn't do anything to help my situation. "Can you turn into animals, then?" I added.

"Sure. If I were to try to get out of here, I'd turn into a mouse or a fly, and then a bird as soon as I got to the water."

"Not a fish?"

"No way," he said. "Sea monsters."

"I forgot about those."

He laughed. "How do you *forget* about sea monsters?"

I shrugged and grinned. "Never seen one. I guess I'm not sure what to picture."

"Something creepy that eats fish," Clement said. "I don't actually know what to picture, either, I just know that the remains of an escapee washed up on the rocks a few years ago and it was a real mess."

I cringed. "I'll take your word for it." I shifted onto my stomach and rested my hand on my chin. "You said anything living. Can you turn into plants? Like, could you turn into a tree?"

He waved a hand in the air in a *so-so* gesture. "I can, but I don't like the feeling," he said. "It's a whole different array of senses. Trees are aware of their surroundings and they can communicate with each other, but it's... I don't know, it's weird. It's a foreign sensation. Trees don't have eyes and so all the messages they get are through touch or chemicals. It can be uncomfortable."

"That sounds amazing."

"It is," he admitted. "It's incredible. Just... not in a pleasant way." He shrugged. "For me, at least. Some people like it."

I stared openly at him. He let me gape, then laughed

awkwardly.

"It's not that unusual in Enchantia," he said. "You don't have to look at me like I'm a zoo animal or something."

"Sorry."

I realized a second later that he'd been teasing me. The corners of his eyes crinkled, and I smirked and shook my head at him.

"I think you're brilliant," I said. My stupid new tendency to turn red every time I opened my mouth resurfaced, and I quickly added, "Your powers, I mean. They're something special. We have magic in Oz but shapeshifters aren't too common."

"It's a real gift." The light faded in his eyes. "I don't know if I'll ever get to experience it again."

My chest clenched. "You have to. I can't believe they're allowed to just shut off your powers like that."

"They're allowed to do whatever they want," he said. "And ogres hate magic."

"Why?"

"I like to think they're jealous," he said.

He was making light of it again, but the pain was still visible in his eyes.

"They're definitely jealous," I said. "Of your magic *and* your roguish good looks."

I managed to hold my blush at bay this time, and Clement grinned.

"What can I say, I'm a man of many talents."

"The prince of the prison."

"The king of the captives."

"The emperor of the..." Too late, I realized I had nothing to finish the sentence with.

"Enclosed," he said, then made a face. "Enslaved? En... captured?" He laughed. "I've got nothing."

"You've got a friend," I offered.

He smiled at me, and this time, the warmth was back at the corners of his eyes. "That's for sure," he said. "Too bad we're both here."

11TH SEPTEMBER

The next day, I finally got to see more than a tiny rectangular patch of the sky. After lunch, my group of inmates--I'd learned we ate in shifts, and that my shift included only about a fifth of the prisoners here--was allowed outside.

I looked up, taking in the vast blue sky. A few tiny clouds drifted merrily across its subtle gradient, as free as I was imprisoned.

Clement turned his face toward the sky, too, and let out a heavy sigh. The air seemed to carry away his stress, and he closed his eyes and let the sunshine settle across his skin.

Beyond a thick barbed-wire fence, the ocean stretched out, brilliant blue and calm. It would have been a stunning scene, if not for the wire in the way.

Despite the fence, the sea provided us with a cool, refreshing breeze that prevented the sun from getting too hot and stirred the hair on my forehead.

"This would be a paradise if not for the prison part," I said.

"A lot of things about this situation would be great aside from the prison part," Clement said. "At least two square meals a day, sometimes three. Our whole wardrobe is provided for. We don't have many possessions, so it's easy enough to keep things tidy, and we get to live right next to our friends. It's great if you really think about it."

I did think about it--about the foul-smelling slop that passed as food and the gray uniforms and my pillow that was literally thinner than some of Clement's books. I'd asked him last night how he got the books in the first place. According to him, some do-gooder from Badalah had gifted the prison with a large library a few years ago. The ogres had destroyed most of the books for fun, but a few of the inmates had rescued what volumes they could and passed them around. The ogres had let them hold onto whatever they'd saved, solely so they could trot them out whenever nobles or lawmakers from the kingdoms came by to tour the prison.

"You're right, this is a palace," I said.

Clement snorted, somehow managing to make it sound dignified.

"Come on, let's go look at the water," he said. "If you get close enough you can almost pretend the wire isn't there. Just don't poke your eye out."

Next to the fence, the sea was close enough that the spray misted across my face every time a wave crashed against the jagged rocks. Clement hadn't been exaggerating the rough water here; I couldn't imagine how a human being would manage to get through those enormous waves to the calm blue sea beyond. The sea birds seemed comfortable enough, though, and sat atop the highest rocks and stared up at us with their beady eyes.

"It's good fishing right there," Clement said, nodding down at the rocks. "Sit here long enough and you'll see a fish get caught between the crags. Makes for easy picking for the birds." He pointed down to a slightly flatter cluster of boulders. "Couple of tide pools, too, when the tide's out."

"How high does the water get?"

"Not much higher than this," Clement said. "Not high enough that those waves go down any."

I breathed in the salty air and reveled in the water that landed on my face. It was *fresh,* in a way that was nothing like any other aspect of the dank, barren prison.

I ran my fingers through the grass beneath us. Calling it a lawn would have been generous; it was mostly dirt worn down with footprints and salty air and the occasional white clump of bird droppings. Still, a few intrepid green blades poked up from the ground as if determined to make the best of their situation.

"I miss green," I said.

Clement followed my gaze to the ground. "There's not a lot of plant life around here, that's for sure."

"It's everywhere in Oz," I said. "I wish I could take you there. I miss the city especially."

"I didn't think there was much greenery in cities, either."

The blue sky and sea before me grew distant as my mind filled with images of home. "My city's different. It's all green."

I could almost see the spires of the palace I called home, emerald and glistening as they pushed up toward our usual overcast, greenish sky. Ma had said that kind of sky in Kansas usually meant a tornado, but in the Emerald City, that was just how things looked. I missed the gentle billows of the clouds' undersides, the way they reminded me of thick down-filled blankets draped across the whole city. I remembered the mellow autumn air, and the clatter of vehicles down on the shimmering green roads, and the way lights glittered among the emerald buildings at night.

"Are your people gardeners?" Clement asked.

I shook my head. "We are, but I don't mean the buildings have ivy growing on them or anything like that. I mean, it's all *green*. The Wizard who ran Oz a long time ago got the idea after seeing how lush the countryside was, according to my mother. He made everyone in the city wear green spectacles to trick them into thinking the walls were green."

Clement raised an eyebrow, looking almost concerned, and I laughed.

"Plenty of people saw right through that," I said. "Slipping glass into spectacles isn't enough to make a whole city forget what the place used to look like. But everyone respected the Wizard. He had his quirks, but people were willing to go along with them, because he was a good ruler. A month or two after I was adopted, Ma and some of the witches of Oz worked together to cast an enchantment over the city. It's all made of emerald and jasper and green granite now."

Clement stared at me. "That must have been an enormous spell."

"It was. But Ma and the witches were always full of grand gestures." I hadn't been old enough to remember the city's transformation, but I smiled at the memory of the glee that had covered Ma's face every time she told the story. "Ma was so excited to become a mother that she says my arrival infused the whole kingdom with some extra life and magic."

I rolled my eyes, as I always had when she'd made the overly grand claim, but it filled my chest with warmth even so. The fierceness of Ma's love for me hadn't faded, even if she had.

"Maybe that's the magic I sensed on you when you arrived," Clement said, playing along.

"Must be."

"You said before you were adopted," he said. "That's kinda cool."

I nodded. "Me and all my siblings. Someone brought me to the palace when I was a baby and asked for asylum in Oz for me. Of course Ma granted it, and adopted me besides. She took in Margaret next."

"Your sister?"

"She was orphaned when an epidemic swept through a Winkie village," I said. "Ma managed to mobilize a team of doctors before things got too bad, but Margaret was left orphaned before they arrived. Ma felt sorry for her and took her in right away. And then Frank came a few years later, and then the twins, and then little Chester and Lucy arrived at the same time as Gertrude, who was already a few years old."

Clement squinted a little, as if he were trying hard to memorize everyone's names. Not that there was any point. It wasn't like he'd ever get to meet them.

My heart clenched. The sea was vast before me and it was easy to imagine myself flying over the water and circling back around to home. But a dozen insurmountable obstacles stood in my way, from this fence to the rocks to the fact that there would still be a warrant out for my arrest, despite the fact that I hadn't done what they'd accused me of.

"Has anyone ever tried to escape over the bridge?" I said abruptly.

Clement sighed. My constant ideas for escape had to be wearing on him.

But he was patient.

"Yes," he said. "Nobody makes it past the ogres."

"I figured," I said. "But I thought I might as well ask."

I couldn't give up. Not when my family was still out there, most likely wondering whether I was even alive.

I stood. Clement reached out as if to stop me.

"Where are you going?" he called, but I was already halfway across the grass.

I couldn't think too hard about this, otherwise I'd panic and never do it at all.

I approached an ogre standing guard near the fence. He picked at one of his nails, clearly bored. I cleared my throat and he glanced up, his gaze partially obscured by a bushy eyebrow.

He grunted at me to go ahead.

"Sir," I said.

Always be polite, the Tin Woodsman had once advised me. *Lead with your heart. Everyone is the same on the inside. We all just want to be respected and loved. When you're intimidated by someone, start by reminding yourself that they just want the same things you do.*

I wasn't sure he'd ever met an ogre.

I cleared my throat and straightened my shoulders. "Can you tell me how to get a letter to my family?"

The ogre stared at me.

"Prisoners in Oz are permitted to send letters to their relatives and receive letters and packages in return, but they have to be reviewed by a prison guard for contraband first. Can you please tell me the rules and process here?"

The ogre blinked. He had an enormous wart on one eyelid.

"Here's the rules," he said at last. "You don't send letters. You don't get letters. That's the process."

My heart fluttered like a caged bird. "I don't need to receive anything," I said, even though that concession was enough to almost make my throat close up. "I just need to get a single letter to my family to let them know I'm all right. I didn't get a trial. They don't know where I am."

"You stupid?" the guard demanded. "No letters. Ain't that hard to understand."

"I understand that's your policy," I said, fighting to stay calm. "However, as you can see, I have some extenuating circumstances."

"Extenu-what?" he grunted. "You're an inmate. I don't give a rat's left whisker about your circumstances."

My shoulders tensed and my throat tightened. "Could I at least speak to the warden?"

The ogre shoved me. I tumbled back and landed on my backside, jolting against the packed earth hard enough to make my whole back spasm with pain.

The ogre burst out laughing. It was an awful sound, grating and wheezing.

"Look at your circumstances now." He guffawed and went back to picking his nails. "Speak to the warden," he muttered to himself, as if that were a clever joke.

I scrambled to my feet. My tailbone twinged. Across the grass, Clement winced in sympathy.

The ogre glanced up. "Get," he ordered.

I didn't stick around to find out if he planned to

punctuate the command with another shove. Clement was waiting for me, still by the fence.

"You should run ideas like that past me before you do them," he said.

"You would have told me not to."

"Exactly."

"I have to get a message to my siblings."

"The only message they'll get is that you're dead, if you keep that up," Clement said.

I waited for his smirk, but he wasn't laughing. This was a warning, and I hated that I had to pay attention.

But he had a point. I wouldn't get back to my siblings at all unless I managed to survive long enough to get out of here.

I sat back down, then, cringing, leaned a bit forward to take the weight off my tailbone. The water still shimmered in the distance, cerulean and full of possibilities I wasn't allowed to explore.

"Something's not right," I said.

Clement glanced sidelong at me. "You just figuring that out?"

I gave him a rueful grin and shook my head. "I mean in Oz. Me being here--it's not right, but it's something like the seventeenth not-right thing I've heard about this year."

There had been little rumors at first, whispers that the Wizard was back or that the good witches of Oz were at risk of turning evil. I'd thought they were all nonsense--the sort of things people came up with when they were bored and didn't have any real problems to gossip about.

But now I was in prison, and flying monkeys had brought me here.

"I should have paid more attention," I said.

Clement drew up his knees and wrapped his arms around them. "I know the feeling. Things in Enchantia haven't been right either."

"Ma dying threw everything out of whack," I said. "I've been so busy trying to hold things together at home that I guess I didn't focus enough on the kingdom."

"At least you have an excuse," Clement said. "I was just complacent. Figured nothing really bad could ever happen in a place like Enchantia." He rested his chin on his knees and stared out at the sea. A giant wave crashed below us with a boom, and a spray of water misted across our faces. "I'm sorry about your mother," he added.

"Thanks."

Across the yard, a group of men started shouting at each other. I glanced over my shoulder. Two of them shoved each other while a third tried desperately to pull them apart.

The ogre I'd tried talking to seemed to wake up. Interest enlivened his face, and he picked up the club he'd had propped against the fence and strode toward the inmates.

I tensed. The inmates saw him coming and stopped fighting. One of them backed up with his hands up, and the other said something. I couldn't hear him from here, but it looked like an apology.

The ogre stood, listening, and then made as if to walk away. Then he turned back and punched the man across the face. The inmate stumbled back and fell to the ground, clutching his jaw.

All around us, guards who'd been watching the altercation burst into loud peals of snorting, wheezing laughter. My skin crawled at the sound.

"Idiots," Clement muttered. "If you're going to get in

a fight, don't do it in the yard."

"Where *should* you get into a fight?" I muttered. The guards were everywhere. They kept an eye on the cafeteria and even patrolled just outside the bathrooms with their barely-shielded toilets and cold showers running from ancient pipes that looked like they'd come straight out of some garbage dump in The Forge.

"Nowhere," Clement said. "Don't get into trouble here. Don't attract attention to yourself. And don't *ever* get the attention of that guy."

He glanced pointedly over his shoulder. I followed his gaze to an enormous, mean-looking fellow who sat alone near a corner of the fence, watching a group of sea birds hunting far out across the water.

"Who's that?"

"Everyone calls him Psycho," Clement said, keeping his voice low. "He's injured three guards and killed an inmate, and that's just in the time I've been here."

I stared. Clement gave me a tight shake of his head, warning me not to get caught looking.

It was hard not to watch the man, though. He was huge, certainly, and he had shoulders like a boulder and a face that looked like it had been sculpted badly out of clay. But I wouldn't have pegged him for a violent murderer. He seemed quiet, sitting there like he was, watching the birds as if in total tranquility.

"How long have you been here?"

"Two weeks."

Now I stared at Clement.

"I figured you must have been locked up for years," I blurted. "You really know your way around."

He shrugged. "I'm a fast learner. And Canine and some of the other guys showed me the ropes, like I'm showing you."

I imagined myself as the latest in a long string of young initiates. It wasn't a happy thought, although I couldn't tell whether that was because I hated being in prison at all, or whether I had just enjoyed thinking that Clement had taken some sort of special interest in me.

I glanced back at the hulking giant in the corner.

"Why the nickname?" I asked. "I'm guessing *Psycho* isn't what his parents called him."

"I hope not," Clement said with a low laugh. "He got the name because he's a total psychopath, I'm guessing."

"Not a play on *psychic*, then?" I tapped my wrist, hinting at the silver cuffs the inmate wore around his massive wrists.

Clement furrowed his brow a little. "I hadn't thought of that. Maybe. I don't know much about him except that we should both stay the hell away."

I nodded, but my attention was already drifting away from Clement's warnings. Far more interesting than Psycho were the guards. They were changing shifts. One of them clapped his replacement on the shoulder with one hairy hand and said something that made the ogres nearby laugh.

"How often do they change shifts?" I murmured to Clement.

He shrugged. "A few times a day. They usually trade off at least once while we're out in the yard. They eat their lunches in shifts, too."

"In the cafeteria?"

"You think they'd eat that slop they serve us?" he said wryly. "No, they've got their own dining room in their quarters."

I studied the retreating ogres. A few of them looked

tired, or at least their hunched backs and slow walks suggested fatigue. Perhaps they'd been on duty for a while; perhaps they paid a little less attention to their captives when they were about to trade out.

"They live here?"

Clement nodded. "Their barracks overlook the bridge back to Badalah. That way they can keep an eye out for escapees even when they're off duty."

"Do the guards ever leave before their replacements show up?" I asked. "Do they get bored? Complacent?"

Clement gave me a severe look. "You're still trying to figure out how to get out of here."

"Of course I am." I lowered my voice. "And to be honest, after only two weeks I'm surprised you're not."

"I'll take the chance if it comes," Clement said. "But this isn't known as the world's best prison for no reason."

The hard-packed earth around us, the dull cement walls that waited inside, and the ogres who were ready to throw punches at the slightest provocation didn't seem like the *best* of anything to me.

But this place did seem difficult to escape from, and that, I supposed, was all anyone outside these walls cared about.

Clement went back to staring out across the water. I tried to follow his lead, but I couldn't stop myself from watching the guards. Surely, among all of them, there had to be *one* ogre who had a spark of compassion buried inside. Finding someone who would help me escape seemed impossible, but finding someone who would let me send a letter to my siblings--or better yet, to the Scarecrow or the Tin Woodman or one of the good witches of Oz--would be enough to keep me going.

I didn't see a spark of compassion, though. I couldn't

even find a spark of basic decency.

Not all ogres were wicked. Not all *anythings* were wicked, Ma had said, and you should never judge someone by their appearance. After all, the Lion had terrified her when they'd first met and he'd turned out to be a downright coward. I had a feeling, though, that all the ogres *here* were terrible, and that was why they'd been chosen for the job.

Well, if I couldn't find one I could talk into helping me, I'd just have to find one I could outsmart.

I watched them carefully, taking note of their faces so I could learn to tell them apart and mentally noting any behaviors that might indicate a special level of stupidity or absent-mindedness. One of the ogres leaned against a post in the fence and picked his nose. Another tapped his club against his leg and let his eyes fall closed now and again, as if he'd had a late night. One of them was staring across the yard at a group of young men, and his flabby lips were drawn into a wide, unsettling smile.

I watched the young men, too. They were clearly goading each other on, trying to convince each other to get closer to Psycho. The ogre seemed to think he was about to witness an entertaining bloodbath.

"Will the guards step in if Psycho tries to kill someone?" I asked Clement. "Or will they just let it happen?"

He started, pulled from some distant reverie, and craned his neck to see what I was talking about. His jaw hardened.

"They'll let him kill them," he said. "That, or they'll try to kill Psycho. Depends on how brave they're feeling."

I tensed, watching the young men. They were full of swagger. One of them spit on the ground and said something I couldn't quite make out, and another shoved the first toward Psycho. The man who'd spit raised his head and feinted toward his friends as if he were about to strike them, then spun around and marched toward Psycho.

The giant in the corner was still gazing out across the water and hadn't noticed the young men, but everyone else in the area had.

"He's gonna die," a man near me crowed in soft delight.

"Guards'll kill Psycho first," his friend muttered. "They've been just looking for an excuse."

"Guards can't kill Psycho," the first man said. "Even so, I'd sure love to watch them try."

The murmurs caught Psycho's attention. He turned, beady eyes scanning the yard, and saw the young man swaggering slowly toward him. The man was trying to act casual, as if he just happened to be moving toward that corner of the fence rather than to any one person in particular, and Psycho watched him with a slight frown.

The muscles in my neck tightened. My heart pounded, reminding me of the beginnings of a panic attack.

Breathe, Ma's voice reminded me in my head.

I let out a long, slow stream of air. Across the yard, the young man took another step toward the hulking criminal.

It was too close. Psycho's massive shoulders tightened up toward his ears and his hands clenched into fists. He rose to his feet.

The yard fell silent.

I heard my next few breaths. The young man froze, staring at Psycho.

And then, abruptly, he turned and ran. He let out a

string of expletives as he ran back into the protective circle of his friends, and they burst into raucous laughter.

"Real big man you are," one of them shouted gleefully.

The man who'd approached Psycho turned red and shoved the guy who'd spoken in the chest. The man only laughed harder, and the others joined in with mocking jeers.

Across the yard, Psycho watched, his face stony and unmoving. Then he sat back down, alone, and continued staring out across the sea.

12TH SEPTEMBER

We were let out into the yard again the next day. In between the pleasant breeze and the beautiful view, I could almost pretend I was here as a tourist, someone just visiting a lovely small isle off the coast of Badalah.

The tension in my shoulders and the way my heart kept fluttering ruined the illusion. My thoughts kept returning to my siblings. Were they all right? Had the prison warden at least sent them a note letting them know what had happened? Was anyone from Oz looking for me, or had they given up and started trying to find a new mayor already? Margaret wouldn't take on the job, I knew that much, and all the others were far too young to even consider it. Was anyone helping Chester with his schoolwork? Had Ethel managed to get the bird that had flown into her bedroom window up and flying again?

My mind spun in circles, stopping on each of my siblings and then moving on again, never able to rest for more than an instant.

And then there was Oz to consider. What was happening in my kingdom? Had anyone attended my meeting with the Munchkin Agricultural Council, or had it and every other important gathering been postponed?

And how was I supposed to oversee the inauguration of the Tinsmiths' Union if I wasn't in Oz? The Tin Woodman would be there, of course, but they'd specifically asked to hold the event at the Emerald Palace because they wanted me there as mayor. And what about the Quadling's new textile mill? I was supposed to cut the ribbon this week. Glinda could do it, I supposed, but again, they'd specifically asked for me.

But I wasn't there. I wasn't in Quadling Country, or in the Emerald City, or anywhere else I was supposed to be this week, because I was *here,* trapped in the literal middle of the ocean by walls and wires, and monitored by ogres that would just as soon murder me as let me post a letter.

"It's your turn," Clement said.

I jumped. A board scratched in dirt was still in front of me, and I was still holding the pebble that was supposed to make my next move.

I blinked, trying to remember the rules of the game, and placed my pebble. Clement considered the board, gave me an approving nod, and the game moved on.

"You all right?" he asked quietly as soon as the other three men playing with us had gotten into an argument about some obscure rule or other. Not that there were actual *rules* to this game. Someone had made it up at the prison some time ago, and it sounded like the game changed a little every time it was played.

I fiddled with the pebbles in my hand. "I'm fine," I said. "Thinking about home."

"You must miss it."

"It's not just that." I shifted on the hard earth. My tailbone was still sore from hitting the ground the day before. "I'm concerned about my kingdom. So much has been happening, but if the Winged Monkeys are back, who's to say it won't all go wrong?"

He examined the board, but his gaze seemed to go way past it and into the stone below. "But why worry? There's nothing you can do about it here."

"I know," I snapped. "That's the problem."

Regret instantly punched me across the chest, just like one of the ogres might. Clement had been nothing but kind to me. I didn't need to get terse with him.

"Sorry," I muttered.

He shrugged. "You're stressed. I get it."

His placid forehead and steady gestures didn't give much credence to his words.

"You don't look like you get it," I said. "How do you do that? How are you so *calm* all the time?"

He laughed softly. "I'm not calm. I'm going crazy."

"You don't look like it."

"Even with my powers locked up, I'm still a shapeshifter," he muttered. "No one else needs to know I'm panicking on the inside, so I don't show them."

I tried to find a hint of panic on his face. Nothing turned up.

"People see what you want them to see," he added. "That's what I was always taught in Enchantia."

It was his turn. He glanced lightly over the board

and placed his pebble. I still didn't quite understand the intricacies of the game, so I placed my next stone and hoped for the best.

"What's that about Enchantia?" one of the men we were playing with asked. His name was Walnut, I'd learned. He was small and wiry, with skin leathery from years of sunshine. I couldn't tell whether *Walnut* was his real name or just a prison nickname, although his round head and wrinkled face suggested he'd picked it up here.

"Just talking about how we see things there," Clement said. "Or how we did, anyway. Things are changing back home, and not for the better."

"You want to talk about things changing for the worse, you come to Floris," Walnut said. "We've got you beat and that's for sure."

"I heard about that," I said. Their situation had been in all the papers a few months ago: The kingdom of Floris, once known for its beautiful flowers and magnificent plant life, had been all but destroyed by a blight. "Sounds like a rough time."

"You going to go or not?" one of the other men asked.

Walnut placed his pebble, and the game moved on.

"It sounds like all the kingdoms are having problems of some kind or other," Clement said. "I guess that's the way of things."

"Hasn't always been," a familiar voice said.

I jumped and swiveled my head to look at Bear. I didn't know when he'd come to observe our game or how I'd missed him, but there he was, sitting cross-legged on the dirt not half a foot from my left elbow as if he'd been there all day.

"Come on, you can't say something like that and expect us not to ask," Clement said.

Bear gave him a slight smile, but didn't say anything more. Our game continued, and eventually Clement and I were both knocked off the board. The other three leaned in, the competition ramping up.

Bear stood with a soft grunt. Despite the sound, his movements were fluid and suggested a man much younger than his years. He gestured at Clement and me to follow him, and we exchanged glances and then scrambled to our feet.

We made our way to the other side of the grass. The yard was a considerable space, perhaps as big as my throne room back at the Emerald Palace. Even so, it wasn't enough to hold this many men without feeling a bit cramped. Bear led us to the emptiest part, a windy spot next to the fence where not even the boldest tufts of grass tried to grow.

"What do you mean, it hasn't always been like this?" Clement said.

The way he spoke was almost indulgent, like he was simply giving an old man the opportunity to tell some stories, but I leaned forward with real interest.

"Things are getting worse all across the twelve kingdoms," Bear said. The wind blasted up from the sea, bringing with it spray and a briny seaweed scent. "They're getting worse, but they're not actually *bad*. You're too young to remember what bad was like."

Clement glanced at me, one of his eyebrows slightly raised. I shrugged.

Bear laced one finger through the fence, careful to avoid the sharp barbs that marred the wire. He hooked it and leaned back a little, letting his weight pull at the whole expanse of fence. I glanced behind us, waiting for a guard to come yell at him, but no one was paying attention to us. Bear had chosen his spot well.

"Back before you were born, or at least before you were old enough to form lasting memories, the world was a darker place. The kingdoms were constantly at war between themselves, and even within their borders there was conflict and brutal poverty and all manner of things that make life less pleasant than perhaps it ought to be."

A smile cracked its way onto my face. "That's what my ma always said."

She'd had a thousand stories from the time before she'd taken me and my siblings into her life, each one featuring some great trouble or other: the beastly Kalidahs who had plagued the forests of Oz, the invasive deadly poppies that had overtaken the kingdom's meadows, and of course the wicked witch Ma had defeated back when she'd been only a little girl.

By the time we arrived, Ma had more or less given up adventuring. We were her adventures now, she had always said, and besides, the beasts and witches of the world weren't what they used to be.

I'd always thought that was a bit of hyperbole, Ma's storytelling abilities coming to the forefront. Perhaps there was a grain of truth to it after all.

"About eighteen years ago there was a splendid burst of magic," Bear continued. "Peace and prosperity spread across the kingdoms. It was a remarkable time to be alive. The magic crept into everything, bringing life and healing and new color to the world." He tapped the wire and glanced over at us. "Of course, nobody believed me. Nobody but me felt the magic, and every time I tried to explain it they called me a crackpot."

His gaze settled on us, challenging and testing us. After a long moment, Clement shrugged.

"I'm not calling you anything."

"Me neither," I said.

Another strong gust of wind blew specks of seawater up onto my face. I took a deep breath in, savoring the fresh air and its hints of distant freedom.

"I've felt the magic every day since then," Bear said. "It's woven into the fabric of life. It inspired me to leave my village and live in the woods." His mouth turned down a little. "Of course, that may be what landed me here. People get suspicious of hermits. Start slinging unfounded accusations." He harrumphed. "People are dreadful, which is the other reason I went to the forest. You can see what good it did me."

"We can all relate to that," Clement said.

I couldn't. Not really. After all, the Winged Monkeys who had kidnapped me weren't exactly *people*. They were animals, and brutish ones at that.

I wasn't sure what Ma would think of me thinking of them in those terms. She had claimed they'd been quite friendly, once, back when she'd owned the Golden Cap that gave her power to command them.

Of course, the Monkeys had also once torn out the Scarecrow's straw and dashed the Tin Woodman to pieces over some rocks around that time, so I thought Ma might have been perhaps a mite too forgiving.

"You still feel the magic, then?" Clement said. He held up one of his silver bracelets. "Even here?"

"Aye, I feel it," Bear said. "Can't do a damn thing to control it, but I still sense its presence through the lands." His bushy eyebrows drew together and lowered, and his gaze over the water grew distant. "Only it's not right anymore. It's changed. Fragmented. The magic used to feel smooth, like a looking glass, and now it's all been dashed to pieces. And there are more pieces every day, so many that I don't see how they can ever be mended."

Bear's words filled me with a cold fear. Whatever was happening out there was getting worse, judging by the inmates' stories about Enchantia and Floris and my own knowledge of Oz. If it couldn't be mended, where did that leave me? Or my siblings, or my kingdom?

Clement nudged my shoulder and shook his head, just barely, as if to say I shouldn't place too much trust in the ramblings of an old hermit.

But I'd been born with more than my share of anxiety, and warning bells had already started to go off in my head.

Clement put a warm, comforting hand on my shoulder.

"Careful, Bear," he said. "Can't have you scaring my new roommate."

Bear fixed his keen eyes on me. Like his posture, his eyes seemed decades younger than the rest of him. Whatever magic he had learned to command while living out in the woods, it had taken root inside him and kept him sharp.

"I don't need to tell this one about the magic," Bear said. "He possesses some of it himself."

Perhaps he was losing his mind after all. I held up my wrists, which were noticeably devoid of any kind of magic-suppressing cuffs.

"One of those mirror shards you're talking about must have slipped sideways and onto me," I said, as if I had any idea whether that was how magic worked. "I don't have abilities."

Bear's eyes narrowed. "That can't be right."

He looked to Clement, who only shrugged.

"You have an aura of magic." An edge of something like outrage heightened Bear's tone. "The same magic that covers all the kingdoms. You can feel it, Clement, can't you? You're from Enchantia. You ought to know about this sort of thing."

"I thought I felt something," Clement admitted. "Sometimes I wonder if these cuffs aren't just suppressing my abilities, but disturbing my senses, too."

Bear lifted his own wrists and glared at his bracelets. "Dampening my powers, chafing my old skin, and now interfering with my ability to tell what's happening out in the world? Son of a pixie, as if things couldn't get worse in here."

"Maybe you're just sensing some of the magic of Oz on me." I barely knew this man, but the urge to try to make him feel better was strong. We were all in a miserable situation, and Bear had so far been nothing but civil to me. It struck me as my duty to be kind in return. "I don't have magic myself, but I grew up surrounded by it. My mother collected powerful artifacts and we always had witches and sorcerers over to the house." These were good memories, full of light and whimsy. I could have grown up feeling jealous of all the people around me, but they'd been generous with their abilities and endlessly willing to entertain my siblings and me with their more dazzling tricks.

Clement smiled a little. "Sounds like a nice upbringing. Almost Enchantian."

"Depends on how odd you like your magic to be," I said. "I also grew up with a stuffed scarecrow and a tin man as godfathers, and a giant lion as an uncle."

His smile bloomed into a full-fledged grin. "What do you mean, a stuffed scarecrow?"

"I mean he's made of fabric and straw," I said. "And a whole lot of brains."

Bear seemed unimpressed. He rubbed his hand over the back of his neck. "That must be it, then. No doubt you've got their residue all over you."

"I'm sure that's it," Clement said. He seemed to share my urge to comfort the older man, or maybe he was searching for his own justification for thinking I had abilities I'd never possessed. "We both must be sensing Jakon's lifestyle back in Oz."

"Sounds like an interesting place, your country," Bear said. A gust of wind whistled up from the rocks. He closed his eyes against the sea spray and took in a deep breath of the fresh air. "I daresay I'd enjoy visiting. You're the mayor there, you said?"

"Yes." The barbed fence felt very close, all of a sudden, as if the yard was shrinking in on me. "I used to be, anyway. I don't know what will happen now."

Clement put a reassuring hand on my arm. He'd done that a few times now, and something about it always surprised and comforted me. This cold, barren prison didn't seem like somewhere friendship could thrive, but Clement had an unfailing warmth that seemed to defy the fence and walls.

"No one knows what the future holds," he said brightly. "For all we know, the magic that Bear claims is fracturing all around the country will send this island crumbling into the sea."

His cheerful voice was not a match for the image that sprung to my mind, of great cement walls and inmates alike tumbling into the churning, monster-infested waters.

Bear gave Clement a stern look.

"You're not particularly gifted at optimism," he said severely.

Clement burst out laughing.

Bear shook his head as if Clement were a lost cause and turned to me. "The conversation is only going to go downhill from here. You up for learning another game?"

"Let me guess," I said. "It uses pebbles, too."

"What would you prefer, rat droppings?"

"Pebbles are spectacular."

He sat with his back to the fence and began gathering up tiny stones. I joined him, and after a moment, Clement shook his head and settled in next to us.

We played, and time slipped by. The hours dragged whenever I was indoors, but out here, where at least I had the salty air and the cries of the sea birds to break up the tedium, it was possible to pretend this was only one chapter of my life instead of the rest of the book.

After a few rounds of the game, which seemed to consist mostly of trying to take one another off the board based on where a handful of larger stones fell when we threw them, Bear began to talk. He really had lived alone in the forests of Arboria, but, he pointed out, that hadn't made him unique.

"Lots of Arborians live in the woods," he said. "We're a spiritual people and plenty go off to the forests to live in harmony with the trees." He knocked one of my pebbles off the dirt board and threw the stones again. "Difference between them and me is that they tend to live in luxury."

I'd known the Arborians were, on the whole, rather wealthy. They bought a fair bit of the gold produced in Draconis, and Ma had once returned from a trip with stories of golden temples high in the mountains and enormous birds that carried the people on their backs. Even as someone living in a palace made of great blocks of emerald, Arboria had sounded magical to me.

The way Bear spoke, though, that wealth wasn't

something to be admired.

"Everything's *gold this* and *precious stones that*," he said. "It grates on the nerves after a while."

"Beauty grates on your nerves?" I said.

He stared at me as though I was something of an idiot.

"How in touch with the spiritual side of the world do you think it's possible to be when you're surrounded with man-made creations all the time?" he demanded.

He threw the stones again. The majority of them fell outside the small circle he'd scratched into the dirt, and he made a face and handed them off to Clement.

"I went to Arboria once," Clement said. "You don't even have roads in half the country. It's not like you were living in a city like Urbis."

"Doesn't have to be a city to get in the way," Bear said. "All those temples and palaces and manors in the mountains are just a distraction. The people think they're closer to their god by living so high up, but I'll tell you the only thing *high* was all their egos."

I glanced at Clement. He met my gaze and suppressed a smile.

"You sound like a real delight to be around, Bear," he teased.

He threw the stones, scattering them in a tight pattern mostly within the circle. He surveyed the board and removed a few of my stones from the board with a wink. That ended the round, giving us all the chance to rearrange our pebbles to our advantage.

"I'm damn delightful," Bear grumbled. "Just not to mountain folk who think they're better than the rest of us because they have gold-plated toilets to say their prayers from."

Clement raised an eyebrow. "You all pray on the

toilet?"

"They're fancy enough they might as well," Bear said. "You're missing the point, boy. True spiritual connection can only be obtained by living simply with the earth. It's even easier if you don't have other folks around jabbering your ears off night and day." He gave the prison yard a dirty look. "Not that anyone has much choice in a place like this."

"We can go find something else to do," Clement offered, eyes twinkling. "Leave you to your thoughts."

Bear growled, and I suddenly understood where he might have gotten his name. "You think you're real funny, Clem," he muttered. "Real funny. Throw the damn stones."

Clement bit back a smirk and took his turn. He even tossed his handful of rocks elegantly. I wasn't sure whether it was the way he carried himself or just the slender, well-built body he'd been blessed with, but I *was* sure I enjoyed watching him play. His face stayed tranquil but his eyes sharpened each time he focused on the board, and his moves suggested he had a deeper knowledge of even this simple game than most.

He threw the stones again, took one of Bear's pieces off the board, and went again. Bear grumbled something about cheating, but I couldn't see any sign of it. Clement was just good at the game.

Still, it looked like he might be going for a while. I let my gaze soften and wander over the rest of the prison yard. My world had shrunk to the size of this island. It was large for a prison, but small for the rest of my life.

Across the grass, another group of men played a game scratched onto the dirt. A couple of men jogged in circles around the yard, trying to work up a sweat. A cluster of older men sat with their backs up against the prison wall, shooting the breeze, and one fellow lay splayed out on the sparse grass, napping in the sunshine.

On the other end of the yard, in the same place as before, Psycho sat next to the fence. A bird sat on his finger, chirruping.

I did a double take. But no, he really did have a small bird perched on his finger, chirping at him in a high voice that carried clearly to me. It was some species of sea bird; I'd seen similar small, dark-feathered creatures hopping on the rocks with the gulls and petrels that always seemed to be fishing or sleeping among the crags of the island.

Psycho smiled, a bizarre expression on his hewn-boulder face, and said something. The bird tilted its head and listened, then danced lightly up his finger and chirped something back.

It was almost like they were having a conversation. Some people could communicate with birds, of course. Given my roommates' abilities and the many talents of the good witches back home, such was entirely within the realm of possibility--or it would have been, if not for the silver cuffs glinting on both his wrists.

He really must be mad.

"Jakon, your turn," Bear barked.

I jumped and took the stones from Clement. They fell from my hand into a neat pattern inside the circle.

Bear nodded his approval. "Much better than the last round," he said. "You're getting the hang of it."

My stomach churned at the words. I didn't want to *get the hang of* prison. I didn't want to be here at all.

I took a deep breath, but even so, the fence kept pressing inward, its thousands of barbs pricking my soul.

13TH SEPTEMBER

I scooped a spoonful of eggs from my plate. Or, rather, I scooped up a mushy clump of the things that looked like they were maybe *supposed* to be eggs. The food wobbled and its juices pooled in the curve of the spoon. We hadn't been given forks today, due to some guy on one of the other shifts attempting to jab some personal enemy in the eye at last night's dinner.

Noise assaulted me from every direction. There had to be almost a hundred guys in here, and they all seemed to be jabbering or hollering at each other. I couldn't imagine what any of them had to talk about; it wasn't as if much ever happened on the island.

Near the door, one of the ogres leaned against the

wall. His eyes drooped downward and the large metal mug of coffee in his hand trembled. He caught it before it fell and saw me watching. I looked away.

They had to slip up sometimes. Ogres were like anyone else. They had to make mistakes. I might be able to grab a key, or overhear some vital piece of information, or learn something that would let me blackmail the warden, or catch someone failing to lock a gate, or--

"You really ought to try to eat," Clement said at my elbow. "It's not good food but it's not the worst we've had."

He shoveled a spoonful of eggs into his mouth. He seemed to have trouble chewing, but swallowed anyway.

"It's just the texture that gets to me," he said.

I poked the eggs around my plate, mixing them with underdone fried potatoes that looked like they'd seen better days.

"Don't all the kingdoms run this jail?" I said. "Did they all get together at some summit and decide we didn't deserve real food? I can't imagine my mother going along with that."

"Everyone sends their worst prisoners here," Clement said. "I don't know that any kingdom really *runs* it. This place has been managed by the ogres for as long as anyone remembers. It's probably nicer than it used to be. International progress and all that."

"It's *much* nicer than it used to be," said Stoker. He always looked especially groggy in the mornings; physiologically, this was supposed to be his bedtime. "The leaders of the kingdoms have actually taken in interest in the place over the last twenty years or so. Before that, they just shipped their criminals off to the ogres with no oversight at all."

The last twenty years. Or has it been the last eighteen years? Whatever magic Bear had talked about must have affected the prison a little while it was busy spreading peace and prosperity across the kingdoms.

If things really were going bad like he'd said, things at the jail could only go downhill.

Anxiety flopped around in the pit of my stomach like a dying fish. The eggs looked more unappetizing than ever.

Down the table, a few of the younger guys I'd seen out in the yard before were making a ruckus, shouting good-natured insults at each other and throwing food into each other's faces. It was like watching a bunch of poorly behaved children and I cringed a little, but no one else paid them any mind. Everyone else was used to them-- and to the food, and the noise, and the walls closing in.

Even the ogres seemed disinterested. Either they were accustomed to the jeering and the mess or they weren't being paid enough to care.

One of the members of the group elbowed another.

"All you gotta do is catch one of his birds," he said. "He'll go nuts, I promise."

"I don't want him to go nuts, you cottonheaded ninny."

"Yeah, that's because you're a chicken," the first guy said. "You're just another one of Psycho's birds." He started flapping his arms and making chicken noises.

Another member of his group started asking why he didn't try to tick off the madman himself if he thought it would be so funny, and got a clump of egg in his hair for the trouble.

And still, no one around me seemed to mind or even notice.

I had to get out of here.

Ideally while I still had all my senses and powers of observation intact.

I couldn't bear to think of who I would become if I stayed in this prison. I'd been blessed with an enormous family and the best education Oz could offer. I was a good mayor--not because of my own innate talents, but because Ma had loved me, the Scarecrow had tutored me, the Tin Woodman had advised me, and the good witches Glinda and Locasta had regaled me with their years of experience governing Quadling and Gillikin countries. I had been raised to be a good leader, and I tried to become a better one every day. But if I stayed here, surrounded by coarse criminals and with only the empty gray walls to stimulate my mind, I would lose my grip on myself.

I couldn't stand it. I pushed my food away. Across the table, Stoker's groggy attention sharpened and Bear raised an eyebrow.

Clement's hand settled gently on my forearm.

"You all right?"

"I'm fine." My voice came out rough. The environment was taking its toll already. "Not hungry. I'm going to head out to the yard."

He considered me, his perceptive eyes taking in everything and his calm face not betraying anything of his thoughts.

"I'll see you in a bit," he said mildly. "Barnabas has an old deck of cards he bartered from one of the ogres. He said he's willing to teach some card tricks to anyone who's interested."

I gave him a tight nod. I was being unfair. Not everyone in the prison was coarse and vulgar. Nor did everyone belong here, if Clement and Bear's stories were to be believed.

I dumped my tray of food into the large metal bin, but I didn't head straight out to the yard. Prisoners in long-term cells, like me, had a little freedom to roam the jail.

Not that anyone did. There was nothing to see, just corridor after corridor of identical cement hallways and locked metal doors. The most interesting room I had access to was the bathroom, which I avoided as much as possible on account of the smell and the mold clinging to the drains.

Still, I made my way down the hallway that connected some of the corridors. It gave way to some storage closets containing mops and big jugs of vinegar, and just beyond that was a small room containing a rickety metal table and a few equally dilapidated chairs.

This room was reserved for the ogres' staff meetings, at least according to word around the prison yard. I hadn't gotten any indication that the ogres actually *held* these meetings. Their protocols mostly seemed to involve higher-ranking guards shouting at lower-ranking ones when they passed in the hallways, usually things like "You're supposed to let them out starting at *that* end of the hallway, you warty cave goblin" that were inevitably followed by a cuff round the head.

That meant the room was usually empty, which meant I had access to at least one window that looked out toward the bridge.

I'd gotten a vague sense of the island's layout when the Monkeys had brought me here. Now, I had a view onto the full breadth of the prison's security measures.

My heart sank. I had expected locked doors and armed ogres. I hadn't anticipated the enormous sensor arches standing on either side of the bridge and the entrance to the jail. There were three in total, each one tall enough for a small giant to walk comfortably underneath.

I'd only seen technology like this once before, during a trip to The Forge. I'd been young at the time, maybe only seven or eight, but had been amazed during our tour of a Forge security facility. Ma had been interested in purchasing some technology to improve safety along the yellow brick road through some of Oz's more dangerous forests. We hadn't ended up needing one of these sensor arches, but they'd stuck with me. Each one could be calibrated to sense almost anything, from magic to certain kinds of metal to life signs that might tip security guards off to animal smuggling.

I didn't know what these were set up to detect, but it was clear anyone trying to leave the island via the bridge would have to pass under all three.

And that was to say nothing of the guards. I'd expected guards. But not this many, and not this heavily armed. There had to be close to fifty ogres roaming around the prison doors and the first stretch of the bridge. Even if I somehow managed to get past them, the bridge itself was patrolled by even more ogres and studded with regular checkpoints.

The only other way out of here was to swim, and I didn't dare, not after hearing about the creatures in the sea.

I was a fool to think I could escape a place like this.

But I had to be a fool. I had to cling to impossible dreams and design unreasonable plans, because to do anything else would be to give up.

I couldn't do that. Not when my brothers and sisters were still out there.

Why hadn't anyone come looking for me? Why

hadn't a delegation from Oz burst down the doors of the prison and demanded to know why the mayor had been unjustly imprisoned?

But of course no one would come for me. Nobody knew I was here.

I couldn't do anything until I knew what those sensors did.

Heart pounding, I crept out of the abandoned meeting room and toward the front doors of the prison. There was a lobby here, an empty cement room that bore only a single decoration, an old sign reading *Abandon Hope, All Ye Who Enter Here*. I couldn't tell if it was supposed to be some kind of joke.

There was no security in the lobby. That was all outside.

People will let you get surprisingly far if you have enough confidence and a good story, the Lion had told me right after Ma had died and the burden of leading Oz had settled fully on my shoulders. *Most people are looking for a leader. If you act like you're in charge, everyone is likely to go along with it. That's what the Wizard did and it worked out pretty well for him.*

I'd taken his words to heart, and they'd served me well over the last year. Assuming responsibility over my kingdom had terrified me, but I liked to think I'd faked my courage so well that nobody outside my family knew how scared I'd been at first.

I straightened my shoulders. The prison's front doors were heavy and difficult to open, but I threw all my weight into it and managed to create a gap large enough to slip through. I marched, head high, through the guards and toward the first sensor.

"Oy!" one of the guards shouted, advancing toward me. "What do you think you're doing?"

I turned, using everything I'd ever learned to keep my face calm. "The warden asked me to deliver a message to the guards in the first checkpoint."

The ogre's face crumpled with confusion. His hand, resting on his waist, tightened around the leather belt he wore there. A large-barreled brass gun was strapped in a holster. I tore my eyes from it and tried to act like my heart hadn't just skipped several beats.

"He said it's urgent," I said.

"What are you talking about?" he said.

Another guard near him shouted, "That's a load of dung. Take him back inside."

I drew myself up to my full height. I wasn't quite as tall as this ogre. Even so, he seemed startled; most of the prisoners seemed to unconsciously try to make themselves smaller whenever they ended up face-to-face with one of the guards.

"What's the message?" the first ogre demanded.

"The warden told me to deliver it to the first checkpoint directly," I said. "It's confidential."

The ogre's lips twisted in amusement. "So he sent a prisoner to deliver it?"

"I'm not just a prisoner. I'm the Mayor of Oz. It's a sensitive matter and there's a reason he asked me to go." I raised my eyebrows. "You can go ask him if you'd like, but if he gets angry at you for delaying me, don't blame me."

The ogre frowned as he tried to puzzle through everything I'd said. The other ogre snapped at him to not listen to nonsense, and a third ogre who hadn't yet spoken guffawed at both of them for not just hitting me and dragging me back to my cell.

The ogre who'd first stopped me seemed overwhelmed by all the input.

That was my chance.

Before I could think, I took off at a dead sprint down the bridge.

I ran underneath the first sensor, and then the second. The screeching peal of bells split the air as they went off. I ran under the third sensor. It went off, too, the sounds blurring into one unending scream.

Adrenaline pumped through me. I bolted down the bridge, each step jolting my body. The sea air whipped against my face and I felt as if I were flying like one of the seabirds, winging away from this place toward freedom.

I would make it. I just had to keep running, keep pushing, keep throwing one foot wildly in front of the other, keep--

A weight slammed into my back and crushed me into the stone below. A brutal blow landed on the back of my head and a yelp I barely recognized as mine merged with the screeching of the bells.

My head throbbed and my vision filled with black clouds. Someone jammed cuffs into my wrists and someone else landed another heavy blow into my side with the tip of his boot. I winced and tried to roll over to breathe, but some ogre's knee was pressed into my back, squeezing my lungs.

One of the guards hauled me up to my feet and threw another punch at my face. My jaw popped and the world tilted on its axis.

"Get him back inside," someone growled.

The next thing I knew, I was being thrown into my cell. Blood dripped into my eye and my lungs burned with exertion and abuse. The guard grabbed my shoulders and spun me around, so quickly I blacked out for a moment with the pain of it, and unlocked my handcuffs. He was none too gentle, and the metal scraped my hands as he roughly removed them.

The guard hit me again, and again, and threw me against the wall. My teeth chattered against one another with the impact.

The ogre pressed me up against the wall with his arm to my throat. He leaned in until his rank, hot breath covered my face.

"Thanks for the fun," he said, and spat onto my cheek.

He left. The door clanged behind him.

Pain consumed me. I sank down onto my bed and tried to breathe.

Every muscle in my body ached. In a strange way, I welcomed the pain. The actual agony of my cuts and rapidly forming bruises was better than the formless anxiety that had swirled in the pit of my stomach since I'd first arrived here. It was better to be able to point to a gash in my arm as the source of my pain; I could *do* something about a gash, even if I couldn't contact my siblings or check on my kingdom or even get a straight answer about the so-called "treason" I'd been charged with.

I sat on the bed and let my cuts ooze blood for a while. I stared at the tiny rivulets of red. They pooled and beaded across my skin like rubies. I could almost imagine some strange jewelry from Quadling Country looking like this. And my bruises, when they turned blue and then yellow mottled with green--those were little pieces of the other kingdoms, little reminders of the land I'd unwillingly abandoned.

Of the land I would keep fighting to return to.

After a while, I moved to the tiny faucet and drain in the corner of our room. It wasn't much of anything, just meant for ensuring we had a regular supply of fresh water even if the guards didn't feel like letting us out for meals or bathroom breaks that day. The light trickle of water poured over my injuries, cool and soothing.

I tidied myself up as well as I could.

Clearly it wasn't good enough.

"What in the love of enchantment happened to you?" Clement demanded the moment he entered our cell, several hours later.

I looked up from where I'd settled, carefully, with the book he'd loaned me.

"Got in some trouble," I said. "Made a questionable decision. Experienced consequences."

"I'd say," he said. "You're the talk of the jail."

My eyebrows flew up. "It hasn't been that long."

"It doesn't need to be when you bust your way through an army of guards and three sensors," Clement said. "Didn't you hear me when I told you to keep your head down? Damn, Jakon, you've already gone mad."

I sat up and winced. "I went mad the minute they locked me in here. I've just been waiting for the right moment to show it off."

Clement shook his head and sat on my bed without waiting for an invitation. He turned to look at me, eyes huge.

"What did they do to you?"

"Does it look that bad?"

He leaned forward. "You ought to have that cut on your forehead looked at. I'm surprised I can't see your skull."

"The prison has doctors?" I couldn't imagine wanting to be treated by anybody who worked here.

Clement didn't answer the question. He was too busy examining me as if he hoped to make a catalogue of every one of my bumps and bruises.

"Are you all right?" he asked. "Honestly?"

I shifted, trying to find a way I could sit on this thin mattress without everything in my body hurting. It wasn't possible.

"I'm better than I have been. At least I did something."

Clement frowned. Clearly, he didn't much follow my logic.

"I've been sinking myself into a pit of worry, being here." I held up my arm, which sported one impressive gash and a scrape that still had a little dirt from the bridge embedded in it. "At least other people can see these injuries."

Clement blinked at me. "How does *that* make anything better?"

I laughed, feeling lighter than I had in days. "I don't know. But it does." I set my book aside. "Do you know what the sensors near the front doors are for? I didn't have metal or any kind of contraband on me, so they must be calibrated for something else."

Clement's frown deepened. "They're for magic."

I snorted, but he didn't laugh.

"You're serious," I said after a minute. "I thought we'd been through this. Twice."

"This isn't me or Bear saying it."

We let this sink in for a moment. Whatever the prison's system, it was clearly falling prey to the same magic that had Clement and Bear's wires crossed.

"Did they go off when you were brought in?" Clement said.

I shook my head. "I came by air. They didn't bother going through the sensors, just dropped me straight down by the front doors."

He considered this. A couple of tiny lines formed

between his eyebrows, then at the corners of his lips. Every moment seemed to take him deeper into a puzzle he didn't know how to piece together.

"You should try using magic," he said finally, giving me a sharp look that seemed designed to bore straight into my soul. "If you didn't have it before, maybe you do now. Maybe all that magic that's fracturing somehow, I don't know... pierced your aura or something."

"Sounds painful."

But Clement wasn't in the mood for jokes. His brow stayed furrowed and the lines on his face seemed like they planned to settle in for a while.

"I'm game," I said at last. "You're going to have to tell me what to do, though."

He bit his lip. "I've never tried to teach a beginner before."

"You can try to teach me to make bubbles in a glass of water," I suggested. "That's what Locasta tried when she and Ma tested me for magical ability."

"Who's Locasta?"

"Good Witch of the North," I said. When this didn't seem to mean anything to him, I added, "Family friend. Bit like a grandmother."

Exactly one of the lines on Clement's forehead smoothed out. His face transfixed me; he was usually so serene that any sign of stress or confusion made him seem like a whole new person.

"Does everyone in Oz get tested for magical ability?"

"Not unless there's a reason to think they might have it," I said. "Ma didn't even know what race I was for sure when I showed up at the palace."

He shook his head a little and another of the lines smoothed out. "I always forget you grew up in a palace. It makes you make so much more sense."

I eyed him. "What does that mean?"

He smirked. "I mean you don't fit in around here. You're too elegant. Too classy."

I burst out laughing. He stared at me, then added, "Sorry, it's not meant to be an insult."

I waved a hand. "I'm not offended. I just keep thinking the same thing about you."

A slow grin spread across his face. "Guess we were meant to be."

Something about the way he spoke sent heat rushing to my face. He didn't blush--or if he did, his skin was too dark in the evening light for me to tell--but his gaze darted away from mine in a way that wasn't usual.

"As roommates," he added. "We were meant to room together."

"Right, absolutely," I said. "I'm glad it worked out this way. I can't imagine what it would have been like to have ended up with Crowbar or one of the others."

"Crowbar would have eaten you alive," Clement said.

I sat up straighter. "I don't know about that."

"I do." He chuckled. "That or you would have ended up as his little servant, scuttling around and obeying his orders."

"All right, now I'm offended," I said.

But of course I wasn't. Clement's teasing warmed me. It felt like home.

"It's getting too dark to see whether you can conjure bubbles," Clement said, glancing up at the high rectangular window. The sky outside was lavender-gray and fading quickly.

We didn't have lights in our cells; that sort of thing was considered a luxury criminals didn't need. We'd been using a candle to read in the evenings. Clement had purchased it from another inmate using the prison's established system of favors as currency, but its wick had almost burned down and besides, we were running out of matches.

"Let's see if you can make light instead," Clement suggested. "Maybe you can light our candle."

"That'd be convenient."

"It'd be better than convenient," he said. "It'd prove you have abilities."

I didn't dare let myself get hopeful. Magic could help me escape from this place in a way running couldn't touch, and that made even the possibility of it dangerous.

If I had magic, I wanted to know. I just couldn't let myself start wishing for it. I already had too many wishes that didn't have a hope of coming true.

"Fine," I said. "Tell me what to do."

"We use wands in Enchantia," Clement said, frowning in thought. "They help us channel our intent. It's a lot harder without a wand."

"We don't have any wands."

He let out a long, thoughtful sigh. Then he leapt up from my bed and lifted his mattress.

There wasn't anything visible there. The ogres regularly checked under mattresses and shook out our neatly folded clothes while searching for contraband. Instead, Clement had carefully tucked his remaining matches into holes in his mattress. It wasn't hard to find holes--like everything else, these were worn with age and use and hadn't been great quality in the first place--but it took him a moment to search with his fingertips across the fabric to figure out which rips and snags held anything but straw.

Eventually, he pulled out a wooden matchstick.

"Try this," he said. "It's not a wand but it's the right

shape. Sort of."

I took the matchstick from him and held it carefully between my thumb and pointer finger. It felt far too delicate to support any kind of magic.

"Usually you need to form a real bond between yourself and your tools." Clement tilted his head. "Then again, using a match to create fire might make it easier."

"Let me guess," I said wryly. "You've never tried it this way before."

"Shocking, I know."

He collected his candle and settled back on my bed, cross-legged and facing me.

I held up the match, feeling as though I were about to get into a duel with a mouse.

"Now what?"

"Now you focus on the candle and imagine it lit," he said. "Take that intention and channel it down the wand."

I positioned my match close to the wick of the candle, as if proximity might help somehow. "Ah, yes," I said. "The wand."

"It physically pains me to watch you use that," Clement said. "Just so you know, if this works and you want to use magic again, you'll have to keep using this match."

"What if it breaks?"

"It's my second-to-last one," he said grimly. "So you'd better hope it doesn't. Focus."

I settled painfully on the mattress and did my best to imagine the candle springing to life. I imagined light and heat, and the way the flame would paint our darkening cell with its warm orange glow.

I took that feeling of heat and tried to push it down the slender stick of wood. There was *something* there, some sense of power and energy. I pushed it to the tip of the wand and urged it to jump the tiny distance to the wick.

Nothing happened.

"Keep trying," Clement said.

I did. Outside, the lavender sky dimmed and stars emerged, a constellation I didn't know dancing partially through our small rectangle.

I imagined flame, but still, nothing happened. Whatever power I had felt had come from my imagination, and it seemed destined to stay there.

But it wasn't as if we had anything else to do, so I kept pointing the match and hoping for a miracle.

Night fell, leaving us in darkness.

14TH SEPTEMBER

To my utter amazement, the guard that let us out to the yard the next afternoon allowed me out, too.

"You're sure I'm not supposed to stay in here?" I said.

The ogre grunted at me and walked away, and Clement only shrugged, so I followed him out.

The instant I stepped out into the yard, the guards let loose with whoops and hollers.

"Look at that bruise!" one of them shouted gleefully. "Size of the wart on an ugly witch's nose!"

I bristled. Aside from whether anyone enjoyed being publicly mocked by ogres, the conception of witches as hideous beasts grated on me.

"Don't react," Clement muttered.

This time, I took his advice.

The ogres kept shouting comments about my injuries and how quickly the guards at the gates had taken me down. My being here appeared to have rallied them and improved morale across the board. Apparently, all it took to cheer up this crowd was a good beating.

"At least you're making people happy," Clement said.

I rolled my eyes.

Digger walked up to us, his shoulders slightly hunched and his eyes squinting against the sunshine.

"We're starting a game of piglet," Digger said.

I cringed inwardly. I had a feeling I might spontaneously combust if I had to play one more game with a handful of pebbles.

I wasn't exactly awash in other options, though. A person could only watch the seabirds for so long, and I had a feeling I'd get in several hours of that this afternoon as it was.

So we sat and played and argued over the minutiae of the rules like any of it mattered. Other groups of men sat around playing their own games or staring out at the ocean. The ogres had let another group out into the yard with us today, and the space felt crowded.

I couldn't resent all the extra people, though. I'd rather everyone be out here rather than locked up in those depressing cement cells, even if it meant I didn't have as much elbow room as I would have liked.

Everyone seemed willing to live and let live today, even the ogres. The afternoon was warmer than usual, and now that they'd all had their fun at my expense, most of the ogres had stopped paying any attention to us. A group of them sat at the far end of the yard where they played cards and were avoided by the inmates. One guard not far from my group dozed openly against the fence. The rest of us did our best to avoid catching their attention.

Not everyone in this group seemed capable of entertaining themselves with pebbles or conversation or daydreams, though. Near our group, the young men who'd been egging each other on about harassing Psycho were back at it, accusing each other of cowardice and pushing each other to "take action," whatever that meant. I watched them out of the corner of my eye.

Their conversations weren't interesting, not exactly. But neither was the game of piglet. It was hard to focus on anything here, so my attention drifted back and forth and occasionally up to the sky above whenever a bird flew across the yard.

Then, abruptly, my focus landed on one of the young men. It took me a moment to figure out what had gotten my attention, and then I tensed.

Three of the young men had just broken from their group and walked past me on their way toward Psycho, who sat in silence at his usual spot by the fence.

Under normal circumstances, I was pretty sure the criminal in the corner could take care of himself, but this time, the men held makeshift weapons. They kept the objects discreetly tucked up their sleeves, but I'd caught a glimpse of a shard of metal filed to a sharp point. They had dismantled some old chair or shelf and turned the pieces into blades.

I leapt to my feet without thinking and dashed across the yard, dodging groups of men sitting on the sparse grass and narrowly avoiding a fist-sized rock in my path. I threw myself between Psycho and the three men.

"Hey, there," I said, voice as sharp and rough as one of their weapons. "We're having a decent day. Stop and think about what you're doing here."

The man nearest me had already raised his weapon. I eyed the jagged point. My heart thudded.

"Leadership means doing good," the Scarecrow had once lectured. "It also means preventing harm."

I wasn't a leader here, but the lessons my family had taught me still crowded my head. I didn't have any reason to protect Psycho, but something about my disastrous failed escape yesterday had flipped a switch inside me. It didn't matter that I didn't have responsibilities here. I was still *me,* Jakon Gale and Mayor of Oz, and Jakon Gale stepped in to counter injustice and violence. This prison had stolen my freedom, but it wouldn't steal me from myself.

"How about you shut up?" one of the men hissed. He glanced over at the nearest ogre, who was fast asleep on the ground with his head pillowed on his arm. "This is the best chance we've got to get rid of this guy. You want him still roaming the prison?"

"He'll bash your head in before he'll talk to you," another man said.

I searched their faces, looking for any hint of humanity or compassion.

There was none. They were young, and angry, and bored. Psycho was nothing to them but a chance to entertain themselves a little and maybe blow off some steam. It turned my stomach.

"What does that have to do with anything?" I took a small step forward, closing some of the distance between the men and me.

He took a little step forward, too, measuring his will and his courage against mine.

He'd be in for a bitter disappointment. I might be plagued by worry twenty-four hours of every day, but I also had an uncle who knew more about courage than anybody. He'd taught me to feel the fear and take action just to spite it. My arms shook from anxiety, but I stood up straight anyhow and tried to pretend I didn't notice the terror slowly pooling in the pit of my stomach.

The first man lowered his blade, not to back off but instead to position its brutal point just inches from my stomach.

"You ought to back off, little man," he said in a low voice. "Else Psycho won't be the only body they'll have to clean up today. The guards already worked you over pretty well. Wouldn't take much to finish you off."

My heart pounded so hard my entire ribcage shook. Stars sparkled in the corner of my vision, and my entire attention stayed fixed on the point of that blade.

I'd never been in a physical altercation. Even yesterday, that hadn't been a *fight.* I'd acted without thinking and gotten beat up as a result, but I hadn't had time to worry about whether I might get myself killed.

But this man's threats were certain, and the blade poised at my gut had the power to lay me out more quickly than any ogre's blow.

"Let's talk about this," I said quietly. "I don't want to make a scene. You don't want to make a scene. The guards are busy playing cards, and you know they won't be happy if you interrupt them."

"They'll all be happy if I get this psychopath out of the way," the man said. "Based on that round of applause you got when you came out here, I bet they'd enjoy seeing you go, too."

"Or maybe they'll just turn on you."

My words sounded distant. The point of the makeshift blade felt alive, a deadly snake on the verge of striking.

The man tilted his head.

"They can come for me if they want," he said. "It's been a slow day. I'd welcome the exercise."

"I've been watching you and your friends since I got here,"

I said, fighting to keep my voice from shaking. "You're bored. I get that. Why take it out on him, though?"

I didn't dare take my eyes off the man's face, so I just jerked my chin back toward Psycho.

"You'll get yourself locked in your cell or worse, sent to the dungeon." I'd heard horror stories about the dungeon; it was dark, and damp, and people down there were kept in total solitude until the guards either let them out or forgot about them completely.

"Or they'll salute me and invite me to play cards." The man smirked. "You clearly haven't been around long enough to know how things are done here."

Clement sidled up to me, keeping a safe distance.

"Davie, Bones, Clank," he said, in a calm, appealing voice. "You really don't want to do this. The guards are going to notice what you're up to any second, and I already know Ogg has been itching to smack someone around. He just about took Fang out in the hallway earlier."

One of the three men, a younger fellow who hadn't spoken up yet, jerked forward.

"Who do you think told us to deal with Psycho?" he hissed. "Why do you think they're all keeping themselves so damn busy?"

"Clank," the first man snapped.

"I'm just saying, boss," Clank said. "These boys oughta know who they're up against."

"Davie, you should know better than to strike a deal with the ogres," Clement said in an undertone.

The leader, Davie, gave Clement a cool once-over. Then he raised his chin and glanced across the lawn. He caught the eye of one of the ogres playing cards, who I'd gotten the impression outranked a lot of the others. Davie nodded at the ogre, and the ogre nodded back.

And then, quietly, they started packing up their card game. I stared aghast as they filed out, grabbing the other guards on the way and waking them where necessary.

When the yard was clear of any kind of oversight, Davie turned back to Clement.

"You were saying?"

I edged a little to the side, as if I could somehow protect both Psycho and Clement at once. I glanced behind my shoulder. Psycho hadn't moved. He didn't seem inclined to defend himself, or even to escape. He just sat there, birds perched on his shoulder and on the ground nearby, and watched us. A hopeless sort of look clouded his stony face.

"Look, no adult supervision," the other man sneered. This must be Bones. He wielded a blade like the others', and his arm twitched forward as if he could barely stop himself from attacking. "Let's deal with all three of them. One for each of us. I'll take the dark one."

He made a move toward Clement.

Fear hit me with the force of a boulder hurtling down a mountain. My heart lurched and my stomach tightened. A scream rose up in my throat and the heat fled from my hands and feet, leaving them frozen.

I tried to shout, to warn Bones away, but no sound escaped my mouth.

Instead, a violent gust of wind burst from me. It escaped my mouth and my eyes and my chest all at once. Without thinking, I threw out my hands to shape the wind and give it direction.

Behind me, the cries of gulls and the squawks of smaller birds filled the air. One of their wings brushed past my ear as it threw itself toward the sky.

Before me, the air kicked up dirt and blades of grass and sent them spiraling. The wind spun in dizzying circles, around and around until it formed a cloud of debris around us that looked like the whirlpools I sometimes saw forming just past the rocks of the prison island. Particles of dirt hit our faces and small pebbles struck our skin with uncanny force.

The other men backed up, and they were shouting, somewhere beyond the roar of the wind and the scream of the power inside me. The column of spinning air stretched into the air, and the point where it touched the earth sharpened. I felt its strength and its precision, and a tugging in the pit of my stomach told me I could control that point--drive it toward the men who'd threatened my friend, use it to punish them for what they'd tried to do.

I could send the full fury of this twister straight into their path, and it was anyone's guess whether they'd survive.

I directed the force of the wind toward them. Davie scrambled back and crouched to the ground, shielding his head from the wind. Bones fell and scrabbled in the dirt for purchase. And Clank--Clank was nowhere to be seen.

As suddenly as the storm had started, it stopped. The last burst of the twister brushed a spray of dirt from the ground, and then it was gone. We stood in silence, surrounded only by the distant roar of the waves and the gentle pull of the breeze.

Clement took a deep, shuddering breath beside me.

"Well," he said at last, looking down at Davie and Bones cowering in the dirt. "He did warn you."

Bear strode toward us, followed by Canine, and Stoker, who had as usual dragged his blanket outdoors to shield himself from the sun. Bear towered over the two men on the ground and leaned toward them.

"You'll keep your mouth shut about this if you know what's good for you," Bear growled. "If you tell anyone--the ogres, the other prisoners, *anyone*--I'll make sure you never see the light of day again, and that's a promise."

He spun around and glared at the other men in the crowded yard, all of whom were gaping at us with their mouths open.

"That goes for all of you," he said. "Don't think I won't find out. Jakon here isn't the only one with abilities he hasn't chosen to share."

On the other side of the yard, Barnabas squinted at me with unvarnished curiosity. He raised one hand and pointed at his own silver cuff, the question all over his face. Bear gave him a tight, almost imperceptible shake of the head.

He gave Psycho a calculating look, but the man I'd rushed forward to protect was staring at me just like the rest of them. He didn't look relieved. If anything, he seemed scared. Bear turned back to me.

"I think maybe you should go back inside," he muttered. "This lot will need to gossip amongst themselves and they might as well get it out of their systems while the guards are still elsewhere."

I couldn't answer. Shock pulsed through me, sending tingles down my arms and making my breath short.

Clement grabbed my arm. "I'll come with."

He all but dragged me from the prison yard. I let

myself be taken.

The hallways and cells were left open during yard time, either to allow us some illusion of choice or because the ogres were too lazy to unlock and lock the doors that many times. A few of the men who'd chosen to stay indoors today glanced curiously at us as we passed, but Clement pulled me toward our room without stopping to say hello.

He put his hands on my shoulders and drove me toward my bed. He sat me down with a firm push, then went back to close the door behind us.

He stood against it with his back against the metal.

"You sure don't have any magic at all," he said. "No special powers in you."

"I didn't know." My voice sounded foreign to my own ears, and when I held up my hands, they looked unfamiliar, too.

Clement folded his arms. "You didn't know, or you didn't feel like telling me the truth?"

His voice made it clear this was a question, not an accusation, but it hit me like a slap anyway.

I stared up at him. My heart pounded.

"I would have told you if I'd known."

He considered me for a long moment, then unfolded his arms and pushed off from the door.

"Well, then, wow. This is a big day for you." His eyes sharpened. "Are you all right?"

"Yes," I said slowly, trying on the word for truth.

I stared at my hands again and wished there was a mirror so I could stare at my face, too. That man out there, the one who had conjured a cyclone out of thin air--that couldn't have been *me*.

"Bear must have been on to something," he said.

"It was you," I said. "You're the first one who noticed.

You're the one who said that thing about the..." I waved my hands around vaguely. I was talking about something so far beyond my knowledge I may as well have been making up nonsense words. "You know, about the... shards... puncturing my... aura."

I jerked my head up to stare at him.

"What even is an aura?" I demanded. "Is that a magical term or just a fancy way to talk about, I don't know, the air around me? Why did wind come out of my mouth even though I couldn't even use a magic wand yesterday?"

"To be fair, it was a matchstick."

"A matchstick is still better than *nothing*," I said, then frowned. "I mean, I think it is. It seems like it should be. I don't know anything about this." My chest shook with my heartbeat and I felt like I was about to throw up the stale toast I'd eaten for breakfast. "I've never done anything like that before. Ma tested me for that sort of ability. Now I've got it and this is the *worst* place something like that could manifest. I'm in prison. Magic isn't allowed here. Someone's going to tell the guards and then I'm going to end up with those silver cuffs, and then I'm never going to get out of here. That's why the sensors went off when I went under them, isn't it? Because I have magic. The sensors could tell it was there, even if I couldn't. You could tell it was there. Bear could tell it was there. Why couldn't I? I've got these abilities and I can't even feel them. That's not going to do me any good, having powers I can't even control. I'm going to--"

Clement put both hands on my shoulders and pressed down, hard.

"Jakon," he said loudly.

I started. I'd been staring off into the distance; now

97

the distance had been replaced by his thigh.

I probably shouldn't stare at that, a voice in my head said, as reasonable and chatty as if it belonged to someone else entirely. *It's rude to stare at people's thighs. I assume it is, anyway. Then again, I was staring first, so really he's just standing in my staring place.*

I shook my head as if I could scare off my internal monologue as easily as I would a fly. looked up to meet Clement's solid gaze. He waited until my attention was fully fixed on him.

Land sakes, he's standing close, the voice continued brightly. *Not that I mind. He's got nice eyes.*

Shut up, another voice said, and I blinked hard and tried to silence all the chattering going on inside me.

The Scarecrow had always advised me to simply observe the voices in my head as I would observe birds passing by in the sky: there, but fleeting and unimportant. He'd tried to teach me to watch my thoughts rather than cling to them, but I'd always suspected that kind of detachment was easier for someone whose brain was made of straw.

Still, I took a few deep breaths and tried to imagine the thoughts as birds. Slowly, gradually, they faded and flew away.

"You're all right," Clement said, and this time, it wasn't a question.

I let out a final long sigh and nodded. "Thank you."

"I've got you," he said. His kindness was so casual; something about it made my heartbeat slow in a way none of my deep breaths had.

"To answer your questions," he said, his grip on my shoulders loosening. "An aura is the energy that surrounds you, magical and otherwise. Everyone has one, but not everyone's has traces of identifiable magic in it. Yours does."

I nodded to show I understood, and he let go of my shoulders and sank onto the bed beside me. He was close enough that our knees touched, and I didn't pull away.

"The reason you weren't able to use the matchstick wand is that it turns out your magic is different from mine," he said. "Everyone's magic is unique. Most people in Enchantia have a similar kind, because we've got similar ancestors and learn similar techniques from an early age, but the way we perform spells isn't the only way. It seems like your abilities are easier to channel without an external aid."

"I don't even know what my magic is," I said. "That... that thing that just happened out there. What *was* that?"

Clement nudged my shoulder with his. "That's the easiest question of all," he said. "You've got a natural-born skill I'd trade my right arm for. You can control the weather." He held up a finger as if to call a pause to his own conversation. "Actually, you can control wind. You haven't tried anything with water yet and I have no idea if you can change the temperature. I suspect wind's not the end of your abilities, though."

I let my eyes rest at the place Clement's thighs had been a few moments before. His mattress wavered in my vision, blurry as I stared far beyond it.

"I can control the wind," I repeated, trying to make them settle in my mind as something real.

"I suspect so."

"Well."

"Yeah."

I raised one of my hands and examined it, searching for any sign of my abilities: sparkles, a deep inner glow, a shimmering visible to the naked eye.

It just looked like a hand.

Clement grabbed my hand and lowered it to my lap. He held onto it, and my heart skipped a beat and then settled into a slow, calm rhythm.

"Will you help me figure out the rest?" I asked.

"Of course."

I took a deep breath.

"Good. We'll learn about my magic. And then, maybe we can figure out how to use it to escape."

For the first time, Clement didn't seem amused or nonplussed by my talk of getting out of here. He held onto my hand and nodded.

"Maybe," he said slowly, as if trying on the idea for the first time. "Maybe we can."

15TH SEPTEMBER

We weren't allowed out of our cell until lunchtime the next day. The ogre who unlocked our door seemed disgruntled. I tensed when I walked past him, waiting for him to grab me and slap a pair of the silver cuffs on my wrists, but he just let me past and trundled off to the next door.

Relief flooded me. Apart from not wanting my powers to be locked away almost as soon as I'd discovered them, my wrists still ached from the handcuffs that had followed my escape attempt.

"I think they're annoyed Psycho didn't get murdered yesterday," Barnabas muttered when he met us in the hallway. He was taller than Clement and me by a bit and had to duck for us to hear him. "Heard some of them complaining about it when they locked up last night."

"It's disgusting," Clement said. "Prison or not, murdering inmates is a shade too far."

"You should bring that up with them," Barnabas said with a smirk. "I'm sure it'd go well."

We went through the food line and received two sandwiches apiece, consisting of slices of dry bread separated by a single thin slice of ham. I still preferred these to the usual slop.

Clement and I sat with our regular group. These men had always been nice enough, but today, they treated me with a kind of hushed respect.

"You did good yesterday," Digger said while we powered our way through the dry sandwiches. "Damn impressive cyclone you called up."

"Tornado," Barnabas said.

We all looked at him, and he set down his sandwich.

"A cyclone is a large, destructive circular storm, often out at sea and usually accompanied by rain," he lectured. "A tornado involves strong winds spiraling around a central point with a funnel-shaped cloud. They're narrower than cyclones and usually form over land."

Digger blinked dully at him and dropped his sandwich onto his tray.

"Incredible," he drawled. "My life is richer for knowing that. Thank you, Barnabas, for sharing your infinite wisdom."

Barnabas raised his thin eyebrows and pressed his lips together. He picked his sandwich back up and delicately separated the ham from the bread.

"You're welcome," he said. "Precision in language is important."

Digger shook his head. "I'll say."

"I'm actually happy to know the difference," Clement said. "I'm going to help Jakon develop his skills if no one ruins it by alerting the guards, and it might be useful to see if he can create *both*."

Canine leaned forward. His nose twitched a little. "You're going to train?"

I glanced around. Plenty of people kept shooting curious looks my way, but no one had dared sit close enough to eavesdrop.

"That's the plan," I said. "What good is having magic if you can't use it?"

Barnabas flinched, and I realized a second too late how insensitive I had sounded.

"If you don't have the cuffs, I mean," I added in a hurry. "If I can figure out how to harness this *thing* I can apparently do, I'd just as soon use it to get all your cuffs off."

I didn't understand what it was like to have magic but not be able to access it. But I had a firm grasp on how it felt to not have any magic at all in a place like this, and that had been bad enough.

"I've heard your stories," I said in a low voice. "None of you should be here."

Interest rippled through our small group. I held up a hand.

"I'm not making any promises," I said. "I don't know if I'll even be able to create a tornado again, let alone use my magic to get those cuffs off. If I can, though, I'll do my best to help all of you out of here. Nothing is right about this prison."

"You going to knock the walls down?" Stoker suggested. He looked more awake and interested than I'd seen him in a while.

"Maybe? I have no idea," I said. "If we get out of here

somehow, though, you should all formally seek asylum in Oz. Once I'm back in my palace with my guards, I can protect you until we figure out what's going on that sent us all here."

"Cheers to that," Digger said, raising his water cup.

We finished eating, but I wasn't eager to go out to the yard. Not yet, not until I was sure the ogres hadn't caught wind of what I'd done yesterday. Clement and I sat together while the others wandered outside.

After a while, he nudged me and gestured with his chin. I tensed and glanced up.

Psycho was standing in the aisle between the tables, his tray clutched tightly in his enormous hands.

He shuffled from foot to foot. "Can I join you?"

It was the first time I'd heard his voice. It was softer than I'd expected, and gentler.

I exchanged glances with Clement, then nodded at the other side of the table. "Go for it."

Psycho awkwardly slid between the table and the attached bench. He seemed too large to fit there comfortably, but he settled in anyway and looked down at his sandwich.

Finally, after a long silence, he looked up.

"I wanted to thank you for saving the birds' lives," he said.

I did a double-take.

"I wasn't trying to help the birds, I was trying to help you," I said.

"I know. But if they'd attacked me they would have gone for the birds next. They used to do that before I arrived--throw rocks at the birds and try to lure them into the yard with crumbs so they could catch them and wring their necks." He winced; this seemed to be difficult for him to talk about.

I hesitated and laced my fingers together under the table.

"Then I guess you're welcome," I said after a moment. "Those guys are jerks."

He nodded and kept looking at his sandwich. "I'm Silas."

I held out a hand. "Jakon."

He shook it. His enormous hand almost devoured mine, but his touch surprised me with its gentleness.

Clement introduced himself, too, and then we lapsed into an awkward but friendly silence. Silas ate quietly, and Clement and I exchanged glances and waited for him to finish. It was one of the strangest meals I'd ever had, but not one of the worst.

Finally, Silas finished chewing his last bite of dry sandwich and looked up. He searched our faces, opened his mouth, closed it again, and took a deep breath.

"Do you guys..."

He trailed off. A day ago I'd been cautious about this guy, but now, he seemed almost too timid to talk to me.

He took another deep breath and gripped his tray with both hands.

"Do you guys want to come meet my birds?"

That was an impossible invitation to resist. Clement and I nodded, and Silas stood. We followed him in silence to return our trays and head outside.

He headed straight for his usual corner of the fence. No one was nearby; everyone knew this was Psycho's territory, and nobody but the jerks who kept taunting him wanted to get anywhere close.

The birds that were already clustered in this area shifted a little as we approached, but none of them flew away. They eyed us with caution, though, and a few hopped backward and stretched their wings as if they were prepared to fly away at the slightest threat.

Silas sat on his usual boulder, and the birds clustered around his feet.

"They're all right," he said, in his soft voice. "These are my friends."

A few of the birds tilted their heads and considered this. I tried to make myself appear small and non-threatening.

"You can talk to birds?" Clement said, keeping his voice low and smooth.

Silas nodded.

"Your cuffs don't get in the way?"

Silas shook his head. He held out a finger, and one of the smaller birds fluttered up and settled on it.

"The ogres can't stop me from talking to birds," he said quietly. "It's not magic. It's just part of me."

"My magic is part of me and these cuffs shut it right down," Clement said, though not with any trace of jealousy. Instead, he looked a little awed. Carefully, he lowered himself and sat cross-legged amidst the birds.

This seemed like a good idea, so I followed his cue and settled next to him.

"I don't really like people," Silas said.

"I've heard," Clement said. He hesitated, then leaned forward and added, "Silas, don't take this the wrong way, but everyone around here says you've killed a few people. I'm starting to think that's not quite right."

I froze and waited for Silas to get angry. He just held out his other hand and waited for another of the birds to fly up and take a seat.

"I know that's what they say." He kept his gaze focused softly on the bird instead of on Clement or me. "It's not true. I've never killed anybody. I don't think I've ever even hurt anybody. But I'm big. When the ogres kill inmates or each other, it's easy to blame it on me."

Clement stretched out a hand, inviting one of the nearest birds to approach him. It hopped a little closer and evaluated him with its sharp, tiny eyes, but didn't get close enough to touch.

"I can't say I'm surprised," Clement said.

"But that's terrible." My voice was a little too loud. One of the birds nearby fluttered its wings and hopped away from me. I lowered my tone. "I don't know why I didn't expect it, but it's still awful."

"Sums up everything about this place," Clement said.

Silas shrugged, the movement barely-there so as not to startle the birds. "I'm big and ugly and don't fight back."

"You're not ugly," Clement said.

It wasn't exactly true. Between his craggy face and his hulking shoulders, Silas wasn't about to win any beauty contests. But I didn't get the impression Clement was lying; he struck me as capable of finding the good in anyone.

I considered Silas again and tried to be more like Clement. He'd had a point; Silas's eyes were a beautiful blue, and his face made me think it might be nice if he ever smiled.

"Is that why the guards told those guys from yesterday to come after you?" I said. "Because they knew you wouldn't fight?"

"They probably wanted to see if I would," he said.

It was a horrible idea, but Silas seemed to have accepted his fate. If I'd thought Clement was a calm person, Silas seemed capable of taking things without any reaction at all.

Or maybe he was just shy. He'd had a reaction when

he'd talked about the other inmates attacking his birds. Maybe he just didn't like to share his feelings with other people.

I couldn't blame him. There were enough men here who would take advantage of any weakness.

"I don't mind what the ogres do," Silas offered after a few moments of silence and fluttering wings. "Not really. My reputation keeps people away from me. Most of the time, anyway. I don't like people."

"No," Clement said thoughtfully. "You like birds."

One of the small black birds had been evaluating Clement since we'd arrived. Now, it jumped forward and hopped up onto his outstretched finger.

A smile spread across Clement's face.

"I hope you decide you like us," he said.

Silas noticed me looking at the bird with interest.

"You want a head scratch?" he said.

It took me a second to realize he wasn't asking Clement or me. The little bird on Clement's finger chirped back, and a small smile appeared on Silas's heavy features.

I'd been right. It did brighten his face.

"You can pet him," Silas said to me. "Lightly, on the head. If you've got fingernails, use 'em. He likes that."

Carefully, my breath suspended, I touched the top of the little bird's head. His feathers startled me with their softness. I did have a little bit of a fingernail, and I did my best to use it to scratch through the impossibly delicate feathers.

The bird closed its eyes and pressed its head up toward my finger.

"I do like you," Silas said. "You can sit with me for a while, if you'd like. The birds are good company."

The afternoon passed more quickly than any day

since I'd arrived here. Silas was right: the birds *were* good company, and so was he. The three of us talked a little and stayed quiet a lot, and sometimes Silas would share the birds' comments. The creatures were surprisingly funny, making wry observations about the inmates in the yard and joking about aiming their droppings on the ogres' heads.

The other inmates in the yard couldn't fail to miss that Psycho had some new friends. Nor could they miss that one of those friends was the one who'd kicked up a tornado in the yard just a day earlier. They observed us from a safe distance, fear mingling on their faces with respect and interest.

The men wearing cuffs in particular seemed to view me with a new kind of regard. It seemed I had entered a secret brotherhood, made up of men whose imprisonment counted for double. Even here, trapped by the walls and wire and sea beyond, I was a free man.

"You ought to bust up the prison," a man I'd never spoken to murmured to me when all we traipsed back indoors for a late dinner. "You've got the power. I've got the plan." He tapped his temple. "I've robbed banks they said no one could penetrate. I could help you get us all out of here."

I blinked, not sure how to respond to this.

"I'll keep you in mind," I finally said, and the man, satisfied, nodded and fell behind me in line.

"This is weird," I muttered to Clement and Silas once we were settled at our table together.

The others in our usual group didn't join us right away. Instead, they sat a bit down the table, not sure whether they were invited.

I leaned forward and caught Bear's eye.

"Guys," I called, waving at them to scoot down. "We

109

don't bite."

Canine grinned, showing off his slightly pointed teeth, and was the first one to slide his tray down the table to join us. The others followed, clearly relieved to have the ice broken.

"Everyone's jealous of you, Jakon," Stoker announced. "The men with magic want to know how you hid your abilities from the scanners on your way in and the ones without it are getting hopeful that they'll start manifesting powers, too."

I picked up a spoonful of unidentifiable glop and tried to figure out what was in it. "They just might," I said. "I didn't think I had abilities until they showed up."

"You must have known," Digger said with a dismissive wave of his spoon.

I shrugged. There was no point arguing this. If I was honest with myself, I only cared whether one person believed me, and he hadn't questioned me again since yesterday.

Silas seemed to have shrunk in on himself. He ate in silence, careful not to take up too much space or bump Canine next to him.

I glanced at Clement, who saw what I was thinking and gave me a subtle nod.

I cleared my throat. "We haven't done introductions. This is Silas."

Silas looked up, startled at being mentioned. The other men looked at him with expressions of mingled interest and caution.

"This is Canine," I started.

I went around our little group, sharing names, and each of the men did the polite thing and offered to shake Silas's hand. Each of them seemed startled at his gentleness--except for Bear, who I suspected had already figured everything out.

"Silas has a real affinity with birds," I said.

I didn't mention that he could talk to them. My magical abilities had been outed to the whole prison yard, and I had no doubt word of my tornado had reached the other inmate groups, despite Bear's threat. It didn't seem right to out Silas until he was ready.

His shoulders seemed to let go of a bit of tension.

"He let us pet a couple of the birds that hang out with him," Clement added brightly. "Best thing that's happened to me since I came to prison."

Silas smiled, just a little.

Canine turned to him, resting his elbow on the table. "You think you could coax your birds into letting me get close?" he said. "I've always thought birds were damn interesting but they know I'm a dog on the inside and always get skittish. I don't want to attack the things, I've just always wanted to touch one. Seem like they'd be nice to touch."

"They're soft," I agreed. "Softer than I expected."

"I'd be happy to introduce you," Silas said, looking down at his plate. He couldn't seem to meet Canine's eyes, but his smile didn't go anywhere, either.

Clement nudged me. I didn't need him to speak to know he was pleased with the way this conversation was going. Clement, I was learning, liked when people felt included, and this had to be a triumph.

Stoker leaned in toward me. "So, are you actually planning to tear the prison down? Couldn't help overhearing that gentleman on the way in."

I rolled my eyes. "Yeah, I'm surprised the ogres aren't already on top of me. No, I'm not planning on breaking the prison down. My only goal is to create another tornado, just to see if I even can."

"You can," Bear said, not even bothering to look at me. "You'll have your powers harnessed soon enough."

"Maybe not," I said. "For all I know, that was a one-off."

He harrumphed and otherwise ignored me.

"Anyway, I have no idea when or where I'm supposed to practice," I said. "I don't think we're going to have an ogre-free yard again any time soon."

I felt eyes on me and swiveled my head to see a whole table full of younger men gaping at me. They quickly looked down or at the ceiling and pretended they hadn't been staring. Far past them, at the table closest to the wall, Davie and Bones and Clank sat in a huddle with their crew, giving me dirty looks from a safe distance.

"If you guys hear rumors that I'm about to bash the walls in, it'd be great if you could do your best to discourage them," I muttered.

Barnabas gave me a reassuring nod. Digger just looked disappointed.

∽

That night, neither Clement nor I could sleep. He paced our cell in the darkness, mumbling to himself under the pretext of talking to me.

"We could try some meditation exercises," he said. "You've got, what's it called? Core-based magic? Core-focused?" He shook his head. "Whatever. It's primarily internal, so our work should be, too. Except the results are external, so we need a bridge. Not the wand. The wand didn't work."

"You don't actually have to solve this tonight," I said.

He looked up at me, startled to find me still in

the room. I could barely make out in his silhouette. The moon was only a sliver outside our small window tonight; its light was no help.

"The ogres are going to find out," he said. "Nobody around here can keep a secret."

"Some of them looked pretty scared of Bear. You think that hint about having some of his own magic available meant anything?"

Clement snorted. His footsteps on the cement floor stopped. "If he had access to any of his abilities he'd have raised hell by now. No, he was bluffing." He resumed pacing. "I wonder if we'd have any luck creating incantations for you to use. I don't know much about incantations but I'm pretty sure you could make up your own, just as a way to focus your attention."

"I don't think I need words," I said. "That tornado came out of me on its own. I didn't have much to do with it."

"You must have, you were using your hands." He waved his own shadowy hands vaguely in the air in a way I was pretty sure had nothing to do with how mine had looked.

"I was just trying to direct the storm," I said. "I wanted to keep it away from you and push it toward the other guys."

"How did it show up in the first place?"

My mind wandered back to the moment the wind had burst into existence. I remembered Davie's weapon hovering too close to my stomach, and Bones moving toward Clement.

I didn't want to tell the truth of it. But Clement wouldn't judge me. He wasn't that kind of man.

"I got scared," I admitted. "I thought he was going to stab you and I panicked."

Clement stopped pacing for a moment to consider this. Several expressions passed across his face, none of which I could identify in the darkness.

I shifted on my thin mattress. It was impossible to get comfortable, even more so now that I was covered in cuts and bruises that had barely begun to heal.

I still didn't regret trying to barrel my way down that bridge. The sensors going off was another shred of evidence that the powers inside me weren't the fleeting result of fractured magic shifting past me for one convenient instant.

I'd had magic when I'd met Clement. I'd had it again when the sensors had started screeching. And I'd had it when that tornado had sprung from nowhere and knocked my enemies flat on their backsides.

"We can practice in here tomorrow," Clement said at last. "If you can control the weather, all you really need is wind and maybe water. We have a window and we have a faucet. We'll figure out incantations and shortcuts and things when we get there."

This seemed to be enough for him. His footsteps moved across the room and his straw mattress rustled as he climbed into bed. He rolled over a few times, and then his breathing settled to a slow, even rhythm.

I stared at the black ceiling. Clement's plan might be enough for tomorrow, but I didn't just need to practice my magic. I needed to get out of here, and that kind of plan was a lot bigger. It carried more risk. And the rewards--stars alive, the rewards were so rich my heart pounded harder.

I might see my siblings again. I hadn't realized how my hope had been wilting inside me, but now it was back and brighter than ever. I had *magic*. Like Glinda and Locasta and the Wizard, I had the kind of power that could free me from this awful place. I could go home to Oz. I could provide my new friends with asylum. As the Mayor, I could approach the other kingdoms about remedying the terrible conditions of the prison and ensure no one was ever put here again without a fair trial.

I just had to figure out *how*--how to wield my powers, and how to use them to get out of here.

I tossed and turned, my thoughts swinging wildly from hope to anxiety and back again. I had to escape. But I had to have a plan. The plan had to be good. If it worked I'd get back to my brothers and sisters. But that was a big *if,* so I needed to have a strategy. The right strategy could get me out of here. If I got out of here, I could answer Margaret's furious questions and reassure Chester that I'd never leave him on purpose and snuggle Lucy until she fell asleep. I could show my magic to the twins and tell Frank all about Silas and his birds. I could help Silas escape, too. But first I needed a plan.

A plan...

It appeared in my mind just as I slipped from consciousness to sleep. The idea came to me fully formed, crystal clear and sparkling. It would work.

One more day.

Just one more day, and then I'd be out of here.

HEIR OF FUGITIVES

1
16TH SEPTEMBER

I stared at the ceiling, heart racing and fingertips twitching against my thin coverlet. Clement was still asleep, and would be for another hour. Dawn had barely begun to shift the deep blue outside the high, rectangular window of our cell, and it was far too early for anyone to be awake.

But I'd opened my eyes half an hour ago, and I could barely close them again long enough to blink.

I'd been in prison for a week now, and that had been a week too long. I wouldn't stay here any longer. I didn't *have* to stay here any longer, because I had an idea, one that would get me out of here and back to the Emerald City before another day was out.

That, of course, assumed Silas felt like cooperating.

Everyone at the prison besides my little group of friends called him *Psycho*, although he was anything but. Silas was a mountain of a man, but even so, something about him felt as delicate as one of the birds that flocked around him every time we were out in the prison yard.

He could talk to the birds, and that--beyond even my own newly discovered magical abilities--might be my salvation.

I rolled over and tried to sleep, then tried to read, but I was too restless for either. Finally, after I thought I was about to go mad, Clement opened his eyes.

I realized too late I'd been staring at him as he slept.

He blinked at me, his eyelids heavy with sleep, and raised an eyebrow.

"Well, that's not creepy at all."

I propped myself up on my elbow. "I know what we have to do."

He rolled onto his back. I thought he'd fallen back asleep, but then he yawned and turned back to look at me. "About your magic? You've got to practice."

"Not my magic." I sat up. The cool morning air bit through my thin gray pajamas. I liked the air; it felt sharp and awake, like me. "Clement, we've got to find Silas."

He was clearly still half-asleep and it took him a few minutes to process my words. Finally, he blinked. "All right. Is he missing?"

I frowned. "No. What are you talking about?"

"Well, we're in jail," Clement said patiently. "We do everything with our cell block group. Silas is in our group. So we'll probably run into him sooner or later."

"Yes, but I need to *talk* to him."

Clement's eyes fell closed again. "I'm not stopping you."

He did fall back asleep this time, his breathing steady and deep.

I couldn't fathom how anyone could sleep at a time like this. Then again, Clement hadn't been the one to come up with my brilliant idea, nor had he stayed awake long enough to hear it.

Well, I could be patient. He'd helped me through every day of the past week. I could let him get a few more minutes of rest.

Because after this, if my plan worked, we weren't going to have time to sleep for a while.

I fell back down onto my mattress and watched the growing daylight shift across the contours of his face. His skin, which was dark and velvety and rich, went through subtle changes as the sun rose. The shadows in the corners of his eyes and under his cheekbones dulled as the light grew brighter, and at the same time, his forehead and the tip of his nose seemed to warm at the first hint of real sunlight. His lips stayed dark, slightly parted and revealing just a hint of his beautiful, even teeth.

I wiggled my foot, ready for him to wake back up.

Finally, he opened his eyes again, and this time, he seemed like he might actually have a shot at remembering anything I told him. I waited in impatient silence for him to say anything to me.

It didn't take long.

He grinned across the room. "What?"

I sat up, feeling like I could just as easily throw myself to the ceiling.

"I had an idea," I said. "Get up. Get dressed. As soon as we're let out for breakfast we've--"

"Got to find Silas," he finished. "I have a vague recollection of you shouting something about that a bit ago."

"I did not shout."

"You kind of shouted," he said. "It's fine, I don't mind. Everyone loves that when they're trying to sleep."

He grinned, his smile easily the brightest thing in the room.

By the time the ogres came to let us out of our cell, I was about ready to crawl out of my skin. Clement followed me gamely as I plowed through breakfast and marched out to the sparse patch of grass that made up the prison yard.

Silas was already there, sitting in his usual spot. Before I'd gotten to know him, it had seemed strange that he'd sit in the same place day after day, surrounded by birds and talking to no one. I'd wondered if he ever got bored, or had perhaps gone mad.

Now that I knew his secret, it was a wonder he ever did anything *but* sit there and talk to the birds. They were good company, better than most in the prison.

I approached him, barely able to slow my steps to avoid frightening the sea birds that sat on his knee and covered the ground around him. I picked my way between the birds' compact bodies, careful to avoid stepping on a webbed foot here or a splayed wing there.

Silas watched me approach, his face impassive but his huge shoulders drawn up toward his ears just a hair.

"Silas," I said, keeping my voice low so as not to disturb the birds--or be overhead. "You're from Skyla, aren't you?"

"Good morning," Clement said from behind me, his tone a veritable lecture.

"Good morning," I repeated. "You're from Skyla, right?"

Silas stared at me, then, slowly, gave me a single reserved nod.

"You can fly, then, can't you?"

He looked down at the silver cuffs on his wrist that held his powers captive. "Not anymore. Not without pixie dust and not with these on."

"Nobody's going to fly you out of here," Clement said, clearly addressing me. He deflated a little; it seemed he'd thought I really did have some idea that could get us out of the prison.

But he hadn't heard my idea yet, not the half of it.

"I would if I could," Silas said. "I'd be glad to take you home. I hate being grounded."

"I know how difficult it is for you to be trapped here." Clement knelt carefully between a few of the birds and reached out his hand toward a curious gull. The gull considered him with one beady eye, then bent his head and allowed Clement to gently scratch the top of it. "It's hard to be grounded when you know what it's like to fly."

Silas hesitated. "You're from Skyla?"

"Enchantia," Clement said. "But I'm a shapeshifter. I used to love shifting into a bird a bit like these."

No wonder the birds seemed to love him. They liked me, too, but approached me with more caution than they did Clement. They must recognize him as somehow being one of them.

"I miss the Skylands," Silas said. He had a deep, gravelly voice, but it was gentle somehow, too, and held barely concealed longing. "I miss the birds back home."

"But you can talk to any birds." I gestured at the creatures all around us. "Not just the ones from Skyla."

Silas nodded.

I glanced from him to Clement, then checked the yard behind us. Nobody was close enough to listen in to our conversation. They were all scared of Silas, and after I'd accidentally knocked a few prison yard bullies to the ground with a small tornado, they gave me room, too.

"There are huge birds in Arboria," I said. "I remember my Ma telling me about them when I was little." I glanced at Clement. "Bear could tell us about them if we asked him. They carry people around. Ma said they don't even have paths up most of their mountains because they rely on the birds so much."

I turned back to Silas and searched his face, silently urging him to go along with my crazy plan.

"Can you call for one?"

He blinked, his eyelids slow and heavy. The rest of his face didn't change, but even so, I saw the thoughts in his head.

Still waters run deep, the Scarecrow had once observed wisely. Ma had rolled her eyes and told him that clichés didn't qualify as intelligence, but the words had stayed with me. Silas was still, and I suspected his waters went deeper than anyone imagined.

"I've never tried shouting that far before," he said.

"That has to be thousands of miles," Clement said. "He'd have to call out all the way across Badalah. That's not physically possible."

Silas shook his head. "It's not like shouting to people," he said. "Birds talk differently. The wind carries the sound."

Ma had told me that, too, and that was the key that I thought might make this whole plan just crazy instead of outright absurd.

"I seem to have some affinity with wind," I said.

Silas's heavy eyebrows tensed. "I can try. I don't know what birds will hear me. I can't always choose who shows up."

"It's worth a try, though, right?" I said.

Clement shot me a look like I'd lost my senses, but he didn't keep arguing. Silas considered the look for a few minutes while he absently stroked a gull's back. A small black bird on his shoulder hopped and chittered, as if providing its input on my idea.

"I'll try," he said at last. "It's better than being here."

I had already planned out the next steps. We inmates had full run of this wing of the prison during this time of day. The ogres who guarded this place were too lazy to lock all the cells up after us. Besides, there was nothing to do indoors except go into each other's cells and mess with each other's stuff, and the ogres always loved when inmates got into that sort of trouble. It provided them with a great excuse to knock us around.

When the guards were changing shifts and had even less reason than usual to pay attention to who was in the yard and who'd gone inside to nap or escape the sun, we slipped indoors.

"Do you have anyone you need to say goodbye to?" I said.

Silas's nostrils flared. "There's nobody I'll miss here."

"What about Bear?" Clement said in an undertone. "What about the others?"

I'd already spent half the night thinking about this. "The second I get back to Oz, I'm using my authority as mayor to offer them political asylum. Then I'm going to Urbis to figure out what the hell is going on with this place."

This was enough for Clement. He nodded and ducked into our cell to collect one of his books. It was the only thing any of us seemed inclined to try to take from here.

I led the way down one of the long cement hallways, Silas trundling behind me and Clement following behind him with lots of cautious glances behind his shoulder.

The hallway terminated in a window, barely low and large enough for a person to scramble through. It would have been a prime avenue of escape if the window hadn't opened onto the narrow edge of a cliff, full of craggy boulders that dropped almost immediately down to the churning ocean below.

Nobody escaped this way, Clement had warned me

when I'd first arrived at the prison. The sea was full of dangers, from hidden whirlpools to sea monsters that would tear a man to pieces.

It was perfect.

I climbed out of the window first. My stomach swayed as I crouched and tried to find purchase on the narrow shelf of jagged rocks outside the window. Two more steps out and I'd fall off the edge of the cliff.

Sometimes, courage is feeling fear and acting anyway, the Lion's voice reminded me in my head.

I had plenty of fear to go around. I'd have to match it with just as much action. I turned and helped Silas out of the window. Clement scrambled out after him, and the three of us stood at the edge of the cliff with our backs against the prison wall and our hands clinging to the boulders that rose up around our knees and made sure footing impossible.

"You sure about this?" Clement said, reaching up to place a hand on Silas's shoulder. "Maybe we can figure out how to sneak to the yard at night and you can call the birds there, when the guards are all indoors."

Silas's face had lost all its color, but he shook his head. "The sooner we go the better."

Clement searched his face, then nodded.

"Let's do this, then."

Silas took a deep breath and opened his mouth. He shouted, and they were words I'd never heard. Sharp consonants gave way to long vowels that carried through the sky.

I clung to the sharp tip of a boulder for stability and leaned forward. Fear tingled through me like electricity, giving power to my magic. I hadn't felt like I was the one to call up the tornado before, but now, I dove headfirst into my terror and tried to use it as fuel. I reached one hand out into the breeze whistling past the prison walls and grabbed at it, like the wind was a ribbon I could catch and control.

My fingers closed around something semi-solid, invisible and light as silk but nevertheless *there*.

I shook the wind, feeling for its currents, and something about it shook me back. We felt each other, the weather and I, and somehow, at a level I couldn't have explained if I'd been given a hundred years to do it, I asked the wind to carry Silas's voice across the kingdoms, and it complied.

Far in the distance, specks of black and gray appeared in the sky. They grew as they approached. Their wings appeared first, and then I could make out the small bumps of their feet tucked beneath their bodies and the graceful lines of their necks. A single white gull fluttered to the rocks around us, and then it was followed by a speckled brown petrel and an enormous gray albatross. More birds landed on the stones, and still, Silas kept shouting.

I never had imagined a sound as beautiful and wild as this could come from a man who looked like him.

Clement, who found beauty in everyone, had been right.

Silas was *dazzling*.

Hundreds more birds flocked through the sky toward us until the blue was almost obscured. Far off in the prison yard, inmates shouted. My heartbeat quickened. The wind whipped around us. And still, the birds kept coming.

They were magnificent, and their numbers took my breath away. But none of them were large enough. Even the massive pelicans and albatrosses were nowhere near large enough to support Clement or me, let alone

125

Silas.

"Keep shouting," I called over the wind and the cries of the birds.

Behind us, heavy-booted footsteps echoed down the cement hallway. I swiveled around and locked eyes with a furious ogre, who ran at me with his club already swinging.

"Get away from the window!" I shouted, but there was nowhere to go. On the left, the boulders that supported us shot straight up to cradle the smooth prison wall; on the right, they gave way to a thin patch of dirt that looked ready to crumble into the sea.

Clement looked to me, his dark eyes so wide they reflected the white of birds' wings nearby. Silas raised his voice as if to force the sound to fight past the thousands of birds still winging their way toward us.

"Get back in here, you flea-bitten mongrels," an ogre shouted.

He reached the window and hollered at the ogre behind him to hoist him up.

Terror flooded me, and with it came fog.

Huge rolling clouds bubbled up from the ocean, as if the sea were a pot that had begun to boil over. I blinked, and in that time the fog somehow reached us. It gripped my limbs, embracing me with cool mist and soaking my thin prison uniform.

Within seconds, I couldn't see my hand stretched out in front of my face. The birds seemed to have no such trouble. There was no more room for them on the cliff or the prison roof high above, so dizzying masses of them circled overhead, concealed by fog but filling the air with their cries.

"Don't panic," Silas said, his voice calm and commanding. "Stretch out your hands. Trust me."

I had no choice but to obey.

The next thing I knew, my clothes were being pulled at by dozens of tiny beaks. They nipped at my hair and gripped my arms with their talons. Their cries filled my ears and drowned out the screaming of the ogres behind us.

With a lurch, the ground gave way.

But it wasn't the ground. It was me.

I was flying.

More wings than I could comprehend flapped around me, and the birds called to one another as if coordinating the massive effort they'd undertaken.

Understanding of what had just happened rushed over me with the wind and the mist.

We hadn't needed three giant birds to escape the Urbis Prison.

We'd needed several thousand small ones.

To my side, Silas said something in that strange bird language. Farther away, concealed by mist, Clement laughed.

I'd never heard him laugh like that. The sound wasn't just joyful, it was *free.*

We were all free.

We flew forward and soon left the mist behind. I managed to turn my head, just slightly; behind us, the prison remained shrouded, and between us and the ogres leaning out the window shaking their weapons and screaming words I couldn't hear, there was *nothing.*

My skin tingled with delight and relief and lingering fear. We had escaped, but there was still a vast swath of sea below us, and it seemed impossible that these tiny birds could carry us for long. Already, a few of them were beginning to flag. Others swept down from the sky to take the weary birds' places.

I could make this easier for them.

I reached out my hand, again searching for the invisible ribbons that connected wind with water and water with sun. I found the one that felt like a cool breeze and gave it a tug.

The wind changed direction, just barely, and the birds flapped harder to compensate.

I twisted the ribbons again, pulling them into an intuitive order that made sense only to a part of my brain I had never encountered before. With each tug, the wind rearranged itself, until finally, we were soaring effortlessly through the air on a jubilant updraft.

"This is incredible!" Clement shouted.

I half expected the birds to take fright at his yelling and drop him, but they seemed to sense our joy. A few gave answering cries of agreement, and a bluebird the color of the sky shot ahead of us and performed a playful series of twirls and dives.

"I've never seen anything like this," Silas said. His voice trembled, and when I glanced over, tears were sparkling in his eyes.

Or perhaps it was just the wind. My own eyes were pouring from the steady rush of air.

Badalah's coastline grew as we approached, vast stretches of sandy beaches interrupted here and there by carefully cultivated green along the rivers.

"Take us as far as you can," Silas said. He looked over at me. "They're getting tired."

"They've already done more than enough," I said. "Tell them thank you." I looked at the birds clinging to the sleeves of my uniform and barreling resolutely ahead. "Thank you. Thank you all."

They didn't acknowledge me; the air grew warmer as we approached the land, and it seemed to take all their focus to keep flying. We hit land and kept going, and as the desert sped away beneath us, the sun heated the air until the birds seemed ready to wilt.

"They've done enough," I said to Silas, gratitude filling me until I felt like I might burst. "Tell them to set us down. They shouldn't suffer on our account."

He seemed in full agreement, and spoke to the birds in words I couldn't understand and in ones I could. Slowly, gradually, we approached the ground. Irregular brown gave way to a clear picture of sand broken up here and there by scrubby brush and the occasional formation of red or beige stone.

They set us in the shade near a river. The trees here were scraggly, with thick, flaking bark and leaves that seemed shriveled by the sun. We stumbled as we landed, our legs overwhelmed with the task of supporting our bodies after that incredible flight.

The birds filled the trees and descended on the river, ready for rest. A few who had been following along with the strange, motley flock winged away and returned after a while, bearing prickly fruits and dead desert mice. They dropped the food before us and landed, chirping and squawking at Silas.

He smothered them with thanks and affection. Clement sat with his arms outstretched and allowed the birds to rest on him, and I leaned against one of the trees and provided scratches to as many birds as came to demand them.

"This is the most surreal moment of my life," I said, while I petted a pigeon with one hand and scratched a seagull with another. A tiny brown wren rubbed her head vigorously against the toe of my shoe. "And I was brought to the prison by flying monkeys."

A giant hawk screamed overhead. Its voice dissipated

across the sands, reminding me how far we must be from civilization.

Silas looked up. The hawk's wings sliced through the blue sky. It circled once, and then it winged its way off into the distance.

"It's safe to sleep here," Silas said. "We're far from anyone else, and he says we're well concealed under these trees."

A sand-colored wren fluttered up onto his shoulder and chirped. He listened, then his impassive face cracked into another transformative smile.

"It seems a few of the birds have offered to stay and keep watch through the night," he said. "There's a village half a day's travel from here. We should leave at dawn."

17TH SEPTEMBER

The birds woke us with chirps and coos before the sun peeked over the horizon. The dark sky shimmered with hints of lavender, promising at the day to come.

I shifted, and a susurration of wings rose all around me. Sometime during the night, the birds had come to rest on and around me, keeping me warm against the desert night. I blinked sleep from my eyes and stroked as many feathered heads as I could manage, murmuring my thanks.

We rose and gathered ourselves. We were a ragged crew, clad in dirt-streaked gray prison uniforms, but the birds fluttered around us and tried to tug our clothes and hair into order. Clement grinned at me.

"Never been groomed by a bird before," he said.

A tiny sparrow nipped at his collar and pecked to get it to lay flat. At our feet, a burrowing owl shuffled across the ground and fiddled with our shoelaces.

"Is this how you get dressed every morning?" Clement said.

Silas flashed the briefest of smiles. "Not usually. They took exception to our appearances."

"We must look bad if *birds* care." I attempted to help them out by adjusting my hair, but the thrasher perched on my head nipped at my finger to warn me away.

Finally, the birds fluttered to the ground or to the trees, and Silas pronounced us ready to depart.

We followed the river. It wasn't the most direct route to the village, Silas said, but the hawk he'd spoken with last night had suggested we'd be more hidden here.

"He doesn't recommend we wade into the river," Silas said as we trudged along between sparse stands of trees. "On account of the alligators."

"Excuse me, what?" I said.

"But he said it might be worth the risk to hide under the water if someone from the prison happens to come across us."

"Are they anywhere close?" Clement asked.

"He hasn't seen anyone yet," Silas said. "Any guards who will be looking for us will have to use the mainland bridge. The birds took us a different direction."

"We'll have to hope they don't figure out where we ended up, then."

Clement clambered over a few knee-high rocks. Silas, being something of a boulder himself, walked around them.

"What are we going to do, anyway?" I said. "After we

reach this village? We can't take the Urbis Express or a train. People are looking for us."

"We'll have to make it to Oz on foot." Clement sounded resolute, as if this idea didn't intimidate him at all.

But I knew how big Badalah and Aboria were, and how many dangers lay between us and the Emerald City.

Most of the birds had gone their own way once we'd started walking, but a small beige wren had decided to stick with us, using Silas as her personal transportation. She hopped up his shoulder and chittered.

"She says there's a stand of salamander succulents up ahead," Silas translated. "They're edible and full of water. She recommends we pick some and eat while we walk."

"I'm happy to do anything the birds advise," I said.

We harvested as many of the succulents as we could carry. They were funny looking plants, with fat, glossy oval leaves speckled with yellow. Their waxy skin reminded me of rubber, but when I broke one in half to investigate, the leaf oozed a refreshing gel that smelled like fresh lettuce.

They tasted a bit like lettuce, too, and the wren had been right about them being full of water. I devoured mine, and they tasted a thousand times better than anything I'd eaten in the prison. She ate while we walked, too, swooping down occasionally from Silas's shoulder to capture a beetle or spider.

Finally, when the sun was almost at its zenith and sweat dripped down our faces, the blocky brown shapes of mud-block houses appeared in the distance on either side of the river. A rope bridge stretched across the water, and people in pale robes filled the streets. There were more trees here, carefully cultivated and heavy with oranges and figs.

The wren chirruped in Silas's ear.

"This is Shajara," he translated. "We might be able to find work and a meal here, but she says we shouldn't get our hopes up."

I frowned at the little bird. "What does that mean?"

Silas shrugged.

We entered the town via a side alley, stepping over a short mud wall and ducking beneath laundry hanging on a line between the buildings.

"I hate to be the one to suggest this," I said, lifting a piece of pale fabric. "But do you think we ought to trade out our prison uniforms for something a little less conspicuous?"

We all stared at the laundry for a long moment.

"I'm not a thief," Clement said finally. "No matter what law enforcement in Enchantia claims."

I ran my hand across the back of my neck. "I'm not a thief either. This would be a loan. Maybe just a loan they won't know about yet. We know the name of this village. Once I get back to Oz, I'll send them money to pay for the clothes and apologize for any trouble."

They considered this, and finally, Clement nodded. "It's better than ending up back in Urbis Prison."

Silas was already reaching for the fabric on the line. "Anything is better than prison."

We changed quickly, replacing the worn prison uniform with equally worn loose trousers and robes with baggy hoods. These clothes were better suited for the desert climate, shielding us from the sun and allowing airflow. We climbed back over the mud wall and hurriedly dug a shallow trench with our hands, then threw our old prison uniforms into the hole and buried them again.

I threw a final handful of sand onto the buried uniforms. That worn-out fabric had weighed almost nothing, and yet, now that I had replaced it with three times as much material, I felt lighter than I had in weeks.

The wren chirped.

"You're right," Silas said. "We'd better not stand here."

Back on the narrow streets of Shajara with our hoods drawn against the sun, we could have been mistaken for residents of the city if it hadn't been for Silas. The largest clothes we'd found on the line still weren't big enough to fit him. The hems of his trousers and robe hovered above his ankles, and the fabric stretched across his broad shoulders as if it was on the verge of ripping.

"Now what?" I said. "We don't have any money."

"We beg," Clement said. "Or we find work."

I glanced around. "I don't think we're going to find work here. Or food."

There were too many people on the streets--not shopping or doing business, but sitting as if they *lived* out here on the mud paving stones. Too many of them had deep hollows beneath their cheekbones and patches on their clothes.

"We should try," Clement said. "We're not going to get far without bread."

I nodded, and we made our way further down the street toward a storefront with a display of flatbread and honeyed sweetbreads in the window. Several beggars sat outside. One shook a tin cup at us, rattling the single coin inside it. The others didn't even bother.

"I'm sorry, I don't have any money," I said to the

man with the cup.

He stared at me, then let loose with a string of expletives. Clement grabbed my arm and pulled me inside.

We approached the counter. A gruff man stood behind it, his apron covered in flour.

"Olive and salt flatbreads half-off today only," he said.

"We're actually here looking for work, if you hav--" I started.

He cut me off with a scoff. "You're all looking for work," he said. "You have money?"

I hesitated. It sounded like a bit of a trick question.

"No," I finally said. "That's why we're hoping--"

"I don't have work." The man's gaze flickered up to Silas, and he seemed to steel himself. He rested his hands on the edge of the counter as if trying to make himself bigger. "Not for anybody but myself. I'll tell you what I *do* have: a family. A wife and two young daughters, and they all need food in their bellies. Are you going to buy something?"

Annoyance flared like fire inside me. "No, we're not," I said. "We're just trying to make an honest few coins--"

"Honest," the man barked. "You think it's honest to come into my shop and beg?"

"We're not *begging*," I started.

Clement grabbed my arm and squeezed. I bit my tongue.

"In that case, sir, good day," I said.

I let Clement drag me out of the shop. The man watched us, his eyes mostly fixed on Silas, until the door slammed shut behind us.

"That was productive," I said.

Clement shook his head tightly at me. He led the way

down the street. I followed, and Silas trundled behind me, walking slowly with the wren still on his shoulder.

We wandered the city, passing homes and shops and village squares filled with shabbily dressed people. I'd thought perhaps we'd come into the bad side of town and that we'd find friendly people on the other side of the river, but when we crossed the rickety rope bridge and explored the other side of town, we found only more half-empty shops and villagers who looked at us with narrowed eyes.

Clement stopped outside a boarded-up shop. He gestured at us to huddle closer.

"You were right, Jakon, we're not going to find anything here," he said. "Look at this place."

Across the street, a middle-aged man and a young woman were locked in a tense, half-whispered argument. He gestured at her basket, and she held it behind herself as if trying to protect whatever was inside. Further down the street, a couple of young men were openly arguing.

"They're all hungry," Silas said. "There's not enough food. Or not enough money."

"There's not enough of anything," Clement said. His hand tightened around the end of his sleeve, and I knew he was thinking the same thing as me: that we'd been wrong to steal the clothes from the line, and that we'd equally had no choice.

"It hasn't always been like this." I nodded at the boards locking up the shop next to us. They hadn't been here long; the wood wasn't new, but the patterns of wear didn't match this location. They'd been put up to block off this window recently.

Clement nodded slowly, and I followed his gaze across the street. Another empty mud brick shop sat there, its doorway and windows empty and the room inside swept clean. A couple of starving children huddled inside, playing games and shooting us the occasional cautious glance with eyes that seemed set too far into their skull-like heads.

"They're all starving," Clement said. The calm of his face didn't match the pain in his voice. "I didn't think Badalah was this badly off."

"They aren't," I said. "At least, the capital city isn't. Or wasn't. Or isn't supposed to be. Badalah has always thrived thanks to its crops of spices and coffee."

Ma and the Scarecrow had told me about the capital city, Kisbu, back when they'd come back from a diplomatic visit. It was beautiful, they'd said, with stunning architecture and some of the best food and most beautiful music in all the kingdoms. They hadn't said anything about poverty or starvation. In my job as mayor of Oz, I'd always had the impression that Badalah was one of, if not the richest of the kingdoms.

"Things are going wrong here," I said. "Just like in the other kingdoms."

Down the street, the young men who'd been arguing raised their voices. One of them struck the other across the face. I flinched as the young man yelped and swung back.

One of the men in the group saw me looking. He stared, then rose up and moved toward us.

"We should get out of here," I muttered. "Now. The desert might be unforgiving but this town is worse."

My companions didn't need telling twice. Bread or not, Shajara held nothing for us. We ducked down a side alley, darted through a drab back garden filled with thirsty, wilting plants, and strode back out into the dry wilderness.

We spent the hottest part of the day resting beneath another stand of trees, far upriver from the village. I stared at the water bubbling past and tried to make sense of what we'd seen back there.

"She says the bark of these trees is edible," Silas said after a conversation with the ever-helpful wren. "It's hard to chew so we'll have to soak it in water or figure out how to boil it. Besides that, there are prickly pears all through this desert and she said we can always call a hawk to help us catch rodents or even desert rabbits."

I reached out a hand, slowly so as not to scare the wren, and scratched the top of her head.

"Why is she being so helpful?" I said. "We haven't done anything for her."

Silas blinked at me as if he hadn't quite understood the question. "She's a bird," he said after a moment.

He seemed to consider that an actual answer. Clement bit his lip and seemed to suppress a smile. I caught his eye, and he shrugged at me.

"It sounds like we won't starve," Clement said. "Which is more than I can say for the people in that village."

"What did you mean, things are wrong there like everywhere else?" Silas asked, staring at me. His eyes were a beautiful blue; it saddened me that no one at the prison had ever bothered to notice them or the kind man behind them.

I sighed and stretched out my feet. I'd taken off my shoes earlier when we'd first sat down to rest, and now I dipped my toes in the water, keeping a sharp eye out for anything that might be an alligator. The water wasn't as cool as I'd hoped, but it was still a sight better than the hot breeze that played around my ears like I'd just opened an oven.

"We got talking at the prison," I said. "Me and Clement and some of the other guys we introduced you to. Things are going wrong in all their kingdoms. Digger said the blight in Floris is just as bad as all the papers made it out to be. There's apparently a curse in Elder that's turning a lot of wolf shifters wild. There are rumors of unicorns disappearing over in The Vale."

"It's not any one thing," Clement said. "Just a whole lot of little ones all coming together to spell a big problem."

"Bear thought it was something to do with the magic in the kingdoms," I said. "He said the kingdoms got a burst of magic a couple of decades ago. Now the magic is fracturing."

Silas frowned. "Nothing bad is happening in Skyla."

I leaned back and stared up. The thin leaves of the trees above rustled together, a pattern of dancing lace against the blue sky. "Maybe Skyla is safe."

"Maybe not," he said. "I left months ago. Maybe the bad things are happening there now."

He frowned, the expression turning his face even stonier than usual.

Clement leaned on his elbow and looked up at Silas. Even when we were all sitting, he towered over Clement and me.

"What did they put you in jail for?" he asked. "Everyone said you were in for murder. Some guys said you'd killed a grown man. Other people said you'd murdered some kids."

Silas's face drooped.

"I don't believe either of those stories," Clement added in a hurry. "I don't think you'd kill a spider."

The corner of Silas's mouth quirked up. "I don't kill spiders," he said. "I take the dangerous ones outside.

The other ones are free to live in my house. I kept one in a corner of my cell. She made a new web every day. It was pretty."

I grinned up at him. "You're a good guy, Silas."

He glanced at me with a slight smile, then looked away, embarrassed.

"I don't know why they took me to prison," he said at last. He patted the wren, each of his fingers almost the size of her head and yet impossibly gentle. "I heard that pirates were coming back to Skyla. They haven't docked there in a long time. I asked about it, and I guess people didn't like me asking."

Clement sat up. "You were imprisoned for *asking* about *pirates?*"

Silas nodded sadly. "I guess I shouldn't have done that. Peter...Peter Pan our leader got rid of them years ago."

"But that's stupid," I said. He flinched, and I waved a hand. "That anyone would get upset with you for that, I mean. I would have asked, too. Didn't pirates cause a lot of trouble in Skyla back in the day?"

"I thought so," he said. "That's why I was worried. But I guess I wasn't supposed to worry."

"What's wrong with the world?" Clement said. "I thought my imprisonment was over something stupid, but yours takes the cake."

I glanced up at him, interested. I'd never been able to get the full details from him, just that he'd been taken to jail for being too "political."

"We escaped together," I said. "We're all pretty good friends now. You finally going to tell me what happened?"

Clement grimaced. "It's idiotic."

"Come on, I'm curious."

"No, I mean, you're going to think I'm an idiot for

thinking this is why I ended up in jail," he said. "I mean, they told me straight out that it's why, but I've got to be a moron for believing them. It's too dumb."

I rolled over and rested my arm on my elbow, then curled my feet up underneath myself so my toes wouldn't tempt any wandering alligators. "You're killing me, Clement. What happened?"

He took a deep breath and closed his eyes, almost cringing from embarrassment.

"I stated, in public, that Snow White is the most beautiful queen we've ever had."

Silence followed this pronouncement, broken only by the bubbling of the river.

Finally, the wren cheeped.

"She said, '*What?*'" Silas translated. He managed to put a bit of the bird's inflection into his voice.

"I echo that sentiment," I said. "*What?*"

"I agree," Clement said.

"You think Queen Snow White is pretty?" I said. "That's why you were in *Urbis Prison?*"

Even my nonsensical accusations of treason made more sense than that.

"According to the prison warden," Clement said. He picked at a blade of the wiry grass that grew on the banks of the river. "I did say she was beautiful. All I can figure is that they thought I was threatening her. But it wasn't a threat. I wasn't planning to harass her or stalk her or anything. I don't even like women like that."

"She *is* pretty," Silas said blankly. "I've seen her picture in the papers."

"She's famous for it," I said. "Everyone knows Queen Snow is gorgeous. Glinda always said even her magic couldn't make her half as pretty, and Glinda is easily the most beautiful woman in Oz after Ma."

Or, rather, she *was* the most beautiful woman after Ma. My mother was gone.

My heart clenched.

"So now you know," Clement said, looking down at his bare feet. "That's my story."

I clapped a hand onto his shin, which was the nearest part of him I could reach.

"I hereby pronounce your entire imprisonment stupid beyond all reason," I said. "Yours too, Silas. I hope everyone in Urbis Prison has a story that dumb, because if so, it should be a piece of cake to get them all released into Oz's custody."

We all watched the water and the leaves for a while, lost in our own thoughts.

"Maybe your problems have to do with the leaders of your kingdoms," Silas said at last. "Clement, you talked about your queen. Jakon, you're the leader of Oz. And I asked about the pirates, who never got along with Peter Pan. Maybe they're trying to attack the kingdoms' rulers by attacking people who support them."

I turned this over in my mind. It was a common thread, that was for sure. I wished I'd asked more of the men back in the prison about their stories and so-called crimes.

"It makes sense," Clement said. "If the magic is breaking apart like Bear said, it makes sense that would weaken the positions of kings and queens all over the world. Lots of them used magic to obtain their thrones, or they use magic to run their kingdoms."

The water flowed merrily past us. It seemed to knock my thoughts loose and let them pass through my head more easily. I'd spent so much time in the prison ruminating over the same few ideas--how I could escape, whether my siblings were all right--that now, the rush of new concepts rushing through my mind almost overwhelmed me.

"How long have things been going wrong?" I glanced over at Clement and Silas, as if they'd somehow have answers about the breadth and depth of the twelve kingdoms. "A year? More than that?" I sat up and wrapped my arms around my knees. This next bit was hard to say, but the words knocked behind my teeth like birds desperate to escape their cage. "Do you think the magic killed my Ma?"

Clement froze. The corners of Silas's mouth turned down.

"I don't know," Clement said at last. "I guess it's possible."

He looked to Silas, but Silas stared out at the water and refused to meet anyone's eyes.

Finally, Clement turned back to me, eyebrows drawn together. "How did she die?" he asked gently.

"She got sick," I said.

Suddenly, I felt as if I couldn't sit here one more second. My toes twitched against the grass and my heart fluttered in my chest, skipping every third beat.

"We should get going," I said.

The wren let loose with a series of chirps. Silas listened intently, then gave her a single nod with his boulder-like head.

"Wren says she thinks we should travel at night from here on out," he said. "We'll be less likely to get caught, and nights get cold around here. We don't have enough birds to keep us warm, so it makes more sense to travel then and sleep during the day when it's too hot to move anyway."

I didn't have to consider the idea long to agree. The village we'd just left hadn't been welcoming, and I couldn't imagine we'd find a better reception elsewhere in Badalah. It would be better to move at night, when people were less likely to notice us traveling the banks of this river.

"I'll take first watch," Clement said. He nodded at me, then Silas. "You guys should get some sleep."

I curled up between the roots of a nearby tree. Wren fluttered down from Silas's shoulder and nestled against me, her tiny body expanding and contracting with every breath. She reminded me of Lucy, who couldn't sleep without someone there to snuggle her.

Except right now, I suspected I was the one who wouldn't be able to sleep without someone else's comforting presence next to me, and Wren saw as much.

I wrapped myself around her and closed my eyes. Ma's face floated before me, and it was a long time before I sank into actual sleep.

18TH SEPTEMBER

We walked through the night. The moon was only a sliver overhead, but a friendly owl joined us at Silas's invitation and cried out to warn us whenever we approached an obstacle, like a patch of thorny bushes or a stand of boulders. We kept to the river for the most part, letting its soft rushing keep us on track.

After a while, the river met up with a road of well-packed dirt amid scrub brush that protected it a bit from the sand that seemed to blow constantly across the land. The wren, who had been napping in my hair, chirped at us to take it, and not long after that we came to a crossroads marked by a tall signpost. The signs indicated that one way would take us to Aboria, and another would take us to Kisbu, the capital city. We turned toward this latter path. The river's soft burbling faded away behind us until there was no sound but our footsteps and the cries of distant nocturnal creatures.

As the night wore on, the hard-packed earth and scrub brushes gave way to rolling hills of soft sand that gleamed blue in the meager moonlight. Stars twinkled overhead, revealing familiar constellations, and the packed dirt road turned into one of wide beige paving stones that seemed protected from sand drifts by some kind of enchantment. The owl, seeming to think we were safe on this featureless path, offered a few long hoots and soared off into the night.

"He said to continue on the path and we'll reach the city before dawn," Silas said.

We kept moving. I hadn't done this much walking in a day in years. The prison hadn't had room for much real exercise, and even back in Oz, I'd spent too much of every day hunched over my office desk or sitting at conference tables across from Munchkin delegations or Winkie representatives. My legs ached from the walking and my worn shoes, but this was a good ache. The pain meant freedom.

As the owl had promised, we reached Kisbu before dawn had begun to glimmer at the edges of the world. We passed under an arch in the city walls, and the guards posted at either side eyed us but didn't stop us. I imagined plenty of Badalahns journeyed in the early morning, before the sun rose to scorch the earth and its inhabitants alike.

We passed through the city, keeping to dark alleys and keeping a sharp eye out for anywhere that seemed likely to have food to share with hungry travelers. Last night's owl had generously caught us a stringy rabbit, which we'd roasted over a small fire, but one rabbit for three men--one of whom was the size of a small mountain--hadn't been quite enough to soothe any of our growling bellies.

"Can you spare a bit of bread?" I asked at the first food stall we saw.

The baker didn't even seem open for the day, and he didn't look at us with much friendliness in his eyes.

"We're happy to work for it," I added quickly. "We're travelers and just arrived in the city."

The man blinked at us. "That my problem?"

"No, sir," I said. "We'd appreciate your generosity, that's all."

He stepped behind his food cart with its worn canvas canopy. He rummaged in whatever was back there, then stood up, a couple of large pieces of flatbread in his hand.

"You can take these," he said. "They're stale but they're all you're getting."

I bowed. "Thank you sir. That's kind. I know times are hard."

He held the bread in the air. "You take it, and then you get out of here. I can't have beggars crowding my stall. Scares off the paying customers, not that there's many of those these days."

"Absolutely, sir, you won't see us again."

"Try the palace if you're hungry. They used to give food to the poor but the doors have been closed for a while now ever since... Well, anyway, they might help."

The bread was stale. It had the texture of leather and was almost as hard to bite through, but I gobbled up my portion anyway. My spirits lifted as the meager meal hit my system; it hadn't been much, but when it came to food, a little was a *lot* better than nothing.

I kept waiting for exhaustion to hit me. We'd walked

all night and sunrise meant it was past time to curl up in an alley somewhere and sleep. But I'd never seen Kisbu before, and the excitement and anxiety of being in a new place flooded me with adrenaline and made it impossible to feel fatigue.

Ma had been right. The architecture of the city was beautiful and unique. White stone buildings with elaborate floral carvings lined some of the streets in the wealthier part of the city, and magnificent statues stood in front gardens filled with cacti and hardy desert plants. People seemed friendlier here than they'd been in Shajara, and eyed us with caution rather than outright hostility if they noticed us at all.

The moment we passed through these beautiful streets and into the poorer part of town, though, the atmosphere changed. Men lurking in doorways watched us with careful eyes, and women tucked their children behind their robes as soon as they saw Silas. Beggars sat with their backs against buildings, sleeping or staring into space, and everyone seemed tired and on guard.

"I don't think it used to be like this," I murmured.

"Nowhere's like it used to be," Clement said.

"I miss Skyla even so," Silas said. "If the kingdoms are all going to be bad, I'd rather be at home."

"I know exactly what you mean," I said.

Clement frowned. "I can't say I miss Enchantia," he said. "I've always wanted to travel. This isn't the nicest way to do it but still, I don't half mind being on this adventure."

I raised an eyebrow. "You *don't mind* being an escaped convict on the run?"

He shrugged and the corner of his mouth quirked up. "Well, when you put it that way. But I've seen more of the world this week than I ever had in Enchantia. It's kind of exciting." He sighed. "I'd enjoy it a lot more if I could shift, though."

I'd almost forgotten about the bracelets on Clement and Silas's wrists.

"I know a few people who might be able to take them off," Silas said. "They're all back home, though."

"We could always see if whoever you know would be willing to come to Oz to remove them," I suggested. "We can't take the Urbis Express, but our friends still can. That's if Glinda can't get your bracelets off, anyway. If anyone can manage it I'd put my money on her."

Silas listened, but his expression was distant, like he was already halfway to Skyla in his mind.

"I've got to get home either way," I said. "I don't even know who's running my kingdom right now. I hope it's the Scarecrow but I'm a little worried it's Frank."

Clement squinted a little. "That's one of your brothers, right?"

"The thirteen-year-old," I said. "Which is far too young to run a kingdom. Margaret's a few years older but she'd let Oz explode before she'd take on a job like that. Margaret doesn't like to be tied down."

Clement laughed. "Sounds like a handful."

"And then some." My gaze softened. Margaret would never take on responsibility for Oz, and I loved that about her. Ma always said I'd gotten all the adventure and Meg had gotten all the fire, and that she and I could do great things together if we'd just learn to combine our talents. Margaret had said that she'd never have the patience to combine her talents with a worrywart like me, but she'd grinned as she'd said it. I missed her.

I missed them all.

"I have to go home," Silas said. He was still distant,

and I got the feeling he hadn't been listening. "I can't continue on this path with you. I need to make my way back to Skyla."

I understood. Thoughts of home sometimes swept me up, too, and there was no resisting that kind of longing.

"Will you be all right traveling alone?" I said.

Silas smiled, and the corners of his eyes folded into bright little wrinkles. "I won't be alone. I have my birds."

"It's so far away, though," I said. "Are you sure you don't want to come to Oz until we can get everything sorted out with the prison?"

He considered this, but only for a moment.

"I have to go home," he said simply. "I have to find my family."

He'd never spoken about his family to us before. And he didn't have to. I knew the pull they must have on him, and I'd be the last person to stand in his way.

We walked quietly along the streets, each lost in our own thoughts. Mine kept drifting to the Emerald Palace. I hoped against hope that my siblings were safe within its walls and that no one had scooped them up and taken them someplace like Urbis Prison. If the magic that was shattering across the kingdoms was targeting the rulers, I could only close my eyes and beg whoever was in charge of that sort of thing to please focus on me and not the young people in my care.

You always take on too much, love, Ma had said, not long before she'd died. *I'm terribly sorry I've always let you, and I'm even sorrier that I'm about to leave you with even more responsibility.*

I had reassured her that I could handle it, that I could govern Oz and raise my siblings and do everything in my power to keep our lives as bright as they'd always been under her watchful care.

And then I'd gone out into the hallway and sobbed. The weight of it had settled on me, not like a heavy cape or load on my shoulders, but like cement that had been poured into my bones and hardened to become part of my body.

The magic that was breaking up and somehow harming each of the twelve kingdoms--that was another weight settling in on my bones, and I had to become strong enough to carry it.

We reached the center of the city. The enormous open square was filled with colorful tents and people bustling about. Tension hovered in the air, the same as we'd felt in Shajara and the poor part of Kisbu, but at least here no one paid much attention to us. People were too busy haggling over wares and trying to strike good bargains to worry about the strangers in their midst.

"I go this way," Silas said, pointing down a wide street that led away from the square.

"Are you absolutely sure?" Clement said.

Silas smiled and the wren on his shoulder tilted her head.

"I'll be all right," he said. "Don't worry about me."

"If you run into any trouble, send a message to me in the Emerald City," I said. "Promise."

"I promise."

I held out my arms, and Silas seemed startled but let me hug him. It was like trying to embrace a mountain.

He hugged Clement, too.

"What will you do?" Silas asked.

Clement glanced at me, as if asking permission, not that he needed it.

"I'm going with Jakon," he said. "If he says Glinda

can get these bracelets off, that's good enough for me. Enchantia's not safe for me anymore."

"Travel safely," Silas said. "Maybe we'll meet again."

"We will," I promised. "I'll make sure of it."

He looked between us for a long moment, and it seemed like words were hovering just behind his lips. His blue eyes seemed full, of worry or gratitude or maybe just relief that he'd be on his way home soon.

"Thank you for being my friends," he said after a moment.

Before we could answer, he turned and trundled off through the crowd, head and shoulders above everyone else. The wren on his shoulder hopped around and stared at us, its tiny eyes wide and unblinking until he turned a corner and disappeared behind a white stone building.

I let out a huge sigh I hadn't meant to hold. Worry for Silas settled in with all my other fears and anxieties, but it was dull compared to many of my other fears. Unlike us, he had an army's worth of birds to keep him safe. I made a silent wish that they'd protect him all the way home.

That, of course, left us without his special abilities or the protection his massive, intimidating frame provided. Clement and me by ourselves were relatively invisible. We'd also be more vulnerable if anyone *did* notice us.

Nerves fizzled in the pit of my stomach.

"We're going to be all right," Clement said, shaking out his shoulders. "It occurs to me, though, that without the birds to tell us what's edible and what isn't around here, we'll need to stock up on food before we leave the city." He massaged the back of his neck and gave me a sidelong look.

"What?" I tensed, not sure I wanted the answer.

"I don't like the way that man down there is looking at us," he said. "Let's move."

One glance was enough to tell me which man he meant. I didn't like the guy's expression, either. He was eyeing us like a predator might, tracking our movements and searching us for valuables.

I gave Clement a curt nod, and we walked on, quickly losing ourselves between the colorful tents. Vendors cried out on every side, advertising spices and figs and bright embroidered scarves.

"Something just occurred to me, too," I said, barely loud enough to be heard over the hubbub around us. "It's going to be harder to get all the way to Oz without Silas. It's not just the food. Those birds gave us directions and warned us whether we might be in any danger, and Silas himself made people think twice before bothering us. You saw that guy back there. He was trying to figure out if we had anything worth stealing. He wouldn't have been so bold when our group included a fellow whose arms were bigger around than my waist."

"That's a good point," Clement said. "We'll have to stay on our guard."

"Even if we do, we've still got a big chunk of Badalah and then the entire width of Aboria to cross before we reach the borders of Oz. And *then* to reach the Emerald City we've still got to get through the desert on our borders."

Clement drew his eyebrows together.

"Oz has a desert?"

"Oz has four deserts," I said grimly. "Our entire border is filled with sandy wastelands. Some ancient witch put them there to discourage trespassers, long before the kingdoms all started getting along. Ma had been working to build roads through them, but she didn't get far before she passed."

"We made it through Badalah," Clement said. "I guess we'll have to get through those, too."

"Badalah's deserts follow the laws of nature," I said grimly. "The ones in Oz, not so much. They *can* be crossed on foot, but it's a sight easier on the Urbis Express."

"Which we can't take."

"Exactly."

We passed underneath a purple-striped tent that covered a dizzying array of jewel-like fruits. My stomach growled.

"What if we change course?" I said. "We can head to Urbis. As a world leader, I can seek asylum there just as well as anywhere else. The warden's paperwork claims the kingdom of Oz sent me to prison, so maybe it would be better to avoid home anyway until things are cleared up. And I'd planned to call a council in Urbis as soon as I got home, anyway, so this would just save us a few steps."

"What about your siblings?"

I bit the inside of my cheek. That was the question that gnawed at me.

"I can send a telegram from Urbis," I said. "Once I'm sure they're all right, I can have the little ones flown in to Urbis until the council meetings are over." I shrugged. "I don't even need to do that, just so long as I'm sure they're all right."

Clement thought for a few moments as we walked in silence, and I let him. As usual, his face betrayed almost nothing, while the slight creases at the corners of his eyes told me he was thinking hard and examining the issue from all angles.

"It's a good plan," he said at last. "Let's do it."

"We still need food," I said. "It's a long walk from here to there."

"What about the palace? The bread seller this morning said they might give us food."

I looked to the large palace, unmistakable with its golden domes. I'd never seen it before, but my mother had described it in detail to me. What else that was unmistakable was the boarded up gates and windows and the excessive amount of palace guards outside. We wouldn't get close, let alone inside to talk to the Sultan or Sultana. It reinforced the idea that something had happened here. I'd met Aladdin and Jawahir once and they weren't the type to hide away. Or at least they never used to be. "I think it's a no-go," I said, pointing out the palace to Clement. "Let's see if we can find work in exchange for food."

Clement's calm dignity turned out to be an asset when looking for work. The seller at the purple-striped tent turned us away with a derisive laugh, but another nearby shopkeeper that didn't seem to be doing so well was amenable to our offer of a few hours of work in exchange for a bag of bruised figs and pomegranates. We arranged his displays and called out to passersby, and by the time he closed up shop for the day we'd earned our fruit and a few flatbreads besides, left over from his own lunch.

By the time we got back on the road, the sky shimmered with red and the evening air nipped at the back of our necks.

I pulled my hood up for warmth. Fatigue had hit me on and off through the day, but I had forced myself to push through and put in a good day's work. Now that no one was watching me or promising food, it was harder to keep myself moving forward.

The city streets emptied quickly, and here and there, doors opened to reveal drinking establishments or gaming dens. The crowd seemed seedier at night, and Clement and I kept to the shadows as much as possible. This wasn't Shajara, and it seemed unlikely that anyone would risk themselves to steal our bag of bruised fruit, but I'd still seen enough hunger here today to be wary.

We passed under a bridge made of beautifully carved stone, then ducked down a quiet alley and up a wide road that led to the edge of the city. A woman with dark kohl around her eyes and red-painted lips called out to us in a sultry voice and crooked her finger at us. Clement lifted a hand, acknowledging her with a respectful wave, but kept walking.

Eventually we reached the edge of the city. Large wooden doors barred the way, and guards on either side looked us up and down, illuminated by the glow of the large torches mounted around the doorway's arch.

"Where are you headed?" one of them asked. Simple leather armor covered his chest, leaving his arms and much of his back bare. He was all muscle--the kind of man who could snap me in half without effort. His cloak hung on a peg nailed into the wall; the evening wasn't yet cool enough to touch a warrior like this.

I straightened, the fatigue from earlier gone. "Out of the city," I said, voice tight.

He chuckled. "No need to get defensive, young master. Only you might want to reconsider. Not many leave the city this late at night. Dangerous creatures prowl the sands beyond. It wasn't so long ago that our own princess nearly died out there. Many of the palace guards did...of course it wasn't animals that did that... no, it was something much worse."

A tremor of fear shimmered through me, but I kept it off my face.

"We know what we're about," I lied, not daring to ask him about what could be worse than dangerous animals.

He shrugged. "On your heads be it."

He pulled a massive lever, which seemed stiff enough that the effort made the muscles of his back ripple. The doors swung steadily apart, opening the paved brick path to Urbis.

"Good travels," the other guard called. "Sure you won't reconsider?"

I shook my head, and he shrugged. The doors closed again behind us, and the light from their torches waned and finally disappeared.

The silence of the desert outside Kisbu's walls echoed in my ears. Overhead, stars twinkled through the night.

Clement lifted his chin, and I took a deep breath of the cool, dry air. We strode forward, toward the great city-state of Urbis.

"Did you notice something strange back there?" I asked.

Clement laughed quietly. "Just one thing? Everything felt strange."

"The people all seemed dazed. Not quite there."

Clement shrugged. "Maybe it's the heat. The sun always makes me feel sleepy."

I shook my head. "That's not it. They didn't look sleepy as such, just a little confused." As I spoke I realized I felt little disorientated too. Like part of my memories were fading.

My eyelids grew heavy again as we walked and I shrugged it off as tiredness. We'd been out in the sun all day. All I needed was a good night's sleep. The wide road drove straight ahead through the dunes and occasional patch of scrub brush, its pale beige surface gleaming dully in the sparse moonlight. Wind whistled past us, rustling our robes and hair. I put one foot in front of another and allowed my thoughts to drift where they would.

My mother had made a journey like this, long ago. She had walked all the way across Oz, accompanied by the Scarecrow and the Tin Woodman and the Lion--or the Cowardly Lion, rather, as he'd been known in those days. She'd had a little dog, Toto, too. I'd never met Toto. He'd died long before I was born. But he was a bit of a legend in our family, a bold little hero who had survived a tornado, the attack of the Kalidahs, and the machinations of the Wicked Witch of the West. *He was scarcely the size of two of my paws together,* the Lion said every time it was his turn to regale us with the story. *And still he had more courage than I did. For it is not the size of one's body that determines strength, my children. It's the size of one's heart.*

Had Ma ever walked until her feet ached and her eyelids felt as if they couldn't stay up a moment longer? Had she said goodbye to friends along the journey? I knew she'd *made* friends. Some of the people she'd met when she'd first arrived in Oz had stayed in her life right until the very end.

I glanced over at Clement, whose eyes drooped as heavily as mine. Would he stay in my life, after this was all over?

I didn't have the answer. I only had hope.

And somehow, when it came to Clement, hope felt dangerous.

He felt me looking at him and glanced over. His face,

shadowed by his hood, was almost impossible to make out, but his eyes glinted in the moonlight and his teeth were easy enough to make out when he smiled.

"You awake?" he asked.

"Barely."

"You think we'll find refuge in Urbis?"

Exhaustion gripped me--not just the tiredness that came from walking instead of sleeping, but also the bone-deep fatigue of being faced with problems that seemed insurmountable.

"I hope so," I said. "I have the right to call a council of world leaders."

"Are you sure they won't just throw you back in jail?" Clement asked. "We did just escape from *Urbis* Prison."

"I can't be imprisoned once I've called a council," I said. Ma had gone over this with me more than once in our diplomacy lessons. "All council members are granted sanctuary until the proceedings are over."

"That's convenient."

Skepticism edged his voice.

I laughed.

"It *is* convenient," I admitted. "On purpose. They put that law in place back when the kingdoms were butting heads all the time. There was an incident where the monarchs of Elder and Aboria kept trying to throw each other in prison to prevent them from voting on issues that affected their shared border. At some point everyone else got sick of their bickering and forbade them all from imprisonment of any kind while a council period was in session."

Clement was silent for a long moment, then a soft laugh emerged from under his hood. "That's got to be embarrassing for Elder and Aboria."

"It's not like it was the current monarchs causing

trouble," I said.

"No, but it was their ancestors. Although I guess we all have ancestors who did stupid things."

"You might," I said, grinning. "I was adopted. I don't know anything about my ancestors. For all you know, they were flawless right back to the beginning of time."

"Sure, they were."

"You can't prove otherwise."

"I guess that explains you," he said.

I faltered over a small pothole in the middle of the road. "What do you mean?"

"I mean you're pretty great," he said, smiling over at me. "You must have come from somewhere good."

Heat rose to my face. I was glad it was dark.

"I think anything good in me came from Ma, truth be told," I said. "My family's always been the best part of me."

Clement put an arm around my shoulder. His touch had come to feel comforting, and I leaned into it.

"In that case, let's get to Urbis as quickly as we can," he said. "And then we'll get you home."

19TH SEPTEMBER

We slept when the moon was high in the sky, taking turns keeping watch. I tried to convince Clement to let me have the first watch, but he insisted, and I was too tired to argue. We hid just behind one of the dunes and nestled into the fine sand. At one point while I was sleeping I began to shiver; I didn't quite emerge to consciousness, but I did feel Clement move closer to me until his back was pressed against mine. His heat flooded through me, and I drifted back down into my dreams of endless desert and mud brick roads.

Eventually he nudged me awake, and I took over while he dropped instantly to a deep sleep. A small desert rodent scurried across the sand. In OZ, the desert mice could talk, but this one was silent in its scurrying.

Silas's birds had reminded me of the creatures of OZ in the way they spoke to him. But unlike the birds that twittered in their own language that Silas could understand, the animals of oz could speak as well as any human. Most of them anyway.

The sun rose somewhere behind a dune, filling the sky with a gradient of lavender and pink. Instantly, the world warmed by several degrees. The shadow of the dune stayed on top of us for a while, and then I used my robe and body to create a sunshield for Clement as he slept.

His face twitched in his sleep. He was more expressive dreaming than awake. How much did he hide from me during the day, to keep his face so calm no matter what troubles we faced?

I didn't want him to have to hide. At the same time, gratitude welled in me for his strength. I felt like a walking ball of barely suppressed panic most days. When he was around, though, he soothed that panic. He acted like everything would be all right, and even when I knew he was acting, I was somehow always willing to be convinced by him.

Finally, his eyes fluttered open. I quickly pretended I hadn't been watching him.

He rolled over and squinted up at the sky.

"We've given up on traveling at night, then?" he said.

"I figure we'll travel when we feel like traveling and sleep when we feel like doing that," I said. "Trying to keep to any kind of schedule out here is ridiculous without the birds keeping watch."

"Fair point." He sat up and stretched. Sand cascaded down from the back of his robes and clung to the tight curls of his hair.

"How are you feeling?"

He looked at me curiously. "I'm good. Why? What's matter?"

I shrugged. "I don't know exactly. It feels like I've forgotten something but I don't know what."

Clement licked his lips. "We are in a strange place, I guess we both feel a bit disorientated."

I nodded as we began our trek, but it wasn't that. It was like part of my mind was missing, but for the life of me I couldn't remember what I had lost.

We kept walking, this time under the scorching sun. Even in the daytime, this road was mostly abandoned. Occasionally, a cart drawn by donkeys would pass us. I tensed every time, but Clement smiled and waved in greeting, and I tried my best to mimic him.

Sweat beaded on my forehead and pooled between my shoulder blades. The hood of my robe shielded me from the direct burn of the sun, but it did nothing to prevent the dry heat or the glare of the sunlight on the dunes. I squinted and kept my eyes closed as much as possible, against the brightness and the occasional gusts of sand that blew across the road. Even the breeze was brutal out here, hot as dragon's breath and twice as strong.

My legs and feet ached. I hadn't gotten that much exercise in prison, and now, after days and nights of walking, my muscles throbbed in protest. Clement looked even worse than I felt. As we continued forward through the Badalahn desert, his shoulders drooped and his eyebrows furrowed closer and closer together.

"Are you all right?" I asked.

He nodded and grunted out an affirmative.

A while later, when his breathing had turned to panting, I stopped.

"You're not fine," I said.

He didn't answer. I grabbed his shoulders and turned him toward me.

"What's wrong?" Was his memory fading like mine seemed to be?

He shook his head. "I'm just thirsty. We didn't think to bring water."

He was right. Like an idiot, I hadn't thought of it before we'd left Kisbu. I hadn't been thirsty last night, either; it had been too cold and I'd been too sleepy and worried.

Now, his words awoke me to the realization that I was parched. My mouth felt sticky and dry, and my whole body cried out for moisture.

There was none to be had.

"There's not going to be a creek around here," Clement said, gritting his teeth. "We need to keep going."

"Eat some fruit," I said. "There's water in that."

He nodded, and we sat at the edge of the road with our backs to the sun and dug into the bag of food. My body responded to the pomegranate juice around the ruby seeds at the first taste, and I practically inhaled the fruit, crunching the seeds to get them out of the way so I could take in more of the tart juice.

But it wasn't enough. The whole bag of fruit wouldn't be enough, not against heat like this.

I knew it, and Clement knew it. And for the first time, the knowledge of our predicament seemed to really hit him. He stared at the pomegranate peel scattered around us and his whole face seemed to droop downward.

Clement was worried.

That meant it was my turn to step up.

I didn't know for sure that I could do anything about our situation, and part of me didn't even want to try. After all, if I tried, I'd know that I hadn't yet exhausted all our options.

The other part of me knew we'd die out here if I didn't do something.

"I've got an idea," I said. "It might be terrible."

Clement blinked at me. He didn't say anything, but it was clear everything right now was terrible, as far as he was concerned, so how could my idea make things any worse?

I held my hands out in front of myself and closed my eyes. The hot wind whipped past us like a dozen ribbons, invisible but as physical as Clement and me. They flapped and waved, pushing sand and heat across the desert.

And there, between the ribbons, like tiny silk threads, was something else.

I took a deep breath and called to the threads, urging their delicate silver strands toward me.

Into my hands, I thought, my mouth moving with the silent words. *Go into my hands.*

The weight of a single silver thread pooled against the skin of my palms, warm and barely there. More strands joined the first, curling against one another and nesting into each other's curves.

"That's a good trick," Clement breathed.

I opened my eyes.

Water glittered in my cupped hands, clear and sparkling in the sun.

I raised them to Clement. "Help yourself."

He drank like a dying man, his lips pressed against my fingers and his eyes closed. The water was hot in my hands, but he didn't seem to care; it was *wet* and full of life, and that was all that mattered.

I filled my hands again, and he drank. I did, too, first by slurping water from my hands and then by coaxing the water in the air directly into my mouth.

"How are you feeling now?" I asked him.

"Better."

"Do you...er...Do you remember everything?"

"My mind is a little fuzzier than usual, but that's probably to be expected in the situation."

"I'm not sure that's it. I've been feeling weird since Kisbu but I can't quite put my finger on what it is."

"Like things are leaving your mind?"

"Exactly."

Clement sighed. "I think we need to pick up the pace. Whatever was happening to the people of Kisbu might be affecting us."

We kept walking. I stopped us every hour or so for water, but even so, Clement seemed to droop more the farther we went. Every step seemed to burden him, and his face grew strained and drawn as the day crept toward late afternoon.

"I've never been to Badalah before," he said, breaking a long silence that had been filled only with dust and heat. "Except when I was brought through it to Urbis Prison. It feels wrong, here. There's some bad magic in this kingdom."

I slowed my steps, and, seemingly without thinking, he slowed to match my pace.

"You're probably feeling whatever's happening in the kingdom," I said. "The people are hungry. Everyone seemed on edge."

He shook his head. "That was in Kisbu. There's nothing ahead of us but desert."

"Is it getting worse?"

"It's getting closer." He licked his dry lips. "*We're* getting closer. The bad magic is in front of us."

I touched his arm and stopped, but he shook his

head.

"We should keep moving," he said. "The sun's going to bake us either way, so we might as well get some road behind us."

It was a reasonable point, but still, I hated the way he seemed to shrivel more with every step. We kept walking, but slowly, not pushing.

"What do you mean when you say *bad magic?*" I asked. "I don't feel anything."

"No, you wouldn't." He adjusted his hood to make sure no sliver of sunlight could touch his face. "Your magic is new and seems to come in bursts. Whatever I'm feeling--it's deep. It's like a pitch that's too low for you to hear. But I've spent my life tuning my ear to those pitches."

I didn't think that was how hearing worked, but still, I got what he was driving at. I was a beginner; he, despite the silver cuffs on his hands, was not.

And, though I never would have assumed it was possible, that put him at a disadvantage.

I steered us around a drift of sand lying across our path. The road was charmed with protection against drifts and sandstorms, but like any other wall, the enchantment seemed to have crumbled here and there. A scorpion skittered across the road, eager to avoid us.

"How can I help?" I asked, then frowned. "Or should we go back?"

"We can't go back," he said. "There's nothing for us in Kisbu besides maybe prison guards."

"This would be a lot easier if we weren't on the run," I grumbled.

Clement managed a dry laugh.

I smiled ruefully. "We just need to get to Urbis. Then we won't be prisoners anymore. And you can get those cuffs off."

"That would help the most," he said. "Once I'm free I can protect myself a little, and I'll be able to sense where this awful magic is coming from." He grimaced. "I can't tell where or what it is right now, just that it's everywhere, it's worse ahead, and it makes me feel sick."

My stomach lurched with sympathy. His suffering hurt me. I didn't like seeing anyone in pain, of course, but for some reason it was worse when it was Clement. He'd been so kind to me, and he was such a decent person. If anyone should suffer, it was the ogres, or whoever had falsely accused us and put us in this situation in the first place.

After I called the council, those were the first questions I planned to explore.

I cast my eyes to the path ahead of us, the endless road that disappeared over the horizon, looking so similar to the way we had just come from. The magic Clement spoke of was invisible and although I couldn't feel it the way he could, there was something about the path ahead that left me feeling uneasy. Maybe it was just the feelings Clement was telling me about that I was attuned to, but there was something ominous about the path ahead.

"Distract me," Clement said abruptly.

I glanced at him. His face was twisted with discomfort. A bead of sweat ran down his forehead; I couldn't tell whether it was from the heat or the strain of resisting the magic.

"Tell me a story," he said. "Something that happened to you, or an Ozian legend. Something that will take my mind off this."

The right story sprang to mind immediately; it had been following me all day, frolicking at my heels like a puppy and reminding me that I wasn't the first one to take on a journey of these epic proportions. Ma had done it first, and, as was usually the case, Ma had done it best, too.

"Dorothy lived in the midst of the great Kansas prairies, with Uncle Henry, who was a farmer, and Aunt Em, who was the farmer's wife," I started.

I knew these words like they were my own name. Ma had told us the story in her words, and the Scarecrow in his, and the Tin Woodman and the Lion and Glinda and Locasta, each of them spinning the tale in their own way and with their own flavor. Over the years, the story had taken up residence in my brain and become part of me.

"Their house was small," I continued, "for the lumber to build it had to be carried by wagon for many miles."

The lines on Clement's forehead eased. He reached for my hand. His skin brushed against mine, clammy cold against dry heat, and I twined my fingers between his and held on.

I told him the story of Ma's journey to Oz, of the adventures she'd found there and the friends she had made along the way. The tension in Clement's shoulders eased as I spoke. The story soothed me, too. It was as warm and familiar as a childhood blanket.

"Kansas sounds amazing. I wish I was in another world right now. I wonder how many other worlds there are?"

It was something I'd thought about a lot, but I didn't know how to get to Kansas and the world my mother called Earth. I wouldn't know how to get back if I did get there and with all its faults, Oz was my home. My mother had used her silver slippers to move back and forth between the two worlds, but the magic in them had long since been used up.

Hand-in-hand, we moved across the earth as the sun moved across the sky. The desert faded from violent white to dusty beige to rust tinged with gold, and the first cool breeze started from the north. A single star peeked out from behind the curtain of early evening, and all the while, my voice carried us.

"Stop," someone shouted, jerking me from my reverie. "Put your hands where I can see them."

Something sharp pressed against the small of my back. On either side, figures rose from where they'd camouflaged themselves against the dunes.

I let go of Clement's hand and raised both of mine in the air, fingers outstretched.

Clement hissed inward, the discomfort back on his face. He raised his hands, too. I dared a glance over at him and saw a sand-colored shadow behind him pressing a dull steel dagger between Clement's shoulder blades.

My heart took off at a gallop, pounding so hard my ribs shook with it.

"We're unarmed." I fought and failed to keep my voice steady. An image of the dagger thrusting into Clement's back invaded my mind. My throat closed up. My skin tingled with fear.

"That's good for you," the same voice growled. It was a man's voice, deep and ragged, and with a slight accent I'd never heard before.

"You're desert raiders," Clement said. He was better at pretending than I was; he sounded cool as ever. "You're the Shifra Clan."

"You did your research," the man growled. "So what made you so bold as to come out into my desert without an escort?"

The blade at my back pressed harder. I arched my back to put space between us.

Clement took a deep breath before answering. "Begging your pardon, I'd forgotten this was part of your territory. We're headed to Urbis. We mean you no harm."

"That's clear enough. The question is what harm *we* mean *you*."

All around us, the shapes that had risen from the dunes surrounded us in a loose circle. They were men, or at least had the shape of men, but were clad head to toe in dune-colored robes with a rough homespun texture that blended with the sand behind them. Only their eyes showed through a small slit in their hoods and wrappings, dark and lined with kohl to reduce the glare of the sun.

They had used some kind of magic to conceal themselves, too. I didn't sense their abilities right away, as Clement probably had, but when I closed my eyes, the ribbons of air that surrounded their bodies seemed to glance off of them in a way that didn't happen with Clement and me.

"We don't have anything worth stealing," Clement said. "You're free to search us."

"We thank you kindly for the permission," the man behind me said.

Hands clutched at me, patting down my robes and digging in my pockets. They found the bag of fruit and flatbread, which one of them took and tucked beneath the folds of his robes, and then they discovered Clement's silver cuffs.

"Nothing worth taking?" the man asked. He seemed to be the only one among them permitted to speak, and even his gravelly voice seemed hushed, as if he had trained it to carry to the edges of the nearest dunes and no more. He was just as concealed as the rest, and I couldn't have picked him out from others no matter how hard I tried. "These are pretty trinkets."

"They can't be removed," Clement said. "Trust me, I've tried."

The man's dark eyes fixed on Clement's face. "Why wear bracelets you can't take off?"

The man lifted Clement's hand and brought the cuff close to his eyes. His fingernails dug into Clement's skin, and Clement caught his breath as he fought to not react.

"You're not a genie, are you?" he asked, voice poisonous with a threat I didn't understand.

"No," Clement said.

The man lifted his steel blade and held it to Clement's throat.

"I said, you're not a genie, are you?" he repeated.

"We're prisoners," I blurted.

All eyes turned on me, including Clement's.

"We escaped from Urbis Prison," I said. "The cuffs are from the jail. They're enchanted and can't be removed."

The leader of the group narrowed his eyes at me, studying me for any hint of a lie, and then he raised his eye and gestured sharply to another of the identically dressed men. That man stepped forward and examined Clement's wrists.

He stepped back and gave the leader a nod.

The leader laughed softly. Goosebumps prickled across my skin.

"Remove his hands," he ordered. "Take the cuffs. We can find a use for them. Then get rid of these two and bury them."

Panic coursed through me, molten and searing.

"You can't murder us," I said. "We won't tell anyone we saw you. Take the fruit. Just don't hurt him."

"We aren't supposed to be on this road anymore," the leader growled. "We'll get in trouble if word gets out, and I don't trust you to keep your mouth shut."

He backed away, and one of his subordinates stepped toward Clement. His large curved blade flashed with the fire of the sunset.

"We'll be missed," I said. "You can't kill us or you'll be found out. I'm the Mayor of Oz. This man is under my protection."

The leader barked a laugh and raised Clement's wrist into the air. "I'm the Queen of Elder. A pleasure to make your acquaintance." He gave me a mocking bow, then added, his voice flat, "Badalah has enough trouble right now to worry about the disappearance of two nobodies." He turned to his lackey. "Kill them."

"We are not nobodies," I shouted out, desperately trying to pull something from my addled brain. "We are on a mission for the Sultan, Aladdin."

The man leered. "There is no Sultan, idiot. Hasn't been since Jawahir's father died years ago. Maybe you should do your own research like your friend." He turned back to the others. "I said kill them!"

The man with the curved blade raised it. I leapt forward to stop him, but it was too late. He brought it down on Clement's wrist.

The blade bounced off Clement's skin as if it were made of diamonds.

I froze and stared. The man wielding the weapon did, too, and then he grabbed Clement's wrist himself and tried to slice through his arm again.

And again, the blade ricocheted off Clement's arm and rebounded, jerking the assailant's shoulder backward.

"Son of a genie," the man cursed. "Damn jail put a jinx on the cuffs. I can't take them."

The leader narrowed his eyes until they almost disappeared between the kohl lining.

"Then kill them," he said. "Bury them far enough out that no one will find them but wild dogs."

"Yes, sir."

The blade at the small of my back pulled away, and I saw its trajectory in my mind's eye: back a little, then forward, slicing between my ribs and into my lungs, then again into my heart. At the same time, the man with the curved blade stepped back and raised his weapon, this time aiming for Clement's neck.

Fear and fury erupted from inside me, and with it came the wind.

A tornado burst from me, the air in my threatened lungs joining with the air on every side to form a tornado of unstoppable power.

The twister was immediate and immense. I threw my hands to either side and held it in place, with Clement and me side by side in the eye of the storm.

The desert raiders' screams filled the air and mingled with the deafening rush of wind. Their bodies rose into the air along with a blinding whirl of sand. Limbs flew every which way as if the men were rag dolls, and their robes didn't even flap in the wind. My storm was too brutal to create such a gentle motion; instead, the fabric streamed out behind them, rigid and pale brown as mud brick walls.

Their bodies spun around us, faster and faster until even their screams were lost in the smothering wind.

"Jakon," Clement said.

I didn't listen. Power rushed through me, power and

rage and uncontrollable fear. The tornado grew, raising the raiders' bodies higher and higher into the sky. The tornado grew opaque around us, thick as it was with sand. The sky darkened and lightning cracked across the top of the tornado, lighting the world with a vicious flash, the branching arms of electricity barely missing the raiders that spiraled high overhead.

"Jakon!" Clement shouted.

He grabbed my arm and shook me. I met his eyes, and, abruptly, the storm died down.

The raiders' bodies plummeted to the dunes all around, hitting with thumps accompanied by the shimmering sound of sand raining from the sky.

The last gusts of wind circled us, carrying sand that glittered in the moonlight.

I held still, hands outstretched, breathing heavily. My heart hammered. My stomach churned. My skin throbbed and tingled with adrenaline and shock and my limbs quivered, first lightly and then in uncontrollable jolts.

Clement's arms wrapped around me.

"You're all right," he murmured, pulling me close. "Everything's all right, Jakon." He rubbed my back in slow circles. "We're alive. You saved us."

I pulled away, still trembling.

"Did I kill them?" I asked, voice shaking. "Are they dead?"

I'd never killed anyone before. I'd never wanted to kill anyone. Even now, when our lives had been at risk--

I couldn't bear the thought.

"Sit down," he said.

His calm voice was impossible to disobey. I sank down onto the sand now scattered across the brick road.

Clement walked up the nearest dune. He crouched over one of the bodies that blended so uncannily with the sand and felt for the pulse in the man's neck. He hesitated, then moved to the next man, then the next.

At one point he stopped and rifled through a man's robes. A moment later, he retrieved our bag of fruit and bread.

"Take his water skin, too," I called weakly. "The one at his waist."

Clement froze. "I'm not a thief."

"I am." My voice cracked. "We'll need a way to carry water. We can't stop and wait for my magic every time we get thirsty."

He hesitated, then unfastened the water skin. He skidded down the sand and knelt in front of me.

"They're alive," he said. "But they're out cold."

My arms began to shake again, this time with relief.

Clement leaned forward and took my hands in his. They trembled violently at first, then, soothed by the steadiness of his skin against mine, slowed and stilled.

"I don't know how long they'll stay unconscious," he said. "And I don't want you to have to do that again. We should keep moving, get some distance between them and us."

I nodded silently and let him pull me to my feet.

We walked at a quick pace away under the twinkling stars and soon left the bodies of the sand raiders far behind us.

"What do you think he meant about there being no Sultan?" I asked once we were far enough away from the men to feel a little calmer.

"What do you mean?" Clement asked, eyeing me curiously. "There's only the Sultana, Jawahir."

"But..." I knew Aladdin. I had met him, had spoken

with him. My ma had taught me all the names of the leaders of all the lands. Jawahir was married to... to... and then it went and I couldn't remember what it was I'd been thinking about.

20TH SEPTEMBER

It took several hours until we felt like we could sleep, and again, Clement insisted on taking first watch. I settled into the sand behind a dune. Somehow or other, while I was half-asleep, my head ended up on his lap. He tangled his fingers in my hair and traced his nails along my scalp.

No one had done that for me since I was young, except for maybe Lucy the times I'd allowed her to do my hair at her pretend salon. I relaxed into his touch, and I didn't let myself think too much about what it might mean. It was enough to know he cared for me in some way or another, and enough to know he would watch over me as I slept. With my eyes closed I recited the names of my siblings and friends over and over in my mind, fearful that I'd forget them overnight. My mind was fuzzy and small things were beginning to erode.

We traded shifts, and I let him sleep until he woke up on his own sometime in the early morning. He looked a little better than he had yesterday, but the strain of the "bad magic" still clung to him. He looked as dazed as I felt though his smile told me he still remembered me.

"We're almost there," I promised.

I didn't know Badalah well enough to make that kind of claim. But right now, truth seemed less important than hope, and Clement was willing to play along.

"We'll be there before you know it," he agreed, and my heart warmed at the shared lie.

We kept walking. My legs and feet still hurt, but I was used to it now. I resumed my story, telling Clement all about Ma's final encounters with the Wizard of Oz and then about Glinda, who had been the one to finally get Ma home to Kansas. It felt good to remember it and to tell it out loud. I wondered what tales of my past I'd forgotten. There were definitely missing pieces and the holes in my memory felt like they were getting bigger with each hour that passed.

"She came back eventually, of course," I said. "She had an awful lot of adventures. Eventually she and Uncle Henry and Aunt Em came back to live in Oz permanently, and she took over when Princess...er... Ozma decided to leave the kingdom. I never met any of them. Henry and Em passed away before I was born, and Ozma never came back home after she left Oz. Said other people needed her more."

"You still had Glinda, though," Clement said. "And the Scarecrow and Woodman and Lion. And Margaret and Frank and Ethel and Gertrude and... no, don't tell me... Glinda?"

"That's the wrong witch. You already said her."

"Locasta," he corrected himself quickly. "Locasta and Glinda are both good witches. And your other siblings are Chester and Lucy."

He grinned, pleased with himself. He was remembering my family better than I was.

"I'm impressed." I linked arms with him. "I feel bad now, though. I don't know anything about you or your family."

"There's not much to tell," he said. "I'm an only child. My parents were well off but not that interested in raising me. Went to a boarding school when I was nine to learn maths and history and shapeshifting, and then I graduated and worked at a wandmaker's for a while."

"You remember everything about your childhood?" I asked, trying to gauge if his memory loss was as impactful as mine."

He gave me an odd look. "I think so. You don't?"

I shook my head. "I don't know. I feel like there are big chunks missing, but I don't know what."

"I do feel a little fuzzy, but I think I remember everything. I remember working as a wandmaker's apprentice like it was yesterday."

"That explains why you know so much about magic wands," I said. "And how a matchstick might work in a pinch."

He laughed. "I don't know anything about wands," he said. "No more than any other Enchantian, anyway. I was a bookkeeper."

"Oh," I said, giving him a sidelong look full of artificial judgment. "That's less exciting."

He chuckled and tightened his arm to pull me in closer. "You clearly don't understand the thrill of a completely balanced expense report."

A scraggly bush on the side of the road quivered as a lizard dove deeper into its branches for protection.

"It wasn't really that interesting," he said. "I was never one of those people who felt like I had a calling. It was just a job to pay for my lodging and the occasional trip to the theater or a nice restaurant. Shapeshifting is the only thing I've ever been really drawn to."

"Why not get work as one of those, then?" I said. "Or is that even a thing?"

"Shapeshifter jobs are competitive," he said. "And there are too many of them in the criminal sector for my liking. Not that avoiding those helped me any." He raised his wrist.

"What about your friends?" I asked. "Did you have anyone special?"

"I'm still close with a few people from school," he said. "Most of them are in different parts of the country, though. I spent a little time with people from work, but we never really clicked."

"What about more-than-friends?" I said. "Did you ever, you know, see anyone? A girl?"

The question beneath the question simmered with heat, and Clement smiled.

"I was seeing this one fellow for a while," he said. "We got on well, but it didn't work in the end. No one's fault. He and I just wanted different things."

If I'd been a better friend, I might have felt some sympathy that Clement's relationship hadn't worked out.

Instead, a spark of interest lit inside me. I tried to smother it to no avail.

"What *did* you want?" I said. "Or what do you want? In someone special, I mean?"

He seemed to bite back a grin, but he couldn't stop

his eyes from sparkling.

"Why, you interested?"

I became abruptly aware of how close he was. Heat rushed to my face, putting the morning sun to shame. Clement laughed and held tightly to my arm so I couldn't leap away.

"I'm just teasing," he said, but he couldn't seem to tear his gaze from my face.

He was searching me for an answer, and I didn't know how to give it.

I liked him. Lands, I liked him. Sometimes when I looked at him the pit of my stomach wobbled.

But I had a kingdom to run, and siblings to protect, and a corrupt prison to investigate, and a council to convene, and magic to study, and--

"I was kidding, Jakon," he insisted, still searching my face.

"It's not that I don't like you," I said.

His face didn't fall, exactly, but his grip on my arm slackened a little.

"I like you a *lot*," I blurted. "You're honestly the best person I've ever met, and I'm so glad we're friends."

The word, *friends,* hovered in the air, and the light in Clement's eyes faded a little bit. Still, he forced his smile back.

"I'm glad we're friends, too," he said.

"That's not what I mean."

He wouldn't meet my eyes. Instead, he looked straight ahead, as if this were an ordinary day and an ordinary conversation.

"Look, birds," he said, voice a shade too light. "It would have been a lot easier if we'd seen those a few days ago. We could have asked for another ride."

I followed his gaze up ahead. In the far distance,

an enormous flock of black birds flew toward us, their wings beating the air and their bodies large enough to shadow the blue sky.

I grabbed Clement's arm, my heart pounding.

"Those aren't birds," I said. "We need to hide."

Clement didn't question me, not until we had dug a hole into the side of a dune and covered ourselves as well as we could with our robes and sand.

Then he peeked out from his hood at me.

"What's going on?"

"Those aren't birds," I said. "They're Winged Monkeys."

His eyes widened. "Are you sure?"

"I'd know those shapes anywhere. They're searching for me."

He nestled further down into the sand. We'd only been able to cover ourselves so well, and I barely dared breathe for fear the monkeys would see us and come swooping down.

They passed overhead, their awkward bodies now so close I could make out the hair on their limbs and their strange, leathery faces. Clement watched them from beneath the cover of his hood, his body as still as mine.

In the center of the flock, two monkeys carried a human figure that struggled and fought helplessly against the captors' strength. I remembered how that had felt. Their hands had been like iron shackles, their arms as much wiry muscle as flesh and bone.

I squinted against the bright sky, but I couldn't see the prisoner's face and it was impossible to tell if it was a man or a woman, an adult or a child. I tried to figure out if Margaret or Frank might be about that size and shape. Had that been one of my siblings?

I had to get back to them. I had to make sure they

were safe.

The monkeys' enormous wings filled the sky. The sound of their flapping rained down on us, and the breeze kicked up by those great feathered wings blew the sand in gusts across the road and the dunes. A puff of sand hit my face, abrasive and powdery at the same time, and I choked in silence rather than risk coughing and giving us away.

Eventually, when I thought I was about to die from the tension of it, the last of the monkeys disappeared into the distance toward the other side of the kingdom and Urbis Prison. We waited for several more long, agonizing moments, just in case there were any stragglers, but it seemed the monkeys kept pace with one another.

I sat up warily, ready to dive back into the sand at the first hint of anything in the sky.

Endless blue stretched out in every direction, and the sky gleamed innocently down on us as if it hadn't just played host to a veritable army of evil.

"How far are we from Urbis?"

"Still a few days at least," Clement said. "I don't know much about Badalah, but the distance from Kisbu to the border is significant."

"We have to move faster."

"I don't know if I can."

His face was open to me, and a twinge of guilt stirred in my chest.

"As fast as we can, then," I said. "I don't want you to strain yourself."

We shook the sand from our robes and clambered to our feet. Dry grains still clung to us and filled the crevices in the fabric of our clothing. I suspected we'd never get it all out.

We kept walking. The hours dragged by, laden down

as they were by heat and discomfort. To entertain myself as we walked, I played with the ribbons of magic in the air.

I twitched one of the wide, hot strands and forced a breeze to circle around our heads and rustle our hoods. At one point, I even managed to knock Clement's hood clean off his head.

He laughed, the expression doing little to lift the fatigue from his face. "Not bad. But can you put it back on?"

He trudged along with the sun beating down on his head while I figured it out. This was more complicated, fighting against gravity as I was, and it took a while to identify which strings I had to pull and when. Eventually, though, I guided an uncanny breeze up his back and over his head with enough force to raise the hood and settle it back in place.

"I told you," Clement said. He had a broad smile on his face, and he shook his head a little as he spoke. "The first time we met, I told you. You have magic."

"Now we both know not to ignore your abilities," I said. "Even with those cuffs on, you're a force to be reckoned with."

"You should see me with them off." He smirked, and then the expression faded. "I'm sorry I haven't been able to help much. I should be helping you figure out your abilities, but I feel like I've got both hands tied behind my back."

"You've helped me plenty," I said. "Especially yesterday."

The memory of the tornado bursting from me returned, and with it came echoes of fear and fury. My skin prickled in spite of the sun.

"I don't understand why I can create tornados

without thinking sometimes and can barely get a hood back on your head at others." I kicked a stone lying on the path. It skipped along the bricks and rolled into the sand along the road. "When it comes out of me like that I almost can't control it."

No, even that was softening the truth. I *couldn't* control it, or at least I hadn't been in control of that violent twister yesterday. I would have killed those men outright if Clement hadn't forced me back to my senses.

"That's the least puzzling thing about your abilities," Clement said.

I raised an eyebrow at him.

"Magic is deeply linked to emotion for most people," he said. "Every time it's come out, you've been cornered and scared. The first time, you were protecting Silas from those thugs. The second time, we were stuck between ogres and a drop into the ocean. And yesterday, we outnumbered five to one by sand raiders."

"So my magic comes out when I'm panicking?" I snorted. "I should have a tornado swirling around me all the time, then."

Clement pushed his hood aside to look at me. "What do you mean?"

"I mean I'm always scared," I said. "I've been one walking anxiety attack after another ever since I was a kid. Ma used to have to come hold me and remind me how to breathe." I still remembered her arms around me and the gentle lilt to her voice as she had counted to three over and over to guide me in pacing my frantic gasps. Margaret had cornered me a few years ago in the Emerald Palace with a ruby-eyed snake, and despite knowing the creature was harmless I'd still had to lock myself in my room for an hour to calm down. Her words after the incident floated through my memory, and I repeated them, slowly. "I was born terrified."

Clement's eyebrows lowered. "But you're the Mayor of Oz."

"I can't let fear stand in the way of my responsibilities," I said. "Oz is too important."

He stared at me.

I let him stare, but after a moment, my skin prickled with the awkwardness of it.

"What?" I finally snapped.

"I don't know, I just…" He trailed off and furrowed his brow. "You're complicated, Jakon."

I rolled my eyes. "It's not that complicated. I'm scared of everything all the time. I had to learn to function anyway."

"But that's incredible."

"It's really not."

My face warmed. His attention on me was almost too much to handle, and I wasn't sure if it was because I didn't like him looking at me with such open admiration or because I liked it far too much.

"Anyway, I wasn't even worried about me those times," I said. "Not completely. I was worried about you."

Something passed over his face, but he turned away and his hood concealed the expression before I could identify it.

"Maybe your strongest emotions are tied to other people, then," he said, then paused. "You managed to escape Urbis Prison because you were worried about your siblings. Your magic manifests when your friends are threatened."

"That's no good," I said. "How am I supposed to learn to harness my powers when the big ones only show up when people's lives are in danger?"

He laughed, then realized I hadn't been making a joke.

"They'll settle," he said. "Powers always do. Every time they appear, you'll get more comfortable with your magic and develop a better sense for how to access your abilities. You're already doing more than you could at first. You figured out how to pull water out of thin air. Nobody even had to teach you that."

I sighed. I had every reason to believe he was right, but my gut churned at the thought of having another of those tornadoes erupt from me at the next provocation. I thrilled with excitement every time I remembered I had powers--but how many people was I going to harm on my way to harnessing them?

"The weird part, at least to me, is the fact that your abilities have manifested at all," Clement said. "Most people's powers show up when they're children. In Enchantia, if you don't have at least *some* abilities by the time you're school-age everyone assumes you won't get them at all. People who do come to powers late in life usually do it through massive amounts of study under the tutelage of experienced magicians. And then there's you."

"A lifetime of nothing, nothing, nothing, and then *boom*," I said.

"I've never seen it before." He shrugged. "But maybe that's my inexperience talking. We're headed to Urbis. Maybe we can find someone there who knows more about how magic works in the other kingdoms."

We fell silent. Our feet kept moving, but we never seemed to get anywhere. The vast desert never changed; the landscape surrounding us held only dunes and more dunes. The cloudless sky stayed the same, too. The only indication that time had passed was the sun, which hit its zenith and kept traveling across the sky.

A hot wind blew sand in our faces. The sun shone down. Sweat dripped down my forehead.

"It's getting worse," Clement said.

I started. I'd almost forgotten where I was; the sameness of the landscape and the oppressive heat had hypnotized me, and I couldn't even remember where my thoughts had been a moment before.

"What's getting worse?"

A second later, I realized I shouldn't have needed to ask. Clement's face told me everything. A muscle in his jaw pulsed and his eyes darted from one edge of the distant horizon to another. He kept walking, but everything but his feet seemed to be pulling back and trying to avoid the path up ahead.

I put a hand on his arm. "Do we need to go back?"

He shook his head, though this seemed to take more effort than it should have. "We have to get to Urbis. Your siblings need you."

"It doesn't do any good if you're too sick to function by the time we get there. Is the pain connected to the memory loss?"

He shook his head. "I don't think so. They are different magic. The pain comes in waves," he said. "I just need water and a minute to rest."

This seemed like an insufficient treatment for the kind of restless pain that skittered across his face and down his twitching arms. It was as if he was being stung by the scorpions we occasionally saw darting across the road, but there were no venomous creatures in sight.

We sat at the side of the road. The sun had fallen far enough to the west that a tiny shadow offered a bit of cover, and I drew moisture from the air to fill Clement's stolen water skin. He drank it all, so I filled it again and he drank that, too. The water seemed to soothe the twitching of his limbs, and he leaned into the sloped wall of sand behind us and closed his eyes.

"You should sleep," I said. "Wait for it to pass."

Anxiety about reaching Urbis and finding out for sure whether the Winged Monkeys had stolen away one of my siblings crawled up and down my arms.

But as I'd told him, fear was no excuse for abandoning my responsibilities, and I had a responsibility to Clement now. I had to keep him safe and well. I'd told the sand raiders that he was under my protection, and I meant it.

"We have to get through Badalah," he protested weakly.

"It's not like we'll reach Urbis today anyway, and it's still a million degrees out here."

I refilled the water skin while I spoke. I could do both at once, now. It pleased me.

"We may as well rest," I said, placing the pouch in Clement's hand. "We'll be more comfortable if we walk after the sun goes down anyway. After all, it's like we said, it's not like we have a schedule to keep anymore."

He nodded without opening his eyes. I hadn't even needed to add that small bit of persuasion; he was already half-asleep.

The sun set and the stars came out, one by one and then in small groups, like guests arriving at a party in their most dazzling apparel.

After a while, Clement stirred. He stretched, and his eyes opened slowly, their sclera the only part really visible in the night.

"What time is it?"

I glanced at the sky, then shrugged. "Damned if I know."

He laughed and sat up, rubbing the back of his head to shake the sand loose. "Sorry, force of habit. I mean, how long was I out?"

"To tell you the truth, I have no idea," I said. "I've been working on a new trick. Watch this."

I raised my hands and tugged at the ribbons of air. A tug, a jerk, and then a tiny tornado erupted in front of me, spinning dark and sparkling sand in a tidy spiral no taller than my knee.

"Well done, Jakon," Clement said, clapping slowly and staring at the tornado. "That's brilliant."

I dropped the ribbons and the tornado fell to the earth with a splash of sand. I gave him a mock bow. "Thank you, I have spent *decades* perfecting my craft."

He laughed, and his laughter warmed the pit of my stomach.

"Are you feeling better?" I asked. He didn't look it. If anything his nap had left him looking more tired than before. His skin, darkened by the sun was paling again except for dark circles under his eyes.

He stretched his arms out in front of him and rolled his head from side to side. "Much. Either the wave of magic passed or I'm rested enough to handle it."

"Good." I smiled and wondered if he was telling me the truth. Maybe he just looked worse than he felt. I patted him on the back, and my hand lingered and drifted to rest between his shoulder blades. There were layers and layers of rough-spun fabric between us, but I still felt the gentle rise and fall of his breath.

"About earlier," I said. "When you were joking about, you know. About me being interested."

He tensed and waved a hand. "No, Jakon, I was teasing. You don't need to--"

"I am," I blurted.

He turned. Silence hung between us, tight enough to snap at a touch.

"I really like you," I said. "And--I mean, you're gorgeous. I'd have to have my head buried in this sand not to have noticed that. It's just..."

I fell silent, trying to find the words.

I *had* the words. I'd thought them over and over while he'd slept. Getting them from my heart to my lips, though--that was different.

"Everyone I love is in danger right now," I said. "Whatever's happening in the kingdoms right now, it's put us all at risk."

"And you have too much to worry about to add a relationship to the plate," he finished.

I nodded and bit my tongue. I took a deep breath.

"It's that," I said. "But there's more, too. You saw what happens whenever you're threatened. I almost killed those men back there. I can't even begin to think of what would have happened if I were any closer to you than I am now. I'm terrified of what I'll do if I get home and find out my siblings have gotten hurt." I held up my hands, shadows in the darker shadows of the night. "I can't control these powers, and if I let myself care about you any more than I do now..."

I trailed off again. Goosebumps rose up on my skin. My power lay coiled inside me, quiet now but as deadly as a viper.

"I understand," Clement said.

"It's not about you," I said.

"I don't think it's about you, either," Clement said. He took one of my hands and held it on my lap. "At least, not yet. When abilities first manifest they can be like separate entities all on their own. Learning to tame them and understand them is like bringing that entity inside yourself, piece by piece, until you figure out where it all fits." He nudged the pile of sand from my tiny tornado with his toe. "You're making good progress."

I filled our water skin, and we clambered back down to the road and continued walking. It was easier at night, when I didn't have to squint against the glare of the sun or push through the heat beating down on us. The last warmth from the day was fading from the sands around us, and I welcomed the cool air that brushed my hair from my forehead.

In the distance, a light bobbed up and down. We'd passed plenty of people on this road over the last couple of days, each time greeting them with little more than a nod and a wish for safe travels, but I still tensed at any sign of life. Every traveller could be a bounty hunter, or an ogre from Urbis Prison, or a soldier from a neighboring kingdom alerted to the security threat we posed.

Clement touched my arm, silently reminding me to stay calm, and I took a few deep breaths and focused on putting one foot in front of the other.

The light grew closer, and I made out the shape of a lantern with a flame glowing at its center. It was carried by a young man with dark hair and thin limbs. Behind him, other shapes clustered in the night: a young woman, dressed in layers of worn fabric, and two small children.

Clement and I nodded to them as we approached one another.

"Good travels," Clement called, voice light and friendly.

"Good travels," the man returned.

When they got closer, I realized the children wore

rags on their feet in place of shoes. The woman and the children stared at us with wide eyes reflecting the lantern light, and the man eyed us with caution all over his features although he looked dazed too.

They were more frightened of us than we were of them. My shoulders relaxed.

The man stopped not far from us. "Where are you headed, travellers?" he asked. "If you're looking for work in Jaf you may as well turn around. There's none to be had."

He spoke from experience, judging by the hollows in the woman's cheeks and the size of his arms, which looked like little more than leather wrapped around bones.

"We're on our way to Urbis," I said.

The man nodded. "I hope things are better there than here. Can you tell me about Kisbu? Is it difficult to find work and lodging there?"

One of the children whimpered. The woman crouched to attend to the child.

I exchanged glances with Clement. He reached into his robes for our bag.

"I can't speak for Kisbu," I said. "We just passed through. We were able to find work for a day without too much trouble."

The lines on the man's forehead smoothed. He shifted the lantern from one hand to the other.

"That's good to hear," he said. He reached down and found the shoulder of his oldest child, and squeezed it like he needed the small girl to tether him to the ground. "Very good."

"Do you know how much farther it is to...to..." An expression of confusion came over Clement's face before it cleared and he remembered the name he was searching for. "...Urbis?"

The man gestured behind himself with his chin, which was sharp from hunger.

"It's another two days from here, one if you walk quickly," he said. "You'll reach Jaf first. It's a small village. You won't find work, but if you've got money there are those who will be glad to trade it for whatever food they can scrape together. That is of course if you can stand it there. The whole town was full of crazy folk. None of them remembered a thing. It was like a spell had been put on them. we left before it infected us. Urbis is just beyond that."

"Thank you," Clement said, giving me a look. The magic was close.

He glanced at me again, the question burning in his eyes, and I gave him a slight nod.

He pulled the bag of fruit out from beneath his robes.

"Please take this," he said. "Your little ones need it more than us."

The man waved him off, but his gaze seemed glued to the bag. Clement held it open, revealing the food inside.

"It's bruised and some of it is getting soft," Clement said. "But it'll keep their bellies full until you can get to Kisbu."

"I can't take your food," the man said.

"Amir," his wife said, sharply but quietly. She pulled the littlest child close to herself.

Both children stared at the bag, their eyes wide. Hunger clung to their faces, and it seemed to take everything they had not to reach for the bag themselves. I saw Lucy in their faces, and Chester.

"Take it. We'll get more in Jaf," I lied.

The man accepted the bag. The moment his fingers touched the fabric they clenched around the material as if he'd been trying to hold himself back and had lost the battle.

"Thank you," he said, voice tight. "Thank you. More than I can express."

"Travel safely," Clement said.

The oldest child stared up at me. I smiled at her, trying to elicit a smile in return, and after a moment a tiny grin flashed across her face. Overcome, she hid her face in her father's robes.

"Thank you," the man said again.

The woman reached for our hands as she passed and squeezed them. Her fingers were skin and bone.

We watched as the family moved down the road toward Kisbu. Clement let out a long breath that sounded like he'd been holding it a while.

"Things are wrong in Badalah," he said. "Things are wrong everywhere. You heard what he said about the people of Jaf. They are losing their minds."

"That's why we need to get to Urbis," I said. "So we can make them right."

And before we lose ours, I added silently

21ST SEPTEMBER

The sun leapt over the horizon, gilding the desert and revealing endless sand on every side. Up ahead, buildings hunkered against the heat, their mud brick sides dark despite the sunrise.

My good mood evaporated as we approached the village of Jaf. The man on the road had warned us about the people, but he hadn't mentioned the dirty looks we'd receive from everyone from the old woman sweeping her front steps to the teenage boy who glared at us as we made our way between the buildings.

The road to Urbis cut straight through the village, so there was no avoiding it. I wished we had, even so. The hostility in the air sent prickles down my arms, and the tightness returned to Clement's face as we moved through the town.

We walked past a storefront with a wide, glassless window. Inside, a couple of flies buzzed lazily around a sparse display of flatbreads and dried fruit.

My stomach growled, loudly enough for a woman sitting outside the shop to hear and shoot me a dirty look.

"They don't seem to like outsiders here," Clement said under his breath.

"Concerning, given that anyone traveling to or from Urbis has to walk right down the center of town," I muttered back. "At least we don't have anything worth stealing."

"They don't know that."

I became acutely aware of the many pairs of eyes fixed on us. I'd never been dinner for a pack of wolves, but I had a feeling this was the moment that directly preceded such an experience.

"We need to get through here quickly," I said. "I don't know what'll happen if one of them tries to attack us, and I don't want to accidentally kill these people. They're just hungry."

No, not hungry--starving. Predatory eyes stared out from sunken eye sockets, and desperation shone from hollow faces. Even the children searched us with a focus I'd never seen on faces so young.

"No wonder that family left," Clement muttered. "This is heartbreaking. Why hasn't the royal family done something?"

"They have their own troubles right now," I said, remembering the boarded up palace in Kisbu. "I'm the Mayor of Oz and I'm traveling to Urbis on foot after breaking out of prison. Based on what Digger told us, the entire royal family of Floris is dealing with famine and disease. This thing that's happening all around the world is affecting more than this little town."

"I wish we'd saved some of our fruit," Clement said. "Those kids could use it."

"We barely had enough for the two kids we met last night," I said. "This town doesn't need a bag of fruit, it needs a miracle."

A man stepped into our path. I tensed. Silently, quickly, Clement put a firm hand on the small of my back. *Don't do anything.*

I took a deep breath, feeling for the familiarity of my lungs expanding and collapsing. *There's always a well of peace inside yourself,* the Tin Woodman had told me once, after I'd gotten overwhelmed at my sister...er... Margaret's sixth birthday party and hidden myself in a closet. *You just have to find it. Listen for the silence behind the noise.* I had to think hard to remember Margaret's name. Whatever was affecting me was getting worse.

I looked at the bricks below my feet and listened. There it was, a patch of stillness just underneath my heartbeat. I leaned into it and kept breathing.

"Where are you folks headed?" the man demanded, an aggressive edge to his voice.

Clement, the master of the calm I always struggled to find, held out a hand with a friendly smile.

"We're headed to er...the er...big city place," he said pointing forward. I tried to help him, but I couldn't remember the name of it anymore either.

"You going to buy food for your travels?" the man asked. He didn't take Clement's hand. "Do something to support the town you're walking through?"

Clement lowered his hand, but his smile remained, calm and pleasant. "I'm afraid we don't have any money."

"You look like you've been fed well enough," the man

said. "There's plenty of meat on your bones."

"Our luck ran out recently," Clement said. "We're hoping to find better fortunes in the city."

"Lucky, having the ability to up and move as it suits you," the man said.

I shifted my weight from one foot to the other. I couldn't tell where this conversation was going.

"I don't suppose there's any work to be had here?" Clement asked.

I didn't understand how he could stay so tranquil, or how he could keep his voice steady and pleasant in the face of his man glaring at us. This man wasn't even the only threat in our environment; nearby, other people were watching the exchange, their posture rigid and their attention on us bearing all the heat of the desert sun.

"No work here," the man said. "And we don't appreciate people who come and add wear and tear to our roads without paying for the privilege."

I opened my mouth without thinking. What wear and tear could two men on foot possibly cause to their road? "Surely these roads belong to the king of Badalah and to the people?"

The man growled. "Badalah has no king. This road belongs to Jaf and the people of Jaf and no one else.

Clement touched my arm, just barely, before I had the chance to speak again.

"We're sorry we can't help," he said. His voice didn't raise; his shoulders didn't tighten. He stayed cool and relaxed, unwilling to meet the tension rising all around us. "We surely would if we could. Times are hard for everyone."

The man eyed him, sharp and skeptical. Clement refused to be ruffled.

Finally, the man's face softened, just barely. "I hope things get better for us all," he said. His voice was still hard, but something almost imperceptible had changed. He stepped aside. "You'll want to move quickly through this town. It's cursed. No reason for you to stay and get cursed with it."

Clement held out his hand again, and this time, the man shook it.

"Thanks for the advice," Clement said. "We'll get out of our hair as soon as we can."

We moved on down the dusty brick road, and while nobody seemed inclined to so much as toss us a smile, nobody moved on us, either.

I let out an enormous sigh once we stepped out of the shadow of the last building on the outskirts of the village. My heartbeat slowed.

"I don't know how you do that," I said, once we were well past the buildings. The featureless desert had begun to wear on me, but I still preferred it to the hostility of the people behind us. "How you stay so *calm* when people are looking at us like we're something to eat."

Clement's eyes seemed focused on something in the far distance, though there was nothing to see but sand and sky.

"I only have a couple of options in a situation like that," he said. "My experience is that I can either get flustered and watch everyone get flustered with me, or I can stay calm and encourage them to stay calm, too."

"You say that like it's easy."

"It's not easy." He took a few steps, then his distant gaze sharpened and he grinned at me. "It's just, I've *been* a lion. I've *been* a giant ice bear. I can't shapeshift right now, but I still know what it feels like to be the scariest thing in the room. It's easier to stay relaxed when you know what it feels like to *know* nobody's going to hurt you, so I just try to remember that."

"Maybe that's why I have so much trouble," I said. "I've never been unbreakable."

I'd meant it as a joke, but my voice faltered on the words. I was fragile, as delicate in my own way as the porcelain people in Oz's China Country.

Ma's death had shattered me. And now, a year later, I hadn't even begun to pick up all the pieces.

Clement wrapped his arm around me. "That's why you have me," he said cheerfully. "And if my mental shapeshifting ever doesn't work, that's what your tornadoes are for."

"We are a good team, aren't we?"

"The very best."

"The man back there. He said there was no king," I mused later.

"So?"

"Badalah is run by the Sultan Ala... I forgot his name.

"The guy on the road told us that the people were losing their minds," Clement reminded me.

"I almost forgot Margaret earlier," I admitted.

"It's something to do with magic," Clement said. "My memory is fading quickly too. I didn't want to tell you, but I've been forgetting important things too. I think the quicker we get out of Badalah, the better."

"Urbis *is* ahead of us, right?" I said at last, finally remembering the name of it. "That's not just a thing people made up to give travelers false hope?"

"I don't feel equipped to make any promises," Clement said. "I hope it's ahead, because otherwise we're going to starve and end up as a pretty measly meal for the vultures."

I shuddered. I'd seen the birds a few times now, circling overhead off in the distance. Each time, my heart skipped a beat before I made out the bird bodies between their enormous wings and proved to myself that they weren't about to snatch me up and take me back to jail.

"I almost think I'd trade Ma right now," I said. "I always thought her journey through Oz sounded terrifying, but a little consistent terror that came with trees and different landscapes beats worrying about monkeys and walking through a desert day after day."

"Oz definitely sounds more interesting than this desert," Clement said. "It's a shame our route didn't just take us all around Kisbu. I wouldn't mind walking that city for days at a time."

"I might have liked that a year or two ago," I said. "It'd make me too nervous, now. Everyone's on edge."

"That's true." Clement sighed. "I feel like I took the world for granted. It used to be all right. I wasn't happy back in Enchantia, but at least *everyone* wasn't miserable."

I glanced over at him. His face was mostly concealed by his hood and I couldn't make out his expression.

"You were miserable?"

He was silent for a long moment. Our footsteps scraped gently against the bricks.

"Not *miserable,* exactly," he said, speaking slowly and choosing his words with care. "I didn't have anything to complain about. I had a good job. I had plenty of food. I wasn't under attack."

I raised an eyebrow. "You sound like you're trying to convince yourself."

"I guess I am." He lowered his hood and wiped the

sweat from his forehead with his sleeve. His gaze had softened and become distant again, or maybe he was looking deep inside.

I savored the expression on his face. His mind seemed remarkable to me, and I loved the way he could be unreadable one moment and then reveal the depth of his thoughts the next through the tiny lines around his eyes.

"I had everything," he said. "I had every comfort and privilege and nothing to complain about, but I didn't have a lot of meaning. Every day was the same as the rest, and the only goal I had was to work my way up at my job and maybe find a nice guy to settle down with. But I never really found that guy. I remember I used to spend whole weeks doing nothing but going to work and then coming home and reading before bed."

"That sounds lonely."

"It was," he said. "Prison was terrible in its own way, but honestly, I had more friends there than I ever had back home."

"You didn't ever spend time with your parents?"

He laughed, without humor. "They wouldn't have been interested. They have their own lives."

I stared at him. He'd said they weren't close, but the thought of his mother and father not even wanting to spend time with him? I couldn't wrap my mind around it.

My mother had led a dazzling life. If anyone in the all the world had a reason to find other adventures more interesting than her children, it had been Dorothy Gale. But she'd always tried to come home in time for dinner, and she'd taken us on her diplomatic trips around Oz. She adored her life but she *loved* us.

I would give anything for one more hour with her,

and I knew, deep at the very core of my heart, that she would have given anything for one more hour with me, too.

"That's horrible."

My voice came out far too loud and startled a lizard sunning on a rock. It twitched and darted behind the stone.

"Sorry," I said. "It's just that your parents are terrible people and I hate them."

Clement stared at me, and then he burst out laughing.

"How do you really feel about it, Jakon?"

"I'm serious," I said. "The thought of anyone not wanting to be with you and build a relationship with you--I can't even imagine it. You're wonderful. You're kind and clever and interesting, and if your parents think whatever they're doing deserves their time more than you do, they're only shooting themselves in the foot." I laced my arm through his. "Forget them. You're part of my family now, like it or not."

"I thought you didn't want to be with me."

"I said I don't have the emotional resources to care about you more than I do without risking another tornado," I said. "That's an entirely separate issue from welcoming a new member into the Gale family. Ma spent my whole lifetime taking in strays, and you're a stray if I've ever met one. You're one of us now. Full stop."

He laughed again, but there was something deeper behind his laugh that made it catch. He swallowed, and when I glanced over, his eyes seemed a little too bright.

"That's nice of you," he said. "Nobody's ever tried to adopt me before."

"Their loss," I said. "Clearly I'm the first person you've ever met who has any sense, which is lucky for me."

Clement tightened his arm around mine. It was too hot to walk close to each other like this, but neither of us let go.

"If the kingdoms are falling apart, I'm glad my broken piece landed next to yours," he said.

The sun dipped toward the horizon. I asked for the water skin and drank everything in it, then stood still and refilled it for Clement.

"I'm almost glad Ma isn't around to see all this," I said. "The Winged Monkeys, the hunger here, the corruption at the prison. She'd do a better job of sorting it all out than I will. But I'm glad that if she had to die, she did it when things were good. She didn't have to worry about us." I frowned at Clement. "Is that terrible?"

"I think it's kind," he said. "I'm sure she wouldn't have worried either way, though. You'll figure this all out. I know you will."

"I'm scared I'll forget her."

"You won't," Clement said, but he didn't look convinced.

"It'd be easier if I knew what was causing all these problems," I said. "I'm convening this council, but I don't even know what to say to them, aside from 'everything is terrible.' At least when Ma was a little girl and Oz was in trouble she could point to the Wicked Witch of the West and say, 'there, that's the problem.'"

"I don't suppose the witch is back?" Clement said. "You said your Ma melted her. Are you sure that killed her?"

"I'm not sure what else melting someone does to them," I said.

He chuckled. "I guess I'm just clutching at straws, with her monkeys being back at all."

I grinned at him. "You believe the conspiracy theorists?"

He stuck the cork back in the water skin. "I guess not. I just wish we were facing *one* enemy. It'd make things easier on you. I want this to be easier on you."

"Nothing in my life is easy," I said. "Not these days. But you sure lighten the load."

He flashed a smile at me. And lands, it was brighter than the rising moon.

22ND SEPTEMBER

We saw the lights of Urbis long before the city walls. The distant sky gleamed with a pearlescent glow, hinting at lanterns and Forge lights and other myriad forms of illumination.

"We should travel when it's dark until we get there," Clement said, and I agreed. We were nearing civilization, and civilization meant guards and people who may have read of our escape in the newspapers. We'd have to get through the great walls and to the city center without getting caught. The fewer people we passed, the better.

Another wave of magic hit Clement as we approached the lights, and I made him sit and rest until it passed. "His pain was increasing at much the same speed as our memories were decreasing. We took turns taking light naps.

Or, rather, Clement napped and I tried to sleep, but only ended up tossing and turning on the sand. The near future played out in my head over and over, each time filled with terrifying new possibilities. In one daydream, we were caught by other travelers before we even reached the city walls. In another, we were accosted by the guards at the city gates and taken straight back to Urbis Prison without a hearing. We might get jumped in an alley, or faint from hunger, or get bitten by a sand viper before we even reached Urbis. I hadn't seen any snakes on our journey yet, aside from the constellation Clement had pointed out, but that didn't mean we wouldn't stumble over one in the darkness. It was like the more my past was forgotten, fear of the future was taking its place in my mind.

Clement's hand settled on my shoulder.

"You all right?"

"I'm never all right," I said, voice muffled from my cheek pressing against my arm, which I was using as a pillow. "I'm a mess. I am a human disaster zone."

As always, Clement refused to meet my anxiety with his own.

"Ah, yes, the utter wasteland that is Jakon Gale," he said lightly. "You are, indeed, a man who cannot command the wind. You aren't guided by a profound devotion to your family. And you *certainly* aren't the Mayor of Oz with all the rights and privileges that confers."

"Those rights and privileges didn't stop me from getting thrown in prison," I said, words still half-smothered.

Clement rubbed my back lightly, just as Ma used to. "The chances of that happening twice seem pretty low," he said. "Especially if we send a letter to your family first thing, before you convene that council."

"Or we'll get kidnapped by violent criminals before we ever make it to a post office."

"I pity the criminal that tries to get through one of your tornadoes."

"I can't just whip up a tornado every time we get into trouble." I rolled over, the sand feeling like boulders beneath me. "If I want cuffs like yours on my wrists, that's the way to get them."

"Jakon?"

I rolled over again and stared up at the midnight sky. Clement's silhouette blocked out a head-and-shoulder-shaped patch of stars.

"What?" I said.

He patted my arm. "Relax."

He spoke so flatly, with such an air of command, that I couldn't help laughing. People telling me to calm down usually just upset me more, but the words, matched with Clement's gift for impenetrable placidity, struck me as hilarious.

"Fine." I rolled over one more time. "You win. I'm calm as a summer's morning."

That was a lie, but I didn't feel as if I were climbing a mountain of anxiety anymore. I hadn't gone back down the mountain, not exactly, but I felt as if I'd at least sat down to take in the view.

"I'm not going to get any sleep like this," I said. "Let's keep walking. If something terrible is going to happen we might as well get it over with."

The better part of an hour later, our first glimpse of Urbis's high walls shimmered at the edge of the horizon. It was difficult to make out the walls, dark as they were at this hour, but the light pouring up from the black line of the walls was unmistakable.

"We're almost there." Clement set his shoulders and gave me a brisk nod. "We've got this."

I took a deep breath and tried my utmost best to believe him.

Slowly, step by step, we moved toward the city. As we walked, my heartbeat slowed and the nervous prickling on the back of my neck settled.

Clement was right. We would either run into trouble or we wouldn't, and if we did, I had magic in my back pocket that might at least protect me long enough for me to declare a council and claim my right to stay out of prison until it was over.

On top of that, there would be food in Urbis, and real beds. I'd have access to money and the freedom to send an urgent telegram to my siblings. This terrible, exhausting, dry stretch of my journey would be over.

I felt better the closer we got to the city walls. But Clement seemed to be getting worse. I noticed his ragged breathing first, and when I reached for his hand his skin was cold and clammy.

"Clement," I said, question and warning both in my voice.

"It's getting worse," he said tightly. "The magic."

"Another wave?" I said. That was two, close together. I drew my eyebrows together. "Do you need to sit down?"

"I can keep going."

"Nice try," I said. "I'm not going to let you make yourself sick."

"We need to get there while it's still dark."

"It can't be much past two or three in the morning. We have plenty of time. We'll still get there before the first shops start opening up." I wrapped my arms around him and steadied him. "It'll be better if we get there just before dawn anyway. That's always the quietest part of the day. We'll be able to slip right through to the city center."

Weakly, he nodded and crumpled at the side of the road. He put his head between his knees and breathed slowly while I rubbed my palm in circles across his back.

"That's nice," he said, and leaned in a little.

I scooted closer to him and pulled him in until his weight was resting against me. He took a deep, shuddering breath.

I wasn't going to post a letter to my siblings first. I was going to find someone to get these cuffs off of Clement. I couldn't stand seeing him like this.

Eventually, the wave passed and we got back on the road. The stars wheeled overhead and the sand glimmered pale blue. It was breathtaking, and I was sick of it. Even the galaxies shining above us, enchanting in their beauty, made my stomach turn a little.

The beauty wasn't enough. The beauty in the sky couldn't compensate for the terrible things going on below--the poverty in Badalah, the magic fracturing across the kingdoms, whatever was making Clement sick. The heavens sparkled with tranquility, but here on the ground, things were horribly wrong.

I walked faster, urged on by a deep urge to do *something*, and Clement kept pace with me. His face remained tight, but he matched whatever discomfort he was feeling with sheer determination, and we soared across the ground like vengeful spirits.

Ahead of us, the walls grew taller. They were still nothing more than a black silhouette against the starry sky, but that silhouette slowly took on a shape: straight on either side, domed on top, the side of a perfect circle surrounding a perfect wheel-shaped city.

The lights grew brighter, too. Even now, in the darkest reaches of early morning, parts of the city were awake and alive. The glow polluted the sky and obscured the stars, and hinted that we might not have as easy of a time passing through as we would have in Kisbu or even the Emerald City.

Still, those lights drew me in. They held promises: of threats, yes, but also of salvation.

I couldn't let fear slow me down. I ran through the plan as I walked, each footfall matched with a task.

Reach the wall.

Get through the gate.

Go to the city center.

Find Clement a magician.

Convene a council.

That was all we had to do and we'd be safe. Together, they formed an insurmountable challenge. But I didn't have to do them all at once. Thinking that way, the Scarecrow had always said, was illogical. As a physical being I could only complete one task at a time, so there was no reason to worry about more than one task at a time.

Reach the wall.

Get through the gate.

Go to the city center.

My breathing grew ragged. We weren't quite running, but this was faster than we'd walked since we'd first escaped the prison. We were so close. The walls loomed overhead. We were almost there, almost to Urbis, almost to safety, almost to--

Clement stopped dead.

It took me a moment to realize he wasn't still next to me, and then I turned. At that moment, he gasped as if he'd been punched in the gut and dropped to his knees, clutching his head.

"I can't," he said, pressing into his temples with both hands. "Jakon, I'm sorry. I can't."

I crouched next to him and reached for his shoulders. He leaned into me, using my body as support.

"What happened?" I demanded. "What's going on? Can you look at me?"

My heart pounded and the back of my neck prickled with sudden cold. We were so close. He couldn't give up now.

"Clement, look at me," I repeated.

"I can't keep going." He looked up, pain shining brightly in his eyes. "Jakon, I'm so sorry. You have to go without me."

I stared at him. It was difficult to make out anything but his eyes in the darkness, even with the glow of the city adding its own pale efforts to the starlight, but I didn't need to see his face to read the hunch of his shoulders or the shaking of his hands.

"Clement, what happened? Is it the magic?"

He nodded, then hissed a sharp breath in between his teeth and squeezed his eyes shut.

I held onto him and waited for his pain to recede. It took a long time.

"You have to go ahead without me," he repeated. "I'm so sorry, Jakon, I wanted to come with you. But I can't. I can't do it."

He buried his face in my shoulder. I pulled him close. His whole body shuddered in my embrace, as if he were being buffeted about by great gusts of wind.

The night lay cool and calm all around us, but for the first time, Clement couldn't meet it. The tranquility he wore like a second skin was gone, revealing only pain and terror.

"The magic is stronger," he said. "There's a massive buildup up ahead. It's going right through my skull."

I put a hand on his shoulder. "We can wait until it passes."

He shook his head. He was all tension and pain; his skin was drawn tight over his skull, and his back felt like stone under my hand.

"It's not going to pass."

"These waves always pass," I said, keeping my voice soothing.

He shook his head again, more violently this time. "This isn't a wave. This is an *ocean.*"

I looked toward the city. The glow rising from above the dark walls seemed ominous now, as if it came not from the ordinary lights of a large city but from something eldritch and far too close.

"Maybe my magic can help you," I said.

He looked up at me, and a bleak smile crossed his features. "How? You control wind."

"And water," I said. "Maybe magic is like weather. Or maybe I can blow it away."

"You're welcome to try," he said, though without much hope.

I raised my hands and closed my eyes. The cool ribbons of the early morning breeze danced around me. I tried to sense for something deeper inside or behind them. Clement had felt my magic when I'd first arrived at the prison. So had Bear. If there was a sea of enchantment in front of us, I should be able to feel it.

But I wasn't Clement, and I didn't even know what I was trying to find.

I tugged on the ribbons and created a vast wind that swept across the desert, kicking up sand. It blew sideways. If the magic was between us and the city, this should throw it all to one side and leave us a clear path.

I looked to Clement. He massaged his temples and shook his head at me.

I tried again. My skills had improved. I could command the wind. But Clement's expression didn't change, and it seemed the air was the only invisible force I could control.

I dropped my hands. "Nothing?"

"No," Clement said.

I stood and paced across the sand, first a few steps toward Urbis and then away. The two places felt no different. Whatever magic had driven Clement to the ground didn't affect me.

That would have been fine, had I been traveling on my own.

But I wasn't traveling on my own, and I didn't intend to start now.

"What about a tornado?" I said. "A tornado brought Ma to Oz. It could get us from here to Urbis's gates in a flash. We can find you a magician right away and get your cuffs off."

I didn't know if I could create that sort of tornado, nor was I certain I'd enjoy traveling in one if I could. Everything about it seemed risky. I'd be willing to face risk, if that meant easing Clement's burden.

"I can't," he said. "I can't get one step closer to that magic."

"It would only take a moment."

"I'll die," he said sharply. "One step closer and I will die, Jakon. I'm sorry. Just go ahead. I'll go back to Jaf."

"They'll murder you."

"I'll be fine."

"I'm not going on without you."

"Then you're not going on." His tone held a chilling

finality.

I stared at him, then at the city. On one side, my friend gritted his teeth against the onslaught of magic threatening to destroy him. On the other, the city that held our salvation called to me with promises of safety and family.

I couldn't choose between them. It would tear me apart.

Ma's voice entered my head, a memory from years past. *You've got to deal with the problem in front of you.* She spoke softly, the way I thought an angel might. *You can drive yourself crazy worrying about what-ifs and what-thens, and they'll never do you any good. Tell me, what's the problem right in front of you?*

This decision was the problem. Loyalty and love pulled me in both directions, and I couldn't choose between them.

That's not what I asked, Ma said, and now her voice wasn't from a memory at all, but from deep inside my mind. *What's the problem right in front of you? You are the Mayor of Oz, and you are a Gale. Your job is to find suffering and alleviate it. What's the problem?*

Clement was suffering. My best friend was in blinding pain.

There you go. Solve that. The rest will follow.

Ma's presence faded out. My throat closed up. I needed her back; I needed her advice and her opinions and her willingness to shoulder the responsibilities that made me feel ready to collapse.

But I didn't have Ma. I only had memories of the things she had taught me.

I crouched next to Clement.

"Does the pain stop if you back up?"

Clement scrambled back like a crab across the sand.

He sat again and closed his eyes. After a moment, he nodded.

"What about to the left and right?"

He frowned up at me, but stood and walked obediently in either direction. He stopped again in front of me and took a few more steps back.

"They're the same," he said.

I turned to look at the city. It held magicians and telegrams, food and beds, high-ceilinged world council chambers and Urbis Express zeppelins that would begin operating at dawn. It held everything I needed, except Clement.

And if I didn't have Clement, it didn't have enough.

"The magic that's hurting you is in the city," I said. "In Urbis."

"It has to be," he said. "Something is wrong in there. It's not just bad, it's evil." He held out his hand. It trembled.

"It frightens you," I said slowly.

He nodded without hesitation. "I know you have to go," he said. "I understand. But you have to be careful. Whatever is happening to the magic in there…"

He trailed off and shuddered.

I squared my shoulders. "It doesn't matter, then, because we're not going to Urbis."

"Just because I can't go any farther doesn't mean you have to give up," he started.

I cut him off. "I'm not giving up. Neither are you."

"What about your brothers and sisters?" he asked. "What about the council?"

"I'll see them, it'll just take a few extra days," I said, forcing a confidence into my voice I didn't quite feel.

A confidence I didn't quite feel *yet*. One of the Lion's admonitions came back to me: *Sometimes, courage means acting first and feeling later.* I had to make a choice and take a step, and trust that I'd made the right one.

It was easier said than done, but I owed it to both of us to try.

"As for the council," I continued, "I can call that just as well from Oz as Urbis and take the Express there later straight from the Emerald City." Something about the words didn't sit right. "That's assuming I want to do that, still," I added slowly. "If something is wrong in Urbis, something *evil*..."

"Then you might not want to contact anyone until you know what's going on," Clement finished.

The weight of that settled on me like a sack of flour. An hour ago, I'd thought I had things all figured out. I'd had an action plan: Get to Urbis. Go through the gate.

Now, I was about to take the first step onto a whole new path, and I didn't know what waited for me at the end.

At least I liked my traveling companion.

I held out a hand. "Come on, let's cross as much of this infernal desert as we can while it's still night. We'll cross the border into Aboria and get to Oz from there."

"What about the desert at Oz's borders?" Clement asked.

A grin spread across my face. "That's what the tornadoes are for. You up for letting me take you on a ride?"

The closer we had gotten to Urbis, the stronger my magic had grown. I could feel it within me, building, swirling around. I knew now that I could control it more than I had before. I could control it because I felt the way it moved within me.

He hesitated, clearly unnerved by the crazy smile

on my face, but I couldn't just wipe it away. I was a madman who'd just taken a mad step toward a mad adventure, and if there was ever a time to learn how to travel by tornado, this was it.

"I might as well practice over this sand," I said. "Beats accidentally dropping us into the treetops in Aboria."

Clement shook his head at me, aiming for disapproval, but his smile was growing to be the mirror of my own.

He reached out and took my hand. My fingers laced through his and my warm, dry palm pressed against his still-clammy one.

"I don't remember," he whispered.

"Remember what?" I asked, gripping his hand tightly.

"I don't remember who you are."

"I needed to get us both out of here before I forgot who I was too."

THRONE OF EMERALDS

23RD SEPTEMBER

Even here in the desert, well outside the walls of the great city of Urbis, civilization made its presence felt. The lights of the city burned at all hours, difficult to see during the day but illuminating the sky with a pearly glow from dusk until dawn. Out on the sand, where Clement and I traveled, bits of refuse teased at the life going on within those towering walls.

We passed shards of broken bottles that suggested someone had come out here late one night to drink. Twenty minutes of walking later, birds pecked at a cluster of fruit rinds and chicken bones. A bit after that, a broken wagon wheel stuck halfway out of the sand, its wood already warping and splitting under the hot Badalahn sun.

"I'm sorry I'm making us walk all this way," Clement said, for what had to be the fifteenth time. His memory of me had faded which burned at my soul, but he knew he could trust me and he knew we were walking away from Urbis because of him.

"I wasn't about to continue this journey without you, especially not with your cuffs preventing you from being able to shift.

Clement was good for me that way. I still felt terrified most of the time, but I'd come to realize over the past week that I'd rather be scared out of my wits with him than alone.

"How long do you think it'll take us to get to ...er... Aboria?" Clement said.

We could see hints of the forested nation up ahead. No trees were visible yet, but there, on the horizon, when we stood at the very top of one of the dunes that filled this part of Badalah, the ground far ahead steadied. The soft, undulating swells of sand gave way to solid land, dotted with specks I took for boulders and parched shrubs.

They were a ways yet, but looking toward that distant horizon gave me hope that the aching in my calves might someday subside and that our memories would be returned to us. Now that we were off the brick road between Kisbu and Urbis, every step required twice the effort, and I felt as if the dry particles that had invaded every crevice of my shoes would never be fully shaken out.

We traipsed across the dunes, up and down, over and over, until I was almost dizzy from it. It didn't help that Clement and I no longer had the easy banter I'd gotten used to over the past few days. He walked beside me, but his memory was so fractured, that he remained silent most of the morning. My memory was almost as bad, but I remembered what we were doing and I had to hold onto that. We stopped during the hottest part of the day and used our hands to dig. I was beginning to sense water, not just in the air but in the ground, too. The sand was cooler a few feet down, and held moisture from some none-too-recent downpour.

We made a hole a couple of feet across, and I drew water from our surroundings to fill it. I closed my eyes, relying on some deep instinct that had nothing to do with vision, and reached out for the ribbons of air and water that made up so much of the world. Silently, with my concentration narrowed to a pinpoint, I wove strands of water together to hold the liquid together and prevent it from seeping into the soil.

Then I lowered my hand into the water. I ordered it to slow down and grow colder, and it did, responding to my thoughts almost as quickly as I could think them.

I opened my eyes. The small pool of water sparkled in the sunlight. Tragically, I hadn't yet figured out how to create shade, but this would prevent us from overheating until the sun fell a little.

"Stick your feet in there," I said, already pulling off my socks.

Clement did, and hissed sharply as his toes touched the water.

"Too cold?"

"Way too cold," he said. "It's perfect." He closed his eyes and lowered his feet down to the bottom of our little pool.

I plunged mine in, too. Our toes brushed against one another, and we didn't pull away.

We arranged the hoods of our robes far enough over our heads that no direct sunlight could reach our skin, and then we sat and waited for the day to cool enough that we could keep walking. Not long after we first sat down, Clement winced and bent over.

"Another wave?"

It wasn't really a question. We'd kept our distance from Urbis's walls, but the magic emanating from the city still managed to overwhelm him a few times every day causing him pain.

He nodded. I reached for his hand and held it as he breathed through the pain. When it was over, he let out a long sigh. Whatever life had been in his face before the magic had hit was gone, leaving his cheeks hollow and his skin tight across his forehead.

"You should slee--"

"I know," he said, before I could finish.

Clement mounded a pile of sand next to himself and draped his body over it. He was asleep in moments, his dark eyelids twitching as he dreamed.

I wondered what he dreamed about. Would he lose more of his memories in his sleep as I did? It felt that every time I closed my eyes, something else went missing from my mind and yet I couldn't ever remember what it was I was losing.

I wiggled my toes on the water and splashed some of the icy liquid on the back of my neck as I silently recited my siblings names again. Perhaps I could form the water into different shapes--into ice we could suck on as we walked, or maybe clouds that could shield us from the harrowing sun.

Yes, that would be worth trying.

I raised my hands, closed my eyes, and began to work.

∼

Clement opened his eyes, then squeezed them shut again.

"Where are we?" he murmured, nestling further into his pillow of sand. He'd pulled his feet out of the icy pool sometime during his nap. Now, he stretched and plunged them back into the water. He shuddered, but it seemed to be more out of pleasure than discomfort.

"Still in Badalah, " I said. "Look." I nudged his knee with my bare toes.

He opened his eyes again, unwillingly.

I gestured up. He blinked, trying to make sense of the thing hovering over us, and then he sat bolt upright and stared upward.

A single, fluffy cloud hovered directly over our heads, close enough that we might have been able to brush it with our fingertips if we'd stood on our toes.

Clement looked from the cloud to me. "You made that?"

"You bet your magic wand I did." I stretched my arms out and cracked my knuckles, more from a sense of showmanship than because anything actually needed cracking. "I can't get it any bigger without it falling apart, but still, it's a start."

"I'll say. Can you move it?"

I reached out for the ribbons of air that floated all around us. I tugged one, then another, and the cloud danced from side to side.

Clement's face broke into a wide grin. "Now that's a trick worth having."

"What, pulling water from the air wasn't?"

He scrambled to his feet and reached up. I jerked the cloud just out of his reach, then swept it down and around him. He spun in a circle, trying to keep pace with it.

My stomach growled. A sharp pang ricocheted through me, a hunger like I'd never felt.

Clement stopped spinning and frowned at me. "Your magic's making you hungry."

"We haven't eaten in days," I reminded him. My stomach wouldn't let me forget that in a hurry.

He acknowledged this with a rueful smile, but shook his head. "Magic takes energy. You need energy to use it, same as you need energy to keep hiking up and down these hills."

I let go of my hold on the cloud. It disappeared into wisps that melted away against the blue of the early evening sky.

"I wish I'd gotten the gift of creating food out of thin air."

"I'd kill for an apple pie right now."

I tilted my head. "Apple pies. Are those your favorite?"

"Apple anything," he said. "Fresh, baked, jellied, dried, I like them all."

I stored this information away with everything else I'd learned about him over these past few weeks. That collection of facts was becoming increasingly important to me in spite of my attempts to avoid getting closer to him than I was already. I just needed to hold onto them and not lose them like I was sure I'd lost other things since stepping into the desert.

My magic tingled in my hands. It had a tendency to spring to life whenever Clement was in danger. I had to keep my emotions under control, at least until I knew better how to wield my powers.

Clement's face twisted. I reached out a hand to steady him before he could begin to sway. The wave of magic coming from Urbis seemed to fade almost as quickly as it had arrived, and he shook it off.

"That one wasn't bad," he said. "Let's get moving. Maybe we can put the city behind us by nightfall."

I nodded my agreement, but it turned out that we had both underestimated how enormous Urbis was. The wall that wrapped around the city like the outer rim of a wheel stayed steady on our left as we walked, and its circular shape made it impossible to gauge when we might expect to be past the city and its brutalizing magic. We used the sun and our shadows on the sand to keep our direction steady, and marched across the dunes until my legs were screaming out for rest.

Finally, the sun set. The city still hulked to our side, the light from within warming the dark sky like cream in coffee.

Clement stopped abruptly at the top of a dune and grabbed my arm. His fingers tightened and he held his breath.

I looked out to where his gaze was fixed and saw it: flickering orange lights in the valley between dunes, and a ribbon of smoke rising from a campfire.

Slowly, silently, we sank to our knees and watched the people below. There were almost a dozen of them, mostly adults but also a couple of young children who played in the glow of the fire.

I surveyed the men in particular, looking for armor or weapons. One man had a bow slung on the side of the large pack he was using as a back rest, and I caught glimpses of a few things that might have been scabbards for swords or daggers. Overall, though, these folks didn't look like warriors. They were family men, travelers like us.

"Should we go around?" Clement asked, his voice under a whisper.

I watched the group. They weren't as emaciated

as the family we'd passed on the road before. These children were rosy-cheeked and happy, and the adults didn't seem as guarded as I might have expected.

Most importantly, they held bowls of steaming stew on their laps, and there was more in the pot hanging over the fire.

"We need food," I whispered back.

"We don't have any money."

"No, but we're not too proud to beg."

We stood and walked slowly down the dune, keeping our hands visible. It wasn't long before the group of travelers noticed us, and their demeanor shifted instantly. A few of the men and one of the women sprang to their feet, and another man gathered the children and put himself between us and them.

Clement and I raised our hands, showing they were empty.

"Good travels, friends," Clement called, his voice full of a carefully calculated warmth. I was beginning to understand how intentional he was about presenting himself. It was remarkable to watch especially as his memory had fled him, the essence of who he was remained.

The group let us approach, but those with blades kept their hands tight on the hilts. The woman with a sword strapped to her waist stepped forward, chin high and eyes as sharp as her blade was likely to be.

"We're sorry if we startled you," Clement said, his voice warm and his steps slow. "We're on our way to..."

"Arboria," I whispered in his ear to remind him.

"...Arboria. We didn't expect to run across anyone else out here."

I did my best to match Clement's demeanor. He'd told me he managed to stay calm in situations like this by remembering what it was like to shift and become a powerful creature that nothing could harm. I couldn't shift, but I did know what it was like to command a tornado with the twitch of my fingers. Silently, I reminded myself that I could whisk us away from this situation in an instant if it became dangerous. I was safe. These people couldn't hurt me.

The tension in my shoulders melted, and I let out a long sigh.

"We're hoping you might be willing to share your meal," I said. "We hope to walk trough Arboria to Oz where my family lives."

The smell of the stew was thick in the air by now, a scent full of meat and spices and herbs. This was no meager hunk of rabbit cooked in water. This was *food*.

The woman narrowed her eyes.

"We were planning to go to...er...the city," Clement said, pointing to Urbis's city walls..

I glanced sharply at him. I hadn't planned on telling these people our full story. But Clement's gaze was clear and calm. Whoever these people were, he had decided honesty was best, and I was prepared to trust him.

"There appears to be some kind of magic in the city that isn't compatible with my abilities. We've decided to go around the city instead, but we didn't plan on our journey being this long. We ran out of food a few days ago."

The woman watched us both for a long moment. Clement kept his shoulders loose and his face pleasant. I did, too.

After a while, she took her hand off the hilt of her sword. The others relaxed, and she gestured at us to join them.

The people sitting around the fire made room, and

soon we were chatting amiably with big bowls of stew on our laps.

I could barely focus on the conversation. The meat in the stew melted in my mouth and golden globs of fat shimmered between chunks of vegetables. The spices overwhelmed my senses, reminding me of times before Urbis Prison when good meals with good people had taken a central role in many of my days.

Clement nudged me. I started and glanced up to see our new companions looking at me expectantly.

"I'm sorry, what?" I said.

"I was asking what Oz is like. You mentioned your family are there."

"Sorry," I said, reddening. "We haven't had a meal this good in quite some time."

"No need to apologize," he replied. "That's not an unfamiliar story in these parts."

"You seem better off than most people we've run into lately," I said.

He nodded. "Our guild found good work in Urbis for a time."

"They're headed home to Kisbu." Clement had clearly been listening to these strangers a lot better than I had. "They were in Urbis making furnishings for a private client."

"One who paid well," the man said, not seeming too offended by my failure to pay attention to their conversation. "There are a few of those left in the world, though they seem to be scarcer by the day."

"That seems true throughout Badalah," I said. "And in some of the other kingdoms, perhaps."

"But not Oz?" the man said.

I cleared my throat. I didn't want to talk; I wanted to enjoy this delicious stew. But I resolved to be a good guest.

"Oz is thriving," I said. "Or, at least, it was when I left it a few weeks ago."

Left. It was a fragile word to describe my rough abduction by the Winged Monkeys.

"And what's it like, when things are good?"

"Out of all the kingdoms, I think ours might be the most diverse within its own borders. We have varied terrain and equally varied cultures."

I told our hosts about the myriad strange cities that dotted our landscape, from the delicate China Country to the glittering green Emerald City. I knew I'd missed places out. The memories of names of towns and cities I knew well only days ago had been lost somewhere along our journey. They listened, some rapt and others smiling as if they thought I was making half of it up for the benefit of the children.

"Shame you're not headed in our direction," the woman said. Her name, I had learned, was Akilah. She led this guild, and the others seemed to regard her with total deference. "It's safer to travel the sands in groups."

"We already had a run-in with some raiders," I said.

Her eyes widened. "They don't usually leave travelers alive."

Kind as they had been, I wasn't about to divulge my abilities to these strangers. If they'd heard news of the escaped convicts from Urbis Prison, my ability to command the elements would be a dead giveaway.

"Clement is gifted at talking people down from bad decisions," I said quickly. "The raiders stole from us, but we escaped with our hides."

"A fortunate gift," Akilah said, giving Clement a respectful nod. "It should serve you well on your way to Oz. You have a great deal of ground to cover."

She caught the eye of one of the women sitting around the fire. Without needing to speak, they communicated something, and the woman moved quietly away from the fire and began rummaging in one of their many large packs.

"We move on tonight," Akilah said. "As I expect you will. It's better to travel the desert in darkness."

"So we've learned," Clement said. "We're beyond grateful to you for this meal. I hope it'll get us as far as the border of Aboria, where we should be able to forage for sustenance until we can find a village and work."

"We'll do you one better," Akilah said, gesturing behind us.

The woman who had left the circle was back, bearing two parcels wrapped in newspaper and bound with twine. She handed the parcels over our shoulders. Mine was heavy, with the pliant, tell-tale shape of flatbread inside, accompanied by something else I couldn't identify.

"This should take you to the border and then some," Akilah said. "I wouldn't rely on finding work anywhere, if I were you. It's in short supply."

"This is too generous," Clement said, his fingers tightening around his parcel.

"Badalah has a tradition of hospitality," she said. "I fear our nation has fallen short of its reputation these past few months."

"This isn't the only kingdom to have fallen on hard times," I said. "Things aren't easy anywhere, it seems."

All around the circle, the guild members acknowledged this with nods and murmurs.

"We expected the situation to be better in Urbis," one man said. "And it is, for the very wealthy."

"That's always the way of things," a woman said,

scoffing. "Meanwhile everyone else bears burdens that grow by the day. But that's life."

"But it's no excuse to let our standards slip," Akilah said. "We're happy to offer you food. I hope you'll have the opportunity to do the same for someone else along the road."

We already had. I couldn't forget the look in those hungry children's eyes when Clement and I had handed their father the last of our fruit.

Clement took up the conversation, freeing me to finish my stew. I sopped up the last of the broth with a crust of bread. By then, the guild had already moved to collapse their small tents and gather their packs.

"Keep your eyes open and ears sharp," Akilah advised us, as we prepared to go our separate ways. "It's a long way yet to Oz."

We thanked her, and then our groups took off in opposite directions, them headed toward the constellation Clement called the Cauldron and us toward the one I called the Dragonette.

Clement tucked his parcel of food into his robes as we walked. I went to do the same when the headline on my newspaper caught my eye.

This paper was from Urbis. Perhaps it would give us a hint as to the terrible magic that had kept us from approaching the city.

We stopped and crouched at the top of a dune, where the moonlight was bright enough to let us transfer everything in my parcel to Clement's. I had been right: Flatbread sat at the bottom of the parcel, topped by dried fruit and meat. We managed to cram them into one bundle, and then I shook out the wrinkled newspaper and tilted it toward the moonlight.

The words were difficult to make out. The moon was

239

only in its first quarter and didn't provide enough light for easy reading.

Fortunately, the sand below us didn't require a great deal of focus to navigate. I drew the paper close to my eyes as we walked and squinted until the words formed.

"CRIMINALS APPROACHING URBIS; CITIZENS ADVISED CAUTION," I read aloud. Beneath the headline, a photograph showed several people on a city street. The photograph didn't look posed; someone had snapped it when the group wasn't looking.

They were around my age, but I could see at a glance why the paper had labeled them "dangerous." The woman who seemed to be leading the group had the kind of intense focus on her face that told me anyone who interrupted her would pay a heavy price. A small dragon perched on her shoulder. I tilted my head, not sure I was seeing it right. But no, it was definitely a dragon, and it seemed content, almost like a pet.

"Citizens of Urbis are advised to be on the lookout for a group of young radicals traveling toward the city," I read. "They were recently spotted in The Forge, accompanied by a dragon witnesses claim is trained to attack on command. Members of the group may be identified by golden rings surrounding the irises of their eyes. Some speculate that the rings exist as a result of a magical initiation into their criminal band; others speculate the travelers are all members of a race that exists beyond the confines of all known maps. Urbis citizens should not attempt to approach, as these individuals are considered armed and extremely dangerous. Anyone with information on their whereabouts should contact law enforcement immediately."

"You have golden rings around your irises," Clement said sharply. "What a ridiculous way to profile people.

What's next, should we turn in anyone with a bald spot or one ear slightly bigger than the other?"

"In all fairness, I *am* a wanted criminal."

Clement snorted. "I forgot about that. I suppose you could be considered armed, too."

I didn't have to look up from the paper to know he was rolling his eyes.

"I'm extremely dangerous," I said. "Not because I can create tornadoes or anything. It's the golden eyes."

"Your eyes are beautiful," he said.

Oh.

Oh.

Heat flooded to my face. I was grateful for the darkness.

"The princess of Enchantia has golden rings, too," he added, far too loudly. "They're lovely. Everyone knows they're one of her best features."

"You think I'm as pretty as the princess of Enchantia?" I asked, trying to keep a teasing note in my voice and not dwell on the fact he remembered her and not me.

Clement didn't say anything.

He didn't have to. I knew a *yes* when I didn't hear it.

I brought the paper back to my face. But the article was short; the final sentence just told citizens of Urbis how to locate their nearest law enforcement office if they didn't know where it was already.

I skimmed the other articles, desperate to find one interesting enough that I could read it aloud and break the pregnant silence between us, but the other stories were dull--a house painter had been charged with embezzling money from his employer, a wrestling match had ended in someone's favor, and the Urbis Express had grounded one of its older zeppelins for repairs. There was nothing to explain the magic that had scared Clement so badly, and nothing more about the gang with the golden eyes.

"Who do you think they are?" I finally asked.

"I don't feel like I know anyone these days. Do you recognize any of them?"

I narrowed my eyes at the paper, but all the narrowing in the world wasn't enough to compensate for the darkness. "I can't see well enough to say."

"I don't suppose you can control the moonlight?"

I laughed. Then I hesitated, because I didn't know whether I could or not. I barely knew anything about my sudden powers.

I stopped and tried to reach out into the night air for the moonlight. I couldn't find it anywhere, not in the ribbons of the breeze or the threads of water that danced between them. I could make that air hotter or colder, faster or slower, but I couldn't find anything that felt like illumination.

"It's all right," Clement said, after I let out a disappointed sigh. "Not every magician can do everything. I can shapeshift but I can't even light a candle without a spell and my wand to help me."

"What happened to your wand, anyway?"

"Cursed if I know," he said.

He'd more than likely lost it at the prison. We'd left only a few weeks ago but already it had almost disappeared into the blackness of my mind.

"Once we get back to Oz we'll try to get it back," I said. "Or you can try to bond with a new one. I'll bet Glinda would love to help you out."

He answered with a wan smile but I could tell he didn't remember who Glinda was despite me mentioning her as often as possible so I wouldn't forget her myself. We kept walking, and I tilted the paper up toward the moon as the slender crescent rose higher into the sky.

These people on the page did look familiar. The intense woman with the slicked-back hair and the dragon--I knew her, somehow. I squinted and studied her profile. The dragon on her shoulder rested its chin on the top of her head and seemed to stare directly at the camera.

The dragon. Of course.

"That's Azia," I blurted, happy to have remembered something so important.

I stopped dead in my tracks and stared at the page. The photograph, black-and-white and distant as it was, seemed to sharpen as my memories of the princess of Draconis flooded into my mind. I'd *met* her, years ago when we'd both ended up in Urbis during some meeting our parents were attending. My recollection of the serious, clever princess was fuzzy, but I'd seen her photograph several times in the intervening years, and now that I'd put the pieces together she was unmistakable.

"And that's Prince Deon," I said. "He just married the princess of Floris. Glinda was at their wedding."

I held the paper up, as if that extra inch might somehow get me closer to the moonlight.

"And that's Princess Blaise, it has to be," I said, gaping at the young woman with the cloud of curly hair. This photograph was in black and white, but I knew that hair was a fiery red, because I'd seen it before in other photographs. "I know her, Clement. I know these people. Or I know *of* them, at least."

He took the paper from me. I gave it up without a fight. He peered at the page.

"They're the children of the royal families," he said. "How does this paper not know who they are?"

"I'd bet you anything they know *exactly* who they are and they're trying to not cause a fuss," I said. "Calling them a dangerous band of roving criminals is one thing. Pointing the finger at what looks like half the kingdoms' heirs is another entirely."

"Then why bother?" Clement said. "Why put them in the paper at all?"

"They must have thought the risk was worth it."

Overhead, a shining star winked at us, as if trying to let us in on the secret. I stared up at it, then turned to Clement.

"Whatever's happening in the kingdoms has something to do with them," I said. "I have no proof and I don't need it. Why else would they all be traveling together right now? Bear said magic is fracturing all across the kingdoms. You can't get within a mile of Urbis. I was kidnapped by Winged Monkeys for no good reason at all and our memories are next to useless-- but maybe this is the reason. Maybe whoever charged me with treason thought it was because I was about to run off and join this group of people who have my eyes and my exact station in life." I shook my head, brushing off the technical inaccuracy of my statement as I would have a fly. "Not my *exact* station, because I'm the Mayor of Oz, not her child. But that's only because Ma went and died on me far before her time." I jabbed the photograph with one pointed finger. "In everything but hard fact, I'm one of them."

"Wonder if Princess Kelis is, too," Clement murmured. "She's got eyes like yours." He glanced up at me. "Is that a thing? Do young royals always have golden eyes that fade as they get older, and I've just never heard about it?"

"I have no idea."

"Whatever's affecting the kingdoms must be affecting the rulers of the kingdoms, too," I said. "Or at least their children."

"The kings and queens we're talking about wouldn't let their children run off like this normally, would they? If Urbis is claiming that these people are dangerous, either Urbis is lying or the leaders of the kingdoms have completely lost control of their heirs. Either way, something's not right."

He handed the paper back to me. I kept studying the picture for hints, but no more were forthcoming.

All I knew was that these people were like me, and whatever was happening to them was bound to end up on my plate sooner or later. Fear of the future settled heavily on my shoulders, and I sighed and prepared to trudge up the next hill.

24TH SEPTEMBER

The Aborian border turned out to be much farther away than my eyes had promised. It was difficult to calculate distances across the desert, and every time I crested a high dune and expected to see the scrub brush right in front of me, the still-distant horizon seemed to laugh in my face.

We walked through most of the night. When the first pink threads of dawn glittered around the edge of the world, Clement doubled over and fell to his knees.

I dropped next to him in an unthinking instant. He bent forward and pressed his forehead into the ground and clenched handfuls of sand that only trickled between the gaps in his fingers.

I didn't have to ask what was wrong. I knew the

ragged rhythm of his breathing.

Anger stirred in me--anger at his cuffs, at the Urbis Prison guards who had caged his magic, at Urbis for whatever magic was making him ill, at the distance that still lay between us and Oz.

"Breathe," I ordered, bending down so he could hear me. I put a hand on his back. His heart raced, each beat so hard it rattled his spine. "Clement, *breathe*. In, two, three, four. Out, two, three, four."

I counted slowly, as Ma always had for me, and he did his best to match my pace.

Eventually, after what might have been minutes or hours, the wave passed. He collapsed and rolled onto his back.

"That one was bad," I said.

It wasn't a question, but he nodded and closed his eyes.

"The pain is excruciating, but I remember again. I remember you."

I searched through my own mind and for the first time in days the holes in my memory had diminished. I no longer felt fuzzy.

"We are closer to Arboria's border. I think we are moving away from whatever magic is making us forget."

"But not far enough from the magic causing pain," Clement added.

"We'd better rest a while." I glanced up at the sky, which still glimmered with a few lingering stars.

The sun would rise soon. It was better to keep traveling through the first of the morning, if we could, and rest when it became too hot, but we didn't have that choice. Not right now.

"Try to sleep," I said.

Clement groaned and opened one eye. "I'm sorry I'm

slowing you down."

I waved him off and settled next to him, my back against the rising slope of the dune. "I needed a break anyway. My legs are killing me."

I could have kept going. But I wouldn't have let Clement know that, not for the world. He always apologized at the end of these episodes, as if there was anything he could have done to stop them.

"You sleep," I said. "We can trade off when you wake up. I'm going to practice my magic in the meantime."

"Maybe you can figure out how to carry us around in one of those tornadoes," Clement said, his voice already soft with fatigue. "Like you talked about earlier. We could cover more ground."

I nodded, but his eyes were already closed. I patted his chest instead to let him know I'd heard, and he sighed and relaxed against the sand.

I left my hand there for a moment, feeling for his pulse. It had slowed, but every beat was still hard and full of labor.

My own heart twisted at the thought. I missed them all so much. I'd remembered their names by reciting them to myself, but I'd forgotten how much I loved them all and how much being away from them hurt. Getting my memories back was a blessing, but it was also a curse. I hadn't even had the chance to say goodbye before I'd been kidnapped. I couldn't bear the thought of what would have happened if I'd never escaped and my sudden departure from Oz had been for good.

Ma's voice echoed in my head, along with the memory of her lying in bed just days before she'd passed. *I've never minded goodbyes,* she had said, her voice frail in a way I'd never heard before. *I've said farewell to so many people over the years, and I always thought it was a nice time to tell people how much they meant to me. I'm not looking forward to this one, though.*

Grief punched me from behind. My stomach lurched and my throat closed up. Fire prickled in my eyes, followed right after by a surge of water that made the sand and the sunrise ripple.

I caught my breath with the softest of gasps.

Immediately, seemingly without conscious thought on his part, Clement's hand shot out and settled on my knee. He wiggled closer and rested his head against my leg, eyes still closed, and fell into a deeper sleep with a sigh.

I ran my fingertips through his short, curly hair. The texture was both coarse and soft, and heat rose from his scalp like it would from the sun within an hour or two. He murmured a little in his sleep, welcoming the gentle touch.

You'll find more love, Ma's voice said in my head.

This was a different memory, this one from a few months before she'd passed, right after she'd broken the news of her illness. She had been full of quintessential Dorothy Gale spirit, light and vulnerable and confident all at once. She was going to die, she had told us, without mincing words, but that was all right, everyone had to eventually.

Nature abhors a vacuum, as they say, she had continued. *Whatever space I leave in your lives is going to be filled by heaps and heaps of new love, and that's a promise.* She had kissed Chester on the top of his head, accepting his grief and his tears as wholeheartedly as she accepted everything else about us. *And it's not like you have to give back how much I love you, either. You get to keep that forever and ever and ever and ever and ever and ever and ever...*

She had punctuated each *ever* with a kiss atop Chester's head, until he had been forced to giggle through his tears.

It had been impossible to comprehend at the time. But now, looking down at Clement's face nuzzled against my leg, I realized she had been right. Love would always find us.

I stretched out my hands, examining the creases and my tan and the light coating of dust that had taken residence on every part of me. These hands were powerful--capable of wielding magic, and just as incapable of controlling it when Clement was in danger.

There was plenty of love in the world. I just couldn't trust myself enough to accept it.

Hours later, I woke to find Clement sitting in front of me, shielding me from the sun with his body. He was sitting cross-legged, breathing deeply and evenly.

I'd seen him meditate like this a few times before, and I'd tried it, too. I was terrible at trying to corral my thoughts. Every time I sat in silence, they crowded in on me, anxiety and frustration and random stray ideas all competing for attention.

But Clement said he'd been practicing for years, and could make his mind as empty as the blue sky overhead.

I sat up and nudged him, and his eyes fluttered open. His gaze was distant, at least until he focused on me. He smiled in recognition.

"This helps," he said.

"With the magic coming from Urbis?"

He nodded. I rose to my feet and offered a hand to

help him up.

"I think I can help even more," I said. "Getting away from Kisbu helped our memories return and the further away from Urbis you get, the better you feel. So let's get away from Urbis."

His dark eyes sparkled. "You figured it out?"

"I have no idea," I admitted. "But I was practicing the whole time you were asleep and my nap recharged me pretty good. I managed to move our water skin a good twenty feet in a tornado."

"We weigh a lot more than our water skin."

"Yeah, but I was also trying not to wake you," I said. "This next tornado is going to be much bigger."

He bit his lip, as if debating whether to say something.

He didn't have to speak. I didn't even have to try to read his thoughts. They were too obviously the same as mine.

"Yes, I might accidentally break our legs and leave us stranded for the vultures."

"You're all right with that possibility?" he asked.

"Honestly? I think I am. Every second we're out here puts us at risk of being caught by law enforcement or Winged Monkeys or more sand raiders. If I can get us home to Oz faster, we should risk it."

"Good." Clement grinned. "I couldn't agree more."

"You're going to want to hang on tight to me."

His grin widened. "I was planning on that either way."

My cheeks flamed, but after reliving that conversation with Ma, I couldn't deny that I adored the way he flirted with me. His attention was a gift that turned this terrible journey into an adventure worth having. It was nice to have him back after the couple of days where he didn't really know who I was. I'd missed the flirting more than

I liked to admit.

We hiked to the top of the dune we'd been resting against. Clement tucked our parcel of food safely in the pocket of his robes and fastened the water skin to his waist. I stood just in front of him and raised my hands.

Every tornado was easier to call up than the last. And this one, which I didn't have to make smaller or quieter for fear of waking Clement, felt like the easiest of all. I tugged at the ribbons of the air and coaxed them into a rising spiral. The wind kicked up the sand and sent it spinning toward the blue sky.

Tornadoes always came accompanied by green clouds, according to Ma. The sky took on an uncanny feeling and the heat in the air was liable to make the back of your neck prickle.

My tornadoes, though--these were something different. Nature didn't create these, I did, and they didn't need the structure of roiling clouds or precise weather to come into being. They just needed me.

The storm of sand and wind rose in front of us until it towered high over our heads. I kept it at a distance, and then brought it closer and closer.

The hair rose off my forehead. Clement gripped my shoulder, the pressure of his fingers betraying the fear beneath his calm silence.

"It's all right," I said.

The voice didn't sound like mine. It was low and confident, the tone of a man who knew exactly what he was doing.

I jerked my hands and pulled the twister toward us. The roar of the wind rose and our robes flapped in the surrounding breeze as the point of the funnel approached.

"Hold your breath and hang onto me," I shouted

over the noise.

Clement didn't need telling twice. He stepped in close and wrapped his arms around my waist, burying his head against the back of my shoulder as he did so.

Power danced and spun within me, and I knew--*knew*, in a way I'd never known anything before--that this tornado would do everything I told it to and not a bit more.

I brought the tip of the funnel toward us. Sand abraded my skin, so I closed my eyes. It didn't matter; I didn't need my vision to feel what the ribbons of air were doing beneath my hands.

I yanked. The tornado jerked toward us and enfolded us in an instant.

My feet rose from the ground, and then we were flying. We spun higher and higher into the air in a dizzying, adrenaline-filled rush of wind and power.

Far beneath me, the tip of the funnel was as precise against the sand as a pen against paper. I controlled it the same way, my thoughts guiding my hands in an effortless pattern that whipped us across the sand toward the border of Aboria.

I forced my eyes open. The world spun in violent circles all around me. It passed too quickly for sight, and if I'd been relying on my vision I would have been lost and sick in an instant.

But my magic held my mind steady in the middle of the tornado. No matter where the wind threw us, my attention stayed steady and guided me across the desert in a straight line, away from Urbis and toward the brushland up ahead.

"Jakon," Clement shouted into my ear. "Jakon, I'm going to be sick."

I didn't want to let go of this rush. Power throbbed

through me. I could get us halfway to Oz before my energy ran out, I knew it. I could have spent all day being thrown in a vicious circle as my attention stayed steady at the base of this magnificent storm.

But concern for Clement was stronger even than the magic coursing through my veins with my blood. I tugged the ribbons, slowing their spiral and lowering us gently, carefully, to the ground.

Our feet touched down on the sand. The wind slowed around us, first whipping our robes and then just our hair and then, finally, nothing at all.

A soft breeze brushed across my face. Behind me, Clement's arms slid from my waist, and he dropped onto the ground.

Before I could ask about him, he raised a hand. "I'm all right," he said. "Just a little wobbly. My stomach needs a minute to settle." He looked up at me, eyes shining. "But *damn*, Jakon, that was something."

It was more than something. The tornado had given us distance. We had landed at the top of another dune, and now the shimmers of texture had turned into a real vision of irregular rocks and low, silver-green bushes.

"You know tornadoes usually form up in the clouds, right?" Clement said, looking up at me and squinting against the sun. "Not on the ground? Maybe you'll get even more power and control if you mimic nature."

I loved these moments when his training in enchantment kicked in and he couldn't help trying to teach me.

"I'll try that," I said. "If we ever see natural-born clouds again." The sky overhead was one shade of blue, with no hint of moisture.

No, that wasn't right.

There were clouds--far ahead, above our new

horizon, which was shadowed with a dark green line that just might be forest.

The sight was a balm to my soul. I held out a hand to help Clement up.

"We're almost there," I said. "Let's walk. I need more food before I try that again."

"And I need to let my stomach settle back where it belongs," Clement said, heaving to his feet. "Instead of migrating rapidly between my throat and my heart like it is right now."

I winced. "I'm so sorry. I sort of thought the wind might hold us steady in the middle instead of flinging us around like rag dolls."

"It didn't make you sick?"

I couldn't stop my smile from taking over my face. "It made me feel like a god."

Clement grinned, and we took off down the sandy slope and toward the next one.

"This is a lot better," he said after we'd been walking a while. "The further we get from Urbis the easier it gets."

I tore off a bite of dried meat with my teeth and chewed. The food restored me. Clement had been right: magic required energy.

"You never responded like this in Enchantia?" I said. "I mean, is the magic in Urbis actually bad or is it just hard for you to process magic with those cuffs on?"

Clement frowned and held up both wrists. The silver cuffs were as strong as they'd been the day we'd escaped Urbis Prison. They still shone in spite of their thin coating of dust.

"I think it's both," he said after a while. "I've experienced evil magic before and I know what it feels like. It's like a taste. Once you know what bitterness tastes like, it's easy enough to identify. But I think even ordinary magic is harder for me to be around than it should be. I don't think your tornado would have made me so sick if I wasn't bound."

"Because you could use your own magic to deal with it or because you'd just transform yourself into a tornado?"

He shuddered. "What an awful thought. No, I mean I could just use my own magic to expel your magic, if that makes sense. Your magic isn't bad, but it has its own flavor, too. I like the flavor but sometimes it overwhelms me--like something that's too sweet. When I have my magic, it's like I'm able to dilute other people's powers until I'm comfortable. I don't know how to explain it."

"That makes sense."

"I'm glad it does to one of us," he said, laughing a little.

I bit off another piece of meat. It took a while to chew, and so I chewed and thought as we walked. Finally, I held out a hand.

"Let me see your cuffs."

The metal was solid, one unbroken ring.

"Do you feel magic from these?" I said. "Do these cuffs have a flavor?"

Clement considered the question for a while. He closed his eyes, then opened them and held one hand over the other cuff. Finally, he shrugged.

"They feel like... nothing."

I bit the inside of my cheek. "I think we may have been overthinking this."

He fixed his gaze on me, curious but cautious.

"I don't think the cuffs have magic of their own," I said. "Just something that *inhibits* magic. Which makes me wonder whether Glinda would even be able to remove them. Maybe they'd just shut down her powers, too, whenever she got close. But if we remove them with entirely un-magical means…"

I trailed off. It couldn't be that easy.

"Lots of guys tried to remove them at the prison," I said doubtfully.

"Yeah, guys with magic," I said. "Or guys using their bare hands and maybe a metal bar from their bed frames. What if we find a guy who doesn't have any abilities but *does* have the tools to cut through silver?"

Clement frowned. "A blacksmith. An ordinary blacksmith."

"Am I crazy?"

"I think we may have been idiots," he said. "We won't know until we try."

"The border of Aboria is right there," I said. "One long walk or two quick tornado trips should get us there. Then all we have to do is find a village and maybe, if we're very, very lucky, you'll be free."

The walk was even shorter than I had anticipated. Knowing something new was up ahead lightened my steps, and finally reaching the bottom of the last dune and hitting mostly level ground quickened them. We didn't even need a tornado to get us the last few miles; the promise of shade and maybe even water we didn't have to conjure from the air was motivation enough.

That first line of scrubby pine trees marked the Aborian border, or at least came close enough. We crossed between their prickly branches, and Clement marked the occasion by running ahead and pumping his fist in the air.

My mind cleared further and the remnants of whatever had taken my memories away dissipated. I felt lighter than I had in days now that the magic surrounding me was no longer fogging my head.

Seeing calm, steady Clement frolicking like a child brightened my entire world. I ran up behind him and jumped, clicking my heels in the air like some happy-go-lucky clown from a pantomime.

We all but danced through the trees, at least until the forest grew thick enough to crowd out the sunlight overhead. Then we slowed to a walk and contented ourselves with breathing in the fresh, piney air and enjoying the dappled shade.

Clement reached for my hand. I laced my fingers through his. *This is beautiful,* he was trying to say without breaking the gorgeous silence, and I agreed from the bottom of my heart.

I had missed the color green. The Emerald City was full of it, and to me, green meant life and love and home. These trees didn't hold the same glow as the walls of my city, but they were a sight better than the endless rolling desert had been. I brushed my fingers across the trunk of an ancient maple and felt the water pulsing deep inside its trunk, threads of moisture coming together to form a veritable river of life beneath the thick bark.

I squeezed Clement's hand, and he squeezed mine back.

After an hour of walking, worry started to nudge at me, reminding me that it would be harder to navigate by the stars with this canopy of leaves in the way. For all I knew, we were walking in circles. But I wouldn't let myself be afraid. Not with Clement's hand in mine and an almost-full parcel of food in my pocket.

We had crossed the unforgiving deserts of Badalah. We could handle a little forest.

"Up ahead," Clement whispered, pointing.

I squinted, and I saw it, too. A gap in the trees, and

a signpost.

A road. It offered both direction—and danger. After all, we were still wanted fugitives, and I didn't know how far the news of our escape had spread.

Cautiously, we stepped out onto the worn wagon road. The peeling paint on the signpost hinted that this path wasn't well-traveled. We were still deep in rural Aboria.

But there was a village, Aspen, and the sign indicated it wasn't far away.

"What's our story?" Clement asked as we walked down the dirt road. "We're dressed in robes from Badalah. I look like I might have come from there, and that lily-white skin of yours has finally tanned enough that people might believe you've actually been outdoors once or twice in your life."

He winked, and I rolled my eyes and grinned. He brushed his thumb across the back of my hand.

"I think we should both claim to be from Enchantia originally," I said. "That'll explain our powers."

"And why were we in Badalah?"

"Working in Kisbu?" I said. "What kind of work do we reasonably look like we might be experts at?"

"Being ridiculously handsome," Clement said.

I scoffed. "You, maybe. We could claim to be merchants. What does Enchantia make that sells well in Badalah?"

"Enchanted toys and gifts sell well everywhere," Clement said. "Although maybe not lately, given how things are looking across the kingdoms. Protective charms, maybe?"

"Amulets," I said. "We sold amulets. We've been there for the last three months and our inventory ran out."

Clement nodded, accepting the story. "Now we're on

our way to The Forge to pick up some automatons to sell," he continued. "We're going the long way because our boss wants us to scour the kingdoms for other interesting trinkets. It'll be important for us to have a boss. It makes us seem less like we escaped from prison, I think."

"We don't like our boss," I said. "But we stay with him because he's promised to give us the business when he retires."

"His name is Willhouby," Clement said. "He's stuck up and has a fluffy white cat with a bad attitude."

I laughed and leaned my head against Clement's arm. "I love your mind."

"I love that I have my mind back again. I can be quite a storyteller when I get going."

"I've noticed that."

My siblings were going to love him. Once we got home, I was going to have a hard time getting him back from the twins.

"How do we explain only having the clothes on our backs?" I asked.

Clement was ready with an answer. "We don't have any money on us because we already sent most of it back to Willhouby. He's a real stickler for making sure he handles the finances when we're on the road. It's part of what makes him successful but it's annoying and it makes us feel like he doesn't really trust us."

"We had enough on hand to get us from Kisbu to The Forge," I added. "But it was stolen by sand raiders. They're the ones who locked that bracelet on your wrist. They bought it from some black-market weapons dealer."

"Perfect." Clement flashed a grin. "I like your mind, too."

The road opened onto a small village. A handful of businesses lined the main street, with houses spreading out behind. It seemed like the kind of town so small you'd have a hard time finding anything you were looking for, but fortunately, every town needed a blacksmith.

Despite being in what I assumed would qualify as the middle of nowhere, the buildings here were beautiful and the residents were well-dressed. The storefronts were immaculate, with golden signs and large windows showing off a variety of goods. The road was paved with broad dark stones, and an enormous temple rose up behind the shops, its golden spires rising above the rest of the town.

"They buy a lot of gold from Draconis," I said to Clement in an undertone. "Ma told me Aborians live in luxury no matter their social class. She said they're the kind of people who'd rather have one plate made of gold than twenty made of tin."

"Gold and tin are both metals, which means the blacksmith's likely to be decent either way."

I chuckled. "I appreciate your practicality."

We found the blacksmith easily enough, but not before we were stared at by half the town. Apparently they didn't get filthy, bedraggled visitors from the deserts of Badalah too often. The stares weren't unkind, but it was clear we stood out.

When we reached the blacksmith's shop, marked by a golden sign featuring an anvil, hammer, and tongs, we slipped quickly inside. The blacksmith himself was a slow-moving, tranquil man. He had to be at least in his sixties, but he had the strength of a much younger man and his biceps looked bigger than my head.

I thought about our friend Silas. I hoped he was well

on his way to Skyla by now.

"How can I help you gentlemen?" the blacksmith asked from behind the counter of his shop, pronouncing each word with care.

A variety of tools and projects filled the space behind him, and heat from his fire pressed against my face.

The man considered each of us in turn, taking his time as he studied our faces. Whatever impressions we might have given him, he kept his thoughts to himself.

Clement raised a hand and pulled his loose sleeve away from his wrist. "We were wondering if you might be able to remove these," he said. "We had a run-in with some thieves in the desert. Got away, but not before they'd clapped these on me."

The man studied the cuffs, his eyes sharp.

"There's no seam."

"They were sealed on with magic," Clement said. "The bandits caught us while we were sleeping. I guess they'd been following us long enough to know I'm Enchantian and had some abilities that would have stopped them if they'd decided to play fair. Fortunately we woke up and got away before my friend was put in a similar situation." He nodded at me.

I held the blacksmith's steady gaze, as if I really were an Enchantian who'd been accosted in his sleep by criminals.

"We're hoping the cuffs can be removed without magic," I said. "It's an unpleasant thing for an Enchantian to be separated from his powers. I'm sure you understand."

The blacksmith gave his counter a slow, thoughtful tap. "Can't say I've had firsthand experience, but I imagine it's a bit like having a hand tied behind your arm. Sure, I can try to get them off."

"We don't have any money," I blurted. "The bandits managed to run off with all our coin. But we're happy to work for you, or to stay in town until we've earned enough to pay you."

The man narrowed his eyes a little, then nodded. "My spiritual beliefs require me to help those in need," he said at last. "I daresay you boys qualify. Cutting the bracelets should be a simple thing if their enchantment doesn't get in my way. I'll do my best."

He gestured at us to come around the counter and follow us further into his shop. He sat Clement down and waved me into a chair that was some distance away.

I couldn't see what was happening, but the blacksmith grabbed a couple of saws and pliers and bent down across from Clement. An unpleasant grating sound filled the air, followed by a clink. I stood and craned my neck to see what was happening. The saw moved again, and then there was another clink as the second bracelet fell away.

Clement raised his wrists and stared at them. Joy suffused his face.

"I can't tell you what this means to me," he breathed. "Thank you so much."

"Happy to be of service," the blacksmith said, as if he hadn't really done much at all.

The man set his tools aside. I caught Clement's eye from across the room, and he beamed. He massaged his wrists and flexed his fingers. I could only begin to imagine what he must be feeling, but even that sent a matching smile across my features.

The blacksmith turned back around and looked at me. His gaze stayed on my face for a long moment.

"I do have something you fellows could help me

with," he said after a moment of consideration.

"Of course," Clement said, jumping to his feet. "Anything."

The man crooked his finger and led us toward the back of his shop. He opened a door. I expected to see a mess that needed cleaning up, or perhaps heavy things in need of moving, but the room was little more than a well-organized storage closet.

"Go in there," the man said. "And stay put."

I whipped my head around to stare at him. "What?"

"The newspapers are full of people who look just like you," the blacksmith said, gazing steadily at me. "People with golden eyes. I don't know what kind of trouble they've gotten themselves into, but whatever it was, my prince got caught up in it."

"You can't imprison us," Clement said, still massaging his wrists. The gesture, which had seemed soothing a moment before, now looked like a threat.

The man glanced at Clement's wrists, then looked back up at his face. They locked eyes, and for the first time I saw a man who was Clement's equal in keeping his emotions below the surface.

The blacksmith gestured at the room. "I did you a good turn. Now you do me one. Go in here and stay here until you're let out."

"We had nothing to do with those things in the papers." My heartbeat sped up and heat rushed to my face. I wanted to run, but there were a dozen sharp tools between me and the door, not to mention the fires and this size of this blacksmith's arms.

He clasped his hands behind his back, his posture entirely unthreatening and somehow more terrifying for all that.

"If you had nothing to do with it, you have nothing

to be worried about," he said pleasantly.

There were a thousand holes in that argument. But the rushing of fear in my ears wouldn't let me settle on any of them.

My palms began to tingle. The ribbons of air in this room seemed to solidify, some cool and others fat and full of vicious heat.

Clement's hand closed around mine, pushing it gently into a fist.

"All right," he said calmly. "We'll go. We don't want any trouble."

I let him steer me into the closet. The man gave us a respectful nod, then closed the door, leaving us in darkness.

25TH SEPTEMBER

The hours dragged, and after a while, I began to doubt whether the blacksmith was ever coming back for us. Finally, we fell asleep together on the hard stone floor, Clement's arms wrapped around me.

My eyes flew open several times throughout the night, always accompanied by a racing heartbeat and what felt like a vice tightening around my lungs. I couldn't think. I couldn't even breathe.

Each time, Clement pulled me close. He didn't tell me to calm down. Instead, he told me stories--funny things that had happened back in Enchantia, or fairy tales he'd heard as a child. His voice lulled me back to sleep.

But eventually, even his stories couldn't keep me calm.

"We've been in here all night," I whispered. I sat bolt upright. "We must have been. We have to escape."

"We told him we'd stay," Clement said.

"Yes, and everyone knows it's morally incumbent upon kidnapping victims to just go along with their captor's instructions," I hissed.

Clement reached for me in the darkness. His hand settled against my knee.

"I just mean that we should probably cooperate," he said. "We're wanted twice now--first for escaping Urbis Prison, and then you for having eyes like the people in the paper."

"I'm not a criminal just because my eyes are a certain color."

"I agree," he said. "So let's wait until he comes back, and then we can explain that. If we've stayed and done as he told us, he'll have every reason to think we're honest, trustworthy people."

"Or he'll think we're easy murder targets," I said. "What's to stop him from killing us in some fit of vigilante justice?"

I couldn't see Clement's face, but the amusement in his voice was plain enough. "Did he strike you as the vigilante justice type?"

"It's not funny."

Clement sighed. "No, it's not. I'm sorry. And you're right, we probably should try to escape." He took a deep breath. "I'll shift. A beetle should be small enough to get under the door, and maybe I can unlock it from the outside."

"He used a key," I said, shaking my head, not that Clement could see that in the near-total darkness. "I heard it when he closed the door on us."

"I'll have to find the key, then," Clement said. "He works here. He'll have to come back eventually. But what if he comes back and opens the door and I'm not there?"

"He doesn't know what your abilities are," I pointed out. "I'll claim that you magically transported yourself through the walls and left me here to die or something."

Clement's hand tightened on my knee. "I would never do that."

"I know that," I said, voice softening. "But he doesn't."

Clement shifted in the darkness. "All right, then," he said. "Was sort of hoping a beetle wouldn't be my first shift now that I've got my powers back, but I guess escaped convicts can't be choosers. I'll see you on the--"

Outside, a door closed with a resounding thud. Footsteps sounded, followed by the scraping of someone pushing metal equipment out of the way.

"He's back," I whispered. My heart skipped a beat and my stomach felt like it plummeted right through the stone floor.

"Maybe he won't come for us right away," Clement whispered. "Maybe he's still thinking about what to do. He's got to--"

Any lingering hope I might have had fizzled as the footsteps stopped outside our door. There was the sound of a key sliding into a lock, then the handle turning.

The door swung open. The blacksmith stood there, and I squinted against the daylight pouring into our little closet from behind him.

"Time to go," he said. "Keep quiet and this'll go easy."

His face betrayed nothing, but his voice simmered with a low threat. I scrambled to my feet and swallowed. My hands tingled again, but one glance at Clement's tranquil face and I pressed my palms against my legs and tried to still the magic that ached to burst from me.

"Right outside," the blacksmith said. "Out the door and into the carriage. Try to run for it and things won't go your way."

He raised his hand, just enough to draw my attention to a blade glittering in his hand.

"I have a good aim," he said, like we were having a nice chat about his hobbies. "I'm a three-time regional knife-throwing champion. Lots of opportunity to practice that sort of thing when you're a blacksmith."

"We understand." My voice trembled, but the magic tingling on my palms stayed where it was.

The short trip from the blacksmith's shop to the waiting carriage was full of possibility and chilly morning air.

And then, all too quickly, it was over. The blacksmith shoved us into the back of the carriage and slammed the door, then methodically secured it with two separate locks.

"Stay put," he ordered through the glass window. "There's a bucket under the seat if you need to relieve yourselves. You try to escape and I won't be so accommodating."

"We didn't do anything," I said.

The blacksmith nodded. "Funny thing is, I believe you." He hooked his small key ring to his belt. "Even so, you've got those uncanny eyes. I'm loyal to my monarchs. And even if I weren't, the payday I expect to get for turning you in will more than cover what you owe me for removing those cuffs of yours." He rapped on the window in warning. "If you're honest boys, as you claim, you'll want me to get paid."

"So much for doing his spiritual duty," Clement

muttered. He folded his arms and leaned against the seat, angry but compliant.

I sat down, too, and stared across the carriage at him. The blacksmith disappeared from the window, and a second later the whole vehicle swayed as he climbed up onto the driver's seat.

I was too tired after my fitful night for much talking, and besides, what was there to say? There was no way to smash the window without the blacksmith hearing, and anyway, while Clement could shift and escape, I was too big to fit through such a small gap.

I could conjure up a tornado, but it wouldn't be so easy to hide the damage from a thing like that now that we were in a land full of trees and boulders and other things that wouldn't settle back into place as easily as sand. The ogres from Urbis Prison probably suspected Clement or I had something to do with the sudden storm that had helped us escape from their custody. News of such a strange storm hitting the forests of a country not known for that kind of weather was almost guaranteed to catch their attention.

We'd just have to wait and hope an opportunity for escape presented itself.

I stared out the window as we traveled. The forests grew thicker for some time, and then we hit a mountain range of dazzling snow-capped peaks and deep canyons. Enormous birds soared through the sky with people on their backs being carried from the forests up to cities that nestled at the tops of the mountains.

The cities were beautiful, I could tell that much from here. Gilded roofs shone like fire with the reflected sunrise, and their many spires seemed to echo the mountain landscape.

But we weren't going to any of those beautiful cities.

Instead, our carriage headed into a deep canyon that looked as if it never saw real sunlight. The wheels jolted as we entered a winding road that cut between the mountains.

Shadows filled the canyon with a sense of solemn gloom. Ferns and ivy crawled among the boulders on either side of the road. Nothing else seemed willing to grow here. I settled against my thinly padded bench.

"Where do you think he's taking us?" I asked.

My voice seemed too loud in the silence of this valley--almost as loud as the creaking of the carriage as it clattered along the road, a noise that in itself seemed offensive to the very nature of this place.

"The capital city, I suppose," Clement said. "Mosa can't be too far from here. If I were trying to collect a reward I'd try to do it there."

We passed a few small villages nestled in the canyon. The buildings were small, moss-covered and tranquil, but I didn't see any hint of the poverty that had suffused Badalah. Everything here was beautiful; everyone we saw seemed well-fed and well-dressed.

Perhaps things weren't so bad throughout the whole world. Maybe it was just Badalah and Urbis experiencing the fracturing magic, and the other things I'd heard whispers of--the famine in Floris, the pirates in Skyla, the political stirrings in Enchantia--were nothing more than the ordinary churn of life.

I had to admit it was possible that the Winged Monkeys weren't part of some grand conspiracy, after all. It was just as likely they'd kidnapped me as part of a personal vendetta. Maybe I had done something to offend them. Maybe I wasn't as good of a Mayor as I had tried to be.

"Maybe we've got it all wrong," I murmured.

We passed by a waterfall pouring from a high cliff face. Its billowing stream transitioned from bright white at the top where the sun kissed the clifftop to the deep silver of water in shade. The base of the waterfall churned and frothed into a large pool, which in turn fed into a river that wandered off and away from the road.

It was a beautiful landscape. I wished I could enjoy it.

Clement nudged my foot with his. "What do you mean?"

"The magic," I said. "Maybe we were wrong in thinking everything's connected. Maybe we just wanted to think there was some master plan, to reassure ourselves that our own lives aren't as chaotic and terrifying as they seem."

I sighed and rested my head against the window. The glass was cold and slick, soothing against my hot face.

Clement reached into the pocket of his robes.

"I'd be tempted to believe that if not for this," he said.

He handed me the folded-up newspaper with its article about the band of rogues headed to Urbis.

"Every trouble we've heard about has something to do with the leaders of the kingdoms or their children," he said. "Even me. I'm no king, but I was thrown into jail for talking about Snow White. If someone's got a beef with her, why wouldn't they make an example out of people like me?"

"Maybe you really were thrown in jail for saying she was the fairest in the land."

Clement scoffed and rolled his eyes, but acknowledged the possibility with a nod.

A recent memory floated through my mind. I

unfolded the newspaper and held it toward the window, the better to see in the dim light of the canyon.

"The prince," I said. "The blacksmith said there was some trouble with the prince of Aboria." I squinted, searching the faces of the gang in the newspaper. They weren't all clearly visible, but a wave of hair above a high forehead, just behind the princess of Atlantice, suggested I was onto something.

I pointed at the sliver of a figure. "That's him," I said. "I'm sure of it. That's Prince Fallon."

Clement didn't seem entirely convinced, and I couldn't blame him; half a forehead was hardly enough to identify a prince.

But I believed it was him.

I had to, if only to force this nightmare to make a little more sense.

The hours passed. We traveled all day and deep into the night. Eventually, I fell asleep curled up on my bench, Clement dozing opposite me.

When the carriage lurched to a stop, I sat bolt upright, heart pounding.

Clement sat up, too, and put a reassuring hand on my knee. His eyelids still drooped with exhaustion, but the eyes under them were sharp.

"We're here," he said in a low voice. "Stay calm."

It was easier said than done. I reached for his hand. I couldn't see much outside, just the side of a building and the flickers of torches.

The blacksmith unlocked the carriage door. He shot us a warning look through the window, then opened the door and stood back.

A guard reached in and yanked Clement roughly by the arm. Magic prickled in my hands. I squeezed them into tight fists.

Clement had told me to be calm. I had to try.

The guard pulled me out next. I didn't have time to look around and get my bearings before a dark cloth descended over my eyes, plunging the world into blackness. The guards bound my hands behind my back with rope. My breath came in heavy pants, its rhythm slightly off with my heartbeat.

"I found these two in a border town," the blacksmith said. I knew his voice by now, slow and steady as it was. "The palace is searching for folks with eyes like his. The other one had silver cuffs on. Said they were from sand raiders. Might have been. Might not. Thought I ought to bring them both."

"Thank you," someone said, likely one of the guards. "We'll take it from here."

This was met with silence, then footsteps, then more silence.

"What else?" one of the guards asked.

Another silence.

"What's that supposed to mean?" the guard said. "Money? You want money?"

"Surely there's a reward," the blacksmith said.

"No, there's no reward. Not for this, not unless you can prove one of these two was out to harm the royal family."

"The palace is looking for fellows with eyes like that," the blacksmith said, raising his voice. "Now you mean to tell me I came all this way for nothing?"

"The palace appreciates you doing your civic duty," the guard said.

"I had to change my horses twice."

"You came a long way. You have the queen's gratitude."

"I don't want gratitude, I want coin." The blacksmith

was shouting now. I hadn't expected to hear this from him.

Maybe things weren't so good in Aboria after all.

"You'll accept gratitude or you'll accept a fine," the guard said. "If the palace decides you deserve coin for bringing these strays here, we'll find you. For all we know these are just two stablehands you have a grudge against."

"Look at his eyes!"

"You're dismissed."

"The boy has golden eyes, just like--"

"You're dismissed," the guard repeated.

Metal scraped against metal; a sword being pulled from a scabbard, perhaps, or a knife being scraped against armor.

I tensed and tried to back away from the conversation, but I ran into a solidly built guard, who grabbed my shoulders and held me in place.

There was a moment of silence, then grumbling, then footsteps, and then the carriage squeaked. The wheels clattered against the stones below and the horses' harnesses jangled. The noise receded, and then the guard behind me steered me forward and marched me away.

My heart felt like a bird that had been trapped inside my ribcage and was desperate to get out. My skin tingled with fear and magic, and I forced myself to take low, steady breaths. Clement was still with me; the guard near him was delivering instructions: *There's stairs here* and *Straight ahead, watch your step here*. His guard was a lot more helpful than mine, so I listened hard and tried to take the warnings before my foot caught on the edge of a rug or ran toe-first into a stone step.

I focused on walking. I didn't know what would happen when we stopped or what kind of hideous dungeon we'd find ourselves in. It was all too easy to daydream, but Ma's words floated through my mind: *What's the problem right in front of you?*

The only problem was the next step, and then the next. I tried to solve them one at a time, pacing my breathing all the way. I knew without the benefit of my vision that Clement was calm. I would be, too.

Finally, after a long descent down a staircase with shallow steps, we stopped. Something creaked. Something else jangled. The air was cool here and filled with the earthy smells of dirt and stone.

Someone's hands brushed the back of my head. The blindfold fell away.

We were in a dungeon, lit by a single torch mounted into the wall by the door. Before us was a large cell. A cot stood in the corner, the room a dank mirror of our space in Urbis Prison.

I couldn't be imprisoned again. I couldn't be left here to rot while magic fractured across the kingdoms and Winged Monkeys roamed free.

I had to contact my siblings. I had to get home. I had to--

Clement cleared his throat loudly. I looked at him, frantic and wide-eyed, and he met my gaze.

"We're all right," he said quietly.

A guard behind us laughed. "I'll say you are."

I took a deep breath. The magic tingling in my hands settled.

The guard nodded at us, and we walked into the cell like obedient little puppets.

"Can you tell us what we're being charged with?" Clement asked politely.

The same guard laughed again. "You're a polite one. Wish all our prisoners were as nice as you, it'd make my job a lot easier."

But he didn't answer. He just nodded to another guard, who closed the barred cell door and locked it with one of the keys around his waist.

"You'll get meals twice daily," he said. "Bucket's in the corner to relieve yourselves; we'll take that once a day."

"How long are we going to be held?" Clement asked, again the picture of civility.

The guard shrugged. "Beats me." He hit the bars of the cell, which seemed driven deep into the stone above and below us. They didn't so much as shake.

"Sleep well," he said.

He left. The others followed.

I grabbed the bars with both hands and pressed my face through the gap, ready to plead our case, but they were gone before I could get a word out.

I stared into the dark dungeon beyond the small glow from the torch.

There were three other cells down here. All empty, thank the Wizard. Being imprisoned was bad enough; being imprisoned within a cell that offered only bars for privacy while other so-called criminals stared at the newcomers would have been infinitely worse.

"This is almost poetic," Clement said.

I turned to find him standing in the middle of the cell, hands on his hips as he looked between our beds.

"It looks just like Urbis Prison," I grumbled.

"Where we first met. We went from that to this and only had to cross an entire desert and the better part of a forest to get here."

"You're not making this situation feel any better." I

frowned. "Why aren't you more worried?"

"I'm plenty worried." But his smile told a different story. He raised his hands, showing off his bare wrists. "But we're not really prisoners. Not this time."

I scoffed. "*You're* not really a prisoner. My powers aren't going to help me out of here. I don't think there's enough room to conjure a tornado strong enough to do anything about these bars." I sighed and ran a hand through my disgusting hair. It was gritty with sand and greasy from too long without a bath. "Still, you should get out while you can."

The thought of watching Clement turn himself into a mouse and run away from me turned my stomach. I couldn't have done any of this without him.

He sat on one of the cots, on the same side as he'd taken back in Urbis Prison. He leaned back, pillowing his head on his hands.

"No," he said.

I folded my arms. "This shouldn't be an argument. If you can get out of here, you should. Go to Oz. Find the Scarecrow or someone who can try to get me out of here."

"No way." He shook his head. "We'll get out of here, but we'll do it together."

"And how exactly do you propose we accomplish that?"

"We just need a key," he said. "Once we figure out the guards' schedule and who has keys, I'll shift to something small and clever and borrow one. I'll let you out, we'll make our way outside, and you'll conjure a tornado to get us out of here. We'll be back on the road within three days."

"What if they execute us within three days?" I demanded.

"They won't."

Clement rolled onto his side and rested his head on his elbow. It was so similar to the way we'd talked back when we'd first met that I felt a slight pang--not of nostalgia, exactly, but of familiarity and fondness. We may have found nothing but trouble in all our time together, but we'd grown closer to each other, too. That was something.

I laid down on my cot, too, and rolled to face him.

"Nobody's going to do anything with us for a long time," Clement said. "You heard that guard. He couldn't begin to answer when I asked what we were being charged with. He doesn't even know. He's got to talk to the royal family or whoever's so upset about this golden eye business, and then they have to figure out if we're even a threat, and they're not going to bother to involve us in these conversations."

"No one ever does," I said. The warden at Urbis Prison had barely had two words for me when I'd demanded to know why I was being held, and that had been a theoretically well-run facility full of guards. This was a single building--the palace, based on what the blacksmith had said.

Clement was probably right. We were imprisoned, but we had time, and, more importantly, our powers.

"We'll be stuck here for a while," Clement said, stretching out and kicking off his shoes. "By the time they figure out what they want to do with us, we'll be long gone."

26TH SEPTEMBER

The door to the dungeon banged open. I sat straight up, bleary-eyed and sore from sleeping on the cot.

Someone bustled into the dungeon. Not a guard--not remotely a guard. This person was a woman, around my age and far shorter than any of the guards had been, with messy brown hair and bright green eyes. Her moss-colored tunic all but glowed in the warm torchlight.

The guard who entered the room behind her went immediately to the door of our cell and unlocked it, then, inconceivably, inclined his head toward us.

I glanced over at Clement. He was sitting up, too, looking as confused as I felt.

The young woman rushed forward. Before I could

comprehend what she was doing, she grabbed my hands and pulled me to my feet. She wrapped her arms around me and pulled me in for a tight hug.

Startled, entirely unable to account for this strange event, I hugged her back.

She pulled away and surveyed my face.

"Goodness, what's your name?" she said.

I glanced at Clement, but he seemed bewildered.

Still, whoever this person was, she didn't seem inclined to execute us just yet. Maybe honesty wouldn't hurt.

"My name is Jakon Gale," I said slowly. "I'm the Mayor of Oz."

Her eyebrows flew up. "I heard you'd disappeared! But I never imagined I'd find you in this dungeon, of all places. You poor thing, you look like life's chewed you up and spit you out a bit." She frowned. "I'm sorry, that's probably rude to say. Only I don't think you can blame me for saying it because you have to know you look awful."

"We're in absolute agreement," I assured her.

She turned to greet Clement, and wrapped him in an embrace, too.

"And who are you?" she asked, once she'd pulled away.

"Clement Augustin, ma'am," he said.

"And are you also a mayor?"

A smile tugged at the corner of his mouth. "No, ma'am, I'm a bookkeeper from Enchantia."

"A noble profession," she said. "Welcome to Aboria."

She turned back to me with a bright smile, then whipped her head around to the guards.

"These men are to be released *immediately*," she said. "You're to take them to guest quarters in the East

Wing and see that they get hot baths and some decent clothing."

She lifted the arm of Clement's robes. The garments had been worn-out when we'd first freed them from a clothesline in a small Badahahn village, but now they were filthy to boot.

"Burn these." She glanced up at Clement. "Unless there's some sentimental attachment?"

"None whatsoever," Clement said.

"Lovely. If there's anything else you need to be comfortable, please let any of the palace staff know. Once you're bathed and rested I'd be delighted if you'd join me for breakfast. We have so much to talk about."

I felt rather like I'd just been hit in the face. "Of course," I said, trying to sound like this was an ordinary and reasonable turn of events.

Based on the smirk on Clement's features, I failed.

"I'm sorry," I said. "I don't mean to be rude, but... Who are you?"

A hand flew to her mouth and she laughed. "Oh, goodness, I'm sorry, I'm running ahead of myself as always." She held out a hand. "My name is Veda. And we're going to be great friends."

A hot bath later and I felt like a human being again. The amount of sand and grime I had left behind in the bathwater was astonishing.

Even more incredible was my face in the mirror. Despite all my efforts to shield myself from the desert sun, my skin had turned several shades darker. I'd never been tan before, not really. It had always been easy enough to hide from the sun in Oz, in between all my time spent in the city and the copious shade from trees in the countryside. Now, my skin bore a golden glow. I didn't look half-bad. This was the kind of face I could wear to breakfast with people who weren't Clement.

Come to think of this, I'd rather look like this for Clement, too.

My skin heated, and my face in the mirror took on a rosy hue under the tan. I ran my fingers through my freshly combed hair, trying to get it to look tousled and carefree.

I wasn't tousled and carefree, of course, but I'd always thought that kind of hair looked good on men, and I had a burning desire to look decent now that it felt within the realm of possibility.

Someone knocked on my door while I was still fussing with my hair. I hurried to answer, and the moment I saw Clement I forgot entirely about how I looked, because he was magnificent. The thin layer of dust that had coated everything out in the desert had been washed away, and his skin gleamed, clean and such a rich brown I felt I could spend hours admiring it. The light pouring from the windows in my room seemed delighted to play with him, dancing its way across his face and through the tight, freshly oiled curls of his hair.

"You look nice," I managed.

"You, too," he said.

We grinned at each other for a too-long moment.

"Are you ready?" he finally asked. "A palace servant is here to show us to breakfast."

Humor laced his voice. This was a far cry from the situation we'd found ourselves in down in the dungeons--or, for that matter, in the blacksmith's closet, the desert, or the prison. I much preferred it.

We followed the servant, a polite young man who seemed several years younger than us, down to a polished wooden door. He opened it to reveal a spacious room with high ceilings and rich furnishings. A small square table, just the right size for four people, sat in front of the fireplace, where a low fire was crackling.

Veda was already sitting at the table. She sprang to her feet when we entered and urged us in, then dismissed the servant with a cheerful smile.

"You both look heaps better," she said. "I'm sure you won't mind my saying so, but you were like something the cat dragged in before."

"We were painfully aware," I said. "I feel pounds lighter now that all that sand isn't resting in my hair."

"I'm eager to hear what kind of journey you've been on that had you in such a state." She tucked a strand of her hair behind her ear. It had been pulled back into a braid at some point, but now bits were doing their best to make a break for it, and stray wisps surrounded her face and brushed against her neck. The overall effect was charming.

The door opened, and a serving girl came in pushing an elaborately carved wooden cart laden with gilt-edged ceramic dishes. The most promising of these was a teapot with a fat ribbon of steam rising from its spout. There had been times in the desert at midday when I'd thought I'd never want to touch anything warm ever again. Now, in the cool indoors of the palace, I wanted to sing at the thought of a hot drink.

"Have a seat," Veda said, ushering us toward the table.

I hesitated, silently trying to calculate the information

I'd picked up so far and determine if any of these seats was better than the others and if I should wait for her to sit first. I'd gotten quite good at analyzing these sorts of diplomatic situations over the last year, but I had no idea who this woman was or why she was being so friendly.

She noticed my caution and took charge immediately. "You there," she said, pointing to a seat and nodding at me. "And you next to him. The queen will sit next to me."

I tensed and glanced at Clement. He looked as lost as I was. We sank into the chairs Veda had assigned. The serving girl transferred dishes from the cart to the table: the teapot, teacups and saucers rimmed with gilt, a sugar bowl and cream pitcher, and four plates covered in gold domes. My face stared back at me from my dome, yellowed and slightly misshapen. My stomach growled at the promise of food.

"The queen should be here momentarily," Veda said. "She's been terribly busy lately but she wanted to meet you the moment you arrived."

"Perks of being a mayor," Clement said with a smile.

Veda tilted her head and pursed her lips a little. "No, I don't think that has anything to do with it. I haven't spoken to her since before I came to rescue you two this morning. She hasn't a clue who you are."

I frowned. "Then why--"

The door opened again, and I fell silent.

I still wasn't entirely sure who Veda *was*, but there was no mistaking the woman who entered the room. Even if I hadn't seen her face in the international section of the newspaper occasionally, her regal bearing and red velvet gown trimmed in gold would have told me immediately that this was the queen of Aboria. She entered, skirts swirling around her ankles and hair plaited neatly into a crown braid on top of her head. A delicate golden circlet topped the crown, ornamented with small rubies.

Instinctively, I rose to my feet. Clement followed me by a fraction of a second.

I bowed deeply. "Your Majesty."

She stared at me, dark eyes slightly narrowed as she studied my face. Something about me seemed to surprise her, or perhaps unsettle her; she examined me for longer than I'd expected and didn't bother hiding her curiosity.

"You look familiar," she said.

I bowed again, more lightly this time. "Jakon Gale, Mayor of Oz, at your service, ma'am."

The queen's eyebrows flashed briefly upward. "Dorothy's boy."

"Yes, Your Majesty."

Her expression softened. "It's been years since I saw your mother last, but I remember her as a delightful woman. I'm so sorry for your loss."

"Thank you, ma'am."

The familiar heat rushed to my eyes, and I swallowed and turned my attention away before the prickling could form into real tears.

"This is my friend and traveling companion, Clement Augustin of Enchantia," I said, gesturing.

He offered a deep bow, which she returned with a dignified nod.

"This is Queen Abigail," Veda said brightly. "And now that the introductions are over with and we all know each other's names, I'd very much like to get to the real question: Who are you exactly and how on earth did you end up here?"

I paused, trying to figure out if she was making a joke. But she seemed nothing if not intent on hearing my answer.

"I told you," I said slowly. "I'm the Mayor of Oz."

"Yes, that's who you are, but who *are* you?" she asked.

I blinked.

The queen took her place at the table, which allowed the rest of us to sink back into our seats.

"To clarify," Veda said, and cleared her throat. "I mean to ask where you came from, whether you know about what's happening in the kingdoms, and if you've run into the others yet." She frowned. "I assume you haven't or you wouldn't have ended up here."

The queen quietly poured everyone cups of tea while I tried to put together the pieces of Veda's question.

"The others," I said. "Do you mean those people in the Urbis newspaper?"

"Perhaps we should back up a few paces," the queen said, handing my teacup to me. "It's clear we're all involved in something here. Mr. Gale, forgive me if this is a delicate question, but are you aware your mother adopted you when you were an infant?"

The cup was blissfully warm in my hands. A pleasant scent rose from the dark brew, black tea with a hint of cinnamon.

"Yes, ma'am," I said.

"And are you aware of any siblings?"

"I have six siblings," I said. "All younger."

"Not them." Veda shook her head. "Your *other* siblings."

Clement glanced sharply over at me, and I knew what he was thinking before he spoke.

"Is Jakon related to the people in the newspaper?"

"I suspect so," Queen Abigail said. "One of them is my son, Fallon."

I looked at her with renewed interest. I'd realized he was in the paper, but the idea that this woman was somehow my brother's mother--and that I had a brother who shared my blood—put a surreal cast over the world.

"I don't suppose Dorothy knew?" the queen said hopefully.

"Ma never knew where I came from," I said slowly. "If I had siblings when I was born, she wasn't aware of it. I'm sure she'd have tried to adopt them if she'd known."

The corner of the queen's mouth turned up. "She's not alone."

"There are several people with eyes like yours," Veda said. "Or at least there were a few months ago when a group of them showed up looking for Fallon. Azia--she's the one with the dragon--and the princess of Atlantice and the new prince of Floris, and several others besides."

"Strange, that you should all have ended up in royal families," Queen Abigail said. "It's clear your birth parents intended a specific kind of life for you."

Something ran under her voice that I couldn't quite identify; confusion, perhaps, or even criticism. She was too much of a queen to reveal her opinions on the subject, whatever they were.

"You don't all look alike," Veda said thoughtfully, considering me with her head tilted. "Not aside from the eyes. But there's something in common between you all, some mannerism or attitude I can't place. It's nothing I could put words to, but Fallon seemed to *recognize* those other people."

I'd been in a large family for most of my life, but the

thought that I might have siblings roaming around out there struck me as strange.

Stranger still was the knowledge that they were all wanted criminals.

"I get the impression they aren't traveling just to build family bonds," I said.

Veda poured a little cream into her tea and stirred. "They all seem to have their own reasons for going off together. Their problems had a kind of relation to each other, but they aren't exactly on the same quest, as it were."

"There have been a number of odd occurrences throughout the twelve kingdoms over the past year," Queen Abigail said. "Fallon and the others seem to be trying to figure out why."

"And how to fix things," Veda added.

Clement nudged my foot under the table. I knew exactly what he was thinking.

"Then it won't surprise you to learn we're on a mission, too. I was abducted by Winged Monkeys a few weeks ago and taken to prison on a ridiculous charge, and I'm trying to get home."

Veda's eyebrows shot up. "Abducted by winged *what?*"

"Monkeys," I said. "They're an Ozian race."

"But are they actually--"

"They're exactly what you're picturing," Clement said grimly.

Veda shuddered.

"While I was there, I heard from the other inmates that things weren't quite right in their kingdoms. The blight in Floris, the plight of the Queen of Draconis..."

I cut myself off. The queen's face had taken on a shadowed expression. She and Veda looked at one another, gazes overflowing with significance.

"What?"

"We've had our own troubles here of late." The queen searched my face. "I'm surprised you haven't heard of them. They were in all the papers this spring."

"I'll admit I haven't paid as much attention to the goings-on in the other kingdoms as I should have."

"You've been busy. It's no small feat, to learn to run a kingdom." She remained the picture of composure, but weight clung to her words.

I felt the burden as much as I heard it. The responsibility she bore was as vague as it was familiar.

"Any challenge that affects our kingdoms belongs ultimately to us," I said.

"My son has been learning that lesson, too," the queen said. "It's not an easy one."

"He's learned it, though, and he's going to solve our problems," Veda said resolutely.

"I don't want to be indelicate," Clement said. "But are your 'problems' magical in nature?"

"Profoundly," Veda said.

Clement leaned forward and rested his wrists against the table. "In that case--"

My stomach growled, loud enough to startle the queen next to me. Veda caught my eye across the table and smirked.

"Heavens, I'm so sorry," the queen said. "I completely forgot we're supposed to be eating."

I hadn't forgotten. But I knew my royal manners, and it would have been a terrible breach to begin eating before the queen.

She removed the cover from her plate, giving us the go-ahead to do the same. The scent of fried eggs and grilled sausages wafted up toward me, overpowering in their richness.

The queen took her first bite, and I dove in, savoring the salt and fat. Veda watched me from across the table, a sparkle in her eye, and I let her. This meal was delicious and I wasn't about to let that amused little quirk at the corner of her mouth stop me from enjoying it.

"Yes, our problems are magical," Veda said, after letting me inhale my food for a few moments. She twisted in her chair and fixed Clement with her intense gaze. "Of course, you're from Enchantia. You might be able to help."

"I'm willing to try."

"The king has been turned into a beast," she said bluntly.

The queen closed her eyes for a brief moment.

Clement gave a low whistle. "Never mind. That's above my abilities."

She shrugged one shoulder and speared a little coin of sausage. "That's the answer we've gotten from everybody so far. Fallon left to see if he could find a way to help."

I nudged Clement's foot under the table this time. He met my eyes, read my mind, and let out a soft "Oh."

"What?" Veda said, sitting up straighter.

"It might be nothing and it might be everything," I said. "Only we've noticed that everything going wrong in the kingdoms seems to start with the royals. The Winged Monkeys kidnapped me directly. The Florian blight started at the monarchs' palace. The pirates in Skyla are Peter Pan's old enemies. Your king got turned into a beast."

"And meanwhile magic is fracturing all over the kingdoms," Clement said.

Veda drew her eyebrows together.

"That's more of a theory than a fact, but I can tell you as someone who can sense magical energy that there's something horrifically wrong with the magic coming out of Urbis," Clement said. "A friend of ours back in prison said it's happening all over the place. Whatever magical energies fill our lands, something is damaging them."

"It's all connected, then," Veda said, not sounding remotely surprised. "Makes sense why Fallon and the others would all be on adjacent missions."

"And it suggests the problem is far greater than we suspected," the queen said briskly. "But we know more today than we did yesterday. Knowledge is everything. With any luck it'll be enough to get us on the right path toward fixing... well, the world."

"That assumes Fallon and the others don't get arrested first," Veda said darkly.

The queen's demeanor hardened. "I can tell you if anyone tries it they'll have the royal forces of Aboria to contend with."

"With all due respect, that might not mean much, Your Majesty," I said. "I was taken to prison without a trial. Being Mayor didn't protect me."

"They can't have known who you were," the queen said, frowning. "There must have been some misunderstanding."

"They knew me," I said. "They wouldn't let me so much as send a letter home."

Again, the queen and Veda exchanged glances.

"We're worried about Fallon," Veda said after a moment. "We've been reading the papers for months now, ever since he left Aboria. We can't seem to get word to him."

The queen sighed. "Every time one of our messengers

arrives where they've been spotted, they've moved on."

"As far as we can tell he's been getting into deeper and deeper trouble." Veda speared a piece of sausage as if she blamed it for their problems. "Only we can't tell what *kind* of trouble. The papers in Urbis keep talking about him like he's done something terrible, only they never say what the accusations against him or the others actually are. We've reached out to anybody who's anybody in Urbis and haven't gotten a clear answer."

"Something untoward must be going on if they're not even willing to talk to his mother and sister," Clement said.

Veda glanced up, startled. "Heavens, I'm not Fallon's sister."

Clement frowned. "My apologies. Who are you then, if you'll forgive my ignorance?"

Veda bit her lip and her cheeks took on a slight pink tinge. "I'm..." She looked to the queen, who only smiled. Veda thought for a moment. "I'm his friend."

The way she said *friend* felt familiar. She talked about Fallon the way I thought I might talk about Clement, were anyone to ask me about him.

"If they wouldn't even speak to you, I'm glad we didn't go there," Clement said.

"He felt like something wasn't right," I explained. "So we came the long way home."

The queen smiled, just a little. "You're good friends, to take one another's counsel so seriously."

"It wasn't so much counsel as an ultimatum," Clement said. "There's evil magic in that city. I couldn't get close to it." He shuddered, the memory clearly still visceral.

Queen Abigail took a sip of her tea and set the cup down again with a light clink. "It seems our lives are all strangely entangled. There's only one thing to do, if we want to learn what's actually happening here."

I agreed. I would have to get home to Oz--faster, somehow--and enlist the help of everyone I knew there. I would need to use my authority as Mayor to contact Urbis, and be sure the various provinces were protected against Winged Monkey attack, and perhaps call a council with the King of the Monkeys to learn what exactly his objection to me was.

I had to go home and be Mayor again.

Veda nodded firmly. "You'll have to go find the others."

I froze, a forkful of egg halfway to my mouth.

"The only trouble is we haven't the slightest clue where they are now," she continued. "They were last spotted in The Forge and the papers claim they're headed to Urbis, but the papers have been wrong before."

"I can't go to Urbis."

"No, but you could catch them on the way."

"I mean, I can't go find them." I looked between Veda and Queen Abigail, noting the frustration and disappointment on their faces but unable to do anything about it. "I have to get home."

"Surely this is more important than running Oz," Veda said. "Your government must have been handling things while you were gone. It can keep the kingdom running for another week or two."

Clement spoke up, his voice calm and firm. "It's not just Jakon's duties. He has six younger siblings, and we have no way of telling whether they're safe right now. If the Winged Monkeys came after Jakon, it's possible they've already kidnapped other members of his family."

Veda's face fell. Queen Abigail pursed her lips.

"Stay the night," the queen said after a moment, in

the kind of decisive tone that made it clear she was accustomed to being obeyed. "We'll send a telegram to the Emerald City. If your siblings need you, we'll find out. If they're fine and Oz isn't in too much trouble, I hope you'll reconsider."

My stomach lurched with impatience. I couldn't bear the thought of sitting in this castle for an entire day and night when we could be traveling.

Clement put a hand on my knee, the gesture hidden beneath the table and gentle enough to settle my nerves in an instant.

"I think that's a good idea," he said softly. "As Her Majesty said, knowledge is everything."

I took a deep breath. *Being a good leader sometimes means listening to your brain and not your heart,* the Scarecrow had often insisted, usually over the Tin Woodman's vocal disagreement.

Here, in this moment, the deep disappointment in the pit of my stomach told me the Scarecrow was right. I wanted to get home and see my siblings' faces more than anything, but there were problems all across the kingdoms. I would be a terrible Mayor if I put my own needs ahead of the world's.

"One night," I said. "I can't promise more than that."

27TH SEPTEMBER

Around twenty-four hours later, Clement and I made our way back to the same room for our second breakfast with Veda and the queen. We'd sent a telegram yesterday right after our meal, and my stomach was in knots waiting to learn if we'd heard back.

"They should have sent the response straight to my room," I said as we walked down a long corridor. "There's no way the Scarecrow wouldn't have answered immediately. If there's no word by this morning, something is deeply wrong in Oz."

Clement shrugged, refusing to share my anxiety. "Maybe someone brought it by while Veda was showing us around the grounds."

"They could have left it on the bed."

"An important communication like that? No, better to deliver it by hand. Perhaps the queen requested to see it first and wants to talk to you."

His calm optimism made me want to tear my hair out. Even so, I was grateful for his sunny outlook, and for him. I couldn't imagine how I would have made it this far without him talking me down from panic at every step.

I reached for his hand. His fingers laced instantly through mine, the touch familiar and full of meaning we ignored.

"I appreciate you," I said. "Even when I'm being ridiculous."

"You're never ridiculous," Clement said. "Nervous, yes. Prone to thinking the sky is falling, a little bit. But never ridiculous."

"Thinking the sky is falling doesn't make me a fool?"

"Well, no. Not when the sky *is* falling. Or, rather, the magic is fracturing." He squeezed my hand. "We're in a world of trouble right now. You're not a fool for recognizing it."

"I wish I could stay calm like you."

"I'll stay calm *for* you," Clement said. "And you can pay me back by making sure my room in Oz has a spectacular view of the city."

"I was going to do that anyway."

I'd already mentally planned out the arrangements. Clement would stay in the Peridot Suite. It was one of the palace's nicer guest quarters, and, just as importantly, it was just down the hall from the rooms I'd taken over from Ma.

She had always reserved it for her closest friends. Now Clement was my closest friend, and I was Mayor. It was only right that he stay in those rooms.

"What are your favorite things to do in the Emerald City?" Clement's voice lightened. He was trying to distract me from my worries; the effort was transparent and wonderful.

"I've always loved the theater," I said. "There's a beautiful performance center downtown. Ma built it early in her Mayorship. They do all sorts of productions, ballets and plays and musicals and magic shows. Ma even brought over some scripts and music from Kansas. She had a soft spot for *Pirates of Penzance,* which nobody outside Oz has ever heard of."

"Speaking of views," Clement said.

We stopped at a window and I caught my breath. This castle was high on a mountaintop, and the scene outside the window flooded me with awe.

The ground beneath the palace plunged steeply down to terrain covered in loose boulders covered in moss and thick ferns. In the distance, high peaks and deep valleys alternated, the morning light casting dramatic shadows. Wisps of cloud snaked between the jagged mountaintops, and the air coming through the slightly cracked window smelled of rain and fresh earth.

"The Emerald City looks nothing like this," I said. "I hope you'll like it anyway."

Clement wrapped his arm around my shoulder. "I'll be happy anywhere as long as you're with me," he murmured.

A whole new kind of anxiety flooded the pit of my stomach, hot and fizzing.

Clement's arm was steady and his body radiated warmth. It was everything I could do to keep myself from turning and burying my face in his chest. I wanted to run my hands along his back, breathe in his scent, and pull him closer than friends should be.

All this time traveling through the desert and trapped in closets and carriages and dungeons, Clement and I had been more or less alone. But I hadn't *felt* alone with him, not completely--not when the open skies left us vulnerable to Winged Monkeys or the roof over our heads was provided by a captor with unclear motives.

But here, in the castle of Aboria, we were welcome and safe. The roof over our head belonged to a queen who seemed to wish us well, and the corridor on either side was empty and silent save for our breathing.

"Clement--"

"Jakon," he said at the same moment.

In the distance, an enormous bird soared between two mountain peaks, the tiny shape of a rider on its back. The clouds drifted. My heart pounded.

"Jakon," Clement said again.

His hand slid down my arm. My breath caught in my throat. He turned me around, and I let myself be turned, let him steer me with his strong hands until we were facing each other.

He looked down at me, the minuscule difference in our height enough to make me feel small. His eyes, normally cool or sparkling with amusement, now burned with a dark light. He searched my face, and then his gaze slipped down to my lips.

I tried to speak, but no sound came out. There was nothing to say. There was only him, me, and the space between us.

He pushed me gently backward. The windowsill dug into the small of my back and my head knocked against the window, pushing it open another inch. A fresh breeze swept past me, ruffling my hair. Goosebumps sprang up on the back of my neck.

Clement leaned forward, his gaze now locked on

my lips. His breath brushed against my face, mild and warm, and he glanced up and met my eyes. His were hungry and so, so sweet.

"I'm going to kiss you now," he whispered.

He bent down toward me. I rose the last inch and closed the space between us. Our lips touched, and my back arched as I pushed myself up and toward him.

My anxiety dissolved. The fear churning in my stomach melted, flooding my body instead with the heat of sudden pleasure. I wrapped my arms around Clement's neck and pulled him in close, closer, until the pressure of his chest against mine made it difficult to breathe.

He pulled away, the sparkle back in his eyes.

"I've been wanting to do that for weeks," he murmured.

I kept my arms laced around his neck. "Since the minute you met me?"

A smile spread across his face, creating little crinkles at the corners of his eyes. "No. It was the moment you stood up for Psycho."

I tilted my head. "In the prison yard?"

"You were scared out of your mind. Scared and bruised; you'd just tried to escape the prison and gotten beaten up for your trouble. I could smell the fear on you. And then you saw him being bullied and stepped up anyway." He brushed a lock of hair from my forehead. "I knew then you were someone I wanted to get to know better."

"I liked you before that," I admitted. "I watched you reading a book and, I don't know, that was it for me."

His smile widened, but one of his eyebrows shot up. "Reading a book?"

"Reading a book."

"That's the strangest thing I've ever heard."

I was silent for a long moment.

"Really?" I said. "That's the strangest thing you've ever heard? Wasn't the Winged Monkeys or learning my entire city is built out of precious stones or being told that you'll spend life in prison for thinking Queen Snow White is decent-looking?"

He laughed. "All right, maybe not. But it's up there."

I ran my hand down along his shoulder blade, savoring the smooth planes of his back. I pulled him close and kissed him again.

It was as if my entire life had been lived in shades of black and white, and now the world was filled with glorious color. The sensation of his lips against mine filled the twelve kingdoms and beyond with glorious possibility.

Possibility, and terror--that I'd do something wrong, that I'd lose him, that the intensity of my feelings for him would send my magic spinning out of control, that I wouldn't be enough.

He wrapped his arms around me and held me. He held my fear, too, and my hopes and my resolve. He accepted it all.

"Ahem."

We leapt apart as if we'd been caught doing something forbidden. My heart raced like a bird's, and Clement cleared his throat and shuffled his feet.

Just a bit down the hall, Veda looked at us with her lips pressed firmly together, clearly suppressing a smile.

"Sorry to interrupt," she said, voice barely concealing her amusement. "Breakfast is ready and Queen Abigail just arrived. I was worried you'd gotten lost."

"Not lost," I said, blushing furiously. "Just, um--"

"Waylaid," Clement said.

"Yes, that. We were enjoying the view."

"I can see that." Veda smirked. "Aboria is a lovely place. I'm glad you appreciate it."

She turned and walked back the way she'd come. Clement and I exchanged glances, then hurried after her, Clement grinning the whole way.

The moment we walked through the door, the queen stopped pacing. She was dressed more simply today, in a dusty blue linen dress with gold embroidery at the hems.

"The telegram didn't go through," she said, without offering a proper greeting.

I appreciated her directness. Niceties would have been anything *but* nice this morning, when all I wanted was word from my siblings.

"Why not?" I asked, striding into the room. "What happened?"

Clement and Veda immediately fell back, as if aware this was as much a conference between world leaders as an update between acquaintances. But I didn't want Clement to stand behind me. I needed him beside me, ready to offer his counsel. I glanced over my shoulder and gestured him closer, and he stepped up and touched my elbow lightly.

"Two of the telegram offices between here and Oz are out of service. The one right at the edge of our border is burning down as we speak." Queen Abigail pressed her lips into a thin line and her jaw hardened. "Sending messages between the kingdoms is no longer a simple matter."

"Burning?" Veda repeated in horror.

"An act of malicious sabotage. The fire was set intentionally. My people are still trying to determine a motive, but suffice to say we will not be able to transmit information between Oz that way for some time."

The timing was too perfect to be coincidence.

"It's our fault," I said. "It must be. The ogres at Urbis Prison have been looking for us. I'll bet that blacksmith found someone to complain to after the palace guards didn't give him a reward for bringing us here, and then the ogres caught wind of it."

"If that's the case they'll likely be on their way here," Clement said.

Queen Abigail shook her head. "The fire certainly wasn't started by ogres. I've been getting word of unrest in that town for a while now. We were hoping it would blow over, but it seems that was fool's thinking."

"Have they started to riot?" Veda asked.

"It's difficult to determine exactly what's going on when the telegram system is down," the queen said. "The messenger who brought news of the fire was dispatched as soon as it started, so he knows as much as you and I do. Even so, I suspect the answer will be yes."

Veda folded her arms and let out a heavy sigh. "Things are getting worse and worse. I don't know how to stop it."

"No one does," Clement said. "It's the same throughout all the kingdoms."

Which left me high and dry, with no news from my siblings and no chance of getting any.

"It gets worse," the queen said. "The Urbis Express in Mosa is also shut down. This time it's due to mechanical difficulties, rather than something more sinister." She began pacing again, the golden hem of her skirt rippling at her feet. "Even so, it means I can't send a messenger to Oz."

"And it means you couldn't go home that way even if you wanted to," Veda said.

"We don't want to," I said. "The Urbis Express is too high-profile. And to tell you the truth, I'd rather avoid anything to do with Urbis right now."

Clement nodded silently beside me.

Whatever was going on in the kingdoms, Urbis was involved--not just involved, but perhaps the source of all the trouble. I couldn't get the pain on Clement's face out of my mind. The way he had fallen to his knees outside the city gates and told me he would die if he took another step toward the city--the memory filled me with dread.

"You might as well go after Fallon, then," Veda said, hope rising in her voice.

Clement shook his head. "If we can't travel to Oz, we definitely can't travel to find someone whose location we don't even know."

Veda's shoulders dropped.

"You can't travel at all," the queen said, still striding back and forth across the room. She seemed as if she'd rather climb through the window and run down the mountain than stand here in this closed room for one more moment.

I knew exactly how she felt.

"You're not safe traveling through Aboria," she continued. "You probably aren't safe anywhere. It's not just the telegram office and that one town. Fighting is breaking out everywhere. Badalah is dealing with the kind of poverty that makes people tear each other's throats out. Elder is facing an absolute epidemic of disease, and I can't seem to get news from Oz one way or another. I had the court librarian scour the recent newspapers and there's nothing, not even a mention that the Mayor had gone missing."

She let out a huge, frustrated sigh, then abruptly stopped pacing and looked at me.

"Walk with me," she ordered. "All of you. I need some fresh air."

Clement and I exchanged glances, but Veda followed behind the queen as if this were a fairly ordinary turn of events.

We walked down the palace's high-ceilinged corridors. Open windows let in the morning breeze and displayed breathtaking views of clouds and steep mountainsides. Across the nearest valley, a massive waterfall plunged from a clifftop, its silvery stream disappearing from sight before the water landed in the inevitable pool below.

The queen marched in silence through the palace and a tall, gilded door. The bracing chill of the overcast morning hit me, along with the earthy scent of damp soil, the rich perfume of roses, and a fragrant hint of coming rain.

Queen Abigail strode along a walkway of marble paving stones toward a rose garden. I'd seen palace gardens before, including my own, but this one was on a whole different, spectacular level. Three flat tiers had been carved into the mountainside, and hundreds of rose bushes filled each layer. Moon-white blooms shone closest to the palace. A bit further ahead, they were buttery yellow and then gold. These shifted to shades of salmon and pink, and finally, on the bottom tier of the garden, so far I couldn't see the individual blooms clearly, roses gleamed with shades of rich reds and burgundy so deep they were almost black. It wasn't the right season for roses to be in full bloom, or at least I didn't think so, but each and every one of these bushes, from the tiny tea roses to the flowers as large as my face, seemed at the height of their beauty.

"This is the king and queen's garden," Veda murmured. "She comes here when she needs to clear her head."

Queen Abigail strode with purpose down a flight of winding steps. When she reached the ribbon of peach and salmon roses, she turned off the path and walked toward a golden-domed gazebo of gleaming white marble adorned with carvings of twining roses.

I followed her up the steps and under the shelter of the dome. Marble benches lined the railing, and a circular grate in the very center of the gazebo held a crackling fire. The flames were small and self-contained, but gave off a warmth that belied the brisk morning air.

"That's a nice charm," Clement murmured as he warmed his hands against the blaze.

The queen leaned against the railing and looked out over the garden. A few drops fell from the sky, as if the clouds had been holding off just long enough for us to seek shelter.

"We're at risk of war." The queen's posture might have hinted at turmoil, but her voice was clear and unwavering. "Aboria is under threat from all sides."

"Not all sides," I said.

But no, I couldn't promise that. Not when I was so far removed from the Emerald Palace and everything that had been happening in Oz. For all I knew, my kingdom wasn't even on the map anymore.

Fear tingled up my spine. Oz could be in any state, and I wouldn't know a thing until I got there. It was more uncertainty than I cared to live with, and yet I had no choice.

"I've always had a good relationship with the leaders of the other kingdoms," the queen said, gently thumping her palm against the gazebo railing. "But it wasn't always like this. Before I married Ezra, tensions and uncertainties plagued him. It was like that for everyone back then. With the uprisings in Aboria and the bad news pouring in from the other kingdoms every day, it's only a matter of time before we all start side-eyeing one another again."

"I can't help feeling this would be easier if Fallon was back," Veda said.

The patter of rain on the dome grew to a dull roar. We would have had to shout over it, so we fell silent instead and watched the water drench the gardens.

It was clever, the way these terraces had been carved into the cliff. Each one was angled ever so slightly downward, and stone drainpipes set on either edge of the walkway funneled excess rain toward a creek near the very bottom of the garden. The creek swelled quickly with the rain, its silver breadth growing fatter by the minute. The water rushed downhill, perhaps culminating in a waterfall like the ones tumbling from the mountain spires all around us.

Clement slipped his hand into mine and brushed his lips against my ear. "This is beautiful."

It was. I wished I could appreciate it more. But my heart was vibrating, and dread filled the pit of my stomach.

It wasn't just Oz I had to worry about. There were eleven other kingdoms out there, and Urbis on top of that. We'd been at peace with our neighbors since before I was born. I couldn't fathom what it would be like to lead the kingdom through challenges more serious than a disagreement over tariffs or the inevitable cultural clash in border towns.

The way Queen Abigail was talking, it seemed I needed to be ready for *war*.

"I don't trust anyone right now," she said.

She spoke so quietly it seemed she thought her words would be drowned out by the rain, but I heard them clearly enough. They echoed my own thoughts.

Distrust causes more problems than it solves, the Tin Woodman's voice said in my head. *Don't be a fool, but don't be so cautious that you accidentally scare people into threatening you.*

I didn't know if I could take his advice anymore. Not when things were this bad throughout the world.

The worst of the shower passed overhead and the rain lightened. A fresh breeze rushed through the gazebo, its scent full of damp earth and something so clean I could only assume it was the smell of the sky.

Queen Abigail closed her eyes for a long moment.

"I don't know what to do," she said at last. "I don't know how to contact your siblings. I don't know how to find Fallon and make sure he's all right. I haven't the faintest idea what's happening in Urbis and why it seems to have spoiled like fruit left too long in a bowl. I'm at a loss when it comes to helping my own husband."

She pounded her palm on the railing one last time and turned around.

"I can and will command armies," she said. "Whatever happens, I will figure out how to lead this kingdom through the coming crises. But I simply do not know what to do with you."

Clement's hand tightened in mine.

I tensed. "With respect, Your Majesty, I was hoping

you wouldn't need to *do* anything with me."

Queen Abigail's expression softened.

"I didn't mean it like that. I'm not going to hold you against your will."

She rolled her lips together, as if debating her next words.

Sometimes people need to gather courage before they say true things, the Lion's voice whispered in my memories.

I stayed silent, waiting.

"I won't stop you if you have to leave. It isn't up to me to chart your destiny." Her words were slow, as if she was feeling them out as she spoke. "Even so, I'm reluctant to let you go." she let out a heavy sigh. "You remind me so much of Fallon."

"Me too," Veda said. "It's your eyes."

The queen nodded. "I look at you but I see my son looking back at me. I don't know where he is or what he's doing or if he's even--" She stopped abruptly, refusing to say the next word.

Veda approached slowly and put her hand on the queen's arm. Queen Abigail gave her a grateful look.

"I'm worried you'll get killed if you leave here, or taken back to prison," the queen said. "I'm worried that if you *don't* leave, it will be too many more months before I learned what happened to Fallon. And to have you take your chances and leave, only to go to Oz..." She trailed off and shook her head again. "I'm sorry. It's selfish."

"You love your son," I said. "It would be strange if you didn't want someone to go after him."

"You're welcome here as long as you want to stay, both of you. You should at least consider remaining put until we can re-establish the telegram lines between here and Oz."

"She's right," Veda said. "Why put yourself in danger if a week or two of repair is all you need to get in touch with your family?"

The pressure of their expectations pressed on me. I knew the fear in the queen's eyes. I felt it myself whenever I remembered that Clement was in as much peril on this journey as I was.

But the fear couldn't stop me. Not when my siblings' fate was uncertain.

"I can't wait one week, let alone two." I gazed at the queen, silently urging her to understand. "You've seen how quickly things have gone downhill here."

"Perhaps they're better in Oz," Veda said, although without much hope.

The queen held my gaze for a long, heavy moment.

"At least stay until tomorrow," she said. "I'd rather you not travel through Aboria at all, but you must absolutely *promise* me you won't travel at night. Turmoil aside, these mountain paths are treacherous in the best of conditions, and you're not used to them."

I ached at the thought of another day here. Clement and I could cover three miles in a single hour; the time between now and nightfall was enough to journey a meaningful distance.

Clement cleared his throat. I glanced at him, and he raised his eyebrows slightly, throwing his vote in with the queen's.

I nodded, though it pained me. "One more night."

The rain subsided a little more, fading back to the occasional belated raindrop hitting the dome with a pronounced *thwap*. The sun peeked out from behind a cloud, then hid its face again.

"I'll find Fallon," I blurted, before the thought had

fully formed.

The queen froze, her breath suspended in sudden joy, and I rushed to finish before she could jump to conclusions that might paint me as a more selfless person than I was.

"After I make sure things are all right in Oz."

Her shoulders fell a little, but the hope on her face remained, precarious and breakable.

"I have to go see my siblings and make sure my kingdom isn't falling into disrepair. Once I'm sure everything is all right there, I'll send some of my forces to look for Fallon."

The hope on Queen Abigail's face cracked. "I've sent a dozen scouting parties. Fallon and his companions remain elusive."

"Then I'll go myself."

The words spoke themselves, but as soon as they were out I knew they were right.

Clement did, too. He met my eyes and nodded, the simple gesture a silent promise that wherever I went, he would do his best to follow.

I didn't deserve it. I didn't deserve him.

"I have to go," I said. "Your son and those people he's with, they're connected to me. Maybe as siblings, maybe as something else. Whatever this is, we're in it together."

Queen Abigail reached for my hands. I let her take them, and she squeezed.

The touch was new. She wasn't my mother. I didn't really know her. At the same time, the familiarity of her warm hands pressing against mine made me ache. She was *someone's* mother, and I knew the flavor of that kind of love.

"How will you manage your kingdom?" Queen Abigail

asked. "Do you need help? I could send someone."

Veda chuckled. "You sound like you're trying to stage a coup."

The queen's eyebrows flew up in horror. I couldn't help laughing.

"I have absolutely no intention--"

"I knew what you meant," I interrupted gently. "Thank you. I think we'll be all right. I'll leave the Scarecrow in charge. He's led Oz before and he's got the best head on his shoulders of anyone I know."

A smile touched the queen's face. "I liked him. Your mother introduced us when I came to Oz for a ribbon cutting. You would have been barely a toddler."

The reminder that this woman had known my mother, if only a little, warmed my heart. She had the same smile everyone wore whenever they talked about Dorothy Gale. People had almost universally adored her. It would have been impossible not to.

"I'd like you to keep up communication with the Scarecrow as much as you can," I said.

The wheels started turning in my head. If I was going to leave on another adventure like the madman I had apparently become, I needed to make sure Oz was bulletproof before I crossed back out of her borders.

The queen still clung to my hands, and I held hers back firmly and met her gaze.

"I know you don't feel like you can trust the other kingdoms," I said. "And I know you have good reason. But you can trust Oz. Whatever's happening out in the world, with the magic and the evil that seems to be rising, we can't let it drive wedges between us. If anything happens while I'm gone, the Scarecrow will know to assume the best of you and everyone in Aboria. I hope you'll do the same."

She answered with a solemn nod. And then, abruptly, she pulled me in for a hug.

"I'm sorry," she murmured against my hair, without letting go. "You just look so much like him."

I leaned into the embrace. Tears sprang to my eyes, hot and prickling.

It had been a long time since I had been held by a mother, even one that wasn't mine.

She pulled back, blinking hard.

"Goodness, I don't know where that came from," she said.

"We're all feeling a little vulnerable right now," I said. "You're not alone."

"None of us are alone," Veda said brightly. She clapped one hand on my shoulder and the other hand on Clement's. "I daresay we're all hungry, though. Aboria has some truly magnificent cuisine and you ought to try at least some of it before you head out tomorrow."

The queen smiled at her and wiped the corner of her eyes with her fingertips. "That's a marvelous idea. Perhaps a picnic at Thorntop would be a good way to spend the afternoon once the rain lets up? I could use a quiet day to visit and enjoy the scenery. The gods know it'll be some time before we get another."

28TH SEPTEMBER

We were up before dawn the next morning. The spectacular mountain views and good company from yesterday's picnic at Thorntop Peak had nourished my soul. It had been a long time since I'd felt true friendship from anyone besides Clement, and Queen Abigail and Veda had turned out to be fountains of kindness.

Now that it was time to leave, I almost regretted having to go.

The queen found us in the corridor outside our rooms. Her elegant gown was the same dusty lavender as the pre-dawn sky in the window behind her, and her golden jewelry was set with white stones that reminded me of the moon.

"I'm glad I caught you," she said, her confident voice

startling against the early morning quiet. "I had an idea last night that's going to make your lives substantially easier. How do you feel about birds?"

Memories of our friend Silas flitted through my mind's eye: flocks of birds clustered around him in the prison yard, his great body held aloft in the sky by a well-coordinated team of seabirds, a dozen dust-colored desert wrens keeping him warm at night.

"Positively," I said.

"I'm in favor of birds, as a general idea," Clement agreed.

"Follow me."

The queen led us through the corridors and eventually up a flight of stone steps. She pushed open a door at the top of the stairs.

I had expected a room, but no four walls lay beyond this door. Instead, the ceiling vaulted upward, and the entire far side of the room opened to the sky through a high stone arch. In the center of the room sat an enormous and magnificent beast with silvery wings and a beak that tapered to a razor-sharp hook.

"Oh, lands," I breathed.

Clement stopped dead and stared at the creature in open admiration.

I'd seen these birds flying in the Aborian skies. The people who lived atop these jagged peaks clearly used them as a means of getting from one mountaintop to another. But seeing one up close was a revelation; aside from the Lion, I'd never seen a creature so majestic.

Veda stood next to the bird, patting its giant cheek and cooing at it. She reached into a bucket slung over her arm and pulled out a limp dead rabbit. The bird twitched its head, and when Veda flung the rabbit into the air, it caught the food in its sharp beak. In one lightning movement, it tossed the rabbit into the air and caught it again, swallowing the creature in a single gulp.

"Good boy," Veda exclaimed.

She stroked the bird's silvery cheek again, and the giant closed its eyes and nuzzled into the touch.

"This is Alabaster." The queen beamed at us, clearly pleased with the awe on our faces. "He's my very favorite of all the palace birds and has graciously agreed to fly you across Aboria."

The bottom dropped out of my stomach. The creature wore a gleaming saddle, but even so, I was queasy at the thought of riding it.

Clement wrapped an arm around me. "In the past month, you've been carried by Winged Monkeys and a flock of Silas's birds," he pointed out, then frowned. "On second thought, I can see why this makes you nervous."

"I'm not nervous," I said, as if lying about a thing could make it true. "Or if I am, it doesn't matter. I'll do whatever it takes to get home faster."

"This will be a more comfortable ride than either of those," he pointed out. "You can actually sit this time."

"They're very comfortable," Veda said, now rubbing Alabaster's beak. He was clearly enjoying the touch; he looked as if he'd just as soon fall asleep as go on a cross-country journey.

"And much faster than walking," I said. "Thank you."

The queen held up a hand. "Don't thank me yet. There's a catch. He can only take you to the border of Oz. He knows he's not allowed to leave the kingdom and I'm afraid we don't have time to train him to make an exception."

"Getting to the border that quickly will save us days,"

I said. "And it'll let us bypass any fighting."

"I'd rather not get thrown in another cell on this trip if we can help it," Clement agreed. "This will be wonderful."

Queen Abigail smiled, then opened her arms. I walked into them without hesitation and gave her the kind of hug I hoped Fallon would have given her if he were here.

"Thank you for trying to find him," she said. "No matter how this ends up, thank you for trying."

I stepped back before I could get emotional again.

Veda called us over and showed us how to mount the bird. He was clearly well-trained and accustomed to people climbing all over him, but my stomach still wobbled as I watched Veda demonstrate the proper technique and explained that we could steer him using the reins just like we would a horse.

"I'll go first," Clement said quietly. "You can sit in front of me. I won't let anything happen to you."

My stomach stilled. I reached for his hand and gave it a grateful squeeze.

Clement climbed atop the bird, who seemed entirely nonplussed by having a stranger on his back. He held out a hand, and I climbed up and settled in. The saddle was soft and roomy, and Clement's chest pressed against my back and soothed my fear.

"I was thinking of turning into a horse and letting you ride me to the border," Clement murmured so that only I could hear. "This is better."

"I don't know about that."

He snorted as he tried to suppress a laugh, and I grinned.

"Saddlebags are filled with rations and coin, in case you run into trouble," Veda said. "There's a little paper and a pencil in the small pocket, too. Scribble a note and leave it with him when you send him back so we know you made it all right."

"How do we send him back?" I asked.

She smiled. "Climb off at the border and tell him to go home. He'll figure it out. He's a smart boy." Her tone changed on these last words, as if she were speaking to a baby, and she reached up to scratch his cheek some more.

"Godspeed," Queen Abigail said, stepping back.

Veda went to join her. The queen wrapped an arm around her and they stood together, watching us with fear and hope all over their faces.

Clement reached around me to take the reins. I took a deep breath and held on tightly to the front edge of the saddle, and Alabaster turned toward the archway and launched himself into the sky.

The ground dropped out abruptly beneath us. I dug my fingers into the edge of the saddle and Clement tucked his arms around me. The bird soared and dipped with the breezes winding their way through the mountains. My stomach thrilled at the height and the movement and Clement's touch.

"This has to be better than Winged Monkeys." Clement's lips brushed against my ear, his words almost lost in the wind rushing past us.

"I'm not sure 'better' means 'good,'" I retorted.

But I didn't mean it. There was something magical about journeying this way, with the warmth of this majestic creature below me and my best friend sheltering me with his arms. And the view--the view was incredible. The greens and grays of Aboria melted into dappled patterns below us, stone and water and plant life existing in a perfect arrangement perfected over millennia. Waterfalls dove down from high peaks into shimmering lakes, and gold roofs glinted in the morning light. Mountain peaks jutted up all around, pushing their sharp points up into the heavens, and Alabaster navigated fluently around them, each tiny adjustment of his feathers precise and perfect.

"Out of all the ways we've traveled so far, this is easily my favorite," Clement said.

I grinned. "What, you didn't enjoy the tornado?"

He tightened his hands around the reins. "Let's call it an acquired taste."

"Better work fast," I said. "We're going to have to take another tornado across the desert at the border."

"Oh, wow, I can't wait," he said, deadpan.

I glanced over my shoulder. "I'll try to make it more comfortable. I think I might be able to suspend you in the very center."

"I hope so."

I leaned back into his chest, and he rested his chin on my shoulder. Alabaster's wings beat a few times, jostling us gently in the saddle, and then he found a fresh gust of air and resumed coasting.

I reached a hand out into the air in front of us. I sensed the routes the bird was taking; the ribbons of air this high in the sky were broad and lacked the subtleties and distractions of breezes nearer land. Alabaster had caught a long, wide updraft, slightly warmer than the ribbons around it, and he was riding it like a child might ride a slide.

It was exactly like Chester's favorite ride at the Emerald Amusement Park and Menagerie, come to think of it. Ma had commissioned the slide when I was young. She'd been inspired by fairs back in Kansas and the world she'd come from. We all liked it, but Chester in particular had never been able to get enough of the polished jasper slide that ended in broad ripples like an enormous, comical green tongue.

I leaned back and shared this observation with Clement. He listened, then cleared his throat.

"You're going to have to tell me more about this 'amusement park,'" he said. "We don't have anything like that in Enchantia. Or if we do, it's very, very different."

"I don't think there's anything quite like it anywhere else in the kingdoms," I said. "Unless maybe The Forge? It seems like the kind of thing they'd invent."

"Is it all slides?" Clement asked. "What do you mean by 'slides'? Like chutes that people use to move things down a hill?"

"A little." I twisted my head to make sure he wasn't joking. "Have you really never ridden on a slide before?"

"I don't think so," he said.

"How does Enchantia not even have slides?"

"We might," he said. "It's not the sort of thing my parents would have taken me to."

Pity echoed in my heart. I'd almost forgotten about Clement's upbringing. He still hadn't told me everything about his childhood, but I'd heard enough to know it had been cold. His parents didn't seem to have loved him the way Ma had loved me, and Clement claimed he didn't miss his parents now, while I would have torn heaven and earth apart just to give my Ma one more hug.

"We're going to make up for lost time once we figure out what the devil's happening with the magic and the kingdoms," I promised. "You're going to go on every ride in the park and then we're going to start over at the beginning. There's a big roller coaster that's absolutely terrifying. I've never been on it. Too scared. But I'll go with you."

"Aww." He switched his reins so he was holding them with only one hand and wrapped the other one around my chest. "What's a roller coaster?"

"It's like a train," I said. "Except mad."

"What else?"

"There's a Ferris wheel, of course."

"A what wheel?"

"Like a big wagon wheel, but you sit in an attached carriage and ride as it circles you around to the top. Everyone says it's a good place to go kiss your sweetheart." My face grew hot, but I kept talking. "We should probably go find out if that's true."

His hand twitched against my chest.

"And there's a contraption that spins around until the force of it pins you against the side so hard you can't move," I said. "I like that one."

"That sounds horrifying."

I shook my head. "Not at all. Plus if you jump up against the wall while it's still picking up speed, it'll hold you there and it's like you're flying for a second."

"I'm willing to try it," he said. "I think I'm going to prefer that Flaris wheel, though."

"Ferris."

"Ferris wheel."

"I think we're both going to enjoy that one. Especially since you can bring cotton candy onto that ride."

"What's that?"

I turned around to stare at him. "You've never had cotton candy?"

"You sound horrified."

"I am. It's pure sugar, but it's melted and spun with a machine into a fluffy cloud."

"Oh!" he exclaimed. "Spun sugar."

"Is that what you call it?"

"It's a delicacy in Enchantia. We flavor it with apples and rose water and serve it with crumbled pistachios and honey."

I snorted. "That sounds amazing but it is *not* cotton candy."

"What's the difference?"

I considered for a moment. "Spun sugar sounds fancy," I finally said. "Cotton candy is the opposite. That's what's great about it."

"Spun sugar is pretty good," he said doubtfully.

I twisted my neck again to meet his gaze. "I'll make you a deal. I'll take you to the amusement park and we'll get cotton candy. And then we'll go home and you'll make me some spun sugar. And then we'll decide who does it better."

A grin spread across his face. "Deal."

I loved imagining the future with him. The thought of spending a day comparing sweets with him in Oz-- sakes alive, it was enough to make my heart leap right out of my chest.

The next few hours passed in blissful calm. The high peaks of Enchantia gave way to smaller mountain ranges, then to rolling hills covered in green grass and jagged boulders. The sky cleared, showing dazzling blue, and then filled again with clouds, these heavy and warm like a thick down blanket.

Clement and I talked, then fell silent and enjoyed each other's warmth, and then we talked again, about everything and nothing.

It was easy with him. Everything was easy, even when it was hard.

In the far distance, a line of pale sand covered

the horizon in a straight line, containing the Aborian landscape like the white edge around a photograph. Only the land it really contained was Oz, and we would be home not long after we crossed that desert border.

Clement coaxed Alabaster downward. The graceful bird soared toward the earth, again putting me in mind of Chester's favorite slide. I clung to the edge of the saddle, anticipating a rough jolt as he hit the grassy hillside, but he landed as delicately as a feather and stood still, waiting politely for us to get our bearings and disembark.

I slid down first, my legs wobbly. Clement climbed down after and immediately petted the bird just as Veda had, stroking his cheek and cooing at him about what a good boy he'd been. I watched them, enjoying their brief connection.

Clement hadn't had enough love in his life. And yet, somehow, he managed to hand out affection like it was an infinite resource.

I slung my arm around his waist and rested my head on his arm. After a moment, I reached out and touched the bird, too. His silvery cheek feathers were impossibly soft, and he closed his shiny dark eyes and leaned into my touch.

"Thanks for the ride," I murmured.

Clement pulled the provisions Queen Abigail had provided from the bird's saddlebags. Everything had been thoughtfully packed into two knapsacks. I found the paper and pencil and wrote a quick message, letting them know we'd reached the border safely, thanking them for their help, and reassuring the queen that I had meant everything I'd said about making sure the relationship between Oz and Aboria remained strong. Then I tucked it away and Clement and I stood back.

"So, uh, go home," I said.

I hadn't expected the bird to understand what I was saying. But he promptly backed up a few steps, tilted his head and looked at us, and then launched himself into the sky.

We watched him go, his silver feathers just darker than the overcast clouds.

I turned toward the desert, which began abruptly, as if someone had poured it directly onto the grass. Perhaps someone had. It seemed like the kind of thing the Wizard might have arranged.

I held out my hand. Clement took it, and together we stepped onto the sand.

"Welcome to Oz," I said.

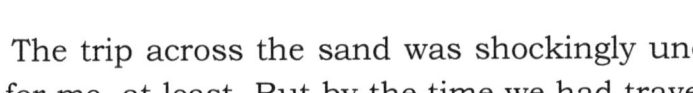

The trip across the sand was shockingly uneventful--for me, at least. But by the time we had traversed the miles of desert in one of my tornados, Clement was looking green enough to fit right in at the Emerald Palace.

"Are you all right?" I asked, steadying him.

He swayed a little, but shook his head. "I'm great," he said, which was clearly a lie.

Guilt bubbled in the pit of my stomach.

"I'm so sorry. I tried to keep you in the middle."

"You did," he said. "Sort of."

I raised an eyebrow.

He smiled wanly. "It was better than last time. Maybe you just need practice. Ideally with someone who isn't me."

"I'll try it with the Scarecrow and Woodman," I said. "They can't get dizzy."

"Lucky them," he muttered.

I led him over to a boulder sitting on the grass of the meadow we'd landed in. I hadn't been entirely sure where we'd ended up, but based on the landscape and what I'd been able to interpret of Alabaster's trajectory, I was pretty sure we'd landed in Munchkin Country.

That was good. None of the various regions of Oz was particularly troublesome these days, but the Munchkins in particular had always been devoted to Ma and, by extension, kind to me.

We sat and ate from the provisions the queen had provided until Clement looked like he wasn't quite so ready to collapse onto the grass. Then, hand-in-hand, we took off across the meadow toward the blue brick road that wound its way between the gently sloping hills.

"I thought you said your Ma took a yellow brick road to the Emerald City," Clement said.

"The yellow brick road goes there. Other roads in Munchkin Country are blue. They're purple in Gillikin Country, red in Quadling country, and yellow in Winkie county."

"But the yellow road--"

"It's confusing. I don't know why the Yellow Brick Road itself isn't *green,* since it leads straight to the Emerald City. I suspect either there was a miscommunication or the Wizard just thought it was funny. He enjoyed a bit of nonsense."

Clement laughed. "Oz sounds like a nonsensical place."

"It's the weirdest and the best."

We followed the blue brick road for the better part of an hour. The clouds melted, revealing warm evening sunshine, and the calls of songbirds all around filled the air with a light, pleasant music.

I was *home.*

One of the Munchkin villages rose up in front of us, and I quickened my pace. I couldn't wait to see the familiar faces of my people and perhaps hear news of what had been happening to the kingdom in my absence.

But something was wrong. My steps slowed as we neared the homes and shops.

The village was quiet. The roads were deserted. The baby blue and cerulean homes, normally so cheerful under a sunny blue sky, seemed foreboding. Empty windows stared at us from either side as we walked down the street.

"Is this normal?" Clement's voice was low and quiet, as if he didn't dare disturb the eerie silence.

I shook my head, unable to speak. I *knew* this village. It was famous. I had been here before, with Ma on a national tour and once with Margaret for a summer festival. It had always been full of life and joy.

Now, it seemed dead.

We passed the house that had crushed the Wicked Witch of the East, back when Ma had first come to Oz. The faded white home had been preserved. A low blue fence surrounded it, and a brass plaque out front told the story of how Dorothy Gale had destroyed her first wicked witch and saved the Munchkins from tyranny.

The house had always unnerved me. It was old and empty, with peeling paint and thin curtains and a veneer of dust. Now, it looked almost at home in this abandoned town.

A shudder ran down my spine.

"This isn't right," I muttered. "Whatever curse is spreading through the other kingdoms is in Oz." Dread pooled in my stomach and fear clawed its way up into my throat.

Clement put an arm around me. "There's no guarantee anyone here got hurt," he said calmly. "It looks like everyone left in a hurry, but that means it's possible they're all safe. For all we know they're in the next village down the road."

Solve the problem right in front of you, Ma chided in my head, throwing her weight firmly behind Clement.

I took a deep breath and took a moment to collect myself. Evening was fast approaching, and the first rays of gold were already touching the shabby white building.

I ran a hand through my hair.

"I have to find out what happened here," I said at long last. "I have a duty to these people. We need to look around." I glanced up, mentally calculating the time between now and sunset. We didn't have long, and I felt queasy at the thought of exploring this abandoned town with only a lamp or two to light the way.

"I agree," Clement said gently. "But I also think we need to sleep. Let's look around the village and stay the night. I'm sure one of these houses has a bed we can borrow."

I didn't want to spend the night here, but even I knew it would be safer than trying to sleep on the open road. If this town had been emptied, it was possible Winged Monkeys had done the emptying. They'd have a harder time spotting us if there was a roof over our heads.

I swallowed hard and set my shoulders.

We made our way quietly through the vacant town. Clement had been right: The Munchkins had left the village in a hurry. Doors stood open, abandoned toys sat in front gardens, and plates still dusted with crumbs cluttered the tables of an empty café. My skin prickled at the deep shadows at the back of the building. It had been a bustling place, full of life and lingering breakfasts. Now, it lurked like a tomb.

"We should head to Boq's mansion," I said, nodding up a side road. "He's a Munchkin I've known almost since I was born. He's getting on in years but he's still a community leader. If anywhere has a clue as to what went on here, it might be his place."

The homes and shops grew slightly larger and fancier as we walked. I turned at the bookshop and led the way to a neighborhood full of comfortable homes, many with Munchkin Country's traditional domed roofs. This street ended in a gleaming blue-and-gold gate, the old familiar mansion visible through its clever latticework.

I put a hand to the gate. It swung easily open.

"Must not have had time to lock up," Clement said.

I smiled, if only for an instant. "Boq never locks it. He says the whole point of a gate is so it can be open to everybody."

His was a confection of a building, all sky blue columns and cheerful gold trim, with beautiful stained glass windows displaying bright patterns of blossoms and songbirds. The front garden overflowed with late-summer abundance, yellow sunflowers and fat-headed pink chrysanthemums and enormous nodding daisies.

Everything about it was bright and welcoming-- everything except the windows, which stood dark and empty in spite of the gathering dusk.

We made our way up the gently curving drive with its gravel of white marble and tumbled blue glass, then up the wide steps to the bright blue front doors. I knocked, out of habit and hope, but of course no one answered.

I touched the latch, but I couldn't bring myself to open the door. The hairs on the back of my neck stood on end.

Clement waited for a moment, then put his hand gently over mine.

"I'll go in first," he said. "I don't know much by way of defensive magic but I can throw a fireball or two if it comes to that."

I'd forgotten we had magic. I'd never had magic of my own in this town before. The abilities I'd discovered back in the prison and my memories of home crashed into one another, each seeking a way to integrate into a new and more complete understanding of my world.

"I'll have a tornado ready," I said.

Thus armed, we nudged the door open together. It swung inward onto a dark, empty foyer.

I strained my ears, but the house was silent aside from the ticking of the enormous silver wall clock that had been in Boq's family for generations. The ticks seemed slower than they should be, and I couldn't tell if it was because the clock was winding down or because I was comparing its seconds against the racing of my heart.

"I don't sense anything," Clement said, relaxing a little. "I think it's just empty."

"That's bad enough, but still better than the alternative."

"Seems we're up against some pretty disappointing options all around."

"Story of my life these days," I muttered. "Feel along the wall on your side, near the door. There should be a little brass switch. Boq had electricity installed by someone from the Forge a few years ago."

Clement ran his fingers along the wallpaper, and I

kept talking, if only to put a dent in the unbearable silence.

"There's no guarantee any of these lights will actually turn on. The house is mostly run using this windmill he set up in the back garden, but either Oz isn't windy enough or he didn't buy a big enough windmill, because the lights only seem to work about half the time. I'm sure there are lamps around here somewhere, but it'd be nice to have the whole room lit up at onc--"

The switch clicked and the lights sprang on. They flickered briefly, then settled into a steady glow from beneath creamy lampshades.

"Thank our lucky stars," I said.

The room was every shade of blue, from the silvery wallpaper to the soft cornflower carpets to the furniture, which had all been painted the same stately navy.

"This color scheme is honestly impressive," Clement said.

"Boq is very devoted to Munchkin Country."

Now that the lights were on, the house seemed much less foreboding. I could almost believe that Boq and his many servants were somewhere in the house, preparing for a banquet or setting up for a party.

"His office is upstairs," I said. "If this situation is political, there might be something there."

"What if it was Monkeys?"

I frowned. "Look for feathers, I guess."

He hoisted his knapsack further up on his back and nodded at me to lead the way.

We wandered the halls, turning on lights as we went. Boq's office was open, but the papers on the desk revealed nothing besides that he had just paid for two large barrels of apple mead and had received a letter from a friend in Quadling Country.

I scoured the letter for any hint of the trouble that had consumed this town, but it was full of nothing but small-town gossip and complaints about the friend's mother-in-law.

I threw it onto the desk. "There's nothing here."

"It's only one letter."

"Shouldn't it be easier than this? If Winged Monkeys attacked this village, wouldn't it be obvious?"

Clement frowned at me from across the room. "I don't know, I've never been in this situation before."

I squeezed my eyes shut. My heart raced in my chest, picking up speed until the beats felt more like vibrations. The ribbons of air floating in the room sharpened in my mind, and my palms grew hot.

"A tornado isn't going to help us right now," Clement said calmly.

I opened my eyes. "Then what is?"

I strode across the room, but there was nowhere to run to. The blue-papered wall rose up in front of me. I pivoted and marched back the other way.

The pacing helped. It gave my heartbeat something to work with.

"It was supposed to be easier than this," I said. "We escaped from an impenetrable prison. We walked across an *entire desert*. We survived a kidnapping in Aboria. And after all that, we made it to Oz. We *made it*. And now I'm home, where things are supposed to be better, but they're not better. This place is a disaster. Everyone is gone, and it's my fault. I'm their Mayor. I'm supposed to protect them from things like this."

"From things like what?" he said. "We don't even know what happened here."

"It wasn't something *good*." I swept my arm, gesturing at the room and the devastated town beyond. "This isn't what a happy, thriving town looks like. Even when the Wicked Witch of the East was running the place there was actually something to *run*."

Clement grabbed my arm as I strode past him. I tried to get free, but he pulled me back and grasped me with both hands.

"Jakon, breathe."

"I'm breathing."

"You're panting. It's different."

I scowled at him, but I did my best to get the shuddering of my lungs under control. He rested his forehead against mine and let out a long sigh, giving me a pace to focus on.

The shimmering blackness at the edge of my vision faded. My heartbeat slowed. Finally, I collapsed against him, burying my face against his shoulder.

"You're not home," he said quietly.

"Oz is home."

"Your *family* is your home."

He pulled back, urging me to look at him. His dark eyes fixed on mine, tethering us together.

"Your home is wherever your brothers and sisters are," he said. "We're not there yet. And when we do get there, things might get harder. We don't know what the future holds. But I do know that whatever happens, we can handle it. That's as much as we need to know right now."

"I would prefer to know the entirety of the future." I grimaced. "I would like to know every obstacle in my path and whether I'm going to be up for the challenge and exactly what the end of all this is going to be."

Clement smirked. "Well, as long as your expectations are reasonable."

I chuckled. I couldn't help it.

"Margaret says I'm melodramatic."

"She's your sister; I think it's her job to say that sort of thing." He grinned. "Which is not to imply she's wrong."

Clement stepped back and turned in a slow circle, surveying the room. Finally, he stopped and sighed.

"I don't think we're going to find anything else here tonight. And I suspect this house has some terribly comfortable beds. Let's go track some down and get a good night's sleep."

"But what about--"

Clement put a finger to my lips. "Not our problem right now."

"But what if--"

"We'll deal with tomorrow's challenges then," he said firmly.

Fatigue crept into my limbs. I held out for a few seconds more, but exhaustion won, aided by the stubborn set of Clement's chin.

I let him drag me from the room. We selected one of Boq's many guest chambers, and I was asleep by the time my head hit the pillow.

29TH SEPTEMBER

I didn't stir. I didn't dream. I slept so soundly that by the time Clement woke me with a gentle shake to my shoulder, I had to blink and rub my eyes a few times before I remembered where I was or what we were doing here.

"What time is it?"

"I don't know, but there's someone outside."

The urgency of his whisper brought me back to my senses in a flash. I sat bolt upright and shoved the china blue comforter away.

"Out there," Clement said, jerking his chin toward the window.

I rushed over and peeked out from behind the curtains. The bedroom window had what was probably a charming view of the town under normal circumstances. Down the curving gravel driveway, past the gates, someone with long red hair and a long white coat was striding down the main street of the village.

No, not someone.

I threw the curtains aside and tugged the window open. The panes swung outward, letting in a whiff of the pink flowers in the window box. I leaned out the window and waved frantically.

"Over here!" I shouted.

She shouldn't have been able to hear me. She was too far away, and my voice wasn't that loud.

But Glinda was a witch, and her senses were far above the ordinary.

She looked sharply over, her figure small in the distance. She hesitated for a moment, then, abruptly, turned town the side road and marched toward the mansion.

I closed the window and turned to Clement, who was staring at me.

"You were right, things do look better in the morning," I said. "Come on, there's someone you have to meet."

He narrowed his eyes, still cautious, but I grinned and grabbed my knapsack.

I paused in front of the room's enormous wall mirror and tried to brush my hair into place. I silently thanked my lucky stars that we'd gotten baths and fresh clothes in Aboria. When I was thirteen or so, Glinda had wrinkled her nose at me and asked Ma if *all* teenage boys smelled like that. When Ma had only laughed, Glinda had sighed and waved her wand at me. I'd reeked of fresh lavender for weeks afterward, and I wasn't looking for a repeat.

I raced down the stairs, Clement at my heels. We

reached the front gate at the same time as Glinda, and she rushed forward and wrapped me in a hug that was somehow delicate and bone-crushing all at once.

"I knew you'd come back," she said into the top of my head. "Even so, it's lovely to find out I really did *know* what I knew, if you know what I mean."

I pulled back and frowned a little at her, as if I expected to see the passage of time in her face. But of course, it wasn't there. It seemed like each year we were growing closer in age, and it wouldn't be long until I looked like her father and then her grandfather. Ma had always called Glinda's eternal youth a great injustice, although I'd privately thought my Ma wouldn't have been quite so beautiful without the laugh lines at the corners of her eyes.

"Things have been absolutely rotten here," she continued. "Do you know what happened to this town?"

"We just arrived last night."

She glanced past me to Clement. "You're not a Munchkin," she said.

He smiled a little. "No, ma'am, I'm from Enchantia."

"Did you come to rescue us?" she asked. "We could certainly use the aid of a great magician or two."

"This is Clement," I said. "He's my friend. Clement, *this* is Glinda, the Good Witch of the South and my dear friend."

Her smile broadened, and she held out a dainty hand for Clement to shake.

"You ended up in Enchantia, then?" She turned back to me and arched one eyebrow. "I can't imagine why the Monkeys would have taken you there."

"You knew I was kidnapped by the Monkeys?"

She laughed, the sound like a bubbling brook. "Everyone knew. Margaret saw everything. We scoured their jungle for you, but the whole place seemed abandoned." She glanced over her shoulder, the mirth on her face fading. "Much like this town."

"They didn't take me anywhere half so nice," I said. "Clement and I met at Urbis Prison."

Glinda's lips parted in shock, and then, as she realized exactly just what I had said, she set her jaw into a hard line. "Urbis Prison?" she demanded. "They took you to *Urbis Prison?*"

Distant thunder rumbled far overhead, although the clouds this morning were too light and fluffy to play host to a storm.

I put a reassuring hand on her arm. "We escaped. Our friend from Skyla helped."

The thunder rumbled again, more quietly this time.

"We made it across Badalah and Aboria," I said. "We were helped by some good people on the way."

I didn't mention the sand raiders or the blacksmith. I didn't want to be responsible for them ending up in the middle of the ocean by day's end. There was no proof that Glinda went in for that kind of retribution, but I also wasn't inclined to play fast and loose with the possibility.

"What happened here?" I said, hoping to redirect her. "The town was abandoned when we arrived."

Her lips turned down. "I was hoping you'd be able to tell me."

"You didn't know?"

She shook her head. "We received a distress call down in Quadling Country a couple of days ago, but there was nothing we could do then. The Winged Monkeys were raiding my palace and the city. We've been doing nothing but fighting them off."

My stomach clenched. "Is everyone--"

"We're fine," she said. "Mostly. The Monkeys are gone but my soldiers are still trying to account for everybody. It's possible the Monkeys made off with a good few dozen Quadlings, but it's equally likely people are still hiding in their cellars or out in the woods. I wasn't able to get away until this morning, and then I arrived, and..."

She trailed off. The deserted town around us all but finished the sentence for her.

"Do you have any idea where everyone might have gone?" I asked.

"Not one," she said. "Fortunately, I don't have to have ideas."

She straightened her long white coat, which flared out to reveal flowing white trousers beneath, and spun on her heel.

"This way," she said, voice again airy. "We're going to solve this mystery, and let's all hope to the Wonderful Wizard that we can stomach the answer."

She strode through the village, her white boots clicking against the dusty blue bricks, and Clement and I hurried to follow. She marched decisively past a dressmaker's shop and a chemist's, then turned left onto a broad, tree-lined path.

I knew this route. I'd been here before.

The path turned into smaller walkways winding like rivers through a broad green lawn, and Glinda marched down the most central of these. They all led to a broad half-circle stage of white marble, overhung with a pale blue canopy and surrounded on three sides by gently sloping grass.

The Blue Amphitheater was home to most of the village's community activities, at least the ones that weren't hosted by Boq. Munchkins came here for symphony concerts and operatic performances, children's plays and community announcements, and all of the town's regular seasonal festivals: the Cherry Blossom Festival, the Midsummer Dance, the Apple Harvest Celebration. The Munchkins were a joyful people, ready to celebrate at a moment's notice.

The empty amphitheater mocked us, its silence a blight on the town's memories of good cheer.

"Don't dawdle," Glinda said kindly.

I started walking again. I couldn't let the gloom that surrounded me slow me down. Not now that there was someone here who might be able to help.

Glinda strode up its shallow steps to the stage, her coat billowing behind her. She stopped in the center of the half-circle and paused under the platform's canvas awning.

She turned slowly around once, then nodded briskly at me.

"This will do. The white background is delightfully free of distractions. Sit, please."

Clement and I obeyed. The cold of the shaded marble seeped through my trousers.

Glinda sat, too, so that we formed a small circle. She pulled her wand out of her jacket and held it aloft.

Clement watched with interest. It was likely the first time he'd seen a wand since leaving Enchantia, assuming the matchstick from our prison cell didn't count.

I smiled a little at the memory.

Glinda waved the white tip of her wand in a slow, precise circle. A line appeared in the air, following the loop she traced--no, not a line. A bubble. She coaxed it with the wand and it grew, first to the size of a cherry, then an orange, and then to a small round melon. A colorful film swam around the bubble's surface, creating strange patterns.

She stopped coaxing and gave the bubble a sharp, staccato tap. I winced, anticipating the pop. Instead, it hardened. The swirling colors gave way to geometric reflections, and the surface took on a glossy sheen that let me see my own face.

"Hold out your hands, please," she said, voice musical.

We did, and the crystal ball settled solidly against our palms.

"Thank you," Glinda said politely.

Clement glanced at me, suppressing a smile. I didn't bother to hide mine. I had missed the Good Witch of the South.

She danced her wand over the curve of the crystal, as if trying to tease the reflections within it to the surface. Her slender auburn eyebrows drew together and her breath suspended.

"I should have been here," she murmured, staring deeply into the shadows and light playing within the ball. "I should have found a way to come."

I kept silent. This kind of magic required concentration.

Glinda's eyes filled with tears, as glossy as the surface of the crystal.

"Those poor dears," she said. "Why didn't I check in on them more often? Perhaps there was warning."

Questions fought their way to my lips. I bit my tongue and forced them back.

"Look," Glinda ordered suddenly.

The surface of the crystal changed. The reflections deep inside solidified and grew brighter. They took on a green glow and formed into shapes--recognizable shapes of blue-clad Munchkins, crowded into a dungeon with emerald green walls. Many of them were crying. All looked miserable.

A few faces stood out: Boq, being supported by two of his adult children. Minnie, the toymaker who had sent me a wooden rocking horse for my fourth birthday. Tripp, the Munchkin around my age who'd shown me and Margaret around on our last visit. And...

"Lands, no," I said. "No, no, no, no, no."

I hunched over the crystal, willing my eyes to be playing tricks.

But there was no mistaking that face. As if to mock me, the view in the crystal narrowed in on the tears streaking down his cheeks.

"*No.*"

It was a shout, wrenched from me without my permission. On instinct, I let go of the crystal ball as if it were red-hot. Clement caught its full weight and stared into its glowing green depths.

"Who are they?" he said. "Those aren't--"

He cut himself off and stared at me.

"Those *aren't*," he repeated.

I let out a shuddering breath.

"They are." Glinda's voice was calm, but underneath those steady tones was a deep and simmering rage. "Those are Jakon's brothers and sisters."

"That was Chester," I said, voice shaking. "He is nine years old. He is clever. He likes to build machines and solve problems." My words grew louder. "He is funny and loves telling bad jokes and he is *being held in a dungeon along with our other siblings and the entire population of this village.*"

I was shouting now, and standing, and pacing across the white expanse of the amphitheater stage as my hands tingled with barely suppressed magic. I was, in fact, surprised to discover I was not *running*, because my limbs were screaming at me to *move, move, move.*

"We have to go," I said. "Now."

Glinda stretched out a hand. "Wait."

"I have to go save them," I said. "Lucy is in that prison. *Lucy.*"

"I agree, but you need to go in with a plan. You saw where they're being held."

"The Emerald Palace dungeons."

I knew those walls.

Worse, I knew the magic they contained.

"You didn't put them there," Glinda said. "That means we're up against somebody who has the power to overrule the charms restricting dungeon access to the Mayor of Oz."

"Someone powerful."

"Someone wicked." She held my gaze. Her jaw was tight with anger, and her lips and cheeks flushed bright red against her pale skin. "Which puts us at an extra disadvantage. Sit down, Jakon. We need to think this through."

My body didn't want to obey, and my heart still screamed at me to run. But my mind understood the gravity of the situation.

I sank back down onto the cold stone stage.

"Your magic isn't enough to rescue them," I said.

She sighed and tapped the crystal ball with her wand. This time, it shattered into dozens of tiny bubbles that floated into the air and away, popping one by one as they realized their usefulness was over.

"My magic has always been weak against wickedness," she explained to Clement. "I'm a powerful witch, but..." She trailed off.

"But even fire struggles when water is its enemy," Clement said. "Magic has inclinations of its own. I understand."

She glanced at me, quickly, and then back at him with renewed interest.

"Precisely. If someone wicked put the Munchkins and the Gale children in the dungeon--and I think we can safely assume that is the case--then it stands to reason that the dungeon is closed to us unless we obtain some wicked magic of our own."

I frowned at her. My heart pounded. "And how do we do that?"

"I suppose we'll have to track down a bad witch." Her face fell. "That promises to be a long and difficult adventure." She gave me a slight, rueful smile. "I'm afraid your mother ran us clean out of wicked witches. I never expected to live to regret it."

We fell silent, each of us thinking hard.

"We might be able to find someone in Enchantia," Clement said. "Do you need a magician who employs the evil arts? Or would a cursed object do just as well? That might be easier to track down on Enchantia's black market, and it would be simpler than trying to convince some self-absorbed sorcerer to work with us."

"An object is enough," Glinda said. "I'd prefer something easy to carry around."

"I knew a fellow once who had a collection of magic mirrors," Clement offered. "I know at least a few of them held evil spirits captive."

Glinda nodded slowly. "Yes, that could work."

I massaged my temple. "It's going to take days to get back and forth to Enchantia. You can ride the Urbis Express, Glinda, but Clement and I can't leave Oz again unless we're ready to risk getting thrown back in prison."

"I have to go," Clement objected. "The collector isn't likely to sell to someone he doesn't know. He's not technically supposed to have half of those mirrors."

Glinda considered Clement with a steady gaze. "I could disguise you," she said at last. "Your magical aura has quite a distinctive signature, but I may be able to mask it as well."

"That still puts us so far behind." I drew my knees up to my chest and wrapped my arms around them, as if the warmth of my body could do anything about the chill growing in my heart. "I've been out of Oz less than a month and an entire village is in the dungeon, not to mention my siblings. Think about how much can happen in two days. There has to be something in Oz."

"Your mother and Locasta and I destroyed almost every wicked object we found over the years. The ones we couldn't destroy, we locked away in a vault hidden in the Emerald Palace's dungeons, which is the one place in Oz we can't get to right now."

"There has to be *something* left," I said, casting my eyes around wildly as if the answer might be here, in plain view of this once-cheerful amphitheater. "Some item, some tool, some *remnant* of a wicked wi--"

I stopped abruptly, staring at the road that led away from the amphitheater, then shot to my feet.

Glinda's blue eyes widened.

"Of course," she said.

"Of course," I said.

"Of *course*," she repeated.

Clement looked between us. "What?"

"Starlight and moonbeams," Glinda said. "It was right in front of us all the time."

She rose to her feet, then held out a hand to help

Clement up.

"Quickly," she said. "Let's hope it's still there."

~

We stood outside the fenced memorial and stared at the dilapidated house.

"You're sure she's still under there?" I asked.

Glinda narrowed her eyes and nodded.

"I put a charm on the body and the house to keep anyone from moving it, at the Munchkins' request."

"I suppose it reassures them to know she's still dead."

"Yes," Glinda said, frowning a little. "If you were to move those bushes you'd still find her feet sticking out from under the house, though she's nothing but a skeleton now."

"But her skeleton will help us?" Clement asked, frowning.

Glinda pursed her lips, gazing at the house with an expression so calculating it hinted at the age and experience behind her youthful face.

"We're not after her body," Glinda said.

A warm breeze set her loose curls to swaying. Beneath the gentle movement, her frame remained statue-still, her eyes locked on the foundation of the shoddy old home.

"She always wore two enchanted items," Glinda said. "The silver slippers, which Dorothy took the day she entered Oz, and an emerald ring. The ring is still under there. It contains a vast magic."

"A wicked magic?" Clement asked.

"She turned it wicked," Glinda said. She held up her own left hand. A delicate gold ring set with an oval emerald sparkled on her middle finger. The emerald seemed to glow with its own subtle light. "Each of the Witches of Oz was granted one when the world was young. They gave us dominion over our respective countries and unconditional access to the Emerald City. Any object that stays with a single owner for so long will begin to take on her essence, and these rings did it better than most. Mine holds a good deal of my magic." Glinda nodded toward the house. "Almyra's ring took on the flavor of hers. It should be more than enough to let me into the Emerald Palace dungeons."

She strode past the plaque out front and through the gate. We followed, but she stopped so abruptly I almost ran into her.

"The trouble is, I can't lift the house." She glanced at Clement. "Not on my own."

He shook his head. "I'm as good as useless without a wand. I can shift without it and do a few small tricks, but nothing like this."

"Could we tunnel underneath?" I asked. "Dig her out?"

They both considered this. Finally, Glinda nodded, though she didn't look convinced.

"It won't be easy. The building crashed right over what used to be a road. We'll have all sorts of brick and rubble to contend with. It'll take time."

Every minute left my siblings and my subjects trapped in a windowless cell deep beneath the Emerald Palace. And that was the best-case scenario. I didn't know who had trapped them there—the Monkey King, or some new wicked witch, or maybe an angry prison ogre trying to use them as ransom to re-capture me. Their identity, motives, and plans were all a mystery. My skin crawled with uncertainty.

My siblings might be released tomorrow. They might also be executed.

"Let's start digging," I said. "It shouldn't be hard to find a shovel. We can take turns with the harder bits. We need--"

"Jakon," Clement interrupted. "We don't have to dig."

"Yes, we do. We have to get that ring."

"No, I mean..." He trailed off, then held up his hands and flexed them gently.

I could have kicked myself. So many times, my magic had risen unbidden to my hands. Now that I was home, it was as if I'd forgotten everything I'd learned to do outside my kingdom's borders.

"I can do it," I said. "Glinda, lift the charm. Then you'll both want to step back."

Clement, who had been serious up until this point, answered me with an enormous grin.

"He means it," he said to Glinda. "We need to get out of the way."

Her eyebrows jumped up in surprise. "What are you going to do?"

"You'll see," Clement said.

She hesitated, eyeing me cautiously, then raised her wand. She pointed it toward the house, which shimmered with white for a moment as her charm dissolved.

Clement led her behind me, past the fence and across the street. Clement beamed at me.

"You've got this," he called.

I nodded, double-checked to make sure they were far enough away, and turned back to the house.

I raised my hands. Prickles of energy rippled across my palms.

The morning's light wind picked up speed and force, growing from a breeze to a gale in a matter of seconds. Ribbons of air rushed past my ears, and I wove them into a spiral as if I were plaiting Ethel's hair or twisting yarn into a rope for one of Chester's inventions. The grass on the monument lawn bowed in the wind, and the decaying shutters on the little wreck of a home clapped against the peeling siding. One of the shutters fell to the ground with a dull crack.

The gale turned to a storm, and the storm turned into a proper tornado, a whirling instrument of force and debris. I focused its slender point at the house.

I had expected resistance. This was a whole home, small and dilapidated though it was, and I was ready to fight to get it into the air.

But the flimsy walls and decaying floor leapt as if they'd been longing to re-experience flight. The whole tiny house flew upward, spiraling around my tornado in a wild frenzy.

I guided the tornado to the side. Its enormity and power were enough to tear up this town, but I had practiced out in the desert, and I kept the earth-bound tip of the storm under tight control. I moved the twister to the side, just enough to reveal the filthy white bones of the witch that had been buried all these years.

And then I set the house down, lightly, on the grass just to the side of its original position, and let the tornado go. The twister's tail rose up into the sky and dissolved, the ribbons of air once more finding their ordinary place in the breeze.

Glinda's boots clicked against the bricks behind me. I turned to face her and couldn't keep myself from grinning at the bewildered look on her face.

"*When* and *how* and *why* did you learn *that?*" she

demanded.

"It's a long story." I glanced over at the wound of earth and damaged brick the house's movement had revealed. "I'll tell you on the way."

"You most certainly will." She stared at me for a moment, then, with decisive briskness, pulled me close, kissed the top of my head, and marched toward the skeleton lying in the dirt, clad in deep blue and black rags streaked with brown filth and speckled with old flakes of white paint.

Glinda crouched next to the body and lifted the skeleton's hand. It came apart, held together by nothing now but its own stillness. She removed the ring from a bone that had once been a finger and stood back up, brushing off her still-immaculate white coat.

She turned to me and straightened her shoulders.

"That's that," she said. "No time to waste." She nodded to the side. "The yellow brick road is that way."

I held out my hands. She came back and took one, and Clement clasped the other. Side-by-side, hand-in-hand, we turned and marched toward the Emerald City.

<<<<>>>>

GOD OF STORIES

30TH SEPTEMBER

The yellow brick road stretched out like a ribbon of sunlight before us. The day was bright and warm, the sky a dazzling blue and the air filled with the scent of early autumn flowers. It was a perfect day, and Glinda's shoulders looked so tight they were ready to snap.

"Someone's coming," she hissed.

I couldn't see anybody on either side of the winding yellow road, but then, I wasn't a powerful Witch of Oz.

"Hide in the bushes," she ordered.

I hesitated.

She gave me a piercing look. "Some monster or other has your siblings and a whole village full of Munchkins under lock and key. I'd rather that monster didn't learn the Mayor was back in Oz just yet."

I couldn't argue with that. Nor could Clement, walking beside me. We left the brick path and ducked behind a stand of shaggy bushes heavy with flame-red leaves and bright orange berries. Behind us, the forest here at the edge of Munchkin Country was dense and full of shadows.

Glinda stood like a statue on the eerily silent road, her hair as red as the leaves and her flowing white coat as immaculate as the puffy clouds overhead. She stared into the distance and waited. Finally, a young Munchkin man came into view over the crest of the nearest hill. He wore a sky-blue shirt and navy-blue trousers held up with suspenders, and his navy cap shielded his face from the sun. He stopped dead when he saw Glinda, paused, and then marched forward with renewed purpose.

"Your Witchiness," he said as soon as he was close enough to be heard. He whipped his cap from his head and lowered into a deep bow, his figure partially obscured from my view by the thick branches. When he straightened, his eyes were bright. "You heard what happened in the villages, then? That the Winged Monkeys attacked? Did you come to save us? We thought you were in Quadling Country."

"I was in Quadling Country," she said. "I only just arrived. You said 'villages.' Is it more than one, then?"

The man's face fell. "It's all of them, My Lady."

My stomach twisted into a knot. No wonder the vast Emerald City dungeons had seemed so cramped when we'd viewed them through Glinda's crystal ball.

Glinda narrowed her eyes. "Then how are you here?"

He twisted his cap in his hands. "I was selling my wares in Gillikin Country, My Lady. I heard the news and went to the Emerald City to demand something be done." His face reddened, with embarrassment or anger or something else I couldn't begin to guess at. "That ended in disaster, of course, so now I'm going home. I hoped at least a few people from my village escaped the raid."

Glinda's face softened. "If your village is the one down this road, then no, I'm afraid not."

His face crumpled, but he fought hard to keep his tears at bay. My heart ached for him. I shared his fear. My loved ones were locked up, too.

"What happened in the Emerald City?" Glinda asked.

"Nothing, My Lady." He sounded almost surprised. "I couldn't get in."

She frowned. "What do you mean? Did the Guardian of the Gate refuse to let you enter?"

The man didn't answer for a moment. He searched Glinda's face, as if unsure what she was asking. Then, slowly, he said, "My Lady... The Guardian can't do anything. Not anymore."

If Glinda had been standing like a statue before, now she was ice. She radiated power without moving a muscle. "Explain that."

He folded his cap in half and wrung it. "The gates are closed." He shuffled from foot to foot. "No one can get in or out, not even the Guardian." He stared up at her. "I thought you knew."

"Who closed the city?" she demanded.

"No one knows," he said. "It just happened."

"When?"

"Yesterday, My Lady."

"And is it every entrance?"

"There's only the one, My Lady." He hesitated. "Well, aside from the back gate."

Glinda's already pale skin blanched.

"But I've never put stock in such rumors, My Lady." The man eyed her, cautious but curious.

I'd never heard of a back gate, but it was clear it meant something to Glinda.

"I see. Thank you for the information." She considered him for a long moment, then added briskly, "You'll not find anybody waiting for you in the village. I suggest you turn at the next fork and head toward Quadling Country. Things are relatively safe there, at least for now, and you'll find shelter and protection at my palace."

He bowed again. "Yes, My Lady. Thank you, My Lady."

She gestured him forward. He shuffled closer, and she bent down and kissed him gently on the forehead. When she pulled back, a bright, star-like mark gleamed.

"It's a witch's mark," I whispered to Clement. "Only the Witches of Oz can give them. It won't protect him from everything, but people don't usually bother people wearing a mark."

"Go quickly," Glinda advised the man. "Things are quiet in Munchkin Country for now, but there's no telling how long the peace will last."

He bowed for a third time, and, at Glinda's nod, hurried past her and down the yellow brick road. He glanced over his shoulder several times, as if checking to be sure she was still there.

Then he disappeared over the crest of the next hill and was gone.

Glinda watched after him for a long, silent moment before gesturing at us to come out from behind the bushes.

"Did you hear all that?" she asked.

I nodded. "What was that about a back gate?"

Glinda pursed her lips. "It's a piece of information far bigger than he thought he was delivering."

I waited for her to explain, but she only put her hands on her hips.

"We can't travel this way anymore," she said after a moment. "We'll have to cut through the forests. If the Emerald City's been closed she'll be keeping a close eye on the yellow brick road."

"Who's she?" Clement asked.

Glinda strode between us as if he hadn't spoken and disappeared behind the bushes. Clement and I shared a glance, then hurried to catch up.

The thick canopy of trees soon blocked out most of the light, and the scent of the Munchkin's autumnal fields was quickly smothered by the dense odor of damp earth and fragrant pines. Ferns and saplings crowded underfoot, and thick patches of emerald moss and mint-green lichen crept up the trunks of the trees.

There was no path here, but Glinda didn't need one. She picked her way as lightly as a bubble through the undergrowth and around branches, and Clement and I bumbled after her as best we could.

Finally, after I'd given up on her telling us anything about what we were doing and why, she stopped and waited for us to catch up. She surveyed the forest, her eyes sapphire-dark in the dappled shadows.

"The Wicked Witch of the West is back," she announced.

My mouth fell open, but no words came out.

Clement's eyebrows furrowed and he looked at me, then her. "Isn't she dead? Jakon told me the story. His mother killed her." He searched my face, as if it held his memory of the tale. "She melted her with a bucket of water."

"Yes, that was supposed to be the way of things," Glinda said. "Filthy old hag."

I had never heard Glinda speak so unkindly of anyone.

"I wondered about the water thing," Clement confessed. "It doesn't seem like that would be powerful enough to hurt a witch, let alone kill her."

"Oh, the water hurt her," Glinda said. "You try not bathing for hundreds of years and then see how you feel when someone dumps a bucket of suds on your head." The corner of her lip twitched. "Of course, Dorothy had infused the water with Goodness, same as I've infused my ring." She held up her hand, where the two witches' rings sparkled side-by-side, her emerald burning with a deep inner light, the Wicked Witch of the East's murky like mud. "I'll admit I was never entirely sure she was dead, but as the years passed and she stayed gone I suppose I got complacent."

She started walking again, and I rushed to keep pace with her.

"How did you get all that from what that Munchkin said?"

"He reminded me of the back gate," she said.

"There is no back gate."

"There most certainly is."

"Then why have I never heard of it?" I scrambled over a fallen log thick with moss. The decaying wood crunched under my foot but didn't give. "I'm the Mayor of Oz."

"There's no reason for the Mayor to know about the gate," Glinda said. "You were unlikely to ever use it. Nobody had in decades. It never crossed my mind to bring it up."

Clement darted around a sapling too tall to trample.

"But what is it? And why does it mean the Wicked Witch is alive?"

Glinda sighed. "The gate is a secret entrance into the Emerald City. It's almost directly opposite the main gate and entirely concealed within the wall. The only people with keys are the Witches of Oz, and neither Locasta nor I have needed to use it since before the Wizard's time. The city was always open to us. The Wicked Witch of the East is well and truly dead—" she raised the muddy emerald ring "—and I happen to know that Locasta is in Gillikin Country protecting it from the Winged Monkeys, just as I was in Quadling Country until yesterday. If the Emerald City gate is closed, and if the city is being controlled by someone who does not have Jakon's best interests at heart, and if the Munchkins and Gale siblings are being held in the Emerald Dungeons..." She waved a hand airily, ordering us to draw our own conclusions.

"That doesn't mean she's the one who closed it," I said. "Whoever it was could have closed the gate after they were already inside."

"Yes, that's probable." Glinda narrowed her eyes and stepped lightly onto a flat boulder, then hopped off the other side. "But it's the Witch. It just is. I feel it in my toes. There's been a nasty flavor to the magic in Oz for a while and it tastes like sulfur and rot."

I glanced at Clement, who shrugged.

"Let's assume it's her," I said. "Did she come back to life?"

"I doubt she ever died," Glinda said. "Dorothy weakened her, there's no doubt about that. But she's a Witch of Oz and magnificently powerful. I suspect she knew she'd met her match in Dorothy and wasn't interested in going head-to-head with her again. She's most likely been hiding, biding her time."

"Until she could come for me."

Glinda's slender eyebrows drew together just a hair, and she pursed her lips.

She wasn't about to say it, but her silence told me the truth: The Wicked Witch of the West didn't see me as a threat.

And, given the situation in the Emerald City, she'd been right to not be concerned.

Dread settled in the pit of my stomach and guilt settled on my shoulders. This was the kind of catastrophe Ma had always been able to keep at bay, and exactly the kind of crisis I wasn't ready to handle.

She had died too young. She had left me too soon. She had given me the most wonderful kingdom in all the world, and I'd done nothing but fail to protect it.

"I don't think the Witch is working alone," Glinda said after a few more minutes of walking. She spoke softly, as much to herself as to us. "I've heard whispers that the Wizard has returned to Oz."

"The Wizard?"

I'd never met him. He'd gone back to Kansas when Ma was a little girl, of course, then ended up in the Land of the Mangaboos some time later, where he'd met up with Ma again. Eventually Glinda had invited him to stay in the Emerald City and had taught him something of real magic, but he was restless. After Princess Ozma had left Oz and handed the city over to Ma, he'd had taken off again, this time on journeys unknown.

I'd always assumed he'd died in the years between then and now. He'd been an old man when Ma was young, and even after becoming a proper Wizard, he was no great Witch. He was still susceptible to age and illness and accident, or so I'd thought.

"Why would he work with the Wicked Witch?" Clement asked. "I thought he was good."

"He's supposed to be," Glinda said. "Unfortunately, one can never be quite sure when it comes to Oscar Diggs."

She marched deeper into the forest, her white coat a beacon amidst the shadows.

Traipsing through the forest was a good deal more pleasant than walking across the deserts of Badalah had been. The ground was uneven here and it took some attention to avoid twisting an ankle, but I didn't mind so long as the shade was deep and the breeze was sweet.

We walked in silence through much of the day, lost in our thoughts. Occasionally one of us would pipe up with a thought: "Maybe the Witch kidnapped the Wizard" or "There's no guarantee it's her; the Monkey King might be behind it all." But for the most part, we were quiet, too focused on getting through the thick undergrowth and considering the thousand possible scenarios that might meet us when we arrived at the Emerald City.

There was no question that we were still headed there, Wicked Witch or not. My siblings pulled me like a magnet, and fear for their eventual fate kept my legs going even when they begged for a rest.

The shadows grew darker overhead, and eventually the sky visible through the thick branches took on a bright orange cast. This was gone almost as soon as it appeared, leaving us in darkness. Glinda pulled out her wand and conjured a glowing bubble that floated along before us and filled the forest nearby with white light and stark shadows. On every side, the forest's nighttime song rose up, crickets and frogs and leaves rustling in the chilly wind.

Then, abruptly, she stopped. The bubble popped. Darkness rushed in.

Ahead of us, deep in the cover of the trees, something growled. My hair stood on end and my heartbeat took off at a gallop. Clement grabbed my hand, his fingers closing like steel bands around mine. He tensed, ready to run.

"Good to see you, too," Glinda called lightly.

The trees before us rustled, and an enormous figure stepped toward us, his body a mass of charcoal curves gleaming against the pitch-black forest.

"Glinda," he rumbled, his voice a low, familiar threat.

I let out an enormous sigh and relief rushed in a thousand tingles across my skin. "Lion!"

Clement tensed even more.

"No," I whispered. "The Lion."

His fingers loosened. I ran forward, heedless of the irregular ground, and threw my arms around the Lion's neck. His mane pressed against my nose with each inhale, ticklish and musky.

"Jakon," he growled. He sniffed me, his huge nose dancing against my neck, and he ran his scratchy tongue affectionately across my face. It was rough enough to scrape my skin.

"I found them in one of the villages at the border," Glinda said. "And not a moment too soon."

"We were worried about you," the Lion said, nudging his nose against my face, checking me for injuries.

"I was worried about me," I admitted. "And all of you."

"We're quite all right," the Lion said.

I tangled my fingers in his mane and scratched the base of his ears, just as he liked. "What are you doing here? You were in Quadling Country when I left."

Left, as if I'd had anything to do with it.

"The Munchkin forests required protecting," the Lion said. "I came as soon as we got word of the Monkey attack. My Lioness stayed home to guard the animals there."

"How is she?"

"Noble and brave," he said, voice rumbling with pride. "And now you should eat and sleep." He nudged me again, almost knocking me off balance. "You smell tired."

The Lion's led us to his den nearby and nudged aside the branches that concealed the round entrance. Glinda sent a few glowing bubbles down into the hole, and they floated dreamily along the earthen ceiling. I crouched and felt my way along the crumbly walls, which sloped quickly downward. Warmth and the scent of fresh dirt greeted me, and in a moment the narrow entrance opened onto a low-ceilinged, round room that glowed in the witch light.

"The foxes dug this for me," the Lion said. "It was very considerate of them."

He prowled to the far end of the small room and sat regally on the floor.

"I haven't got any blankets," he said. "But I'll keep you warm. Come lean against me." He blinked slowly at Clement, who crouched at the mouth of the den. "Who is this?"

"This is Clement," I said. "He's kept me alive these past weeks."

I held out a hand, and Clement, hesitating a bit, stepped forward to take it. I pulled him gently down to sit next to me against the curve of the Lion's body. "Clement, this is the Brave Lion."

Clement's face relaxed a little, and he inclined his head. "The King of the Forest," he said. "Jakon has nothing but good things to say about you, Your Majesty."

"That's because he knows I'll bite him if he doesn't." The Lion chuffed out a laugh.

Clement hesitated, clearly unsure what the noise meant, then chuckled. He leaned up against me and sighed.

Glinda sat near the mouth of the small den, back straight and white coat spread about her. Between the four of us, there was very little room to move around. Ordinarily I would have found it claustrophobic. Tonight, the closeness of my family soothed me.

"Where have you been, Jakon?" the Lion asked.

"It's a long story," I said, and then I told it anyway, skimming over the unpleasant details. The Lion tended toward overprotectiveness, and I had a feeling his services were needed more here than at Urbis Prison, much as I enjoyed the mental image of him tearing into one of the ogre guards.

"You have been a noble companion," the Lion pronounced once I'd related how we'd finally ended up in Munchkin Country. He fixed Clement with his large amber eyes and inclined his head. It was the kind of respectful nod one king might give to another. "Oz owes you a great debt."

"I'm just glad if I could help," Clement said. "And I'm sorry I had to stop Jakon from going to Urbis."

"That seems rather for the best," Glinda said tightly.

I shifted toward her. "Why? What's been happening in Urbis?"

"No one knows," she said cryptically. "That's why I'm cautious." She laced her fingers together and rested them primly on her lap. "What I'd really like to know is what's been happening in the Emerald City. I don't suppose you have any information, Lion? We heard the city has been closed down, but not why or by whom. I imagine you know what happened to the Munchkins?"

"I know they were taken," the Lion growled darkly. "And I know who's responsible."

"The Witch?"

The Lion's eyes widened with surprise for a brief moment, and then he bared his teeth in a snarl.

"I went to the Emerald City to demand the help of the Emerald Army after we heard of the first attack on a Munchkin Village," he said. "Jakon wasn't there, and no one at the palace would answer my inquiries. Me, King of the Forest, treated like a child asking questions out of turn. I left, determined to rid Munchkin Country of the Monkey plague myself. Moments after leaving the city, I turned back to see the Witch of the West descend from the sky and march through the city gates, the Wizard with her. They closed the gates after themselves."

"And you couldn't get back in?"

"I tried. For hours I tried, ramming myself at the gates and attempting to dig beneath the walls. Before evening fell, the Wizard rose from within the city in one of those enormous balloons of his. He floated away. I don't know what he was doing with her or whether he plans to return. For his sake I'd advise him not to." He ended this last word on a low growl that rumbled through his body and vibrated my back.

"If he flew out, couldn't you just fly in?" I asked Glinda. "Or you, Clement. You could turn into a bird and unlock the gates from the inside."

"I wish it were that easy," Glinda said. "The walls around the city prevent people from going to and fro using magic. A witch and a shapeshifter would be entirely rebuffed. The Wizard managed to get out by mechanical means. I don't think any of us have the skills for his kind of humbuggery."

"You've forgotten the back gate," Clement said quietly. "We can still get in. Or Glinda can, at least."

"You'll come with me," Glinda said. "The key opens the door. Then anyone can go through it. That might be our only chance at rescuing the Munchkins."

The Lion's ear twitched. "They are in the city, then?"

"Worse than that," I said. "They're in the Emerald Palace's dungeons. So are my brothers and sisters."

His tail swished abruptly, hard enough to almost knock Glinda sideways.

"Mind that whip of yours, please," she said, sitting back upright.

"Apologies," the Lion growled. "Only I'm rather in a mood to hunt."

"So are we," Glinda said. "And we will. But first these boys need food and sleep. I'll conjure up some supper. You give them enough room to lay down."

The Lion grumbled his agreement, and Glinda pulled out her wand and began chanting a light incantation.

I was asleep before the food appeared.

1ST OCTOBER

I ate well the next morning, revived by a long night of sleep against the Lion's gently heaving side. Glinda tucked into her food with a heartiness that belied her elegant appearance, all the while rehashing everything we knew.

The Emerald City was locked.

All the residents were trapped inside, under the unquestionably cruel rule of the Wicked Witch of the West.

The Wizard had come to the city with her and left on his own, and no one knew why he'd done either.

And, most importantly, the Munchkins and my siblings were still locked in the dungeons. Glinda had confirmed it with another conjured crystal ball, and the look on tiny little Lucy's face had threatened to rip my heart into pieces.

The deck was well and truly stacked against us. I knew I should be afraid, and I was. But it was impossible to give into fear with the Lion next to me. His courage was the stuff of legend, and I felt as if it had seeped into me as we'd slept.

"We'll be all right," Clement said, picking up on my thoughts, as usual. He clapped a hand on my knee and leaned against me. "With a team like this going against her, that Wicked Witch should be quaking in her boots."

"And if we can't intimidate her into submission we'll just throw a bucket of wash water on her head," Glinda said. "It bought us a few decades last time."

"I don't think it was the water," I said.

Glinda acknowledged this with a smile. "The Wicked Witch was scared of your mother. We'll just have to teach her to be scared of you, too."

"You ought to growl at her if you see her," the Lion advised seriously. "That tends to frighten people."

I laughed and scratched his neck under his mane. "I'll give it a try."

The forest was cheerful by the time we set off through it again, though even at midday the shadows here remained deep and green. The Lion made his way between the trees with an uncanny grace. It seemed impossible that any creature so large should be able to traipse in near silence across the forest floor, but he did it, reminding me with each step that he was both the beloved "Uncle Kitten" of my earliest childhood and an apex predator capable of commanding every beast in the forest.

"You still haven't told me much about your new abilities," Glinda said as we walked. Her voice, light and bubbly as ever, held a hint of sternness, as if I could somehow be held accountable for not keeping her up to date on my life from Urbis Prison. She'd used the same tone a couple of years ago when she'd learned from Margaret, rather than me, that I'd finally talked to a boy I'd liked at Ma's annual Emerald Ball.

"I was hoping you'd be able to tell me something," I said. "These powers came out of nowhere."

"Well, you are adopted," she said philosophically, which did nothing to answer any of my questions.

"Did I ever show an inclination for tornadoes when I was little?" I asked.

Her laughter rang out through the trees. "Gracious, no. You were terrified of Dorothy's stories about the tornado that brought you here. A command of cyclones is the last kind of magic I'd have expected you to develop."

She sounded a little too amused.

I cleared my throat. "I wasn't terrified of Ma's stories. I was just worried a tornado might pick up the Emerald Palace and take us all back to Kansas, and I thought the Kansas prairie didn't sound as nice as the Emerald City."

"Where is Kansas, anyway?" Clement asked. "I'd never heard of it before you told me your ma's story."

"No one knows," I said. "Ma always said it was past the edge of the world."

"It's farther than that," Glinda said. "And also closer. It's a matter of dimensions."

Clement's eyebrows wrinkled together. He had no idea what she was talking about. Neither did I. But I'd long ago given up on trying to understand what and where Kansas was. It's boring, Ma had said once when trying to explain it. It's boring and flat and doesn't contain single man-eating plant to my knowledge, and who wants to live in a place like that?

"Shame I don't know how to send the Wicked Witch there," Glinda mused. "I daresay she'd hate it."

Light glimmered up ahead, brighter than anything I'd seen in the forest so far. Beyond the dark silhouettes of the trees, a vast green plain spread out toward the horizon.

We stopped at the edge of the woods. In the middle of the plain, the spires of the Emerald City sparkled up from within the gleaming green walls.

"See?" the Lion said. "The gates are closed. They can't be opened."

"Fortunately, that's no trouble for us," Glinda said. "Come on, this way."

We crept around the edge of the plain, keeping to the cover of the trees. The forest circled the city on all sides, and the vast fields of grass between it and the city rippled in the noon breeze. The sky overhead shone a bright and dreamy blue, nothing about it hinting at the evil at the center of my kingdom.

"You're sure it was the Witch of the West you saw?" I asked the Lion in an undertone. "Not that I'm doubting you, but I'd rather be sure who we're up against."

"A wise precaution," the Lion said. "It was her. It's been many years since my mistreatment at her hands, but hers is a face I couldn't soon forget."

"It's hideous," Glinda said. "Which is not to say that goodness and beauty are always compatriots, for they certainly are not. But the Witch of the West has a sort of ugliness that seems to have boiled up from within."

"She's entirely bloodless, or so you'd think from the shriveled whiteness of her skin," the Lion said.

"And she has one eye," Glinda said. "There's nothing wrong about that, of course, but the eye she's got is a nasty bloodshot thing, and far more powerful than I'd like."

She glanced toward the city. The highest peaks of the palace were visible above the wall. I shrank in on myself, as if doing so could do anything to hide me.

When we reached the opposite side of the city wall, Glinda raised her wand. She cast a shimmering shield of white light around us, which faded after a moment as if it had never been.

"That will conceal us for a few minutes," she said quietly. "Enough time to get from here to the walls. Lion, are you sure you want to come with us?"

He shook out his mane and stepped forward, head thrown back and proud. "She doesn't scare me."

"She scares me." Clement put his hand in mine. "Let's go get her anyway."

Glinda nodded briskly. "In that case: Run."

We took off across the field toward the vast, towering circular wall. I clung to Clement's hand. Glinda jogged out ahead, the tail of her white coat barely skimming the grass, and the Lion brought up the rear, his heavy paws thudding against the earth with each step.

We reached against the wall and Clement and I leaned against it, both breathing hard. The Lion paced back and forth behind us, scanning the skies, and Glinda crouched down at the wall's base.

The huge emerald bricks looked impenetrable to me. They fitted tightly into one another without thick grooves or gooey mortar there to hint at potential weakness. There was no gate here, at least not one my eyes could identify, but Glinda ran her fingers along the bottom of the wall with purpose.

"Ah," she cried softly. She pressed her fingertip into a tiny dent, so small and insignificant I never would have noticed it. She glanced over her shoulder, then pulled off her ring and fitted the emerald into the dent.

It slid in, a perfect key into a perfect lock, and the entire brick jerked downward and sank out of sight, leaving a rectangular crevice in the bottom of the wall.

Glinda put the ring back on her finger.

"Ladies first," she said. "Lion, watch your head. You'll barely fit."

She swung her legs into the crevice, then slipped the rest of her body through the gap. Her shoes clinked lightly against the sunken emerald brick and she turned around to face us. She was buried in the earth almost to her shoulders, but seemed unharmed.

"Quickly, now," she urged, before turning, crouching, and disappearing from sight.

I swallowed and sat on the grass with my legs dangling into the gap. The shadows in the crevice were too deep to allow me to see anything, and Glinda seemed entirely gone. I took a deep breath and pushed myself forward into the hole.

My feet landed on a hard, smooth surface, and I crouched, just as Glinda had. I ducked and moved forward, feeling my way down a gradual slope. When I reached the bottom, I found myself in a glittering, emerald-walled tunnel. Brass lamps, tinted green with the reflection of the walls, hung from the ceiling and gave the corridor a warm glow.

"Welcome to the Witch's Walk," Glinda said, hands on her hips. She looked around, seeming pleased. "It's in excellent shape for having been abandoned all these years."

"The rings?" I said. "The rings were the key?"

"It means the Wicked Witch could come through here same as us," she admitted. "But I doubt she'll bother.

She has control of the main gate. Who needs a tunnel when you have the front door?"

Clement appeared behind me, followed by the Lion, who had to wriggle a little to squeeze his massive body through the dark slope to the tunnel.

Clement let out a low whistle. "This is something. It's so green."

"Wait until you see the Emerald City," I said.

"Let's get to the palace in one piece first," Glinda said. "Once the witch is dealt with we'll have all the time in the world for sightseeing."

"Unless she kills us first," I muttered.

The Lion growled behind me. "We shall not die at the hands of such a cowardly villain as this witch who steals cities without having the courage to face her Mayor head-on. Don't give into fear, Jakon, it won't help you."

Clement grinned. "Yeah, Jakon."

I rolled my eyes, but my heart lightened a little. I'd always been easily hurt when Meggie or servants' children who lived at the palace had teased me. But I loved being teased by Clement. The sparkle in his eyes transformed every jab into a delight.

"Onward," Glinda ordered. "The Lion is right. We don't have time for fear. Our loved ones need saving."

The Witch's Walk was long and full of nonsensical twists and turns. No corridors branched off this winding path, and no variances in the lamps or green walls existed to provide a sense of distance or location. It was dreamlike, this passage, and I was almost able to forget the danger that lay at the end of it.

Eventually, the path sloped up and terminated in a forest-green door with a tiny brass peephole. Glinda stood on her tiptoes and peered through.

"Coast is clear," she said. "But I'm afraid you're all dangerously conspicuous. Hold still."

She pulled out her wand and waved it over our little group. In an instant, Clement's and my clothes melted from shades of brown and cream to greens, and the Lion's gold fur shifted to a bright, grassy hue. Glinda's own white coat and trousers changed to a pleasant mint, and threads of shimmering emerald wove through her red hair.

"Don't you think a lion is still going to catch people's attention?" I asked.

"A lion will," she said, replacing her wand in an inner pocket of her now-colored coat. "But they will not assume he is the Lion." She pursed her lips. "At least, I hope not." She pulled a slender golden rope from her jacket pocket and held it up. "Lion, I'm terribly sorry, but would you mind?"

He raised his head and shook out his mane. "A truly courageous man has nothing to prove," he said proudly. "You may."

He lowered his head, and Glinda, suppressing a smile, slipped the rope around his giant neck and knotted it to form a collar and leash. The Lion submitted graciously.

Glinda turned back to the door, checked the peephole again, and turned the brass handle.

The door opened onto a quiet, dim alley. A few refuse bins and green crates lined the walls; beyond that, the narrow space was empty.

"We're right near Captain Jasper's Smoke Shop and Pearview Park," Glinda said in an undertone. "Jakon, can you lead us to the palace from here? I'll take up the rear and keep an eye out for anyone who might take it in their heads to follow us."

I knew the area; Ma had taken my siblings and me to Pearview Park often, to play in the fountains and climb the fragrant trees. I nodded and slipped ahead. Clement fell in beside me, and the Lion lingered a few paces back, his steps lithe and loping.

Everything seemed normal in the city; or, at least, normal enough. People in green garb bustled down the sidewalks, ducked into shops, and loitered on street corners. Servants in shamrock-patterned dresses or chartreuse caps did the shopping; men and women in pine-green suits and sage top hats adorned with greenery read newspapers outside cafés; shopkeepers in their pale green aprons swept the stoops outside their establishments.

But the air held a tense quiet, and there were no children on the streets.

"No one will look at us," Clement muttered.

I hadn't noticed it until now, but he was right. People walked about as if this were a normal day, but their eyes stayed fixed on the ground. That was wrong. The residents of the Emerald City were famously friendly and notably confident. This was where Ozians came who intended to make a name for themselves, and ordinarily it was impossible to take three steps without receiving at least a smile and a nod or a "Good day, sir!"

"At least you're not likely to get recognized," Clement said.

He had a point. In between my newly tan skin, my overgrown hair, and my outfit that was nothing like the proper attire I usually wore as Mayor of Oz, the chances of anyone recognizing me had been manageable. Now that no one would so much as look my way, they were downright tiny.

A man in a crisp emerald-green suit with gold

braiding marched in front of us. A military cap perched smartly on his head, and a short forest-green cape fluttered out behind him.

I put a hand in front of Clement to stop him, and we let the man go past. He didn't look at us, but even so, my heart sped up a few paces.

"Who was that?" Clement asked under his breath.

"Palace guard," I said.

He glanced sidelong at me. "You don't think they'd help you?"

"Depends on what the Wicked Witch did to them," I said.

Glinda came up behind us and murmured her agreement. "Narcissa has a gift for enslaving and controlling people. We should assume everyone is an enemy until proven otherwise."

"Narcissa?" Clement asked, then waved off his own question. "Wicked Witch, got it."

"It's much too pretty a name for her, I agree," Glinda muttered.

She nudged me in the back, and I kept walking, keeping an eye out for anyone who might be interested in stopping us. The number of guards grew the closer we got to the palace, until finally there seemed to be one on every street corner. A few glanced at the Lion as we walked, but he did an impressive job of slinking and cowering as if Glinda's lightweight leash was capable of doing anything to rein in his magnificent strength.

"Jakon." Clement gestured toward a board outside a pub. It was covered in faded papers in every shade of pale green, each one advertising concerts or lightly used housewares or housekeeping services.

And there, in the center of the board, on a yellow-green page that looked newer than all the rest, my face glared out at me.

WANTED, it said. JAKON GALE FOR CRIMES AGAINST OZ.

My stomach dropped.

"They're everywhere." Clement gestured with his eyes toward the other side of the street, where my face was plastered on the side of a building. Another poster fluttered on a lamppost up ahead.

Suddenly, the protection of my longish hair and traveling clothes didn't feel like enough. I looked down, as if a slight change of angle could possibly do anything to hide my face.

"This throws a wrench in the gears," Glinda said. "I could attempt to make you invisible, but I'm quite sure the Witch has erected wards to prevent that kind of magic from taking effect within the palace walls. She won't take chances."

A guard walked down the sidewalk toward us. I turned and pretended to be looking at a display of top hats in a shop window, and the Lion shielded me with his body. The guard gave him a sharp look as he passed, and the Lion cowered and offered a convincing frightened whine.

"Change of plans," Glinda said. "We can't keep marching to the palace in broad daylight, and we certainly shouldn't attempt to liberate the prisoners today. We need sleep and a strategy. Fortunately, I know where we can find both. Follow me."

She ducked down a side alley. My heart pulled me onward to the palace, but my mind knew better than to go against a Good Witch's orders, so I followed her as she walked with purpose down increasingly narrower streets.

We passed a few pawn shops and a seedy-looking

apothecary with a window full of sinister green glass vials. Abruptly, Glinda stopped and rapped on a tiny dark door tucked between a secondhand shop and a bar with cobwebs at the top of the doorway.

Someone shuffled inside. A moment later, an elderly woman with stooped shoulders and a button nose opened the door and eyed us warily.

"What's this, now?" she murmured, but stepped aside to let us in.

We crowded into a narrow entrance hall with lime-green wallpaper and a series of green coat hooks interspersed among crooked picture frames holding children's drawings. Some of the pictures were yellow with age, others as fresh as if they'd been drawn yesterday.

"This is Mama Jade," Glinda said, unbuttoning her coat. A few white ruffles peeked out from beneath its sleek lines. "She is without question the most important person in Oz at this moment."

"I don't like the sound of that," Mama Jade said, taking us in with a cautious squint. "Who's all this, now?" Her brilliant green eyes sharpened as she looked at me. "Don't tell me. It isn't Dorothy's boy?"

I held out a hand. "Jakon Gale, ma'am."

She took my hand in both of hers and gave it a motherly shake and a pat. She peered up at me, the top of her frizzy gray head barely tall enough to reach my chest.

"I daresay that's why you're here," she said to Glinda. "He's not supposed to be in the city. Word is she had him sent clear out of the country."

"She did, and our intrepid young Mayor found his way right back," Glinda said.

Mama Jade narrowed her eyes at the Lion. "You

must be the one they call King, then, for all that green on your coat."

The Lion inclined his great shaggy head to her.

"So who's this?"

"Clement Augustin, ma'am," Clement said, holding out his hand. "A friend of Jakon's."

She answered by clasping his hand and giving him the same shake-and-pat she'd given me. "Then you're welcome, whatever it brings down on my head."

Glinda removed her coat and placed it on one of the wall hooks. "You'll have nothing brought on your head if all goes according to plan. We only need a bed for the night."

"That I can provide. The Wizard knows I've got enough of them. You're lucky you came when you did, I'm between flocks at the moment."

Glinda smiled warmly, her eyes sparkling, and turned to the rest of us. "Mama Jade is a refuge in a storm for a great many children in this city," she explained. "She takes in foster children when the orphanages overflow and helps find homes for them."

I hesitated, memories clicking into place in my head. "You're the Stork Lady," I blurted.

Mama Jade's face cracked into a broad smile.

"The what?" Clement said.

I looked at the squat little woman with fresh eyes. There she was, the lady from Ma's stories, with her button nose and laugh-lined eyes and string of lime-green beads around her neck.

"She brought Ether and Gertrude and Chester and Lucy to our family," I said. "Ethel and Gertrude spent most of their early years in a Quadling orphanage until the Stork Lady told Ma about them. And she brought Chester after his father died when he was a baby, and saved Lucy after her parents were killed in a wagon accident in Munchkin Country."

"That's right," Mama Jade said. "I'd have kept bringing her little ones if she hadn't taken ill, witches rest her soul. She had a heart and a palace big enough for all of them."

My eyes burned, and suddenly Mama Jade's face swam through a screen of hot tears. I blinked them back and looked toward the pictures on the walls. Their colorful scribbled lines wobbled.

Mama Jade's soft hands closed around mine again. "She was a good lady and no mistake. And now her son needs a bed, which is something I can give."

She turned and led the way up a dark, rickety flight of stairs with each step painted a different shade of green. The brush strokes were visible and clumsy, with paint smudged up onto the walls on either side.

"You'll have a good meal, too," she continued. "And we'll keep all the curtains closed just in case those nasty Monkeys take to flying around the city again."

"Oh?" Glinda said.

Mama Jade wrinkled her little nose. "They like to circle around in the evenings. Can't tell if they're looking for something or just trying to stretch those great vile wings of theirs. Either way we're lucky; they don't come down these poor streets much."

She tossed a grin over her shoulder, and then we were at the top of the stairs and in a bright, cluttered kitchen lit by swinging brass lamps.

Mama Jade seemed skilled at putting together a feast at a moment's notice, using whatever was in the cupboard. She rummaged through her pantry and soon had us all working, peeling carrots and chopping potatoes. I volunteered to dice the onions; it was good to have an excuse as to why my eyes kept watering.

"Is everyone in the Emerald City this nice?" Clement asked, mincing up garlic beside me.

He was good with a knife, I noticed. Perhaps he'd enjoyed cooking in his old life.

There was so much I still didn't know about him. I hoped silently for a future that would give me time to learn it all. Then I hoped he'd want to stick around that long.

"I don't know about everyone," I said. "But we're a decent lot in Oz. At least when a Wicked Witch isn't ruining things."

"If this is what it's like when things are ruined, I can't wait to see what they're like when you're in charge." He grinned. "The Emerald City is beautiful. I wish I'd had more time to appreciate it today."

"Is that why you're still sticking with me?" I said. "Hoping for a chance to enjoy the architecture?"

"That's most of it. I'm a sucker for a good colonnade."

I chuckled, but the laughter was superficial, even forced. I let it die and searched his face.

"You know you don't have to come with me tomorrow, right?" I said. "You can stay here. I'm sure Mama Jade wouldn't mind."

His eyebrows twitched, and his smile faded. "Do you not want me? I might be able to help."

"What I want doesn't matter," I said. "It's just... You don't have to feel like it's an obligation. This isn't your kingdom or your fight." I glanced toward the window, where patterned green curtains shielded us from the view of the street. "We're risking our lives just being in the city. You don't have to put yourself in danger for people you don't even know."

His expression softened. Another lump rose up into

my throat, this one hard and pulsing with my heartbeat.

It wasn't that I didn't love having him here. But him being here was more than I had any right to ask for. He could have a life back in Enchantia. He could have a life here, if he wanted, and he didn't have to pay for it with his safety.

"I just mean that I don't expect anything from you," I said. "You don't have to risk everything for political asylum. You'll have that either way as soon as I get my throne back from the Witch. I made a promise."

"That's not why I'm planning on going with you tomorrow."

"Then why?" I demanded. "Why are you risking your life for people you don't even know?"

"Do you really have to ask?"

The words settled around us. I knew what he was implying, but I couldn't make sense of it—couldn't understand why he'd put himself in such danger for someone as silly and frightened and troubled as me.

He was handsome and strong and smart. He knew how to tell a good story and understood his magic in a way I doubted I'd ever understand mine. He was kind and generous and had looked out for me from the first moment we'd met.

Meanwhile, I couldn't even think about my mother without crying like a child.

Why would he even think to put his safety in my hands, when we were up against someone as strong as the Wicked Witch?

Clement leaned close under pretense of sliding his garlic into a small bowl, until his lips almost touched my ear.

"Where you go, I follow. To the ends of the earth if it comes to that."

"It's dangerous. You heard what Glinda said, the Wicked Witch isn't even scared of me. What if—"

"What if I spend my life running away from the one person who makes it feel worth living?"

His words hung in the air, a challenge and a solution.

"I'm not going anywhere, Jakon." He brushed his lips against the side of my head in a kiss so gentle it might have been a breeze. "Not unless it's by your side."

2ND OCTOBER

We got up early while the streets were still quiet. Mama Jade pushed spinach and cheese tarts into our hands as we lined up in the lime-green hallway and whispered at us to be safe, and Glinda poked her head out the front door and sent a discreet spell in either direction.

"We're clear for at least a block," she murmured over her shoulder. "That'll get us to Celadon Street, and then we can cut through an alley to Myrtle. Viridian Avenue will be the real challenge."

"We can avoid it and go in through the back," I suggested. "There's a servants' entrance just off Reseda."

She nodded and slipped through the door. The rest of us fell in with the Lion bringing up the rear. His tail whipped back and forth, low to the ground.

Tall green buildings jutted upward on every side, as sharp as the peaks of Aboria. Light shone from a window here and there, but for the most part, the city still slept. Beyond the high peaks of the skyscrapers, the early-morning sky roiled with black clouds.

I had the advantage of stunning views from all through the Emerald Palace, but from down here on the ground, the looming buildings seemed about to collapse in upon us. And that was good. The more the buildings shielded us, the better our chances of staying hidden.

We kept to the walls and scurried like rats, relying on the shadows and our own silence to get us to the palace in one piece.

Guards patrolled, even at this early hour, but it was no great trick for Glinda to cast shielding spells that lasted long enough for us to dart from one hiding place to another. Even so, I cringed every time I saw one of those caped uniforms or heard their boots clicking against the green granite sidewalks.

My heart pounded as we approached the Emerald Palace. Unlike most castles, it wasn't shielded from the rest of the city by a gate or moat or sprawling lawn. Instead, the building took up several blocks in the heart of the city, its smooth emerald walls flush against the sidewalk. The palace walls along Reseda Street were pockmarked; people had come to chip off pieces of emerald when Ma had first transformed the city, either to take as souvenirs or sell as precious stones. Locasta had put a stop to that soon enough with a charm, but no one had ever tried to patch up the irregular holes.

The servants' entrance was an unassuming dark green door, marked only with a brass plaque reading PRIVATE. I reached for the handle.

Glinda caught my arm.

"Shouldn't touch an outside door," the Lion growled softly behind me. "She'll have cursed it to keep you out."

"We'd better not try, either," Glinda said. "She'd as soon light me on fire as let me through, and I can't say she likes the Lion any better. But she doesn't know you." She raised her eyebrows at Clement.

He squared his shoulders and reached for the latch. It opened easily, and we hurried inside and into a hallway lined with lockers and coat racks—an entrance hall for any servants who didn't live at the palace full-time.

A single housemaid stood in front of one of the lockers. She froze with her apron halfway tied and stared at us.

"Glinda!" she exclaimed, then clapped a hand over her own mouth. "Sorry, Your Witchiness," she added, though the words were more of a mumble between her fingers.

She lowered her hand and locked eyes with me, then dropped into a sudden awkward curtsy that sent her frilled green cap tumbling halfway off of her head.

"Mayor Jakon," she whispered, panic and hope warring on her face. She was Margaret's age, maybe a year or two younger. "You're back. You're here. You're alive. You mustn't be seen."

"It is the Wicked Witch, then?" I whispered back, my voice barely more than a breath.

She nodded, face draining of color. "She's horrid, Your Mayorness. She said you were dead. She told everyone you'd been killed by her Monkeys."

"Where is she?"

"In the Grand Hall," she said. "She spends almost all her time in there, performing wicked magic and commanding those hideous creatures of hers. But she's got guards all over the palace. The building's crawling with them."

"Are they my guards?" I whispered. "Or hers?"

"Hard to say," she said. "They were yours, once. I know their faces. But there's nothing behind their eyes no more."

It was only as much as I'd expected, and yet hearing it aloud twisted my stomach until I felt ready to vomit.

"We mustn't kill any of them if we can help it," Glinda said.

"They're traitors to Oz," the Lion rumbled.

"They haven't a choice," she said sharply. "Nor any control over their actions at the moment. You can knock them out cold with a swipe of your paws or carry them by the back of their uniforms and lock them into closets, but no biting."

The Lion grumbled his reluctant agreement. The housemaid watched him with wide, fascinated eyes.

"You'll run into fewer guards if you use the servants' stairs," she offered. "She doesn't much bother to have the guards watch us. She figures we're all too scared to fight her." She straightened her shoulders. Her disheveled cap and half-tied apron did little to ruin the effect. "Well, she's wrong. I'll go with you."

I put a hand on her arm. "You mustn't."

"I want to help."

"And you will," Glinda said. "Who else is awake?"

"Most everybody's awake, but almost nobody's at their posts," the maid said. "I came early to get a head start on some of the Witch's mending. She tears holes in her clothes just to have people fix them for her, and beats us if we don't get them straightened up right away."

Glinda rolled her eyes. "Charming as ever, and thank goodness she's saving her energy for the important things." She scoffed, then composed herself and took the housemaid's hands. "We're about to charge through this palace with magic a-blazing, and I can't bear the thought of any of you innocents getting caught in the crossfire. Stay here. Warn anyone who comes into work to keep away from the Grand Hall."

"What about the servants who live here?" the girl asked. "I can't tell them all."

"They'll have to fend for themselves, I'm afraid. You help whoever you can and leave the rest to us."

The maid nodded and straightened her cap.

"You can count on me," she promised.

Her courage, such as it was, overwhelmed me. She hadn't asked to be in this situation. Anyone with an instinct for self-preservation would have run the moment they saw me, or rushed to tell the powerful Witch who sat on my throne that she was under attack. But this housemaid, several years my junior and with none of my power or support, was ready to do whatever she could to help me.

I took her hand and inclined my head to kiss it, bowing to her as I would have to any queen.

"You're the backbone of Oz," I said.

Her cheeks flushed bright pink.

"I'm just doing my job, sir," she stammered.

"And isn't that incredible," Glinda said kindly.

The maid blushed even more deeply. Clement suppressed a smile and took my arm, steering me around and toward the other end of the hall.

"Better give her space," he murmured, a laugh bubbling beneath his words.

Glinda strode up ahead of us and stopped in front

of the door. She put her hands on her hips and turned around, scanning the hall with her sharp blue eyes. After a moment, she raised her hand and crooked a finger.

From across the room, a sturdy green umbrella flew from a jade umbrella stand and landed in her grasp. She held it out to Clement.

"It's not much, as wands go," she said. "And you've no time to bond with it. But a little unpredictability might help when it comes to firing spells at a Wicked Witch. After all, Dorothy melted her with a bucket of water once, and who could have expected that?"

Clement, looking unconvinced, took the umbrella. He turned it over in his hands, feeling the sturdy forest green canvas and carved green glass handle. After a moment, he shrugged and propped it up over his shoulder.

He nodded to Glinda, and she nodded to me, and the Lion pawed the ground eagerly behind us all. Glinda opened the door and strode forward into the palace.

She managed to knock out two of the guards we passed before they even saw us. A third opened his mouth to sound an alarm and was promptly silenced by one firm swipe of the Lion's paw, and a fourth fell asleep in the middle of a corridor after Clement flourished the umbrella in his general direction.

By the time we reached the Grand Hall, I dared to feel almost confident in spite of the pounding of my heart.

"Remember, leave her to me at first," Glinda whispered, just around the corner from the Grand Hall. "For all she knows, you three are powerless against her. Once I've got her engaged, Clement, you jump in and cast whatever you've got her way, and Jakon—"

"I'll imprison her in a tornado," I said, reciting the plan she'd made me memorize last night. "I'll pin her at the top of it while you and Clement throw every spell you've got in her direction."

"Remember, I can't kill her," Glinda said quietly. "The Witches of Oz can't move against one another, not to the death."

"Fortunately I have no such restrictions," the Lion growled.

She pressed her lips together and nodded. "Let's go."

We sprinted toward the Grand Hall's tall double doors. Glinda disposed of the guard on the left with a quick immobilizing charm, and Clement knocked out the one on the right with a flourish of his umbrella, the tip of which sent a stream of sparks directly into the man's face until he dropped, unconscious, to the corridor floor. Red burns streaked across his skin, but he seemed otherwise unharmed.

"Oops," Clement whispered. "Wasn't what I planned."

"Still not bad for umbrella magic," I muttered.

Glinda burst through the double doors, wand aloft and coat swirling behind her.

"Wicked Witch of the West, your time of reckoning has come," she declared, her voice echoing up into the room's vaulted emerald ceilings.

The Witch, lounging on the throne at the far end of the room, didn't so much as twitch. She fixed me with her one bloodshot eye; the emerald walls on every side tinted her sickly yellow skin with a hint of green.

"I'm surprised it took you this long to get here," she said.

Her voice, calm though it was, prickled my skin like nails on a chalkboard. There was something deeply unpleasant about the way her words creaked on the vowels and hit the consonants with too much force; it was as if she had never learned how to speak and instead had to force the words out in a mechanical approximation of language.

Fear rippled down my spine. I thought back to the housemaid, ready to risk her life for my, and steadied my feet against the floor.

"You've been telling everyone I was dead."

"Mm," she said. "Yes."

She kept staring at me. The sclera of her eye was mottled yellow and red, the pupil a sickly yellow-brown the color of mud.

"I've come to take my throne back."

She blinked, her eyelid so thin I could make out the pupil beneath it. "Have you, now?"

I took a step forward in spite of everything in my body hollering at me to retreat. Evil power radiated from her; the whole room felt poisoned with it. I could do nothing against a creature this ancient and wicked, but I had to try, because if I didn't fight her, Chester and Lucy might have to. That thought was unbearable.

"He's not alone," Glinda said.

She pointed her wand at the witch. A stream of bubbles erupted from the tip at the Wicked Witch's wrinkled, papery face. I winced, anticipating Narcissa's reaction to such a feeble attack. She shot to her feet with a yelp as angry red welts rose up across her skin.

"This isn't your fight, princess," she snarled at Glinda, stepping down from the throne dais.

"All of Oz is my fight, you wicked old thing," Glinda snapped.

She lifted her wand again, but this time, Narcissa was ready. She strode forward, fingers raised and gnarled. A brass brazier full of hot coals flew across the room and spilled in Glinda's path, sending a trail of burning embers hurtling toward her.

"Jakon!" Clement shouted, swishing his umbrella wildly through the air.

A bucket shimmered into being in front of me, full to the brim with rippling water.

He'd meant for me to use it to douse the coals, I was sure, but I had a better idea. I picked it up and bolted down the length of the room, holding the bucket aloft.

I sloshed the contents of the bucket square into the Wicked Witch of the West's hideous face.

Water soaked her hair and dripped down her hooked nose. It drenched her black gown and pooled into a puddle at her feet, and she gaped at me in horror.

"I'm melting!" she screamed, her voice hideous and twisted.

And then she laughed, throwing her head back and cackling, until the echoes of her laughter multiplied and filled the room with the screeching of a dozen banshees.

"You're an idiot," she said. "An idiot descended from an idiot. Your fool mother tried the same trick and thought she'd killed me, stupid child that she was. I can see the apple hasn't fallen far from the tree."

"It damaged you badly enough," Glinda said with a grimace.

Beside her, the Lion growled loudly enough to raise the hairs on the back of my neck.

"That was a character failing," Narcissa said. "I've remedied it."

She raised her hand and, with a twitch of one crooked finger, threw a fireball at Glinda's head. Glinda encased the flames in an enormous bubble and snuffed them out. Narcissa threw another fireball, this one at me. Clement threw himself in front of me and opened his umbrella; the fire smashed against the canvas and fizzled out.

The Lion let out an enormous roar.

His huge body galloped past us, all muscle and rage. The Wicked Witch snapped her fingers, and a wall of flames roared up and immobilized him in a ring of fire. He roared again, but the heat was hurting him; he tucked his tail in close and cowered, drawing his fur as far from danger as possible.

I grabbed Clement's arm. "You have to help him."

He shook his head, jaw tight. "He'll be all right for the moment. I'm here to protect you."

"The rightful Mayor has come to take back his throne," Glinda said, striding toward the Witch with her wand outstretched. "You can give it to him now and hope to live to see another day, or this morning will be your last."

Narcissa cackled. "You're not permitted to kill me, Glinda, dear, and neither of these two even could."

She flicked her fingers again and drove a stream of flame toward Clement and me. Again, Clement shielded us both with the umbrella. The green glass handle shimmered with bright magic under his hand as he forced it to resist the flames. Even with all his efforts, the heat from the fire stole my breath.

I raised my hands, prepared to surprise Narcissa with my powers, but Clement shook his head.

"Let Glinda wear her out a little," he muttered. "Then she and I can hit her full-force. Besides, Glinda and I have to douse the flames around the Lion first, otherwise your tornado might kill us all."

I clenched my fists. "You may have to finish her off. Are you prepared for that?"

Clement gritted his teeth and leaned forward against

the witch's barrage of flames. "For you? Absolutely. Though I wouldn't be upset if you managed to throw her headfirst against a wall."

My stomach seized. I had never committed that kind of violence against another person, not ever.

But I could do it today. My memory of little Chester's tear-streaked face was reason enough.

Clearly deciding enough was enough, Glinda interrupted Narcissa's jet of fire with a stream of bubbles that boiled toward the flames and smothered the fire as fast as Narcissa could conjure it.

The witches battled back and forth, flame and water and sparks flying in the air all around us. Clement joined in, flailing his umbrella and firing jets of white light that hit the witch and made her cry out in pain.

And all the while, I stood back and watched, clenching my fists and feeling the magic build within them.

The ribbons of air in this room were a tangled mass of hot and cold, fast and slow, but I could coax them to order. I could tame this mess and use it for my own purposes.

I unclenched my hands. Tingles raced across my palms and up my fingers.

"Clement," I shouted. "Help the Lion."

He met my eyes, reading my intentions, and nodded. He conjured bucket after bucket of water and threw them onto the flames around the Lion. It was slow going; the witches ignored him, locked in their own brutal combat.

Narcissa shielded herself from Glinda's attacks with a sickly yellow cloud of smoke. It smelled of sulfur and rot. I choked on it, the magic in my hands fading. Glinda coughed, wand still raised.

"He's not here for the throne," Narcissa said from

behind the wall of roiling smoke. "Are you, little mayor? You're here for your brothers and sisters."

Fury boiled up inside me, drowning my fear. I would murder her. I would throw her to the wall and crack her spine across my throne. I would smear her remains across the emerald walls of this palace and throw whatever was left out the nearest window.

And then, and only then, would I go find my siblings and welcome them back to a world where the Wicked Witch of the West could do no more harm.

I tugged on the air. A few hot current shifted toward me, but they brought smoke with them that clawed down my throat and scratched my lungs. Across the room, Glinda doubled over, wheezing as she tried to catch her breath.

"Only they're not your real brothers and sisters, are they?" the Wicked Witch called. "Your real family is traipsing across the twelve kingdoms right now, most likely halfway to Urbis."

I froze.

The queen of Aboria had hinted as much. I'd considered the possibility—accepted it, even.

But Narcissa knew?

A dozen sickening possibilities raced through my mind like so much debris in a tornado. Narcissa had scattered my birth family. Narcissa was my birth mother. Narcissa intended to use my birth siblings, these strangers, in some hideous plot to fracture magic across the kingdoms and steal my throne and my true family from under my nose.

My hands, halfway raised before me, trembled.

What did she know?

What had she been hiding?

"I don't belie—" I started, and then my arms were

wrenched behind my back.

The rank, moist breath of a Winged Monkey warmed my ear.

I hadn't heard them coming. I hadn't paid enough attention, and if Glinda or Clement had noticed, I'd been too much a fool to listen for their warning voices.

The creature panted, then let out a grating screech. Other screeches answered on either side. Monkeys had Clement and Glinda, too, and four of them had thrown an enormous net over the Lion that bound him in spite of his snapping jaws and flailing paws. Slight flames still flickered around him; flames and pools of water that spread across the emerald floor. Glinda's wand was nowhere to be seen, but Clement's umbrella lay on the ground in front of him, the green canvas crumpled and one of the spokes broken and bent.

"Take them to the dungeons," Narcissa said, triumph deforming her papery face. "Add the Lion to my menagerie. Throw the others in a cell." She met my eye and smiled, baring a mouth full of rotting yellowed teeth. "You tried, little mayor. Comfort yourself with that."

The monkey behind me yanked on my arms and dragged me from the room.

⁓

I paced the small, sparse green room where the Monkeys had thrown the three of us. Calling it a room was generous: This place was a box. There were no windows here, no bars, and no doors besides the one a Monkey had locked with a large brass key.

The dungeons beneath the Emerald Palace were sprawling; I had no way to tell from here where my siblings and the Munchkins were being held, and no way to get from this room to that one.

"You stashed your wand right under her nose. Are you sure you can't just magic the door open?" I asked Glinda for what had to be the fifth time.

"I don't dare," she said, with the patience only a being as old as time itself could muster. "The Witch will have placed a curse on the door preventing my magic from working on it."

"Best case scenario, it does nothing," Clement said from where he sat with his back against the wall. "Worse case scenario, it kills us."

"Witches can't kill witches."

"I mean you and me," he said.

"And then I'll have to sit in this horrid little room with your corpses," Glinda said. "I'd rather not."

I'd rather not do a lot of things. I'd rather not stay locked up in this oppressive green box, eerily lit by lights buried deep within the translucent walls. I'd rather not be imprisoned in my own palace. I'd rather not live in a world where shattered magic forced kingdoms into poverty and violence and I'd rather not have maybe-siblings out there in the world doing the-Wizard-knew-what.

And, speaking of the Wizard, I'd rather he hadn't teamed up with the Wicked Witch to take over the city in the first place.

Even if he'd been coerced, there was nothing and no one who could have made me turn against my city like that.

I slammed a hand against an emerald wall, which did nothing but make my palm ache. "I could try to rip the door off its hinges with a tornado."

Clement made a face. "What are the chances you crack our heads open in the process?"

"Exorbitantly high." Glinda was sitting not far from Clement with her back to the wall and her legs stretched out in front of her. The fabric of her coat spread out like a blanket beneath her slender white trousers. She smoothed the material and stretched out her fingers.

These gestures, small as they were, passed as restlessness for the ever-composed Good Witch. I wasn't sure whether to be relieved or terrified that she was upset by all this.

"Darling, you may as well sit," Glinda said.

"I can't."

I kept marching from one side of the cell to another, then back again.

A key slid into the lock on the door and I tripped over my own feet. I skittered away, palms tingling.

I'd expected a Monkey, or at least one of the palace guards Narcissa had magicked into a mindless automaton.

Instead, the Wicked Witch herself stood in the doorway.

"Jakon," she said. "Come with me."

"I will not."

"You will," she said. "Or I can kill your boy toy. It's up to you." She cast Clement a dismissive look, her bloodshot eye barely lingering on his face.

"Jakon, you don't—" he started.

"Fine," I said.

I still had my magic. Perhaps I'd find a moment to use it against her.

She held the door open and waited for me to go through, then locked it behind us. She strode down the high-ceilinged emerald corridor, boots clicking on the faintly glowing green floor.

"Well?" she said.

I fell in a step behind her.

"If you're going to kill me you may as well stage a public execution," I snapped. "Let the Ozians know exactly what kind of reign to expect."

She considered this for a moment. I had time to regret my words, and also to realize I'd meant them. A public execution would take time to arrange, and we needed nothing if not time.

"I'm not ready to kill you," she said at last. "I will eventually, but not yet."

She kept walking. Other corridors branched off from this one, all identical, forming a maze that only the most experienced guards could navigate without a map. Ma had built the dungeons like this on purpose, to deter the rare criminal from escaping. I wondered if she'd have put so much thought into her plans if she'd known I'd eventually become their victim.

"The thing is, it would be a dreadful shame to kill you before you knew the truth of your pitiful life," Narcissa said. "Your self-righteous little mother pushed me into years of misery. I'd be doing her memory a disservice if I didn't pass on her generosity."

To my left, a far-away, high-pitched cry echoed along a cavernous corridor. The witch turned briskly in the other direction, grabbing my arm and digging in her nails as she dragged me away from the noise.

"I don't know what you're talking about." I wrenched my arm away.

"Yes, that's the point. You are your mother's idiot, aren't you, boy?"

I didn't give her an answer. She didn't deserve one.

"Here's the truth," the witch said. "Take it as you will. Glinda, the so-called Good Witch of Oz, was responsible for your mother's death."

She let the words sink in. I didn't believe them, not for a second.

"Of course she was," I said. "That's what everyone calls her behind her back, isn't it? Glinda the Murderer. Glinda the Mayor Killer. With all due respect, Narcissa, if you think that's the most evil rumor you could plant in my brain, you've lost your touch."

She fixed her bloodshot eye on me. "It's the truth. Ask her yourself."

"Sure, I will," I muttered. "Right after I confirm that she's been commanding the Winged Monkeys and discover proof that she stole my bicycle when I was six."

"No one is all Good," Narcissa said with a sneer. "It's possible to be all Wicked. But nobody, not even almighty Glinda, has managed the other thing."

She came to a stop, and I realized with a jolt that we were back outside the door of my cell.

"Right," I said. "Well, thanks for the talk. It's been enlightening."

I wasn't normally sarcastic like this, not when I was afraid. But something about her face—about knowing that she was sitting on my throne and commanding my people—lit a fire in me that was hotter than any of the ones she'd thrown about upstairs.

"You don't have to believe me," Narcissa said. "I'm sure it'll be easier for you if you don't. After all, everyone always says Mayor Jakon is a bit of a coward. And the truth is terrible."

Anger boiled up in the pit of my stomach again. I opened my mouth to retort, but Narcissa had already opened the door. She grabbed me by the arm, again digging her nails in so hard they hurt me even through the fabric of my shirt, and threw me back into the cell.

I stumbled forward and landed on my hands and

knees, hard enough that I knew it would leave bruises. Narcissa slammed the door behind me.

Clement scrambled over to help me up.

"What did she want?" he asked, fear and relief battling it out across his face.

I massaged my knees, wincing. "Not much. Just trying to scare me." I glanced over at Glinda, who was watching me with her lips pursed and eyebrows drawn together in concern. "She tried to convince me you killed Ma."

Glinda blanched.

"It's such an absurd lie," I said, hobbling across the room with Clement supporting me. "We knew she was evil. Now we know she's stupid, too. Maybe we can use that to our advantage."

Glinda looked down at the floor. I stopped, my heart aching in sympathy.

"It's all right, Glinda. Don't worry. I'd never believe something like that."

"Thank you, Jakon," she said with a gentle smile. "You're kind to believe the best of me." She took a deep breath, then swallowed and looked at the floor again.

Something about her expression stopped me in my tracks. I watched her face, my stomach sinking.

"Glinda?"

"Yes?"

"Are you all right?"

She pressed her lips together and her delicate eyebrows drew close.

"Jakon, darling, this isn't the best time or place for this conversation." She took a deep breath. "But I suppose we'd better have it anyway."

I hesitated. I wanted to tell her that it was all right, that we didn't have to have any kind of conversation right now except for the one where we all came up with ideas on how to best escape this miserable prison cell.

But I couldn't make myself say the words, not when her eyes were shimmering with tears.

"Glinda?" I said again.

Don't say it, I urged her silently. Don't. Don't.

"My love, it's true. I didn't mean to kill Dorothy, but I did it."

I stared at her.

The seconds passed, first crawling and then racing and then crawling again.

Glinda's bottom lip trembled. She swallowed, the tiny movement of her pale greenish throat suddenly huge and meaningful. A sudden tear trailed down her cheek, sparkling like an emerald in the eerie green light, and she wiped it away with the sleeve of her coat.

I kept staring.

Finally, with as much effort as it would have taken me to tunnel straight through the emerald walls and to freedom, I managed to form a single sentence.

"What do you mean?"

She bit her lip and another tear spilled out. "I'm so sorry, Jakon. It was an accident."

An accident.

Ma, dead, was an accident.

Horror surged up within me and wrangled a cry from my throat. Heat flooded my palms, magic so hot it threatened to burn my skin.

"What do you mean?" My voice sounded like it belonged to someone else. "What happened? What did you do? What did you do?"

I couldn't believe it. I shouldn't. I didn't want to.

But damn the Wizard and the Yellow Brick Road, her face didn't hold a hint of a lie.

Rage joined horror, and I stepped toward her, suddenly aware of my height and my strength. She had a wand, but I had anger.

Stars, did I have anger.

I raised my hands without thinking. The air in the room sprang to life, streams of it whipping her curls across her face. Her hair, ordinarily as bright as a flame, was almost black in the dim green light, and something about that felt right, that she should look so different in this moment.

"Jakon," Clement said.

His voice barely made a dent in the roaring in my ears—or was that the roaring of the wind? I couldn't tell. It didn't matter. The wind picked up, and Glinda opened her mouth and closed it again as if she couldn't breath against the gale.

"Jakon!" Clement snapped.

He threw his hands toward the floor and a translucent white wall burst up between Glinda and me, sealing her in on one side and Clement and me on the other.

The wind on her side of the wall died down, and she gasped for breath. I could just make out her face through the white curtain.

Someone was screaming, and it took some time to realize the someone was me.

"What did you do? How could it be an accident? You're a Good Witch. Ma trusted you! I trusted you! How could you?"

Clement sat, quiet and unmoving, and on the other side of the wall, Glinda began to sob.

My legs crumpled beneath me, and suddenly, my words were gone. The wind stopped blowing. I sat on the hard emerald floor, knees drawn up to my chest, and stared through the white wall at Glinda.

She met my gaze. "I'm so sorry," she whispered.

I held up a hand. Magic and fury still throbbed just beneath my skin.

"No," I said. "Just... no."

She pressed her lips together and nodded, and we sat like that for a long time, Clement's white wall shimmering silently between us.

3RD OCTOBER

Fatigue clung to my bones when I awoke some time later. I didn't know when I'd fallen asleep, or how. My head was cradled on Clement's lap, and Glinda was still watching me through the barrier, her tears now dry and her face full of an unbearable concern.

Clement stroked the side of my face, his touch gentle and full of kindness.

I didn't deserve his kindness.

I opened my mouth. Nothing came out.

"Hush, love," he whispered, bending over me. "Give yourself a moment."

"I shouldn't have—"

"She knows," he said.

"I was so angry."

"I know," he said, smoothing my hair. "We both do."

Slowly, I sat up. Shame filled me. I forced myself to meet Glinda's gaze anyway.

"My sweet boy," she said, her voice muffled by the curtain of magic. "I'd hoped you wouldn't find out like this."

Answers sprang to my lips: When were you going to tell me? Were you going to tell me? Why? Why? Why?

I didn't trust myself to speak any of them aloud. I wasn't sure what else might come out.

I took a few slow, deep breaths: one, two, three, four, out, two, three, four.

Clement rubbed small circles on my back, as he might have for a small child who'd just woken from a nightmare.

"Would you lower the wall?" I asked after a long moment. "I want to talk to her."

He took one of my hands and pressed his palm against mine. It took me a moment to realize what he was doing.

"My magic is under control," I said. "I can feel it tingling but I'm not going to do anything."

"Still, I think maybe a window might be better." He laced his fingers between mine. "I trust you, but a little distance might make it easier."

I swallowed and nodded.

Clement crept toward the wall and held a hand out. His face contorted with focus; it was difficult for him to use magic without a wand.

A circular gap opened in the shimmering white wall, exactly the right height for Glinda and I to see one another while remaining seated.

She twisted her hands in her lap. Caution tightened her face, and she watched me, waiting for me to take the next step.

I folded my hands in my lap, too, twining my fingers together as if that would keep the magic under control.

"Tell me everything," I said, in a voice as calm and measured as I could muster. It still shook. "Please."

Glinda hesitated for a long moment, searching my face, her eyes darting back and forth, dark in the emerald light.

"What I'm about to tell you will change everything," she said. "Are you prepared for that?"

"You just told me you murdered my mother," I said, before I could stop the words. "I think I can deal with anything else you'd like to throw at me."

I pressed my lips together and looked down at the ground, focusing on one point in the shimmering emerald floor until I was sure I had my tongue back under control.

"I killed your mother," Glinda said, voice tight. "Not murdered."

"Is there a difference?"

"Yes, child, and it's vast."

I took another deep breath. Clement settled back beside me and placed a comforting hand on my knee.

"I want to know the truth," I said at last. "Whatever it is."

"Very well," she said. "I'd planned to tell you this story eventually. It's important that you know that. I hoped you'd have more time to get your feet under you. To grieve Dorothy. To become comfortable ruling Oz." She lifted her hands, palms up. "We don't always get what we want."

It was the understatement of the century. I pressed my tongue to the roof of my mouth to force back a sharp retort.

"The truth is, you were brought to Dorothy as a baby," she said. "You know that part. What you don't know is who brought you and why."

"Does Narcissa know this?" I interrupted.

"It seems she does. It shouldn't come as a surprise. She has access to many of the same arcane arts I do."

"So you both knew? But no one bothered to tell me?"

Glinda acknowledged the terrible truth with a silent nod.

"Let her talk," Clement murmured.

"You were brought to Dorothy by two women," Glinda continued. "One young and one old. They told Dorothy your story, that you born from a dalliance between a goddess and a human."

I frowned. That was ludicrous.

And then, as quickly as I had first doubted her story, I believed it. Why else would the powers of storms and cyclones spring to my fingertips at my slightest command? It made sense that I would be a goddess's castoff. And where else would I have ended up but at the palace of Dorothy Gale, a woman ready to take in every stray that came her way?

"What was my birth mother's name?" I asked. "Where did she come from?"

I knew nothing of gods and goddesses. Oz was a land of witches and wizards; goddesses belonged to the people of places like Aboria.

"Her name was Aphrodite," Glinda said.

Aphrodite. I mouthed the word, rolling its syllables silently around my tongue and lips, tasting it for familiarity.

I recognized nothing.

"She had too much to drink one night, as the story goes, and met a charming human man who swept her off her feet and apparently made her forget she was the goddess of fertility." A slight trace of humor tugged at the corners of Glinda's mouth, though not enough to create an actual smile. "Unfortunately, her father, a powerful god called Zeus, wouldn't have been pleased to know his daughter was pregnant. She hid from him and gave birth to you in secret. The only person who knew was an elderly midwife who understood Aphrodite's problem. She couldn't take you back to the home of the gods, not without incurring her father's wrath. Nor could she stay on land without raising the suspicions of the gods and goddesses of Mount Olympus."

Olympus. Another word that meant nothing to me, and everything.

"Where is that?" I asked.

"Far beyond the borders of our world, past the edge of the sea," Glinda said. "It's a place like Kansas, hard to get to if you don't already know the way."

"So the midwife helped Aphrodite find a home for Jakon," Clement said.

"In exchange for a considerable sum of gold," Glinda said. "Aphrodite, being a goddess, wasn't about to take chances with her child. She and the midwife delivered you to the Mayor of Oz, believing this would ensure you received the best of everything. Dorothy fell in love with you at once, and a heap of good fortune followed your adoption and filled the kingdom. Dorothy always attributed these blessings to you bringing her so much happiness and making her a better mayor, but I knew different. Oz was filled with the kind of luck and magic that can only come from a goddess of love."

"The other people like me," I said, heart racing. "The one with the golden eyes, who are traveling the kingdoms. They're demigods, too, aren't they? Children of other gods and goddesses."

"It would explain your similarities," Glinda said.

"It would explain why so many of them ended up in royal households, too," Clement said. "Aphrodite wasn't willing to leave you with anyone but the ruler of Oz. Maybe other goddesses had the same thought."

"None of those children were as lucky as you, of that I'm quite sure," Glinda said. "Nobody could love quite like Dorothy. She told me where you came from. I used my crystal ball once to look back on the moment of your arrival, and the moment you were placed in her arms..." Glinda trailed off. A moment later, she touched her fingertip to the inner corner of her eye and smiled. "Well, I've never seen that expression on anyone's face, before or since, and I've been around for a very long time."

My stomach clenched with pain. I knew the force and strength of Ma's love. Living without it was like living without air.

"She said you filled her heart to the brim," Glinda said. "She couldn't imagine it holding a single drop more love. Then she went and adopted Margaret and her heart grew to accommodate your sister."

A smile rose unbidden to my face. Ma had told me that part before. *You never have to worry about not having enough love for both of them,* she'd said, before adopting the twins. *Your heart will expand to hold anything you throw at it, and that's a promise.*

I hadn't realized her words had applied to grief, too. Every time I thought I had cried as much as I could cry, or missed her as much as I could miss anyone, my heart expanded to squeeze in just a little more agony.

Glinda watched me, her gaze sharp and fixed on my face.

"Three years ago, Dorothy came to me and told me she'd been given a diagnosis," she said. "She'd been to all the best doctors in the Emerald City and they'd said the same thing, that parts of her body were growing too quickly and devouring other parts. Everyone's body has to exist in a state of balance, and our old cells have to die to make room for new ones. Dorothy's old cells were growing out of control instead of dying. There was nothing the doctors could do. The sickness would only get worse. She would experience a great deal of pain and suffering, and she wouldn't get better."

"Did you try to heal her?" I said. "You're a Witch of Oz. What's medicine compared to that?"

"I would have saved her if I could. There was only so much I could do," Glinda said. "I told her I could control her pain, conceal it from her awareness, and give her perhaps two good years without suffering. Once the disease overpowered my magic, I would remove the spell, and she would die. The other option was to try to fight the disease, which would require her to be aware of all her symptoms as they progressed, and we'd have almost no chance of saving her in the end anyway. She chose the first option."

"So you could have saved her." My palms tingled, jolts of electricity sparking along my fingers in the form of tiny lightning bolts. "You didn't even try!"

Clement put his hand over mine. He winced at the lightning. I clenched my hands and forced my power back inside.

"I did as Dorothy asked," Glinda said. "It was her life. Her choice."

"But you could have fought the disease."

"Yes, and I would have lost," Glinda said calmly. "Your mother knew that. She didn't want you to see her die like that. Those two good years seemed better to her than three or four of pain and exhaustion."

"So she gave up," I said, hot tears welling in my eyes. "She left us."

"She took those two years and tried to fill them with a lifetime of love," Glinda said firmly. "She put her affairs in order and she made sure each one of you knew you were the center of her universe. And she didn't leave you alone."

"That's news to me," I said.

"Darling," Glinda said, tilting her head. "She didn't take anything back. Your future together is done, that's true. But the love she gave you? You get to keep that. Forever."

I swallowed hard and rolled my eyes up toward the faintly glowing ceiling. Tears pooled, setting the whole world to wobbling, and I blinked, over and over, each time hoping the next blink would get them under control.

I couldn't let her words sink in. Not now. If I did, I would shatter.

Glinda seemed to understand. She cleared her throat, and her voice gained a brisk edge.

"Your mother didn't leave you without friends, either," she said. "I've been watching over you and your siblings. I put protective spells over you the day her disease won out over my magic, and I've been keeping you all safe since she died."

"Safe?" I shot to my feet and paced the cell. Heat vibrated in my palms, but I kept them clenched and forced the energy into my footsteps instead. "Is that why I ended up in Urbis Prison? Are my siblings safe in these dungeons?"

Glinda blanched; her skin turned a sickly gray-green.

"Jakon," Clement said, his voice a plea and a warning.

"The Flying Monkeys came back," Glinda said. "Like I said, my powers aren't limitless. My focus was divided. I had to protect my people; I couldn't keep an eye on everyone, not at every moment. The Monkeys took advantage of that, and now you and your siblings and the Munchkins have paid the price."

I chewed on my bottom lip. "Did everyone know? Did the Lion know? And the Scarecrow and the Woodsman?"

"No," Glinda said. "This has been my burden. You're the only one I ever planned to share it with, and only when you were older."

We were all silent for a long moment.

I turned Glinda's words over in my mind as I marched from one side of the cell to the other, then back again. Anger churned inside me.

She had failed to stop my mother from dying. She had failed to shield me from the Winged Monkeys. She had failed to protect my siblings from the Wicked Witch of the West. I looked at her, and rage tingled down my arms and across my palms.

But when I focused on all that fury and hatred, I couldn't quite attach it to her.

It would have been easier to have someone to blame. I wanted to be furious at Glinda, to rail and throw tantrums and accuse her of everything that had gone wrong in my life over this past year.

But wanting to be mad at her wasn't enough.

She was a victim in all of this, just like me—a victim of the Witch and the Monkeys, yes, but also a victim of life. Illness didn't discriminate. It picked on people who deserved it and people who didn't, and I knew in my heart of hearts that there was nothing Glinda could have done to shield Ma from that random throw of the universal dice.

My anger roiled, but it had nowhere to go.

"The Wicked Witch was wrong." I stopped pacing and stared at the wall directly in front of me. Soft green light pulsed deep within the walls. It was beautiful, or it could have been in another time and place. "You didn't kill Ma."

"I didn't save her," Glinda said. "It's the same thing."

"If there's a difference between murder and killing, there's a difference between killing and letting death happen."

It took everything I had to get the words out, but once I did, the sharp twisting in the pit of my stomach lessened just a bit. I took a deep breath that shuddered all the way down to the bottom of my lungs.

"You did what Ma asked you to do. You helped more than any of the rest of us could have."

"But I didn't save her."

"Neither did I."

I turned to face her, and she gazed at me through the circular gap in Clement's wall.

I glanced at him. He gave me a tiny smile. A moment later, the shimmering white curtain melted down into the emerald floor.

Clement let out a huge sigh that reminded me of just how much effort that spell had taken to sustain.

He was good to me. Too good.

Slowly, I walked across the room to Glinda. I wasn't ready to hug her, not quite yet, and she wasn't about to push me. But I sat cross-legged across from her, close enough to touch.

"So how do we get out of here?"

The tension in the room cracked. That question that implied a plan, and plans were a good sight easier to manage than life-altering confessions.

"I had a thought about that while you were sleeping," Glinda said. "Tell me what you think."

∽

I stood with my back pressed against the wall, my hands raised toward the door of our cell.

"You sure about this?"

"Not remotely." Clement squeezed Glinda's tiny sparkling hairpin between two fingers. The hairpin seemed comically tiny, especially when I considered the magic he was expecting it to channel; but then, I supposed almost-nothing was better than actually-nothing.

"It had better work," Glinda said from my right, grimacing. "This witch won't destroy herself."

She raised her wand and pointed it toward the door. An enormous crystal ball hovered in front of her, three times the size of the one she'd used back in the Munchkin village. It reflected the lights pulsing in the emerald walls, their images dark and shimmering in the heart of the crystal.

"Three," Clement said, bracing himself against the wall to my left. "Two. One."

I raised my hands. The magic that had been threatening to burst from me all day exploded in a vicious swirl of air. I couldn't breathe against the rush of wind against my face, and I was glad.

"Go!" Clement shouted.

Glinda flicked her wand forward, and the giant crystal ball flew toward the door. At the same moment,

Clement jabbed his hairpin in the same direction and covered the ball in a blinding web of sparks.

I threw the full weight of my compact tornado behind the crystal ball. It smashed against the door.

The door jolted. The hinges creaked. A series of cracks appeared in the emerald at the corner of the doorway and radiated outward in lightning-like fractals.

"Again!" Glinda shouted.

I pushed my hands forward, forcing every last ribbon of air in the cell into the whirling cyclone. The still-sparking crystal ball spun around faster than my eyes could track, but I felt its power and threw it at the door again.

If Clement or Glinda tried to shout again, I couldn't hear them—or perhaps they couldn't gather the breath.

It didn't matter. I was a creature of instinct and fury now, fixed on the door that stood between me and my siblings.

It had never had a chance. The fifth time the crystal ball smashed against it, the door cracked apart and wrenched itself from its hinges. I raised my hands, prepared to give it one final smash that would send the metal skittering clear down the corridor outside.

Clement grabbed my arm and yanked, hard. His mouth was open in an agonized gasp; his eyes were bloodshot, and a vein throbbed in his temple.

As if I'd just caught myself reaching for a hot stove, I jerked my hands back.

The wind died down. The sparks around the crystal ball faded, and it dropped to the floor with a clunk and popped like a bubble.

Breath rushed back into my lungs.

Clement doubled over, gasping.

On my other side, even Glinda seemed a little red-faced. She fanned herself with a hand, eyes wide.

Ahead of us, the door dangled crookedly from a single hinge. The metal of the door curled outward where the crystal ball had struck it, leaving a jagged hole that would have been big enough to wriggle through if it the door wasn't already hanging by a thread.

"Good job, us," Clement said once he'd gotten his breath back.

I straightened my shoulders. My hands still fizzed with lingering magic.

"Let's go," I said. "I want the Wicked Witch dead."

Narcissa seemed confident in the strength of our cell; between our crumbled door and the exit from the dungeons to the ground floor of the Emerald Palace, we ran into only two guards, both of whom were easily handled by one of Clement's sleeping spells.

He seemed to have developed a real connection with Glinda's hairpin; he jabbed it in the air and swept it in fancy patterns with a confidence I'd never seen in his spellwork.

"It's a precision instrument," he said when he noticed me smirking at him. "Imbued with the power of a Good Witch of Oz. I could do worse."

I nudged the dungeon door open. A dark corridor lit from overhead by glowing braziers was just beyond. A single palace guard stood at the far end, facing away from us.

I gestured at Clement, and he offered me a mock bow and poked his hairpin directly in the man's direction.

The guard crumpled and his body hit the floor with a muffled thud.

We crept forward. The dungeons had disoriented me, but I knew the rest of the palace well enough to navigate it in the dark. I'd spent my life exploring these halls, racing Meggie and Frank and testing one of Chester's wheeled inventions and playing hide-and-seek with Lucy and the twins, who could always be counted on for a game.

Clement took down every guard we passed, usually before the guard had even noticed us.

He was more than capable of handling things, but I kept my hands raised anyway. I hadn't seen Winged Monkeys patrolling the palace yet. No doubt the Witch kept them on hand only for special tasks, like kidnapping and throwing people in dungeons. Still, I wouldn't be caught empty-handed, not when I could crumple their wings with a tornado instead.

Clement dispatched the guards outside the Grand Hall and we stopped just outside the tall doors. This felt like a repeat—like a second chance, but also a reminder that last time, we'd failed.

I couldn't get distracted this time. Whatever the Wicked Witch knew, Glinda likely knew, too, or could figure out. I didn't need to listen to the Witch.

I just needed to destroy her.

"Remember the plan," Glinda whispered. "Jakon, stay behind us until it's time. Make sure she doesn't have fire going that'll hurt us if it gets fanned by wind."

"And then hit her with everything I've got."

The pain and fear and grief of last night and this morning still lingered, fresh and raw. If anything, my greatest challenge would be holding my powers in until I was ready to use them.

Glinda nodded toward the door, urging me to open it. I cracked it open and peered inside, then froze.

"Is she there?" Clement whispered.

I shook my head frantically at him and gestured at my ear: Listen.

"They're headed this way," a voice said.

It wasn't a familiar voice, not exactly, but I recognized the face shimmering in the enormous mirror that stood on the dais next to my throne. I'd never seen the mirror before, but it had to belong to the Wicked Witch; its glass was a faded, disconcerting yellow, and hairline cracks branched across the mirror's surface, their pattern eerily like the bloodshot veins that sprawled across her single eye.

"All of them?" Narcissa demanded.

The face in the mirror—the Wizard, whose round, wrinkled face and bald head had beamed at me from a dozen different portraits and photographs throughout my life—frowned a little.

"Not all of them, but nearly. There are just two more to collect."

"My Monkeys can manage two," Narcissa said. "Particularly now I've got that meddlesome Glinda in my dungeons. This will proceed smoothly now that she's out of the way. I do wish you'd kill her for me."

"I won't kill Glinda," the Wizard said. "She taught me all the real magic I know."

"What's that got to do with anything?"

"I won't hurt her," the Wizard said firmly. He looked to the side for a moment, thinking, then added, "Well, not seriously."

Narcissa snorted; the sound disgusted me. "You've chosen an odd time to grow a conscience. No matter. Once we have them all, we can complete our plan, and Glinda will be even less of a threat than she is locked up beneath my palace."

My palace. It wasn't hers. It would never, ever be hers.

I slammed my hands against the double doors. Wind and muscle combined to blast them inward; they smashed against the emerald walls and ricocheted back, but by then we were already in the Grand Hall.

"Oscar Diggs, you have broken my heart," Glinda announced, glaring at the Wizard through the mirror.

His wrinkled face drained of all color. Then a huge, fake smile spread across his features. He looked jovial, even kind.

"Glinda!" he said brightly. "What a pleasant—"

She hit the mirror with a giant crystal ball. The glass cracked apart, and jagged pieces skittered across the floor.

"Go!" Clement shouted at me. "Don't give her time to—"

It was too late; a jet of flame erupted mere inches away from me. I leapt back, concentration shattering just like the mirror.

Another jet of flames rose to my other side, so hot my face felt like it might melt.

Clement waved his hairpin, muttering under his breath, his dark eyes focused intensely on me. A moment later, a shimmering white wall formed around my body, much like the one that had separated me from Glinda back in our cell.

Another jet of flame burst from the emerald floor right in front of me. Clement cried out, but the wall shielded me from the worst of the heat.

"Jakon, it's time," Glinda called.

I found my footing. The room shimmered palest green through the curtain. My hands tingled and wind sprang to life between my fingertips.

I dug deep, gathering everything into the space between my palms. Anger. Devastation. Terror. The knowledge that I would never see my mother again, and the equally bone-deep realization that it was up to me to protect my siblings and give them the life Ma had wanted for them. The air between my hands shook and vibrated, concentrating in force and power until the rage of a full tornado was barely contained.

"Now!" I screamed.

Clement dropped the curtain, and the storm burst from me. There were no ribbons of air now. No currents. No delicately woven strands of wind and weather.

There was just rage, pure and unleashed.

The Wicked Witch of the West saw the tornado a fraction of a second before it swept her up into the air. Her eye widened and her mouth fell open, but by then it was too late. The cyclone threw her through the air, a giant abusing its plaything.

The Witch screamed, or perhaps that was the storm, whistling through every crevice and corner of the Grand Hall. The twister ripped tapestries from the walls and yanked braziers from the high ceiling. The Emerald Throne itself resisted for only a moment, and then it too was wrenched from the floor and whirled so quickly it was only a green blur.

Narcissa struggled to find her balance. I couldn't see her in the whirling storm, but I felt her, a fragment of evil stuck inside my magic like a splinter in my thumb, relatively tiny but infinitely painful.

I drove the cyclone toward the wall, but she learned quickly; no matter how I tried to smash her against the hard emerald walls, she managed to move toward the center of the twister, just enough to avoid bashing her head.

A burst of heat flared through my body. At the same moment, one of the tapestries whirling in the storm burst into flames. The wind roared through the room, but I could hear her in my head.

Clever little boy, she cackled, voice mocking and ugly. *I suppose your whorish birth mother left you something after all.*

I shoved the tornado toward the wall again. She managed to dodge it by throwing her body toward the center of the storm.

"Glinda!" I shouted. "Clement!"

I didn't know what they were doing. I couldn't pay attention to them; everything in me was focused on the cyclone and the dot of black fabric whirling through the air.

"I'm here," Clement shouted from somewhere near my right ear. "We're both right here."

Another burst of heat flared inside me, sharp and painful. A second tapestry burst into flames, then another. Soon, everything in the tornado that could burn flared with evil flames. In moments, the storm before us was a deadly spiral of fire and poisonous yellow smoke.

"Glinda!" I screamed.

"I'm trying!" she shouted.

Her wand flickered at the edge of my vision, but whatever she was doing, it wasn't enough. The moment one of the Wicked Witch's fires went out, another flickered to life, and each one lanced through my body with agonizing heat.

"Glinda, Monkeys!" Clement shouted. "Behind you!"

My resolve wavered, and so did the tornado. I'd meant for this storm to surprise and devastate Narcissa, but the blinding flames whipping through my Grand

Hall were hurting me more than her. Now, the Winged Monkeys were here, too.

I couldn't fight them all.

Something crashed behind me. I didn't dare turn to look; the tornado wobbled, and it took all my concentration to keep it spinning.

Another burst of flames shot through me. Clement screamed. Glinda skidded and crashed into my back, wrapping her arms tightly around my shoulders.

"Jakon," she shouted into my ear. "I need you to trust me."

I couldn't answer. I stared blindly at the swirling blaze, trying to feel my way to the Witch so I could attempt one more time to slam her against something solid.

Glinda raised both hands and pointed her wand at the twister. She began chanting, a rhythmic string of words in an ancient language.

The Good Witch's magic burrowed into the base of my tornado. Her spell took root within my magic, its power cool and bright. A spark of white flared near the floor and spiraled up the storm, dousing the Wicked Witch's flames as it went.

Glinda kept chanting, her wand pointed steadily toward the cyclone. The ribbon of white light reached the Wicked Witch, and she let out a blood-curdling scream loud enough to be heard over the roaring of the wind.

It still wasn't enough. Not quite.

"I'm going in," Glinda shouted, not taking her gaze from the cyclone. "Throw me toward her."

I turned to stare. The storm wobbled.

"No. Absolutely not."

"Jakon." She spoke with firm command, her voice

holding the authority of thousands of years as one of the most powerful beings in Oz. "Stop stalling. Throw me in."

"What are you going to do?"

Glinda's eyes were clear and shone with reflected white light. "I'm going to kill her."

"You can't." Dread filled me. "Witches of Oz can't kill other witches."

"But I'm going to try."

"I can't—"

"Jakon, now."

She stepped forward. In an instant, before I could stop it, the storm picked her up and sent her flying. She spiraled, a cool, beloved presence amid the chaos.

Behind me, Winged Monkeys screeched and Clement cried out, his voice sharp with pain.

There was nothing else to do. I focused on Glinda's figure, her body a spot of pure sunlight in the already bright tornado. I squeezed my eyes shut and pushed her toward the Wicked Witch.

Goodness advanced on evil. Cool white light reached the sickly yellow-black sliver near the heart of my storm. And then Glinda consumed her, a flash of light so bright that nothing could survive it—not even Glinda herself.

The tornado shattered into a million tiny pieces. Fragments of sunshine and starlight crashed against the emerald walls, and I dropped to my hands and knees and let go of the magic with a gasp.

Glittering chunks of my throne chased one another in a wicked descent to the floor and clinked, emerald pinging against emerald. The last bits of light sparkled and plunged to the ground all around us, some dissolving and others turning to ash and burned bits of tapestry and coal.

A long moment later, three emerald rings dropped to the ground in front of me, two murky and dull and the third shimmering with a deep inner light.

Behind me, the Monkeys stopped screeching.

There was a long silence.

"Where am I?" one of them whimpered, his voice impossibly young and afraid. "What happened? Where's Mother?"

No one answered. I stared at the empty emerald dais and struggled to breathe.

"Where's Glinda?" Clement asked, crawling toward me. Blood streaked from a cut on his forehead.

I reached for the rings. My fingers closed around them, their physical reality hitting with the devastating, life-altering truth.

"Gone," I said. "The Witches of Oz are gone."

I stood before a door in the sprawling, shimmering dungeon.

"Open it," I ordered.

The guard, his soul back in his eyes, scurried to obey. He unlocked the enormous brass door with a key on his belt and bowed to me.

"Your Mayorness," he murmured.

I marched past him. The Munchkins filling the cavernous space shrank back, then exclaimed softly to one another as they recognized me.

"He's back," someone cried.

"The Mayor is here," someone else said. "It's Mayor Jakon!"

I scanned the room, my gaze skimming across the

faces that turned toward me bearing both shock and hope. The crowd rippled and parted, and finally, finally, my siblings rushed toward me.

"Jakon!" Lucy screamed, her voice high-pitched enough to shatter glass.

She launched herself at me and wrapped her arms around my middle, squeezing harder than I would have thought possible for a six-year-old Munchkin.

Chester, Gertrude, and Ethel followed close behind, clinging to me until their collective weight threatened to pull me down to the ground. Frank hung back; his face was drawn, his eyes red and swollen, but he grinned, and his shoulders collapsed with relief. Meggie wrapped her arms around him and squeezed, hard, hugging him for me since there was no way I'd be able to wrest my arms away from the littles.

"I knew you'd find us," Meggie said, head high and eyes as fierce as ever. "I knew nothing would keep you away from us for long."

"Not prisons or deserts or dungeons or witches," I said.

I twisted my head and kissed the top of Ethel's head, then Chester's. They reeked of old sweat and unwashed hair. I'd never smelled anything so sweet.

I could have stood there for hours, melting into the web of small arms that grabbed at me from every direction. But Meggie was sensible.

"I've been in this dungeon long enough," she announced. She turned toward the Munchkins and raised her voice. "Everyone, there's the door. March."

4TH OCTOBER

I woke long before dawn to a sky thick with gathering rain clouds. Lucy snored on the floor next to me; Chester and Frank lay curled up on my other side. A huge pile of blankets surrounded and engulfed us. Across the room, on my bed, Meggie snuggled with Gertrude and Ethel. None of them, not even Meggie, had been willing to sleep in their own rooms.

Clement was here, too, dozing on the emerald green couch by my window, wrapped in a worn quilt Ma had made for me years ago. The Lion snored on the floor next to him with his great head resting on his paws. Gashes striped his golden back, evidence of his struggle against the Winged Monkeys that had locked him in the witch's menagerie.

The wounds would heal. We would all heal.

Outside the window, another flock of Winged Monkeys took off across the pre-dawn sky. Their silhouettes, just visible against the dark green-gray of the clouds, no longer filled me with dread. The moment the Wicked Witch had died, the curse she'd had them under had lifted. Their wrinkled faces and sloping shoulders hadn't changed, but their eyes had.

"I'm sorry," a young Monkey had told me last night as I'd passed him on my way back from the dungeons. He had pulled a small red cap from his head and twisted it in his hands, unable to meet my eyes. "I don't know what I did, but I'm terribly sorry for whatever it was. If you'd like to throw me in jail I promise I'll go quietly."

I hadn't thrown him in jail. I hadn't done anything to any of them, aside from invite the Monkey King to a council at the palace next week, to discuss what had happened and figure out what we needed to do to repair the shattered trust between the Monkeys and the other peoples of Oz.

Frank shifted, and I realized his eyes were open and fixed on me.

"Hey," I said softly.

He rested his head on his crooked arm. "You came back for us," he whispered over Chester's sleeping form. His skin glowed faintly in the green lights of the city outside my bedroom window.

Lands, I had missed the freckles on the bridge of his nose. Frank was thirteen now, old enough to start considering himself something of a man, but I couldn't see a man when I looked at him. Not yet. His wide dark eyes and delicate nose were still those of my little brother. He was a sensitive soul, the kind of kid who cried whenever he heard of animals getting abandoned and who had once given all his pocket money to a little girl on the street because "she looked sad." I couldn't imagine what being in the dungeons had done to him.

I reached a hand across Chester, whose breath didn't change, because Chester could and did sleep through everything from thunderstorms to accidental explosions resulting from unattended science experiments.

Frank took my hand without hesitation and held on tight.

"We missed you," he whispered. "It was awful without you."

"I missed you, too."

I couldn't have come up with a more fantastical understatement. I had ached for my siblings. My life had been all wrong without them. I had been all wrong.

"We thought we'd never see you again." Frank's eyes immediately welled with tears at the thought.

I squeezed his hand. "I'd never leave you for good."

"You don't always have a choice," Frank said. "Ma didn't."

My heart clenched.

Ma had been given a choice. I still didn't know that I understood why she'd done what she did. I wasn't sure I ever would. But I knew, in the very center of my soul, that she'd made the decision she thought was best for us.

"Glinda did, though," Frank added, eyes shimmering. "She really saved us, didn't she?"

"She really did."

I thought about Glinda, and there was only emptiness where sorrow should have been.

But I knew that feeling. I'd gotten it at times when Ma had died. I'd felt guilty, then, worried it meant I hadn't really loved her enough. The Woodsman had understood, though. He'd taken me for a long walk through the fields outside the Emerald City. I still remembered his words.

Grief comes in a hundred different flavors, he had said, his footsteps clanking on the soft earth beneath us. The grass had swayed in the breeze, rippling and shifting from light to shadow like the Lion's fur did sometimes when he breathed. Sometimes it'll knock you on your back. Other times it'll feel hot, like anger. And sometimes it'll feel like nothing at all.

Is that really grief, though? I'd kicked a dirt clod and sent it crashing through the grass.

The Woodsman had put his arm around my shoulders, the metal cool and smooth and somehow comforting in spite of that.

It's all just your heart's way of trying to help you through, he had said. Hearts are clever. Sometimes it decides you need to not feel anything at all for a while, just to get you through the day, and that's all right. It doesn't mean you loved your Ma any less.

I had loved Glinda. No matter what she had done, or how angry I'd been at her, she had been my family.

"Does Locasta know what happened?" Frank asked.

"She will soon, if she doesn't already."

"Why didn't she come to help?"

"No time," I said. "Anyway, she was guarding the Gillikins. If she hadn't, your cell in the dungeon might have gotten even more crowded."

He shuddered, a shadow passing over his face. "It was awful down there. I don't even want to see the color green for a few days." He glanced around the room and made a face.

"Your whole home is green," I pointed out, biting back a smile.

"At least we've got texture up here," Frank said,

in the scathing voice only thirteen-year-olds could produce. "The dungeons are just green, green, maybe some pulsing lights in the walls, and then more green."

I chuckled. I couldn't help it.

Behind me, Lucy whimpered and twitched in the grip of a nightmare. I scooted so our backs were touching, and she settled back down with a sigh.

"You're in luck," I whispered to Frank. "We're headed to Gillikin Country after everyone wakes up."

Frank's eyebrows shot up. "To see Locasta?"

"Better," I said. "We're going to the godfathers'. I need to catch them up on everything that's been going on here. Plus, Gillikin is the only area that managed to fend off the Wicked Witch. I want to see what kind of shape they're in and figure out if they can maybe help the Munchkins and Quadlings rebuild. Munchkin Country wasn't bad when I went through, but Glinda said the Monkeys turned a few Quadling cities into rubble."

"I hate the Monkeys," Frank muttered.

I shook my head, fixing him with a stern gaze. "No. You can hate the Witch all you want. The Monkeys were her victims, just like the rest of us."

He pursed his lips, then sighed. "I know," he admitted. "I'm just mad."

I bit the inside of my cheek to force back another smile. "You can be mad. Maybe the Woodsman will take you out to break bottles with a slingshot."

The Woodsman was a big advocate of "feeling your feelings." He'd taken me to punch pillows or throw rocks more than once during my own early teenage years, usually after Meggie had surprised me with some upsetting prank or other.

"That would be nice." Frank's eyelids fluttered;

433

sleep was coming to reclaim him. "I'm glad you're back, Jakon."

His breathing soon settled to a steady, even rhythm. Across the room, Clement opened his eyes, smiled at me, and closed them again.

I rolled over and tried to go back to sleep. Outside the window, storm clouds continued to gather.

∼

Hours later, crammed into our largest carriage and armed with luggage and the better part of a dozen umbrellas, we clattered up the Yellow Brick Road. The city gates were still stuck shut by some lingering spell, so we had spent the early morning leading hundreds of Munchkins through the Witch's Walk and out of the city.

Now, a stream of coaches, wagons, and horseless carriages filled the street in front of and behind us. Some of the coaches had been loaned by the palace stables maintained just outside the city walls, and others had been sent by generous residents of Quadling Country in response to the single telegram I'd managed to get out across the one line that hadn't been destroyed by the Winged Monkeys.

"He's going to get wet," Chester announced from the front bench, pressing his nose to the glass of the window so he could watch the Lion, who stalked along beside us. "It's going to rain and he's going to get soaked. Perhaps I could use some of the luggage straps to invent a wearable umbrella. I think that would be quite a good invention, don't you, Jakon?"

"He's a lion," Ethel glanced up from her book. "He lives in a forest. He's accustomed to weather."

"That doesn't mean he would prefer to get rained on," Chester said, voice taking on a professorial tone. "Necessity is not always the mother of invention. Sometimes the mother of invention is comfort."

"I think it would be nice!" Lucy piped up from her perch on my lap. "You can use my umbrella if you want."

"Nobody can use anybody's umbrellas," Meggie said. "They're all in the compartment at the back of the carriage."

"We are capable of stopping," Chester said severely.

Frank smirked. Ethel rolled her eyes and went back to her book. Gertrude, who had been gazing out the window on the other side, looked over with a start.

"Sorry, did someone want my umbrella?"

Next to me, Clement grinned.

The conversation flowed and jumped from one topic to another. I let my attention wander away from the words and let the cadence of their voices wash over me.

For the first time in a long time, peace settled over me. My stomach didn't wobble. My heart didn't race. Nothing threatened me, and the ache that had been inside me since Ma's death had softened a bit. I rested my head against the back of the carriage and let out deep sigh. A few raindrops pattered on the carriage roof, the sound rhythmic and comfortable.

Clement reached for my hand and laced his fingers between mine.

Meggie noticed.

She bit her bottom lip and glanced up at me, eyes sparkling. She jerked her head subtly toward our entwined fingers, then met my eyes again, the question all over her face.

I answered by resting my head on Clement's shoulder. Meggie's face cracked into a broad grin.

I was never going to hear the end of this.

And land's sakes, I hadn't realized how much I'd missed her teasing.

An hour or two later, we split off from the caravan of Munchkin carriages onto a road paved with purple bricks. Not long after, the rolling fields gave way to thick forests and winding mountain paths. Overhead, the clouds dispersed to reveal a starry night sky, framed on every side by silhouetted trees. Slowly, steadily, we climbed a pine-covered mountain, then pulled off near the peak onto a broad avenue paved with deep purple cobblestones and illuminated by glowing lanterns hanging from the branches of the trees.

Gertrude jerked awake. "We're here," she announced with a startled gasp. She looked around, still surfacing from her nap, and hit Ethel repeatedly on the arm. "Ethel. Ethel. We're here."

Ethel, who was a much heavier sleeper, only murmured something indistinguishable and sank back against the bench.

The carriage clattered to a stop at the end of the well-lit driveway. The coachman, who looked a little sleepier for the wear, opened the door. He surveyed the inside of the carriage and realized almost half its occupants were asleep. A soft smile curved under his thick green-dyed mustache.

"Would you like help carrying them in, sir?" he asked.

"Please," I said. "Thanks, Basil."

He touched his cap. "Happy you're home, sir."

I handed Lucy over to him. Clement clambered out next, and I coaxed Chester close enough to the carriage door that Clement could scoop him up. I carried Gertrude, and the others followed. We marched as a motley parade to the door of the godfathers' beautiful mountain lodge, and Ethel skipped ahead to bang on the door.

Lights turned on inside. Dogs barked. Familiar footsteps clanged toward us. And then the door flew open to reveal the Scarecrow standing there with a pitchfork in hand, the Woodsman right behind him.

"I'll tell you what I told the last Winged Monkey—" the Scarecrow started.

He fell silent. He couldn't blink; his painted eyes wouldn't allow it. But he gaped at us in surprise, and behind him, the Woodsman's triangular tin eyebrows shot upward with a soft scraping sound.

"Jakon," the Scarecrow said, staring between us all. "Children. What are you doing here? Why aren't you in the Emerald City? We heard some dreadful rumors, but—"

"But we'll hear all about that later," the Woodsman interrupted. He guided the Scarecrow out of the way and gestured at us. "Come in, come in. Scarecrow, be a dear and put the kettle on. I'll help bring in the luggage."

Once the children were tucked up in the beds the godfathers kept ready for them, Meggie, Clement, the Lion, and I joined them in front of the fire. The coachman had been offered a bed but declined, saying instead that he wanted to walk down to the village to visit his brother's sister-in-law, who, he said, was "quite a nice lady and a bit of a looker, too, if you don't mind my saying so."

I'd been happy to let him go. The thought of being back in a world where people visited each other and flirted with pretty people reminded me that, no matter what, the world kept turning. It was an assurance I'd sorely needed.

The Scarecrow handed out steaming cups of calming poppy rose tea, and the Woodsman poked the fire until the flames were high and warm. The Lion curled up in front of the heat and chuffed contentedly. Meggie sat on the floor with her back resting against him, and Clement and I snuggled close together on a plush loveseat.

"I think you have a story to tell us," the Scarecrow said, fixing his painted eyes on me.

The Woodsman sat rigidly on a wooden chair across from the loveseat. He preferred hard surfaces; they were easier to rise from.

"Give the boy a moment to breathe, Scarecrow," the Woodsman chided. "He looks as if he could use it."

The Scarecrow dropped into a well-worn armchair with a crocheted blanket draped across the back. "Of course," he said, giving me a deferential nod. "My apologies, Jakon, I always forget how important breathing is to you."

Clement leaned forward, face alive with interest. "You don't have to breathe at all, then?" he said. "Either of you?"

"Of course not," the Scarecrow said kindly. "I'm made of straw. Use your brain, dear boy." He tapped his own burlap head, which was stuffed with straw and pins given by the Wizard "to keep him sharp."

The corners of Clement's lips twitched.

"Excuse me for being rude," the Scarecrow added. "But who are you?"

"This is Clement," I said.

Clement held out a hand and smiled. "I'm a friend of Jakon's."

The Scarecrow shook his hand, and then the Woodsman did, too, his tin eyes glancing between Clement and me until a soft smile passed across his face.

"We were friends of Dorothy's once," the Woodsman said.

He reached out and took one of the Scarecrow's soft, floppy hands. They exchanged a look, full of nostalgia and the love that had built up between them over decades.

"I'm glad Jakon has a friend," the Scarecrow said.

Meggie coughed on her tea. I shot her a stern look. She only coughed harder. The Lion patted her on the back with one of his giant paws, mistaking her suppressed laughter for choking, and she quickly gathered her composure.

"We've been terribly worried about you," the Woodsman said, leaning forward. "We heard about your kidnapping, of course."

"I went to the Emerald City to try to help as soon as it happened, but nobody knew anything," the Scarecrow said.

Meggie nodded her agreement. "All we were sure of was that the Monkeys were involved. We were about to mount a proper search all through Oz, and then first Monkey attack happened in the north and Locasta asked the Scarecrow to come back."

"We thought it was an isolated incident," the Scarecrow said. "I planned to go right back to the Emerald City, but then Woodsman and I wound up protecting the town at the bottom of our mountain from the Monkeys."

"He built a trebuchet," the Woodsman offered mildly. "It's quite impressive."

I widened my eyes. "You built a what?"

"A trebuchet," the Scarecrow said. "A trebuchet is a type of catapult that uses a—"

"I know what it is," I said. "I'm just trying to imagine you using one."

"We had help from some strong Gillikins," the Scarecrow said. "There are five trebuchets in these hills, all capable of launching boulders into the air above the city. Of course, the boulders then come back down, which required most of the Gillikins to hide in their cellars or the forest during the attacks, but that's better than getting carried off by the beasts."

"No wonder you held out better than the rest of Oz," I said.

"We were worried our attentions had been improperly divided," the Woodsman said. "We heard a rumor a few days ago that the Emerald City was facing similar troubles. We were planning on leaving things here in the hands of the Gillikins and going back to the city in the morning to see if there was truth to the rumors, and to make sure the children were all right."

"Then yesterday, the Monkeys stopped fighting quite abruptly and flew off," the Scarecrow said. "And before we could leave for the Emerald City, you showed up at our door." He tilted his head and small wrinkles appeared between his eyes. "The children are all right, aren't they?"

I glanced at Clement while Meggie snorted into her tea.

"They are now," I said. "But there was a bit of trouble getting there. And I have some bad news about Glinda."

The Woodsman leaned forward, joints creaking.

I told them the story from the beginning, from the moment the Winged Monkeys had whisked me from the Emerald City to Clement's and my daring escape from Urbis Prison, with the help of our Skylan friend Silas. I skimmed over the journey across the desert and

Aboria, dwelling only on the magic fracturing outward from Urbis, and then I told them everything I knew about the Wicked Witch of the West and the traitorous Wizard of Oz.

I didn't tell them what I'd learned about Ma. I couldn't speak of that yet, especially not with Meggie in the room. But I did tell them about Glinda's final battle with the Wicked Witch, and the sacrifice that had saved us all.

The godfathers stared at me. The Scarecrow's face drooped with heavy wrinkles, and a few drops of oil leaked from the Woodsman's eyes.

When I finished, they were silent for a long time.

"I thought she'd outlive us all," the Scarecrow finally said. "Even the Woodsman, and he can be patched up better than I can."

"She saved us," I said. "She saved all of Oz."

"I hope the cost was worth it," Meggie said.

I sipped my tea. I felt as though I ought to chastise her for minimizing Glinda's gift, but I couldn't dismiss the same unsettled concern from my own thoughts.

The last Wicked Witch of Oz was dead, but the magic shattering its way across the world still threatened our safety. I couldn't begin to predict the impact it would have on my kingdom. The Queen of Aboria had seemed prepared for outright war.

I didn't know how to prepare for a war. I didn't even know how to rule an Oz that had only one great Witch left.

"We have to rebuild," I said. "And I need to get things sorted out between the Emerald Palace and Urbis Prison. I assume the Wicked Witch is the one who charged me with treason, and those charges won't hold up as soon as the world hears what happened here. But there are other problems coming toward us, and we need to do something about whatever's happening in Urbis."

"On that note, I forgot to tell you something," Meggie said.

All eyes turned to her. She set her tea on the floor and leaned forward. The Lion flicked his tail around her and onto her lap.

"Some people came looking for you after you got kidnapped," she said. "They said something about Urbis and that they wanted your help."

Clement inhaled sharply; I leaned forward, sending the tea in my cup sloshing forward.

"What people?" I said. "What did they look like?"

"They all looked different, but their eyes were like yours." She bit her lip, as if debating whether to say the next bit. "They said they were your brothers and sisters. Your real brothers and sisters."

The edge to her voice rankled me.

"You are my real sister," I said. "Full stop. End of story."

She smiled a little and buried her fingertips in the fluffy end of the Lion's tail.

"Well, your blood siblings, then."

Perhaps they weren't the children of other goddesses. Perhaps they'd come from the same one.

Or perhaps sibling meant something else to gods. For all I knew, they had a whole different way of thinking about families.

"What did you tell them?" I asked.

"I said I didn't know where you were," she said. "They didn't want to stay and wait for you. They said they were going to Enchantia to try to track down another sibling, but told me to tell you to join them if you can."

"Did they say why?"

She shook her head. "Just that it was important."

Clement watched me, studying my face for thoughts and impressions.

I had plenty of thoughts. Curiosity tugged at me, along with anxiety and concern and hope that perhaps these siblings and I might be concerned about the same problems spreading across our world.

But in spite of all the thoughts, I only had one decision.

"Out of the question," I said.

Clement wasn't convinced. The lines on his forehead argued as loudly as his voice could have.

"I could go," he offered after a moment. "I could find them and see what they want."

"You can't go back to Enchantia," I said. "The charges against me should get easily dropped, but yours might stick."

"Don't you at least want to meet them?" Meggie asked, her voice equal parts curious and cautious. "I mean, they are your family."

"I already have a family."

She bit her lip and frowned at me. She was trying to find the right words for something, and I stayed quiet, sipped my tea, and let her think. Meggie taking time to consider before she spoke was a rare occasion and I intended to treat it with the respect it deserved.

"I don't think Ma would approve," she said finally, speaking more to her teacup than to me. She stroked the Lion's tail, deep in thought. "I think Ma would want you to go find them."

I watched her and waited.

"It's just..."

She looked to the Lion, who blinked slowly at her.

"It's just that I don't think Ma would want you

to reject anyone who wanted to be your family," she blurted. "Not until you'd given them a chance, at least. You know her. She never turned anyone away, and it sounds like these people could really use your help."

"Oz needs my help, too."

"Oz has plenty of protectors," she said. "We're down a witch, but Locasta and the godfathers are still here, and, I don't know, maybe I can even step up and pitch in a little bit with mayor stuff if you want to go find these people."

I raised an eyebrow. Meggie did not, as a rule, offer to assist with mayoral duties.

"I'm not saying I want to take over your job long-term," she added sternly. "I just... I know Ma would want you to go see if you have a connection with these people. They seemed nice. And you know how Ma felt about family."

We all knew. To Ma, family was everything—and her family included anyone and everyone who wanted to be part of it.

"You shouldn't use Oz or us as an excuse to avoid meeting them," Meggie said. "That's all. That's all I have to say."

She picked her teacup back up and drained it. The Lion rumbled his approval of her speech and nuzzled her cheek with his enormous nose.

"I agree with Margaret," the Scarecrow said. "If these are your siblings, there's a great deal you could learn from them, about the troubles in the kingdoms and perhaps about yourself. The pursuit of knowledge is always worthy."

"But it's not everything," the Woodsman said. "What does your heart tell you?"

I fell silent and tried to listen to my heart. It pounded.

"That I'm scared," I said with a rueful almost-laugh.

Meggie rolled her eyes but managed to not say anything.

"But what are you scared of?" Clement asked gently.

That was the real question, and I took a deep breath and gave it some real consideration. It was difficult to tease apart the threads of my anxiety, but I tugged on them one by one until a few thoughts came loose.

"I'm scared to leave Oz again," I said. "The last time I left the kingdom, the Wicked Witch kidnapped my brothers and sisters."

"That won't happen again," the Woodsman said firmly. "We'll stay with your siblings until you get back."

"All three of us will," the Lion growled. "Now that the Monkeys have returned to their senses, the Munchkin forests can handle themselves and I can stay with the children."

"What about your own kingdom?" I asked.

"The Lioness can manage things in Quadling Country," he rumbled proudly. "She's quite capable."

I took a deep breath. "All right, then, what about the kingdom? I'm the mayor. I can't just leave Oz, especially while we're rebuilding."

"I ruled the Emerald City once when your Ma was still young," the Scarecrow said. "I can do it again."

"And Locasta can help," the Woodsman said. "She's older and wiser than any of us. I'm sure she and Scarecrow would have no trouble managing the kingdom for a bit."

"You shouldn't have to—"

"But we can, and we're happy to do it," the Woodsman said. The fire flickered, illuminating the side of his tin face with dancing tongues of gold. "We're your family, Jakon. We respect you as the Mayor of Oz, but we also love you as our child. If you need to go, you need to go. We'll carry your responsibilities here."

"I can't ask you to—"

"No, you can't," the Scarecrow said, tapping the side of his head. "Because we've already offered."

I fell silent. Their promises and my fears mingled in my mind.

Finally, Meggie propped her arm on the Lion's back and rested her head on her hand. "Jakon?" she said. "I love you as family too and all, but you've got to stop overthinking things. You always do this and it drives me crazy. Go find your siblings. Help them. Figure out what's happening in the kingdoms. We'll be fine."

"You got thrown in the dungeon last time I wasn't around to keep an eye on you."

"Yeah, and then you got thrown in the dungeon too," she said. "You're not that impressive."

I laughed.

"They'll be fine," the Woodsman said. "We'll protect them with our lives and do our best to keep Oz in one piece for you. Cross my heart."

I let out a heavy sigh. Clement nodded at me, his eyes warm with encouragement. He, just like the rest of my family, trusted me even when I didn't trust myself. Now, in some kind of circular logic, I knew I needed to trust them back.

Doing it was another matter.

"I'll think about it," I said.

Meggie rolled her eyes so far back in her head I was worried they'd get stuck.

"You're killing me, Jakon," she said. "But fine. I'll leave you alone about it for a couple of days, on one condition."

I raised an eyebrow, anticipating something about

her royal duties or how much authority she'd have over the younger children while I was gone.

Instead, she leaned forward, eyes alight.

"You have to carry me around in a tornado," she said. "I've wanted a tornado ride since I was like two and Ma told me her Kansas story for the first time, and I will literally kill you if you run off before I get one."

Clement groaned. "You don't want it. I promise."

"Jakon?" she said, her voice a warning.

I shook my head, but couldn't stop from smiling. "You're out of your mind, Megs. But yeah, I'll send you flying. Tomorrow." The poppy tea had hit me, weighing down my eyelids and making my limbs feel soft and droopy. "Tonight, I just want to be here with you all, and maybe get some sleep."

"Deal," she said. "I'll give you a week. But this isn't over."

I grinned, sleepy but overjoyed to be back in her exhausting presence. "With you, it never is."

She leaned back against the Lion with a contented sigh. I let my head rest on Clement's shoulder, and before I knew it, morning had arrived.

5TH OCTOBER

After a long breakfast and much discussion, we loaded ourselves back into the carriage for the journey home. The godfathers had made it clear that Locasta had things in Gillikin Country under control, which meant I needed to get back to the city and make sure the telegram lines the Monkeys had destroyed were rebuilt first thing.

Our coachman had taken me up on my offer to let him stay in the village for a few days, seeming eager to get in as much time with his brother's beautiful sister-in-law as he could. The Scarecrow and Woodsman, who weren't worried about comfort or sunburn, drove, while the rest of us crowded together for the ride back.

The journey was faster this time, now that we didn't have a crush of Munchkin traffic to navigate, but I still had plenty of time to get lost in my thoughts.

Meggie's words rang in my head. They held some truth. Ma would have wanted me to go find my so-called blood siblings and try to connect with them. But I'd also promised her I'd do my best to lead Oz in her absence. I couldn't do that from Enchantia.

Clement seemed to understand how crowded the inside of my mind felt, and he engaged in lively conversation with my siblings and let me think. They played I Spy and Twenty Questions and what seemed like every other game Ma had ever taught us, and eventually, when the afternoon was starting to fade to evening, our carriage stopped clattering along the Yellow Brick road and stopped in front of the gate.

I jumped out of the carriage and approached the towering doors. I rapped on one, hard.

The little door to the external antechamber to the side of the gate flew open, and the Guardian of the Gate marched out, the big golden key on his belt swinging. He eyed me warily.

"Mayor Jakon," he said with a bow. "The gate remains closed. The Wicked Witch's magic has it stuck fast."

My stomach fell. The Witch was dead; her spell should have worn off by now.

"Have any city magicians tried to unlock it?"

The Guardian frowned. "I haven't been able to contact any of them, Your Mayorness, not without leaving my post."

I sighed and went back to the carriage.

"We'll have to go through the Witch's Walk again," I called, loudly enough that everyone inside and out could hear me. "The gate's still shut. I'm going to have to get a message to Locasta somehow. Maybe she can open it."

Clement leaned forward from where he sat trapped by Lucy sleeping on his lap.

"Maybe not," he said. "You might be able to."

I glanced back at the enormous gate. "I'm not sure I want to risk a cyclone. I can probably shake the gates loose, but I'd rather not damage the walls if I don't have to. There are homes right up against the wall on the inside. I don't want to hurt anyone."

He shook his head. "I don't mean a tornado."

Beside him, Chester sank back down, disappointed.

I squinted at Clement. "What do you—"

"The rings," he said.

Of course.

I tugged on the gold chain around my neck. I hadn't dared try to wear the witches' rings myself, but they were there, all three of them, pulsing with their own unique magic.

"Stand back, everyone," I warned. "I have no idea what this is going to do."

I slipped Glinda's ring onto my finger. It shouldn't have fit, but it did, enchanted as it was. My heart clenched.

She was gone.

Her ring was here.

She wasn't.

I pushed the thought away tried to fit the emerald into the keyhole. I tensed, hoping the gate would unlock and fearing it would explode or electrocute me instead.

Nothing happened.

I sighed and turned back to my family and driver, who were all watching me.

"It's no good," I said. "We'll have to go around. And we'll have to go on foot, because that carriage isn't going to make it."

It was a long trek around the city. When we reached the other side, the walls were smooth, curved, and frustratingly unbroken. The entrance to the Witch's Walk had been wide open when we'd left, with Munchkins pouring out in a steady stream. At some point since yesterday, the door must have fallen shut.

"I think it's over there," Meggie said, pointing. "I remember when we came out, I could see that tall pine tree straight ahead." She nodded toward the forest at the edge of the fields surrounding the city.

There were lots of tall pine trees there, and they all looked more or less the same. Even so, I hopped down from the carriage and scoured the block for a keyhole. There was nothing, of course.

The Lion sniffed along the base of the wall, his tail twitching. He tensed as he caught a scent, then bounded forward along the wall.

He stopped amid a tell-tale patch of trampled grass.

"This one," he said, pawing at a brick. "It smells of Munchkins."

Lucy looked up from where she'd been trying to braid blades of grass. "How do Munchkins smell?" she asked, and began sniffing the air, and then her own arm.

"Like lollipops and sunshine," the Lion said generously.

Lucy beamed.

I crouched and searched the wall for the tiny gemstone keyhole. I didn't need to look for long. The keyhole itself was tiny and barely a dent in the huge emerald brick, but the ring was drawn to it like one magnet to another. I slid Glinda's ring into the peculiar lock and the emerald brick slid inward and down, just as it had before.

"It worked!" I called back to the group, as if they

could possibly have missed it. I sat and swung my legs into the gap.

Clement's hand landed on my shoulder with force.

"Wait," he said, voice low and urgent.

I froze. He crouched next to me and put his hand into the gap, as if feeling for the temperature inside the Walk.

His lips tightened into a frown and he angled his body so the others couldn't see his face.

"Something's different," he muttered.

My heart sank. "Different how? Good-different or bad-different?"

"I don't know," he said. "There's magic in the city. More than there was."

I hesitated. Glinda had killed the Wicked Witch. The Monkeys and guards had returned to their senses. Our problems were supposed to be over, at least for a day or two.

"Narcissa was probably suppressing Emerald City magicians," I suggested finally.

He shook his head.

"It's bad-different, then."

He grimaced. "Maybe. I think we should go ahead, just you and I. The others don't have magic. We can make sure everything's safe before we bring the children in."

He didn't have to tell me twice. I dropped into the hole and turned around to face the others.

"Clement and I are going to go in first," I said, forcing my voice to play at cheerfulness. "We want to be sure everything's safe."

Meggie narrowed her eyes. "Why would it not be safe?"

I met her gaze and held it, then shook my head very

slightly. She considered me, then shrugged.

"I guess the Witch's curse might be still wearing off for some of the Monkeys," she said, her voice as falsely light as mine. "You go ahead. We'll eat the sandwiches we packed. Don't be too long."

I thanked her with a quick nod. She quickly gathered the youngest children and started issuing orders to pull out the picnic blanket and start unpacking the sandwiches. Frank hesitated, watching me with sharp eyes, and I forced a smile.

"Don't worry, we're just being cautious," I said. "Back in a few."

He nodded, unconvinced.

I ducked into the Witch's Walk and Clement followed close behind me. We moved quickly under the glowing bronze lamps, darting along the twists and turns as if we were confident that nothing would be around each next corner.

And nothing ever was. The corridor was quiet and calm. The lamps burned. Our footsteps clicked against the floor. And all the while, my heart raced.

"Have you given any more thought to going to Enchantia?" Clement asked after what felt like the fifteenth mile of underground corridor.

"I can't."

"Can't give it more thought or can't go?"

"Yes," I said. "Both. Not until things are back to normal in Oz. Last time I left, a Wicked Witch took over my throne. I can't begin to imagine what will happen if I leave again."

Clement nodded but didn't answer.

Finally, the ground sloped up toward the door that to the alley.

We'd traversed half the city from underground, and

nothing had happened. I hadn't even heard anything from over our heads—no shouting, no explosions, nothing that would indicate the Monkeys had taken over or another curse had ravaged the buildings over our heads. Whatever magic Clement was feeling, it wasn't doing its best to destroy the city.

I breathed a sigh of relief and pushed open the door. At first, everything seemed normal. The alley was dim and abandoned, as alleys tended to be.

Even so, my skin prickled. I looked to the sky, but it was a clear, ordinary blue. No eldritch wind whistled between the buildings; no strange curse discolored the green walls on either side of us.

I hesitated, then let the Walkway door fall closed behind me. It slammed into its frame with a deafening crack.

Clement jumped, and I reached instinctively for his hand. We froze, listening for hints of Monkeys or witches or brainwashed palace guards, but there was...

Nothing.

Absolutely nothing.

The city was silent.

We glanced at one another and pulled our hands apart. I raised mine, feeling for every breeze that was close enough to be pulled into a twister. Clement tugged Glinda's sparkling hair pin from his dark hair and held it aloft. We crept toward the street together, each soft step echoing in the alley, and peeked around the corner.

"Are you seeing—" Clement started.

"Oh, no," I muttered at the same time. "No, no, no."

I straightened and took a few bold steps into the street. Just feet away, a shamrock-green horse pulling a wagon stood facing me, one of its front hooves raised and a few strands of its mane suspended in a breeze.

The hoof didn't come down. Not a hair twitched. The horse stayed, silent and unmoving, its dark eyes unnaturally still.

"Did the Wicked Witch say anything about freezing the city?" Clement asked faintly.

My heart pounded. This horse could spring back to motion at any second, and if it did, it was likely to trample me before it saw me in its path.

But the creature stayed still, its mane stiffened by a breeze that had passed by long ago.

"It's everyone." Clement turned around, taking in the strange scene all around us.

People stood like statues all around us. Two women sitting outside a small bistro had paused with their forks raised halfway to their mouths. A small child chased a cat had been frozen in the act, both of them moving so quickly their feet scarcely touched the pavement. Just outside a shop, an aproned shopkeeper lectured a young employee. The shopkeeper's mouth was wide open, trapped mid-word, and I half expected a fly to buzz in and explore.

But the flies were frozen, too. A small one with an iridescent green shell was already a hand's breadth away from the horse, its body suspended in midair in spite of the lack of movement on the part of its translucent wings.

"The Witch must have done this before she died," Clement said. "Unless..." He trailed off, not wanting to say it.

"She's dead. She's definitely dead." I held up the chain around my neck. "I have her ring. She never would have given that up."

"She tricked your mother once before."

I shook my head. "No. Maybe Narcissa would have

tried to pull that. But Glinda wouldn't."

Clement walked slowly around the wagon. The driver stared ahead, unblinking.

A horrible thought struck me.

"Do you think they know they're stuck?"

Clement paused and touched the horse's cheek with careful fingertips.

"No," he finally said, though sounding uncertain. "No, I don't think so. I think they're just... suspended."

My thoughts flickered back to a story he'd told me once, about a monkey that had been frozen in midair during a dinner party. That story had almost doubled me over with laughter. This story, the one I was living, filled me with deep ripples of fear.

"Is this compliments of the Wicked Witch?" I asked.

Clement closed his eyes and ran his fingertips along the horse's cheek. He closed his eyes in concentration. His face screwed up a little, as if the featherlight touch caused him pain.

Finally, his eyelids fluttered back open.

"I don't think so. This doesn't taste like her magic."

"Then who did it?" My voice rose. I fought to keep it under control. "Who did this? How do we fix it?"

Clement frowned at me. Tiny creases appeared between his eyes. "I have no idea. But it feels familiar."

I waved vaguely at him; a voice in my head screamed more, more, more, but I couldn't make my mouth shape the request.

"It reminds me of Urbis," Clement said slowly. "Not as bad. Not exactly the same, especially now that my cuffs are off. But it's similar."

My stomach spasmed.

It was supposed to be over.

We'd won.

Everything was supposed to be better now.

"We'll figure this out," Clement said.

He wrapped his arms around me and held on tight. I closed my eyes and nuzzled into his embrace. I pressed my ear against his chest and listened for his heartbeat.

It was steady. It was like him.

"We have to go tell the others," I said, pulling away. "And then we'll figure out what to do."

I turned and stared at the horse's glassy eye. The horse stared blankly back.

The children huddled near the fire burning merrily just outside the palace walls. It crackled brightly and gave off a pleasant heat against the evening's autumn chill.

"Do it again," Lucy ordered.

Clement grinned and pointed his hairpin at the flames. They turned bright purple and emitted a shower of silver sparks before fading back to orange.

Lucy clapped her hands, delighted.

"What I want to know is how you've managed to create a fire that burns without fuel and doesn't ignite the surrounding grass," Chester said politely.

Clement shrugged. "Magic."

"Yes, but what are the principles behind the magic?" Chester asked, fixing Clement with a solemn stare. "All inventions, even magical ones, are guided by a set of scientific laws that must be followed."

"That's true," Clement said. "All right, the principle behind this fire is that it does use fuel. Except instead of consuming logs or grass, it uses the air and my own inner power."

Chester tilted his head and narrowed his eyes. "Doesn't that mean that you have less magic?"

"It does. But I have a lot of magic, and the fire requires very little."

"Wait, does that mean you'll run out eventually?" Gertrude asked, leaning forward.

"Only if I never replenish my stores," Clement said. "Fortunately, that doesn't happen very often."

I met his gaze from across the fire. Reflected flames danced in his eyes. He grinned at me, and I grinned back.

It was almost possible, sitting with my family around me, to forget about the uncanny horror of the frozen city just beyond the emerald walls beside us. I could imagine we were simply on an adventure—one of Ma's picnics, or a camping trip, or a hike she'd sent us on "to get all that energy out!" I could even imagine that Ma herself would be waiting for us back at home, eager to hear tales of whatever scrapes we'd gotten ourselves into.

I watched my siblings, and my mind drifted to my other siblings—to the golden-eyed people who had been wandering the world and come in search of me. I wondered what sitting next to a fire with them might be like. Would we have anything in common? Would they view me with suspicion, or would we find enough similarities to make us feel like a real family? Would they care about Oz as deeply as I did, and would I find myself just as invested in their homes and journeys?

I thought I might. The force of Queen Abigail's hugs back in Aboria had told me that Fallon and I, at least, had something in common. We knew what it was like to have mothers who loved us fiercely.

Did the others have loving parents? Did any of them

have siblings of their own? Would they be as kind as Clement was to my little brothers and sisters amid their endless questions and requests?

"Jakon!" Ethel said, elbowing me in the side. "It's your turn!"

I came to with a start. They were all staring at me. The fire flared and turned the Woodsman's face a brilliant shade of orange.

Clement smiled. "If you could choose, would you rather have the power of flight or invisibility?" His words were light, but his gaze searched my face.

"Oh," I said. "Um... Invisibility."

"I'd rather fly," Lucy announced.

"We already know what you'd rather do," Gertrude said. "It's not your turn, Lucy."

Lucy's lips turned down into a pout. Frank pulled her onto his lap.

"It'll be you again in a minute, Luce," he whispered. "And then it'll be your turn to be It. Better think of a good question."

"Two more questions," the Lion rumbled. "Then it's time for bed, cubs."

"It's been a long day," the Scarecrow agreed from his spot a bit further from the fire than the rest. "Your growing brains require rest."

"Will the city be better in the morning?" Gertrude asked, eyes fixed on my face.

I forced a smile. "We don't know yet. Probably not. But don't worry, Uncle Clement and I will figure it out."

"We sure will," Clement said. "All right, Frank, it's your turn."

Frank pursed his lips in thought. "Would you rather hiccup every time you blink?" A grin spread across his face. "Or fart every time you speak?"

"Ew!" the twins shrieked.

Lucy and Chester dissolved into hysterical giggles, then began repeating the word "fart" to each other. Meggie rolled her eyes at me, but she was as glad as I was to see them laughing.

An hour later, after the giggles had subsided, they were all tucked up into their respective beds: Lucy and Chester lying next to the fire, the twins snuggled up against the Lion not far away, and Frank lying near the emerald wall and staring up at the stars.

After she tucked the twins in, Meggie sat next to Clement with her knees tucked up to her chin. She stared at the flames. The Lion watched her, blinking slowly every now and then. The Scarecrow and Woodsman stood just outside the little circle of sleeping children, leaning against one another and talking softly.

I stood some distance away, watching the little group in the pool of firelight. I loved them so much I could barely breathe, and that made the next decision so much harder.

"I'm going to go for a walk," I said quietly to the Scarecrow. "I need to clear my head. Would you keep an eye on everyone?"

"Both eyes," he said with a gracious bow. "A clear head is important."

He turned around and stared into the carriage. The Woodsman fixed his gaze on the sleeping Lion and twins. They would stay there until morning if I asked them to, untiring and unblinking.

"Would you like some company?" Clement asked.

I nodded, and he was at my side in an instant. Meggie watched him go, smiling a little.

She liked him. They all did.

We walked, hand-in-hand, around the curve of the

emerald wall. The further we got from the fire, the colder the air seemed. The grass bent and rustled under our feet. In the forest beyond the field, an owl called out a few times and fell silent.

"Look at the moon," Clement murmured.

It was enormous overhead and still almost full. Its halo radiated through the sky, blurring the nearest stars, and I could just make out the pattern of a face in the craters and dips.

"Have you ever seen the moon up close?"

Clement raised an eyebrow like I'd lost my senses.

I laughed. "Through a telescope, I mean."

"Oh. Yeah, a couple of times. One of the wandmakers I worked with was an amateur astronomist. I was over at his house once and he showed me the sky."

Unbidden, a tiny flame of jealousy leapt up inside me. "Sounds romantic."

He laughed. "Not remotely. His wife was there along with a few of our colleagues. It was some holiday party."

The flame flickered out, leaving a lingering warmth.

"Now, this has the potential to be romantic." Clement wrapped his arm around me.

I laced mine around the small of his back and leaned in close.

"Only you didn't come out here to woo me, did you?" Clement asked.

I shouldn't have been able to make out his face well in only the light from the moon, but after so many nights trudging across the Badalahn desert together, I knew his silhouette and the shards of reflected moonlight in his eyes as well as I knew my own heart. Perhaps better.

"I was thinking about everything earlier."

"I saw that," he said.

He kissed the top of my head. I took a deep breath.

Clement already knew the paths my thoughts had trod, but he waited anyway, just to make sure I said them aloud.

"I have to go find the others," I said. "My... siblings."

No matter how many times I'd thought the word, saying it was something different. Speaking aloud made things real.

My brothers and sisters, all children of a mysterious goddess, were out there somewhere right now, perhaps looking up at the same dazzling moon that shone over our heads now.

Clement tightened his arm around me. "I think you do."

"I don't want to."

"I know."

"But I can't abandon the Emerald City to its fate."

"If the curse on the city has something to do with Urbis, those people are your best shot at saving it," Clement said. "I don't know how they'll help. I don't know what they're doing. But these problems that have been knocking you upside the head one after another—they aren't coming from nowhere."

"Nothing exists in a vacuum," I said.

That was one of Ma's phrases, a constant reminder that everything was connected. The tin mines in Quadling Country affected the tinsmiths in Winkie Country, which in turn influenced the prices of tinned goods in the Emerald City. Natural disasters in other nations impacted our imports and exports. And the magic shattering outward from Urbis had, perhaps, turned all of my birth siblings' lives upside-down in different ways, just as it had mine.

"I'll come with you," Clement said.

I looked up at him, searching the dark, moonlit lines

of his face. "It's not safe for you to leave. You have asylum here. Meggie said my siblings were in Enchantia, which just happens to be where you were accused. It's not safe."

He shrugged. "What about our journey together has been safe?"

"But I can protect you if you stay here."

"I didn't come all this way with you because I wanted to use you as a shield," Clement said. "I care about you."

"I care about you, too," I said. "And that means I can't let you put yourself into danger again to help me."

Clement let out a soft sound somewhere between a scoff and a laugh. "I didn't realize you had to let me do anything."

"I didn't mean it like that."

"I'm not one of your subjects, Jakon," Clement said. "I don't want to be."

I tensed and tried to pull away, but he tightened his arm around me.

"What do you want, then?" I asked.

"I want to be your partner," he said softly. "To stand next to you. To hold your hand and face the same direction together."

I frowned. Thoughts rampaged through my mind, crashing into each other before they could fully form.

"But why?" I said finally.

Clement chuckled. "If you haven't figured that out yet, you're not as smart as I thought."

"You can't like me that much. I'm a mess."

"You're my mess," Clement said firmly. "And I more than like you."

I blushed, the color no doubt invisible in the darkness but enough to warm my face in spite of the cold breeze.

"I more than like you, too," I said.

"Really?"

I turned to face him and leaned forward until my lips almost touched his.

"Really, really," I said. "You have no idea."

He leaned forward the final inch. Heat flared in the pit of my stomach, and I kissed him until I was out of breath.

"This is where I belong," he whispered. "And I'm not budging."

"Want to bet?"

I put my hands on his shoulders and pushed, until he was forced back against the emerald wall. I kissed him again, using myself as a shield between him and the rest of the world.

This time, he didn't complain.

6TH OCTOBER

"I don't want you to go!" Lucy said, wrapping her arms around my legs.

"Lucy, you're being a child," Ethel said severely from the carriage window. "Jakon has to go because everyone in the Emerald City is frozen. Your cat? She's frozen. She can't move at all, not even if a mouse runs right past her nose, and Jakon can't fix it unless he and Uncle Clement go to Enchantia." She looked at me and narrowed her eyes. "Right?"

"Right." I crouched in front of Lucy and held out my arms. She dove headfirst into them, and I pulled her in close. Her soft hair tickled my nose. "I'll be back. I promise. I always come back."

"He did last time, remember?" Frank asked, also crouching down next to me and patting Lucy on the back. "He came and got us from the dungeons. This time we'll just be at the godfathers' house. You love the godfathers' house."

"I want Jakon to come with us," she whined.

"I want to come with you, too, snugglebug." I kissed the top of her head several times. "But Ethel's right. I have to go find some people who can help me make the city all better."

She jutted her bottom lip out. I kept kissing the top of her head. She wasn't going to get her way, but she'd know she was loved. I could guarantee that much.

Eventually, I talked her into the carriage and shut the door.

"They can take us as far as the turnoff to Munchkin Country," I said to Clement as we loaded the last of the bedrolls in the carriage's storage compartment. "Then we're on our own."

"We've had plenty of practice there."

"I hope you're ready for another tornado ride across the Ozian desert."

He grimaced.

Clement and I fell into step beside the carriage with the Scarecrow and Woodsman on either side. The Lion prowled on ahead of us, watching for danger.

"We'll take good care of them," the Woodsman said as we walked. "Don't worry."

"I know you will." I sighed. "I can't help worrying. They've already been through so much. First Ma, then their imprisonment, and then Glinda."

My throat closed up.

Glinda was gone. Ma was gone. Now, Locasta was the only mother figure we had left. She adored us, I knew, but she was usually busy managing the wild Gillikin Country.

I kicked a loose chunk of yellow brick off the road. It skittered off into the field.

"I just want to go one year without having to grieve a member of my family."

The words came out stronger than I'd meant them to. They were more angry, more petulant. I pressed my tongue to the roof of my mouth and forced myself into silence.

"I'm glad you're grieving them," the Woodsman said. "Many years ago, after I lost the heart I'd been born with, I also lost a woman who had once been very dear to me. I couldn't love her without a heart, and when she left me, I didn't feel the grief that should have been there."

I shoved my hands in my pockets. "That sounds nice."

The Woodsman shook his head. "It was dreadful. Grief is the price we pay for love."

"Just as fear is the price we must pay to reach true courage," the Lion said.

"They come hand-in-hand," the Scarecrow said with a nod. "I couldn't seek brains until I understood that I was stupid."

"In Enchantia, we say that light can't exist without the darkness, just as the darkness means nothing without a little light," Clement said. "And magic is only spectacular because we know it's possible to live without it."

"You're all being very wise," I said with a grimace. "I'm not particularly enjoying it."

Clement chuckled and reached for my hand. The Scarecrow patted me on the back, his stuffed arm rustling.

"You can't help being sad now and again," the

Scarecrow said. "Best thing to do is to look for a little meaning in it."

Chester opened the window of the carriage and stuck his arm out. He waved it frantically. I jogged up alongside him, heart pounding.

"What's wrong?" I asked.

"Remember when Ma and the Lion fell asleep in the poppy field when they first came to Oz?"

I frowned up at him. His eyes were alight and his round cheeks held a barely suppressed grin.

"Yeah?" I said. "About it?"

"Well, who made them fall asleep?"

I hesitated; it was clearly a trick question. "Um, whoever planted the poppies?"

"The Wicked Witch of the Rest!" Chester exclaimed.

He immediately dissolved into giggles. Lucy joined him, bouncing up and down on her seat in the carriage, but Meggie leaned over.

"The Wicked Witch didn't make Ma fall asleep, it was the poppies," she said. "And the witch didn't plant the poppies, they were just there."

"It's a joke," Frank said.

"Yeah, Meg, it's a joke," Chester said, looking insulted.

"I have one!" Ethel exclaimed. "Was the Munchkinland tornado a good actor?"

I raised an eyebrow at her. Chester bit his fingernail and screwed up his face in thought.

Ethel, who couldn't wait to deliver the punchline, shouted, "Yes! Because it brought the house down!"

Gertrude cracked up.

Meggie considered for a second. "That one was pretty good."

"It was amazing," Ethel said with a grin.

"My turn!" Chester said. "Which city has the most plants?"

"The Emerald City," Gertrude shot back. "Because it's full of greenhouses."

They continued in this vein for a long while. It warmed my heart. Even without Ma, without Glinda, and without me, if only for a while, my siblings had each other.

Perhaps my other siblings needed each other, too. Perhaps they needed me.

∽

We parted when the sun was high overhead. I hugged each of my siblings in turn, then hugged them again, and then I grabbed Lucy and Chester and gave them a few extra long squeezes. I breathed in the scent of Lucy's hair and did my best to memorize Chester's wide eyes, and Meggie watched me over their heads and gave me a solemn nod. She would take care of them as best she could. She would try to fill in for me, as I had tried to fill in for Ma.

Finally, the Lion stepped between me and the carriage and nudged me away.

"Let them go," he said. "Be brave. They'll be here when you get back."

I swallowed and blinked back the prickling in my eyes. The Lion nudged me with his large nose and licked my hand. His tongue was scratchy enough to scrape my skin.

"Thanks for that."

He fixed me with his amber eyes. "I tolerated plenty of your sloppy kisses when you were a child. You can accept one of mine."

I grinned and threw my arms around his neck. He rumbled deep in his throat, not quite a purr but something close.

"They'll be all right," he said. "We'll protect them with our lives."

"I know you will," I said.

I straightened and cleared my throat.

"Scarecrow, you remember what I said about Aboria."

He nodded. "My memory is impeccable. I won't forget. They're our allies."

"We should assume the best of every nation during these troubled times," the Woodsman said.

"But we must still protect our borders and our people," the Lion said.

"Good leadership requires that we strike a balance," the Scarecrow said. "I'm confident we can do that. No fear, Jakon, the kingdom is in safe hands."

I looked around at my godfathers, each of them so different and full of his own unique strengths. "I wouldn't leave the land with anyone else."

I didn't want to leave it at all. I didn't want to leave them.

"I'll be back as soon as I can," I said.

They nodded. They already knew.

Clement touched my shoulder. "Daylight's fading."

I took a deep breath. "You're right. I just…"

I looked at the carriage. Five faces peered back at me from the windows and open door.

"I love you," I said. "All of you."

"We know," Meggie said. "Go. Go so you can come back."

I swallowed. Clement handed me my knapsack, freshly loaded with food and money. I gave the carriage one last, lingering look, then set my shoulders and turned toward the yellow brick road leading into

Munchkin Country.

I only made it a few steps, but I couldn't turn my back on them. So I spun around and walked backwards, waving all the while. The Scarecrow leapt up onto the driver's seat, and the Woodsman climbed carefully up to sit next to him.

The horses began walking. My siblings leaned out the window and waved and blew kisses as they receded up the road to Gillikin Country. I blew kisses back until the carriage disappeared into the trees. And then, finally, when they were out of sight, I let my tears spill over.

I wiped them on my shirt sleeve, aware of Clement's gaze on me.

"I'm pathetic," I said. "I know."

"That's not what I was thinking." He dug into his knapsack and pulled out a handkerchief. He handed it to me and wrapped an arm around my shoulder. "I was thinking that I've never had anyone love me as much as you love those children." He laughed. "To be honest, I don't think anyone's ever loved me as much as you love Lucy's littlest toe. That's nothing to be ashamed of. It's beautiful."

"I definitely love you as much as I love Lucy's littlest toe."

The words were out before I could consider them. Clement fell suddenly and noticeably silent, and I reddened.

But I didn't take it back.

"You ready for another long journey?" I asked finally.

He considered, staring into the distance up the yellow brick road. A few other paths branched from it, blue brick roads leading through the woods and fields to different Munchkin villages. A stand of autumn-flowering cherry trees waved in the breeze up ahead, and across the yellow road, the leaves of the maples were beginning to change.

"I'm ready," he said at last. "On one condition."

"What's that?"

"That when we get back to the Emerald City—and we will—you'll finally take me to that amusement park. I want to try cotton candy, and I want to go on Chester's favorite slide, and I want to kiss you at the top of the Fleris wheel."

"Ferris."

"Right, that."

I stopped walking and glanced over at him. "You don't have to wait, you know."

"The Emerald City is frozen," he said. "I don't think the rides are working."

I bit my lip. "To kiss me, I mean."

A smile appeared at the corner of his mouth. His dark eyes sparkled.

He kissed me on the lips, long and deeply, and then he kissed my forehead, too. I breathed him in, his scent warm and clean and smelling somehow like home.

And then we fell back into step together, side-by-side and hand-in-hand, and journeyed up the road and toward Enchantia.

KELIS
DAUGHTER OF SNOW WHITE

GRAB THE NEXT BOXSET IN THE KINGDOM OF FAIRYTALES SERIES

MEET THE TEAM

The Kingdom of Fairytales Series was a team effort. Below are the people that made it possible:

EQP Management: Rhi Parkes & J.A. Armitage

Our authors: J.A. Armitage, Audrey Rich, B. Kristin McMichael, Emma Savant, Jennifer Ellision, Scarlett Kol, Rose Castro, Margo Ryerkerk, Zara Quentin, Laura Greenwood and Anne Stryker.

Our Editor
Rose Lipscomb

Our Beta Team
Nadine Peterse-Vrijhof
Diane Major
Kalli Bunch
Stephanie Woodwood

Our Proof Reader
Tina Merritt

And to all the wonderful people who loved the world we created and reviewed our stories.
Thank you

READING ORDER

SEASON ONE
SLEEPING BEAUTY
Queen of Dragons
Heiress of Embers
Throne of Fury
Goddess of Flames

SEASON TWO
LITTLE MERMAID
Queen of Mermaids
Heiress of the Sea
Throne of Change
Goddess of Water

SEASON THREE
RED RIDING HOOD
King of Wolves
Heir of the Curse
Throne of Night
God of Shifters

SEASON FOUR
RAPUNZEL
King of Devotion
Heir of Thorns
Throne of Enchantment
God of Loyalty

SEASON FIVE
RUMPELSTILTSKIN
Queen of Unicorns
Heiress of Gold
Throne of Sacrifice
Goddess of Loss

SEASON SIX
BEAUTY AND THE BEAST
King of Beasts
Heir of Beauty
Throne of Betrayal
God of Illusion

SEASON SEVEN
ALADDIN
Queen of the Sun
Heiress of Shadows
Throne of the Phoenix
Goddess of Fire

SEASON EIGHT
CINDERELLA
Queen of Song
Heiress of Melody
Throne of Symphony
Goddess of Harmony

SEASON NINE
ALICE IN WONDERLAND
Queen of Clockwork
Heiress of Delusion
Throne of Cards
Goddess of Hearts

SEASON TEN
WIZARD OF OZ
King of Traitors
Heir of Fugitives
Throne of Emeralds
God of Storms

SEASON ELEVEN
SNOW WHITE
Queen of Reflections
Heiress of Mirrors
Throne of Wands
Goddess of Magic

SEASON TWELVE
PETER PAN
Queen of Skies
Heiress of Stars
Throne of Feathers
Goddess of Air

SEASON THIRTEEN
URBIS
Kingdom of Royalty
Kingdom of Power
Kingdom of Fairytales
Kingdom of Ever After

BOXSETS
AZIA
BLAISE
CASTIEL
DEON
ELIANA
FALLON
GAIA
HALIA
IVY
JAKON
KELIS
LYRIC
URBIS

www.ingramcontent.com/pod-product-compliance
Lightning Source LLC
LaVergne TN
LVHW041208250326
834689LV00022BA/179/J